The Freddy

ANNIVERSARY COLLECTION

The Complete FREDDY THE PIG Series
Available or Coming Soon from The Overlook Press

The Freddy
ANNIVERSARY COLLECTION

THE FIRST THREE FREDDY BOOKS IN ONE VOLUME

Freddy Goes to Florida

Freddy Goes to the North Pole

Freddy the Detective

Walter R. Brooks

illustrations by Kurt Wiese

INTRODUCTION BY MICHAEL CART

THE OVERLOOK PRESS
Woodstock & New York

If you enjoyed this book, very likely you will be interested not only in the other Freddy books published in this series, but also in joining the Friends of Freddy, an organization of Freddy devotees.

We will be pleased to hear from any reader about our "Freddy" publishing program. You can easily contact us by logging on the either THE OVERLOOK PRESS website, or the Freddy website.

The website addresses are as follows:
THE OVERLOOK PRESS:
www.overlookpress.com

FREDDY:
www.friendsoffreddy.org

We look forward to hearing from you soon.

First published in the United States in 2002 by
The Overlook Press, Peter Mayer Publishers, Inc.
Woodstock & New York

WOODSTOCK:
One Overlook Drive
Woodstock, NY 12498
www.overlookpress.com
[for individual orders, bulk and special sales, contact our Woodstock office]

NEW YORK:
141 Wooster Street
New York, NY 10012

∞ The paper used in this book meets the requirements for paper permanence as described in the ANSI Z39.48-1992 standard.

A CIP record for this book is available from the Library of Congress.

Book design by Bernard Schleifer and Yellowstone Ltd.
Type formatting by Bernard Schleifer Company
Manufactured in Spain
ISBN 1-58567-346-3
1 3 5 7 9 8 6 4 2

INTRODUCTION

THE FREDDY THE PIG BOOKS by Walter R. Brooks are classics of American children's literature. Though they languished in out of print limbo for years, the twenty-six titles in the series are finally enjoying a remarkable renaissance of reader and critical interest, thanks to their re-issue, in beautiful facsimile editions, by The Overlook Press.

Now, to celebrate the 75th anniversary of Freddy's inaugural adventure—*Freddy Goes to Florida*, first published in 1927 as *To and Again*—Overlook is publishing the first three "Freddy" books in one deluxe volume: not only *Florida*, which launched the series, but also *Freddy Goes to the North Pole* (first published as *More To and Again*) and *Freddy the Detective*.

Though the peerless porker is only a supporting player in the first two of these timeless titles, many of the qualities that quickly made him the "star" of the developing series are present in his character from the outset—his cleverness, his imagination, his ineffable way with words, and his enduring capacity for friendship.

And speaking of friends, many of the other characters who will be major players in later titles—Mrs. Wiggins the cow, Jinx the cat, Charles the rooster, Henrietta the hen, Alice and Emma the ducks, Hank the horse, Mr. and Mrs. Webb the spiders—were not only also present at the creation but were already fully developed, richly realized characters. And, indeed, it is this capacity for characterization that is one reason the Brooks books have attained classic status. As the distinguished Canadian critic Sheila Egoff has written, "the animals are not parodies of human beings but they exhibit the qualities that we would like to think we humans instinctively possess."

The qualities to which she refers are ones that I cited in my Introduction to an earlier and rather limited re-issue of a few of the Freddy titles: "the joys—and responsibilities—of friendship, of sharing and caring, of loyalty and constancy, of kindness, compassion, and forgiveness, and above all of helping."

In this way the Freddy books are a celebration of community and of the human/animal condition at its very best. No wonder that Egoff wisely concludes, "They shine with the joy of being alive."

They shine, too, with their celebration of rural and small town life in America. In fact, next to the Oz books of L. Frank Baum, they are the first important works of *American* fantasy. Indeed, the critic Roger Sale has said, "if L. Frank Baum has a successor, it is Brooks."

Brooks, though, was certainly the better writer and his easy, conversational style was, for its time, ground-breaking in its use of the American vernacular, of slang, and of comic regionalisms—many of them invented by Brooks, who relished Yankee dialect and routinely employed it in letters to his friend, the writer and editor Frank Bellamy.

His characters' use of archaic-sounding exclamations—"Well, set fire to my coat tails;" "Pickle me and preserve me;" "Well, tear off my collar and necktie!"—are among the richest sources of the Freddy books' enduring humor.

The naturalness of the Brooks style—though controversial at the time—helped give modern American children's literature its contemporary voice, sound, and style—another reason that the Freddy books have come to enjoy classic status and have found a new readership among today's children. Even the magisterial Anne Carroll Moore, the longtime coordinator of children's work for the New York Public Library and the "inventor" of children's book reviewing in the 1920's, admitted she was "impressed by the ease and naturalness of Mr. Brooks's writing."

It is for this reason that even the earliest Freddy books—like the three titles in this volume—never sound dated or stilted in the way that so many other children's books of the 1920s and 1930s do. Indeed, the sound of Brooks's language remains so savory that it's no wonder that Freddy is now available, unabridged, in audio versions.

Perhaps even more remarkable is the fact that the books' humor, too, remains fresh and contemporary. In part this is due to its being rooted not in situation but in character and in gentle satire. Brooks, whose personal family tree was filled with bankers and politicians, loved lampooning the wealthy and self-important (even including our national bird, the eagle!). In this respect he was operating in yet another quintessentially American framework and was a direct descendant of the Down East humorists of the 1830s.

Actually, a whole book could be written about Brooks's encyclopedic use of humorous devices (the nearly two chapters I devote to them in my book *What's So Funny? Wit and Humor in American Children's Literature* only scratch the surface) but, for now, it is enough to note that it is his abiding humor and wit—especially his gloriously inventive wordplay—that further elevate his work to classic status.

That humor is captured and even expanded by the immortal Kurt Wiese illustrations, which grace each of the twenty-six Freddy titles. And their happy collaboration with Brooks's texts creates an aesthetic whole that is larger than the sum of its individual parts, giving the books still another classic dimension. Happily, Wiese's contribution has been given long overdue attention in the Overlook edition of *The Art of Freddy*, just published in this year of the droll pig's 75th birthday.

A final reason for the enduring importance of the Freddy books is their author's respect for his audience. Brooks's adamant refusal to write down to children was, for its time, pioneering and provided an inspirational example for such later important American writers as Robert Lawson and Robert McCloskey, both of whom wrote in his tradition.

"Children are people," Walter stoutly maintained; "they're just smaller and less experienced [than adults]. They are not taken in by the smug playfulness of those who write or talk down to them as if they were dull-witted and slightly deaf."

No wonder, then, that the Freddy books have always appealed not only to children but also to adults who share the sensibility, heart, and humor that Brooks communicated so well. Indeed, long before the Overlook re-issue of the entire series began, the Friends of Freddy was established to keep the flame alive. And yet I doubt that even these stalwart fans could have imagined that every single one of these classic books would ever be available again and—better yet—would be finding new readers of all ages every day. And not just in America, for Freddy is soon to appear in German and Japanese editions, as well. Perhaps even his publisher is a bit surprised by all of this!

And speaking of his publisher, hearty thanks are due The Overlook Press for giving readers such a happy opportunity for celebrating and—through its larger project of republishing all twenty-six Freddy books—for refocusing attention on a series of American classics that were, for too long, overlooked! And while I'm at it, here is a heartfelt cheer, too, in this age when size matters so overmuch, for small, independent publishers everywhere who so regularly take courageous treks into territory where the larger and mightier fear to tread.

—MICHAEL CART

C O N T E N T S

Mrs. Wiggins he dotted all over.

FREDDY GOES
TO FLORIDA

After clearing his throat he began to crow.

I

CHARLES
the
Rooster

came out of the front door of the chicken coop and walked slowly across the barnyard. It was still very dark in the barnyard, for it was half past four in the morning, and the sun was not yet up.

He shivered and thought of his nice warm perch in the coop, but there was a reason why he did not go back to it. Mr. Bean, the farmer, did not have very much money, and could not afford to buy an alarm clock, and he relied on the rooster to wake him up bright and early in the morning. The last time Charles had overslept, Mr. Bean had been very angry and had threatened to have him fricasseed with baking-powder biscuit for Sunday dinner. Charles did not like getting up early, before any of the other birds and animals were stirring, but he felt that it was better to get up than to be fricasseed. And so this morning he hopped sleepily on to a post and, after clearing his throat several times, began to crow: "Cock-a-doodle-doo! Cock-a-doodle-doo-oo-oo!!"

The eastern sky grew brighter and brighter and pinker and pinker, and for a long time nothing else happened. Then some robins began talking together in little quiet voices in the big elm tree that grew by the barn, and a young chipmunk came scampering along the fence and stopped on the post next to Charles and started to wash his face with his paws, and down in the house where the pigs lived there was a great grunting and squealing, so that Charles knew that the pigs were beginning to think about breakfast. And he crowed some more.

And at last, far off across the fields, where the sky came down to meet them, there appeared a little spark of bright gold, that grew and grew until it looked like a bonfire, and then like a house on fire, and then like a whole city burning up. And that was the upper edge of the sun, coming up from the other side of the world, where all night long it had been shining on Chinese pagodas and the Himalayas and jungles in Africa and all the queer places where people work and play while we are sound asleep.

And just as the edge of the sun came into sight, the head of Mr. Bean, the farmer, appeared at his bedroom window. He had on a white cotton nightcap with a red tassel, and his face was completely hidden behind his bushy, grey whiskers, so that nobody, not even his wife, had ever seen what he really looked like. And he was looking out to see what kind of a day it was going to be.

As soon as Mr. Bean poked his head out of the window, Charles hopped down from the post. His day's work was already done, but although he was still cold and sleepy, he did not go back to the hen-house. For his wife and her eight sisters were up by that time. "And nobody could get a minute's peace in all that cackle," he muttered angrily. "I'll go take forty winks in the barn."

"Good morning, Charles," said Hank, the old, white horse, whose stall was nearest the door. "Touch of winter in the air this morning."

Charles flew up and perched on the edge of Hank's manger.

"Touch of winter!" he exclaimed. "I guess there is! It's cold, that's what it is—downright cold!"

"Well, we've got to expect it now," said Hank. "Snow will be flying in another month or two."

"Ugh!" said Charles, and shivered.

"There's less work for me in winter," said Hank; "though I must say I prefer the summer. I've got a touch of rheumatism in my off hind leg, and these cold nights set it aching."

"Of course," said Charles sympathetically. "They would! It's a shame. You ought to have a blanket or something to cover you, and this barn is a terribly draughty old place. But Mr. Bean, he never thinks how the animals and birds suffer; he sleeps warm under his feather bed and four patchwork quilts—*he* doesn't care as long as *he's* warm! Now, take me. Every morning, winter and summer, I have to get up before daylight, crawl out of my comfortable coop, and crow and get things started on the farm, just because he's too stingy to buy himself an alarm clock. Doesn't matter how cold and rainy it is, it has to be done. And if I miss a morning, what do I get? I get fricasseed, that's what!"

"It seems sort of hard," said Hank.

"I guess it does! And now winter's coming. I detest winter! But I've got to get out, just the same, and wade around in the snow and freeze my bill. I wouldn't mind so much if I was warm the rest of the time. If there was a stove in the hen house, and a couple of good wool blankets to sleep under. That hen house ought to have a cellar under it, too—the floor's as cold as stone."

Hank sighed. "Yes," he agreed, "it's a hard life. There's no denying it. But what can we do about it?"

A little twittering voice answered from high up under the roof. "Why don't you migrate?" it said.

They looked up, but it was dark in the roof, and they could not see anything.

"Who are you?" asked Charles. "And what are you talking about?"

"I'm a barn swallow," said the voice, "and I'm talking about migrating. We birds all migrate every year, and I don't see why you can't do it too, if you don't like the winter."

"Oh, you don't!" said Charles rather crossly. "Well, suppose you tell us what you're talking about. If it's worth listening to. We can't keep track of everything you little unimportant birds do."

Charles, being a farm bird, felt very superior to all the wild birds, and he puffed out his chest with importance. But the swallow only laughed.

"You needn't be so grand," she said. "After all, you've never been outside your own barnyard, and you have to do as you're told, or you get fricasseed. And I've traveled thousands of miles in my time, and I don't take orders from anyone."

"Well, of all the—!" Charles began angrily. But Hank shook his head at him.

"She may have something interesting to tell us," he said. And then he asked the swallow politely if she would explain to them what migrating was.

So she told them that every fall, when it began to get cold, the birds gathered together in big flocks and started south. They traveled hundreds of miles, and some of them went to Florida, and some went to Central or South America. All winter long, she said, it was sunny and warm down south. There was never any snow, never any cold winds, and there was always plenty to eat. And then in the spring they came back north again.

When she had told them this, she dropped with a twitter from the roof and shot like an arrow out through the open door into the warm sunshine.

"Do you believe it?" Charles asked when she had gone. He felt it beneath his dignity to pay much attention to anything a swallow could tell him, although he was really very much interested.

"Yes," said Hank. "I have heard of it before. And it sounds pretty good. But it wouldn't do for me, I'm afraid. It's a long road to Florida. If I could fly, though, I won't say that I wouldn't try it."

"I can't fly," said Charles. "Not much, that is. But I would walk a good many miles to find a place where it is warm and sunny all winter, and where I shouldn't have to get up in the morning till I got good and ready. It wouldn't be any fun going alone, of course, but if we could get up a party—"

"If you could get up a party," said Hank, "I won't say I shouldn't like to go myself."

Charles jumped down from the manger. "I'm going to see some of the other animals," he said. "If they're interested, we'll have a meeting tonight and talk it over." And he went out into the yard.

The more he thought about it, the more excited he became. He went out into the orchard and talked to an oriole and a couple of blackbirds, and the tales they told him of the lazy life they led in the tropical, southern sunshine fairly made his mouth water. Then he went to see the pigs and the cows and the other animals, and they were very much interested and said that they had all been dreading the long, cold winter, and that if he really knew of a place where it was warm and sunshiny they would be very glad to go there. So he invited them to come to a meeting that evening in the cow barn, where he would tell them all about it, and those who wanted to go could talk it over and decide when to start.

The meeting was a great success.

II

NOW, all This time, Charles

had not said anything to his wife and

her eight sisters about what the birds

had told him, and he had not invited them to the meeting.

"She always disapproves of everything I do," he grumbled,

"and her sisters always agree with her. It will be a much better meeting if she doesn't come. I can tell her about it afterwards." His wife's name was Henrietta, and she was a very busy hen, for she had ten little chickens to take care of. And so she was sometimes rather cross to Charles, who never did much work and used to get in her way a good deal.

That night, when Charles started out, she called him back and asked him where he was going.

"I have to attend a business meeting," he said importantly. "I'm expected to make a speech."

"H'm, much good *your* speech will do anybody!" said Henrietta; but she was busy putting the chickens to bed, and Charles slipped out before she had time to say any more.

The meeting was a great success. Nearly all the animals on the farm came, and the cow barn was crowded to the doors. Charles spoke long and eloquently and drew glowing pictures of what their life would be like in a southern land, lolling under the orange trees and telling stories and cracking jokes all day long. The pigs, who had come in a body and sat in the front row, applauded heartily, and the cows mooed and the ducks quacked and the dogs barked, and even the mice, who sat in a row on one of the rafters, squeaked excitedly.

"Now, my friends," said Charles, when he had told them all he had learned from the birds, "I have placed before you these facts. It remains for us to act upon them. I, for one, intend to follow the example of the birds and go south for the winter. It is true that it is easier for the birds than it is for us. The birds can fly across rivers that we shall have to swim or wade, and across mountains that we shall have to climb. I do not conceal from you that it may be a hard journey. But it is my experience that nothing that is worth getting is easy to get. However, I shall be glad to hear what anyone else may have to say, and I accordingly throw the meeting open to discussion." And amid prolonged cheers he hopped down from the seat of the old buggy from which he had addressed the meeting.

Then for quite a while the animals were much excited and all talked at once. All of them hated the thought of the long, cold winter, and when somebody—I think it was Freddy, the smallest and cleverest of the pigs—shouted: "Why don't we start tonight?" they all gave three cheers and started toward the door.

But just then Jock, the larger of the two dogs, a wise old Scotch collie, got up.

"Ladies and gentlemen," he began, "you have all heard what my friend the rooster has said, and I think we all agree with him that it would be fine if we could all go south this winter." ("Yes, yes!" cried all the animals together.) "But there is one thing that I think we have forgotten. I am not a fine speaker like Charles, but I just want to say that we must not forget our duty. We cannot all leave Mr. Bean, for he could not get along without us—"

Here Charles interrupted excitedly. "Mr. Bean!" he shouted. "What do we care for Mr. Bean? What has he ever done for us? *He* can sleep warm these winter nights; *he* can have feather beds and stoves; but *we* don't have such things—*we* don't matter! Why doesn't he warm *our* houses for us? Why—"

"Yes, yes, Charles," said Jock quietly. "But listen to me a minute. Mr. Bean feeds us and gives us a place to live and looks after us when we're sick. We can't just desert him, can we?"

"Well, perhaps you're right," said Charles unwillingly.

"Of course I am," said Jock. And he went on to say that, while those of them whom Mr. Bean did not need during the winter could go south if they wanted to, he thought the others should stay. "I can't go," he said. "And one of the horses should stay to take Mr. Bean into town when he wants to go. And one of the cows and some of the hens ought to stay, too, so he will have eggs and milk. That is all I have to say." And he bowed and sat down.

A long discussion followed, but as all the animals wanted to go, none of them except Jock would admit that they were needed on the farm. They talked louder and louder, and grew more and more angry at each other, and it seemed likely that the meeting would break up in disorder, when there was a loud ear-piercing "Meeaooouw!" and Jinx, the cat, bounded through the doorway.

In the silence that followed, all the mice upon the rafter gave a horrified squeak, and then they rose as one mouse and tiptoed softly into a convenient hole.

"Hello, folks," said Jinx breezily. "What's all the row? I could hear you way down by the millpond, where I was hunting frogs. Better make less noise, or you'll have old Bean out here with his shotgun. What's the matter anyway?"

"Fine!" he said when they had told him. "Fine! That's a great idea, Charley, old boy! Didn't think you had it in you. But see here. No use quarrelling about who's to go and who's not. Draw lots; that's the way to do it. Now you say only one cow can go. Well, here's three of 'em—Mrs. Wiggins and Mrs. Wurzburger and Mrs. Wogus. Here, Jock, you take three straws in your mouth, one long one and two short. Now let 'em draw, and the one that gets the long straw goes."

Jock got the straws, and the cows drew. Mrs. Wiggins won.

"All fair and aboveboard, you see," said Jinx. "Now, horses next. Step up, please; it's getting late."

As soon as the cat had taken charge of things, the meeting became more orderly, and arrangements for the departure of all those whom Mr. Bean would not need during the winter were quickly made. Then, when everything was decided, Charles got up again to make another speech. There wasn't really anything left for him to say, but he was fond of making speeches, and he spoke so beautifully that everybody liked to hear him, although when they got home they could never remember anything he had said.

"Now, my friends," he began, "before we break up this distinguished meeting, I should like to give you one thought to take home with you in your hearts—something to carry away with you as a memento of the kindness and good-fellowship we have enjoyed here together tonight. As I look about me this evening upon all these bright, eager young faces, gathered together here under one roof it is borne in upon me—" But what it was that was borne in upon him they never knew, for at that point he stopped suddenly and climbed hastily down from the buggy seat. His wife, Henrietta, had come in the door.

She marched straight down toward him between the rows of silent animals, and caught him by the wing.

"'Bright, eager young faces,' is it?" she exclaimed angrily. "*I'll* give you a bright, eager young face!" And she boxed his right ear with her claw. "*I'll* give you something to carry home with you!" And she boxed the other ear. "I never heard such nonsense!"

Charles hunched his head down between his shoulders. "But, my dear!" he protested.

"Don't you 'my dear' me!" she said. "You come along home, where you belong. Staying out all night like this! Revelling and carousing with a lot of silly pigs and cows that don't know any better! The very idea!" And she pushed him unceremoniously toward the door.

But before they reached it another figure appeared—a short, bearded man in a long, white nightshirt and carpet slippers. Mr. Bean had been awakened by the noise, and had come out to see what was the matter. He had a lantern in one hand and a carriage whip in the other, and on his head was the white cotton nightcap with the red tassel.

"You animals go to bed!" he said gruffly. Then he turned around and stumped back to the house.

In thirty seconds all the animals had gone and the cow barn was empty, except for Mrs. Wiggins and Mrs. Wurzburger and Mrs. Wogus, who lived there.

III

THE next Morning

M as soon as Mr. Bean had left the house, Jinx, the cat, who had been pretending to be asleep under the stove, jumped up on the table and got a pencil and a piece of paper, and carried them out and laid them down under the big elm tree beside the barn. Then he looked up among the branches, and pretty soon he saw a bright little eye peeping out at him from behind a limb.

"Good morning, robin," he said politely. "I wonder if you'd do me a little favor? We animals are going to migrate this fall, but as none of us have ever been south before, we don't know the way, and I thought perhaps you'd be willing to draw us a little map."

The robin hopped a little way along the branch and cocked his head and looked down at Jinx with his right eye. "I don't know what made you think that," he said. "I don't know why I should do anything for you. You're always chasing me, and there's never a minute's peace for me or my family when you're in the barnyard, and you ate up my wife's third cousin last June. But I suppose you've forgotten all about that."

"I certainly haven't," said Jinx. "It was a most regrettable incident, and I was really terribly upset about it. I had no idea that robin was any relative of your wife's, and when I saw him prowling around your nest, I thought he wanted to steal your children, and of course I didn't stop to make inquiries then. Afterwards, when I found out what a mistake I had made, I would have done anything to restore him to you. But of course it was too late."

"Rather late," said the robin dryly, "since there was nothing left of him but a few tail feathers."

"Well, let's not rake up old scores," said Jinx. "What's done is done, as the saying goes. And if you'll make this map for me, I'll promise never to chase you or any of your family again."

"Well, that's fair enough," said the robin. And he flew down, and picking up the pencil in his claw, began to draw the map that would show them exactly how to get to Florida.

Meanwhile all the other animals who were going were packing up and making their farewell calls on those who were to stay at home. For they had heard Mr. Bean say that he was going to drive into town the next morning, and they thought that would be the best time for them to start on their journey, because he wouldn't get back until late in the afternoon, and by that time they would be many miles away.

Nearly everybody in the barnyard was happy but Charles the rooster. He sat alone in the darkest corner of the henhouse, his tail feathers drooping miserably. For his wife, Henrietta, had positively refused to let him go.

"Go south in the winter, would you?" she had said. "Never in my life have I heard such a pack of nonsensical notions! What right have you to go traipsing off over the country—you, with a wife and children to look after? Not that you ever do look after them. Who's going to get Mr. Bean up in the morning, I should like to know?"

"He can wake himself up," said Charles. "He doesn't have to get up so early in the wintertime anyway."

"Well, you're not going—that's flat!" said his wife. And that settled it. When Henrietta put her foot down, there was nothing more to be said.

Some of the animals, too, had held the opinion that the cat ought not to go either, since it was his duty to keep the mice out of the barn where the grain and vegetables were stored. But that was easily arranged, for some of the mice wanted to go, and so Jinx promised that he would let them alone if the mice that stayed home would keep away from the barn while he was gone. This pleased the other animals, for although Jinx was a wild fellow, rather careless of appearances and a bit too free in his speech, they all felt that he would be a good animal to have with them in a pinch, and no one knew what dangers might lie in wait for them on the road to Florida.

Indeed, a number of the more timid animals who had been carried away by enthusiasm at the meeting in the cow barn had not felt so anxious to go when they had thought it all over. All the sheep had backed out, and most of the mice, and all of the pigs except Freddy. The pigs were not afraid; they were just awfully lazy, and the thought of walking perhaps twenty miles a day for goodness knew how many days was too much for them.

At last the great day came. Mr. Bean harnessed up William to the buggy early in the morning, and drove off to town, and then all the animals gathered in the barnyard. From the window of the hen-house Charles watched them unhappily. They were all so merry and excited, and the pigs had come up to see Freddy off and were all talking at once and giving him a great deal more advice than he could possibly remember, and Hank, the old, white horse, was continually running back into the barn for another mouthful of oats, because he didn't know when he should get any good oats again, and Alice and Emma, the two white ducks, had waddled off down to the end of the pasture to take one last look at the old familiar duck pond, which they wouldn't see again until next spring. It made Charles very sad.

"Why don't you go out and say goodbye to them, Charles?" asked Henrietta. It made her feel bad to see him so unhappy, for she really had a kind heart, and way down inside of it she was very fond of him. But he was so careless and forgetful that she often had to be quite cross to him.

"No," said Charles mournfully. "No. I shall stay here. They've forgotten all about *me*. *They* don't care because I can't go with them. *They* don't remember who it was that gave them the idea in the first place. No, let them go. Heartless creatures! What do I care?"

"Nonsense!" said Henrietta. "Go along out." And so Charles ruffled up his feathers and held his head up in the air and marched out into the yard.

All the good-byes had been said and the travellers were ready to start. The barnyard was silent as they formed in a line and marched out through the gate into the road that stretched away like a long, white ribbon to far distant Florida. First came Jinx, with his tail held straight up in the air like a drum major's stick. Then came Freddy, the pig, and the dog, Robert, who was Jock's younger brother. After them marched Hank and Mrs. Wiggins, and the procession was brought up by the two white ducks, Alice and Emma, who were sisters. The mice—Eek, Quik, Eeny, and Cousin Augustus, ran along the side of the road so as not to be stepped on.

The stay-at-homes crowded out to the gate, waving paws and hoofs, and calling: "Good-bye! Good-bye! Don't forget to write! Have a good time and remember us to Florida!"

Overhead a flock of swallows darted and turned on swift wings. "Good-bye!" they twittered. "We'll see you in a week or two. We start south in about ten days ourselves."

Charles stood on the gatepost and watched the little procession march off down the road. Smaller and smaller it grew, and then it went over a hill, and the white road was empty again. But long after it had gone Charles sat on. And his tail feathers drooped, and his head dropped down on his chest, and a great tear splashed on the gatepost. But luckily no one saw him cry, for the animals had all gone back to their daily tasks.

At least that was what he thought. But Henrietta saw him from the window of the henhouse.

IV

AND

SO

The animals started out into the wide world. Although it was late in the fall and the branches were bare, the sun was bright and the air was fresh and warm.

For some time they walked along together in silence, for they were a little sad at the thought of the comfortable home and the good friends they had left behind. But the smiling valley through which the road ran was too pleasant to be sad in for very long, and pretty soon Freddy, who was very clever, began to sing a song he had just made up. And this is the song he sang:

Oh, the sail Or may sing of his tall, swift ships,
*   Of sailing the deep blue sea,*
But the long, white road where adventures wait
*   Is the better life for me.*
On the open road, when the sun goes down,
*   Your home is wherever you are.*
The sky is your roof and the earth is your bed
*   And you hang your hat on a star.*

You wash your face is the clear, cold dew,
*   And you say good night to the moon,*
And the wind in the treetops sings you to sleep
*   With a drowsy boughs-y tune.*

Then it's hey! for the joy of a roving life,
*   From Florida up to Nome,*
For since I've no home in any one spot,
*   Wherever I am is home.*

There were a good many other verses—too many to put down, for Freddy made them up as he went along, and there was a chorus to each verse that went like this:

Oh, the winding road is long, is long,
*   But never too long for me.*
And we'll cheer each mile with a song, a song,
A song as we ramble along, along,
*   So fearless and gay and free.*

"We have to go across that valley and those hills."

And pretty soon, as their spirits rose, and they thought of the adventures that lay ahead of them and the merry life they would lead, they all began to sing. They roared out the chorus with a will, and even the mice sang in their little, squeaky voices. The mice had got tired walking by this time, because their legs were so short, and so Mrs. Wiggins had invited them up on her back, which was so broad that there was no danger of their falling off, and they could sit there and enjoy the scenery and watch everything go by, just as you do from the window of a train.

All the morning they went steadily on. Every now and then they would have to go to one side of the road to let an automobile or a farm wagon pass them, and every time that happened the people would stare and stare. "Why, just look at those animals!" they would exclaim. "Did you ever see anything like that in your life ?" And after they had gone by, the people would stop their automobiles or their horses and stare after them until they were out of sight.

About noon they climbed a steep hill, and from the top they could see ahead of them a broad valley, very much like the one through which they had come. And beyond the valley were more hills.

"This is all strange country to me now," said Hank, the old, white horse. "I've driven as far as this with Mr. Bean, but I've never been down into that valley. We'd better have a look at the map."

"There's a stream crossing the road halfway down the hill," said Robert, the dog. "Let's go down there.

So they went down and camped beside the stream, and the larger animals went in wading and splashed each other and laughed and shouted, and the two white ducks, Alice and Emma, swam about looking like two white powder puffs, because that is what they like to do best. But Jinx, the cat, stayed on the bank and studied the map that the robin had drawn for him, to see if they were going in the right direction.

Then, when the animals were tired of splashing about in the stream, they came up on the bank and rested, and Jinx showed them the map. "We have to go across that valley and those hills, and then across another valley, and more hills, and then we come to a river," he said. "And we follow the river until we come to a village, and there we shall find a bridge."

"But will the people in the village let us cross the bridge?" asked Eek.

It was funny to see him and the three other mice sitting peaceably beside the cat, but Jinx had promised not to chase them, and they were not afraid. Cats very seldom make promises, but when they do, they always keep them. Their word is as good as their bond.

"I have heard Mrs. Bean say to Mr. Bean," Jinx answered, "never to cross a bridge until you come to it. So we'd better not worry about this one. And now don't you think we'd better be getting on?"

So they got up and started down the hill. Halfway down they had their first adventure.

They heard an automobile behind them and turned out to let it go by. It came along, rattling and bumping, for it was not a very good automobile, and as it passed them, a man with a big, black moustache leaned out and stared in surprise.

"Hey, sonny," he said to the boy who was driving, "wait a minute. Look at them animals. By gum, I never see anything like that before!"

The boy, who had a very dirty face, stopped the automobile, and they both stared back at the animals.

"There's nobody with 'em," said the boy. "Who do you suppose they belong to?"

"Dunno," said the man, and began to get out. "But we'll just drive 'em down to my place, I guess. If they do belong to somebody, we'll get a reward for 'em, and if they don't, we'll keep 'em ourselves. The cow looks like a good milker. Can't say much for the horse, though. Homely brute!"

Hank gave a loud snort at this, for while he was not a vain horse, he had a proper pride in a neat appearance, and he thought the man's remark insulting. Which indeed it was.

"That's a nice pig," said the boy. "We haven't had roast pig in a long time, pa."

"Nor roast duck," said the man, and he licked his black mous- tache and looked greedily at Alice and Emma. "I'll get a rope and tie the cow, and you take some stones and drive the dog away." He reached into the car for his rope.

This was too much for the animals, who had been undecided what to do.

"I don't care for these people *at all,*" said Mrs. Wiggins emphat- ically. "Robert, you and Jinx chase that dirty-faced boy away before he can pick up any stones. Don't hurt him; just give him a good scare. I'll attend to the man." And lowering her horns she galloped straight at him.

Now, cows are almost always good-natured and peaceful animals, and the man was very much surprised. He tried to dodge behind the car, but she scooped him up in her horns and tossed him high in the air. And as he went up, Mrs. Wiggins put her forehead to the back of the automobile and pushed it ahead so that it would be under him when he came down. Which he presently did, with a thump, on the automobile top. He bounced once or twice like a rubber ball; then, frightened but unhurt, peered over the edge of the top at Mrs. Wiggins, who was walking around the car and shaking her horns and mooing in a terribly frightening way. She was really laughing, but the man didn't know that.

Meanwhile the dog and cat had chased the boy away across a field. And he was even more badly frightened than the man; for after

FREDDY GOES TO FLORIDA / 33

they stopped chasing him, he kept on running, and after he was out of sight, they could still hear his terrified yells.

"There! I guess we settled *them*!" said Mrs. Wiggins. And she sat down in the road and bellowed with laughter until the tears ran down her cheeks, and the man with the black moustache shivered with fear. Mrs. Wiggins was very fond of a joke.

Pretty soon the animals started on again, and when they had gone half a mile or so, they looked back and saw the man climb slowly down and get into the automobile. But he did not come after them: he turned round and went back up the hill, and went home another way.

Mrs. Wiggins was a character. That means that when she did anything, she always did it in a little different way than anyone else would have done. And she did a good many things that nobody else would ever have thought of. There were two spiders, Mr. and Mrs. Webb, that lived up in the roof of the cow barn. Of course they had heard everything that had gone on the night the animals had had their meeting, and the next morning Mrs. Webb slid down a long thread and landed on Mrs. Wiggins's nose. At first Mrs. Wiggins shook her head and asked the spider to get off; she tickled. But

Mrs. Webb crept up close to the cow's ear and said: "I want your advice about something."

This flattered Mrs. Wiggins, because very few people ever ask a cow's advice about anything. So she said she would listen. Now spiders have very little voices, and even animals, who hear better than people, have to be very close to them to understand what they say. So Mrs. Webb crept still closer to Mrs. Wiggins's ear, and said: "Mrs. Wiggins, me and Webb have been talking it over, and we'd like to go on this trip with all you animals. It's cold here in the winter, and there are very few flies, and we have to sleep most of the time. Do you suppose it could be managed?"

Mrs. Wiggins thought and thought, and finally she said: "I'd be glad to do you and Mr. Webb a good turn, because you keep the cow barn clear of flies in the summer. As far as your coming along goes, that isn't bothering me, for you can ride on my back. But I've been wondering how you could catch enough flies to keep you alive."

"That's just the difficulty," said the spider. "We'd be travelling all day, and even if we spun a web at night, when we camped, the flies wouldn't get caught in it till next morning, and then we'd be gone."

Mrs. Wiggins thought some more, and then she said: "I've got it! Suppose you spin a web between my horns! Then you'll have it with you all day, and you can catch plenty of flies." And Mrs. Webb was so delighted that she danced about on all her eight legs, and tickled Mrs. Wiggins's ear terribly, and then she ran up her thread as fast as she could and told her husband. And so they went along on the trip to Florida.

This was just the kind of thing Mrs. Wiggins was always doing.

The animals went on down the hill and across the second valley. They met a few people, in automobiles or on foot, but the people only stared and did not try to stop them. Then about four o'clock Alice and Emma, who had got tired and were riding on Hank's back, began quacking excitedly.

"There's something funny coming down the road after us in a cloud of dust!" they said.

"Automobile, probably," said Hank.

"It's too small for an automobile," said Alice.

"Then it's a man," said Mrs. Wiggins.

"It's too small for a man, and it comes too fast," said Emma.

Then they all stopped and looked, and away back on the road they saw a tiny cloud of dust coming along at a great rate, and they could not imagine what it could be. And then the wind blew the dust aside for a moment and they all set up a cheer. For they saw that it was Charles, the rooster, and Henrietta, his wife. And if you don't believe that a hen can run fast, you should have seen them coming down that road.

In a very few minutes they had caught up with their friends, and then there was a great shouting and laughing and asking of questions, but they were both so out of breath that they could not speak for quite ten minutes.

Henrietta spoke first. "Good gracious, what a day I've had!" she exclaimed, fanning herself with her wing. "Yes, we decided to come. Charles felt so bad this morning when you all started out. So I got my sisters to take his place in the mornings. There are eight of them, you see. That makes one for each day in the week, and one over, to look after the children, or help out if one of the others is sick."

"But can your sisters crow?" asked Freddy.

"Crow?" said Henrietta. "Of course they can crow! Any hen can crow if she wants to, better than any rooster that ever was hatched."

"Why don't they ever do it then?" asked Jinx.

"Good gracious, what a silly question, cat! The roosters would never get up at all in the morning if the hens started to crow. They'd loaf round and sleep all day. They do little enough as it is. But at least they're out of the hen house early in the morning so their wives can get some work done. H'm! Crow indeed! I guess not!"

The animals were all glad to have Charles and Henrietta with them, and they went on for a way, and camped that night under a big oaktree by the roadside. For a time they sat about and told stories and jokes and made plans for the future, but they were all tired, and one by one they dropped off to sleep. Before Charles's eyes closed, he looked drowsily up at the starry sky above him, and at the long, mysterious, white road by which they had camped.

"What a wonderful time we're going to have," he muttered sleepily. "This is the first time since I was a chick that I haven't had to worry about getting up in the morning.

> *"Oh, the winding road is long, is long,*
> *But never too long for me.*
> *And we'll cheer each mile . . . mile'th song . . . song . . ."*

His voice trailed off into silence, and he was sound asleep.

"Here I am," she said, "down among the fishes."

V

AT the First

glimmer of daylight next morning Charles awoke. He stretched his wings, flapped them a couple of times, and then, before he knew what he was doing, gave a loud crow.

He had perched on a limb of the oaktree, and just under him Hank was standing, fast asleep. Horses can sleep standing up as well as lying down, because they have four legs and don't fall over, and Hank had gone to sleep that way because the grass was wet with dew, and he thought if he lay down in it, it would be bad for his rheumatism. When Charles crowed, Hank opened his eyes.

"Goodness!" he said. "You startled me! I thought you were not going to crow this morning. You said you were going to sleep till ten o'clock."

Charles looked foolish. "I suppose," he said, "that I've got so in the habit of getting up early and crowing that I do it without thinking."

"Well, in that case," said Hank, "I don't see why you complain so much about it. If you do it without thinking about it, it's just like breathing, and nobody ever complains about having to breathe."

"No," said Charles, "that's gospel truth!"

"I expect," said Hank, "that you've complained about it for so long that you do that without thinking, too."

This was a little hard for Charles to understand, but he thought about it for a while. And then he said: "You're right, Hank. I never realized it before. I don't really mind getting up and crowing a bit, now I come to really think of it. But," he added in a whisper, "don't tell Henrietta I said go."

By the time the sun was up the animals were all up too, and getting their breakfast. Hank and Mrs. Wiggins ate the long, juicy grass that grew beside the road, and Freddy ate the acorns that had fallen from the oaktree, and Charles and Henrietta and the mice ate beechnuts from a beech-tree near by. Charles and Henrietta ate the nuts whole, but the mice held them in their forepaws and stripped off the husks with their sharp little teeth and ate the sweet kernels. And Mrs. Wiggins gave the dog and cat some milk, and the spiders sat up between Mrs. Wiggins's horns, where they had spun their web, and caught flies for breakfast.

They all breakfasted well but Alice and Emma. Ducks like to eat the juicy weeds and things that they find in the mud at the bottom of ponds, but of course there wasn't any pond handy, so Alice and Emma ate a few beechnuts that the mice shelled for them, and said that they would wait for the rest of their breakfast until they came to the river.

It was not until early in the afternoon that they came down a long hill into another valley and found the wide, swift river that the robin had marked on the map. Here they sat down and rested while the ducks dived for their meal in the shallow water under the bank.

Mrs. Wiggins was very much interested in the diving. "I do wish I could do that," she said. "Just think how exciting it must be to be down among the fishes and see all the queer things that grow on the bottom, and look up at the sky through the green water!" She had been leaning over the edge as she talked, and all of a sudden the bank gave way, and down she went into the water with a terrible splash, and there she was, sitting in the river with the water up to her neck.

The animals all rushed to help pull her out, but they could do nothing for her, for she was quite helpless with laughter. She laughed and laughed. "Here I am," she said, "down among the fishes where I wanted to be. Nothing like having your wishes come true."

But suddenly she stopped laughing. "Goodness me!" she exclaimed. "Where are Mr. and Mrs. Webb? They were sitting on my head when I fell down."

She clambered hurriedly up the bank, and then they all searched the bushes along the shore for a long distance downstream. But the spiders were nowhere to be found.

"Well," said Mrs. Wiggins at last, "I guess they're gone. They won't drown— that's a comfort. They'll float down and land somewhere, but the current is pretty swift, and they may go miles before they can get ashore. I don't suppose we'll ever see them again. I hope this will be a lesson to me—cutting up silly on the bank like a two-weeks-old calf!" She was very angry with herself.

The animals all agreed, however, that it wasn't her fault, and pretty soon they started on again. They followed the river for some time, and by and by saw the white houses of the village and the high arches of the bridge ahead of them.

"I vote we wait till after dark to go through the village," said Robert. "Those people are sure to chase us or try to lock us up or something, if they see us."

This seemed a sensible plan, so they sat down by the river to wait. Pretty soon they heard a rattling and a puffing coming along the road, and then an automobile came into sight, and in it were the man with the black moustache and the boy with the dirty face. And behind it ran a black dog, twice as big as Robert and three times as fierce-looking.

As soon as the man saw the animals he stopped the machine. "Now we've got 'em, sonny," he said. "Here, Jack," he called to the dog. "Sick 'em, Jack! Go after 'em. Chew 'em up!"

The dog growled and bounded across the road, but Mrs. Wiggins lowered her horns and shook them threateningly, and Robert barked, and the cat arched his back and spat, and even Freddy squealed angrily. And the dog stopped.

"You'd better not bother us," said Mrs. Wiggins. "I don't want to," said the dog. "I haven't got anything against you. But he'll beat me if I don't."

"What do you stay with him for if he beats you?" asked Robert.

"Where could I go if I didn't stay with him?" asked the dog.

"Come along with us," said Robert, and he told him where they were going.

"That's fine!" said the dog, and he walked toward them, wagging his tail.

"Hey, Jack!" called the man angrily. "What's the matter with you, you useless, good-for-nothing cur? I'll beat you within an inch of your life!" And he picked up a stick and started after the dog.

But now that Jack had found some new friends, he wasn't afraid of his cruel master any more. He turned with a growl, and before the man could lift the stick, he was flat on his back on the road with Jack's forepaws on his chest.

Then the man changed his tune. "Good Jack! Good old boy!" he said. "Let me up, that's a good dog." But Jack did not move, and the other animals came and sat in a ring around the man, and the boy jumped out of the automobile and ran away across the fields yelling, just as he had done before. I don't know that I blame him.

After a while, when they thought they had scared the man enough, they let him up, and he walked over to the automobile without a word and got in it and drove off. Then Jack told them that he had lived with the man for five years, and that it had indeed been a terrible life, for the man hardly gave him anything to eat, and he beat him nearly every day.

"I guess Mr. Bean is a pretty good master after all," said Hank. "At least he never beats us, and if some things aren't just as we should like to have them, it's because he's poor and can't afford to have them better."

"You don't happen to have a bone about you, do you?" asked Robert. "I haven't had a good gnaw since I left home."

"The farm where I have been living is just a little way back along this road," said Jack, "and I buried two good bones in the orchard yesterday. If you'll come with me, we'll get them. Can you spare the time?"

"There's plenty of time," said Robert, "because we can't start on until after dark." So the two dogs raced off together to get the bones.

All this time Mr. and Mrs. Webb had been floating peacefully downstream on the swift current of the river. Spiders can float, because they are very light. But they can't move round much on the water, because it is so slippery under their feet, and for every step they take in one direction they slide two in another. So Mr. and Mrs. Webb just set still and sailed along and admired the changing scenery of the banks.

"I don't know why anyone should want a private yacht when they can travel like this," said Mr. Webb. "It's delightful. Though I must say I am sorry to miss the trip to Florida."

"No use crying over spilt milk," said his wife. "Or spilt spiders either, and that's what we are. We'll never see *those* animals again. Even if we could get over to the bank and climb up to the road before they came along, they'd go right by without either seeing or hearing us."

"But," said Mr. Webb, "they spoke of crossing a bridge further down the river. If we got to that before they did, we could try to make them see us, anyway."

"Now, that's an idea," exclaimed his wife. "You've got a head on you, Webb. I always knew you did have, in spite of what my father said about you before we were married."

"I know what he said well enough without your repeating it every five minutes," grumbled Mr. Webb. "He said I didn't have gumption enough to catch a lame fly without wings. That's what you're thinking about, I suppose."

"No," said Mrs. Webb, "I was thinking about the time he said you'd never be hanged for your beauty, and you ought to—"

"That's enough," said Mr. Webb crossly. "You'd be better occupied thinking about what we're going to do when we get to the bridge than raking up all those old things. There it is just ahead of us."

So Mrs. Webb stopped talking, and they began to think up a plan, and by the time they were almost to the bridge, they had decided what they would do.

The current bore them swiftly down toward one of the arches, but under the arch some dead branches were sticking up through the water, and they caught hold of these and climbed up over them to the bridge.

"They haven't come by yet," said Mr. Webb, after they had examined all the footprints of animals that were plainly marked in the dust on the floor of the bridge. "There have been some horses and dogs along here today, but no cows or pigs or cats or ducks."

So they both climbed up to the iron beam on one side of the bridge, and each of them fastened the end of a thread to the beam, and then they dropped down, spinning out the thread as they went, and carried it across the bridge and fastened the other end to the iron beam on the other side. They did this several times, until they had a bridge of threads, strong enough to hold them both, right across the roadway and about ten feet above it. Then they walked out to the middle of it and waited.

Of course they did not know that the animals had decided to wait until after dark to cross the bridge, and by the time the sun had gone down and the stars had begun to wink out, and lights to twinkle in the houses, they commenced to be worried. But there was nothing to do but wait, and at last they heard the shuffle and patter of many paws and hoofs, and the animals came down the road and on to the bridge. They were walking as quietly as possible, so that the people in the houses would not hear them, but spiders can see in the dark, and when Mrs. Wiggins's nose was just under them, they each slid spinning down a thread and landed on it.

Mrs. Wiggins gave a tremendous sneeze that nearly blew them off, for they had tickled her nose dreadfully, but they hung on tight.

"Dear me!" said Mrs. Wiggins. "I do hope I'm not getting a cold, being out so late in the night air!"

But Mr. Webb had crawled up close to her ear, and he said: "It's us, Mrs. Wiggins—the Webbs. We waited for you on the bridge."

Then Mrs. Wiggins told the other animals what had happened, and they were so glad that they gave a loud cheer, and they all said how happy they were to have the Webbs with them again, and how clever the spiders were to have thought of such a good scheme. And all the villagers came to their doors and looked out to see what the noise was, but by this time the travelers were across the bridge and didn't care.

That night they camped in a deserted barn, and it was lucky they did, for toward morning a heavy shower came up. But the roof was still good, and though most of them woke up when the rain started, they were dry and warm, and soon they went back to sleep again with the pleasantest sound in the world in their ears—the soft drumming of rain on shingles.

VI

SO for **T**WO weeks the animals travelled on toward Florida.

"It must be a long way," said Hank. "The weather doesn't seem to get any warmer."

"But it doesn't get any colder, either," said Mrs. Wiggins, "and down here the leaves are still on the trees. When we left home, the trees round the farm had all shed their leaves and were ready for the winter."

"Well, I don't care how far it is," said Hank. "We're certainly having a good time. I shall be almost sorry when we get there."

Nearly every day now large flocks of birds passed by them overhead, southward bound. And one morning the same swallow who had first put the idea of migrating into Charles's head dropped down from the sky and circled about over them. She had left home two days earlier, and she gave them all the news of the farm, and messages from their relatives, and told them that Mr. and Mrs. Bean were well, but that they felt very bad that the animals had left them.

"At first," she said, "Mr. Bean thought someone had stolen you, but then somehow he guessed that you had decided to go to Florida for the winter. I heard him tell Mrs. Bean that he hoped you'd have a good time and come back safe and sound in the spring. And he said that he was going to try to make things more comfortable for you, although he didn't know how he'd manage it, because he didn't have money enough to fix things up the way they ought to be."

When the animals heard this, they felt a little sorry that they had left Mr. Bean without saying good-bye. "But we'll bring him something nice from Florida when we go back," they said.

So far they had kept away from the cities as much as possible, because they were afraid that the people would not understand that they were migrating, and would try to lock them up and keep them.

And when they had to go through villages, they always waited till late at night, when everyone was asleep. But at last one day, away off in the distance, they saw a little speck of gold, that glittered and sparkled in the bright sunlight.

They wondered and wondered what the gold thing could be, but none of them knew, and pretty soon, as they went along, the road turned into a street, and there were houses on both sides of it and trolley tracks down the middle. And the speck of gold grew bigger and bigger. It looked as if a great golden balloon was tethered among the trees ahead of them.

"We're coming to a city," said Robert. "We'd better turn off this road and go round it."

"I wish I knew what the gold thing is," said Freddy, the pig. Freddy had a very inquiring mind.

Just then a little woolly, white dog with a very fancy blue ribbon around his neck came along, and Freddy asked him.

The little dog stuck his nose up in the air. "Don't speak to me, you common pig," he said.

"Eh?" said Freddy. "What's the matter with you? I only asked you a civil question."

"Go away, you vulgar creature," said the little dog snippily.

"Oho!" said Freddy. "You're too stuck up to talk to a pig, are you?" And he laughed and ran at the little dog and rolled him over and over in the road till his white coat and blue ribbon were both grey with dust. Then he stood him on his feet and said: "Now answer my question."

Then the little dog meekly told him that the thing that looked like a golden balloon was the dome of the Capitol, and that the city they were coming to was Washington, where the President lives. And when Freddy had given him a lecture on politeness and had helped him to brush the dust off himself, he let him go.

"I'd like to see the President," said Hank.

All the others said they would too, but they were afraid to go into the city because the people might lock them up, and boys were sure to throw stones at them.

But Jinx, the cat, said: "I vote we go, just the same. I don't believe the President will let them do anything to us. And we can see the Capitol and the Washington Monument and maybe go up to the White House and call on the President."

So they decided to go, and started down the street toward the city. All the people came out on their doorsteps to watch them go by, but nobody bothered them, and by and by they came to the Capitol. They stood for a long time and admired the big, white building, with its many columns and its gilded dome, and then they walked round to the side and admired it some more, and while they were standing there, two senators in silk hats came out and saw them.

"I didn't know animals ever visited the Capitol," said the first senator.

"Neither did I," said the second senator. "But I don't see why they shouldn't. I think it's rather nice.

Then a third senator came out and joined the other two, and he said: "By George! I have heard about these animals! They belong to one of my constituents. They're going to Florida for the winter, and I believe they're the first animals that ever migrated. This, gentlemen, is one of the most important occurrences in the annals of this august assemblage. I'm going to order a band, and take them round and show them the city."

So he went in and ordered the band, and told the other senators, who put their heads out of the windows and smiled and waved to the animals.

"What's a constituent?" asked Mrs. Wiggins.

But none of the others could tell her, and to this day she has never found out.

Pretty soon the band came, and they struck up "Marching Through Georgia," and went up the wide avenue toward the White House, and the animals marched behind. First came the senator in his high hat, and then Charles and Henrietta, and then Mrs. Wiggins, with the mice sitting on her back, and then the two dogs and Freddy, the pig, and then Hank, with Alice and Emma on *his*

back, and last came Jinx. They all walked in time to the music and held their heads up and pretended not to see any of the people that crowded the sidewalks, as everyone always does when he is in a parade. Beside them walked twenty policemen, to keep the people back and to prevent them from pulling the tail feathers out of the ducks or chickens to keep as souvenirs.

They went all over the city, and the senator showed them all the fine buildings and parks and monuments, and last they came to the White House. And there was the President out on the front porch, smiling and bowing to them, and as they filed past, he shook them each by a claw or a paw or a hoof. Even Eek and Quik and Eeny and Cousin Augustus overcame their timidity and put their tiny paws into the President's big hand. They were all very proud.

And then they went on with the band playing a different tune every ten minutes, and the people cheering and waving handkerchiefs. When they got to the edge of the city, the band stopped and the senator made them a speech, which began:

"Friends and constituents, I am very sensible of the honor which you have done me today. To welcome a delegation of the home folks to the Nation's Capital is one of the few pleasures that cheer the burdened brow of those whose stern duty it is to keep their shoulder always to the wheel of the ship of State. And that reminds me of the story of the two Irishmen."

He told the story, and the animals laughed politely, although they did not see anything very funny about it, and that is why it is not written down here. Nor is the rest of the senator's speech written down, for the animals did not understand much of it, and I am not at all sure that the senator did either. But all agreed that it was a stirring speech.

Then the senator said good-bye to the adventurers, and the band played "Auld Lang Syne," and the animals went on their way.

"Well," said Mrs. Wiggins with a sigh, as she dropped off to sleep that night, "we certainly had a grand time. But I do wish I knew what a constituent is."

VII

ONE afternoon

As the animals were marching along southward, they came to a deep, dark pine wood. It was a warm day, for they were getting near Florida now, and the road was very rough and stony. They were all hot and tired and cross. Even the good-natured

Mrs. Wiggins grumbled as they plodded along between the rows of tall, gloomy trees.

"I wish these woods would come to an end," she said. "I never saw such a place! Nothing but pine needles—no grass, no water. And it's almost suppertime, too."

Robert put his nose up in the air and sniffed. "I smell rain," he said. And just as he said it, there came a long, low grumble of distant thunder.

"Well, we have got to find a shed or a barn or something," said Hank, the old, white horse. "I'm not going to stand under a tree in a thunder shower for anybody."

"My goodness!" said Henrietta crossly. "What's the good of *talking*! Why don't you *do* something? Jinx, why don't you climb a tree and see if you can see a barn?"

This was sensible advice, so Jinx climbed up to the top of the tallest pine he could find. When he came down, he said: "I saw the sun going down in the west, and I saw a thunderstorm coming up in the south. And the woods go on for miles and miles. But about half a mile farther along there is a little log house. And there is a chimney on the house, and there is smoke going into the chimney."

"Coming out of the chimney, you mean," said Hank.

"I mean just what I say," said Jinx. "There is smoke coming from all parts of the sky and gathering into a cloud and pouring down the chimney."

"Fiddlesticks!" exclaimed Henrietta. "I never heard of such nonsense!"

"I don't know whether it's nonsense or not," said the cat, "but that's what I saw. If you're so smart, why don't you climb up the tree and take a look yourself?"

Henrietta didn't dare climb the tree, so she said: "Fiddlesticks!" again in a very loud voice, and walked off.

It was getting darker and darker, and the thunder was rumbling and rolling and coming nearer and nearer.

"Well, there's no use quarreling about it," said Mrs. Wiggins. "If there's a house, there's a barn, and if there's a barn, maybe we can get into it, out of the rain. I'm going along." And as this was a very sensible speech, they all started along after her.

Pretty soon they saw the log house. It sat back from the road, and was almost hidden by the trees and bushes that grew close up to its walls, so that if Jinx had not seen it from the treetop, they might have walked right by and never noticed it. And sure enough, round the top of the chimney was whirling what looked like a cloud of smoke. It whirled round and round, and then plunged down, and as the animals had never seen smoke going the wrong way before, they just stood and stared at it.

"What did I tell you?" said Jinx.

But Henrietta didn't answer him; she went up close to the house and looked and looked; and although it was getting pretty dark, she saw that it wasn't smoke after all, but a flock of birds, who were coming from every direction and dropping down the chimney.

"There's your smoke!" she exclaimed scornfully. "Chimney swallows! They live in the chimney, and they're going home to sleep. Smoke, indeed! That's the cat of it! Jumping at conclusions!"

"I'll jump at you if you say any more," said Jinx, "and pull all your tail feathers out."

"Come, come," said Mrs. Wiggins. "Stop your fighting, animals. If there are swallows in that chimney, it means that there hasn't been a fire built in the house in a long time. And *that* means that nobody lives there. Let's get inside."

Bang, bang-bingle BOOM! went the thunder. And the animals made a rush for the door and got inside just as the rain came down with a swish and a rattle.

There was only one room in the house, and in it were two chairs and a table and an empty barrel and a pile of old newspapers. Opposite the door was a big fireplace, and beside the fireplace was a neat pile of firewood. But everything was very dusty. Nobody had lived in the house in a long time.

Outside, the rain was coming down in torrents, and the thunder and lightning were very bad indeed. But the animals were happy because they were dry. Only the mice, Eeek and Quik and Eeny and Cousin Augustus, were rather frightened, and at the first really sharp flash of lightning they dived down an old mouse hole by the fireplace and didn't come up until the storm was over.

After the thunder and lightning had gone farther away again, and the rain had settled down to a good, steady, all-night pour, Robert said: "It's getting cold. I wish Mr. Bean was here to build us a fire."

"There are some matches up here," said Charles, the rooster, who had perched on the mantel over the fireplace.

"I believe I could build one myself," said Robert. "I've seen him do it often enough. Chuck down a couple matches, Charles."

"And what about all those swallows in the chimney?" asked Henrietta. "I suppose you never thought about them!"

"We'll invite 'em to come down and sit around the fire with us," said Robert. He called up to the swallows and invited them down, and pretty soon they began dropping down in twos and threes. They circled around the room, and then took their places in rows along the walls, for swallows don't perch as other birds do, holding on by their claws—they hang themselves up by the little hooks they have on the tops of their wings. There were so many of them that the log walls were covered with them, and they looked like a beautiful, shining black tapestry.

Then Robert built the fire with newspapers and wood, and he held a match between his teeth and scratched it on the floor and dropped it on the papers. He singed his nose before he got through. but at last he got the papers to burning. Then all the animals had to

Bang, bang—bingle BOOM!

squat down on the hearth and blow the fire to make it go, because he hadn't built it very well. But at last it burned up brightly, and then they all sat round and talked.

"I'd like to know who lived in this house," said Charles.

"Nobody knows," said the oldest swallow, who was hanging just over the door. And all the other swallows said: "That's so," and rustled their wings.

"Nobody lived here in my grandfather's time," said the oldest swallow.

"That's so," said the other swallows again.

"And nobody lived here in my great-grandfather's time."

"That's so."

"And nobody lived here in my great-great-grandfather's time."

"That's so."

"And nobody—"

"Excuse me," said Robert politely, "but I don't think you need go any farther back. Don't people ever come here at all?"

"Once in a while—" the swallow began slowly. Before he could go on, the youngest swallow piped up: "That's so."

The oldest swallow glared at him crossly, and his mother spanked him soundly for speaking out of turn. For it is a custom among the swallows for the oldest and wisest one to do all the talking, and for the others to say: "That's so" when he has finished. They do this because there are so many of them, and if they all talked at once in their little twittery voices, nobody would be able to understand what they were talking about.

"Once in a while," the oldest swallow went on, when the little swallow had been spanked and sent off to cry softly in a corner, "men come out to this house to look for the money that is supposed to be hidden here. It is said that a bag of twenty-dollar gold pieces is concealed in or somewhere near the house. But if that is so, nobody has ever found it."

The animals were all very much excited at this piece of news. Of course they could not use money themselves, but they thought how nice it would be if they could find the gold and take it back to Mr. Bean, who needed money so badly. Then he could buy all the things he wanted, and could repair the barn and the henhouse, and perhaps put stoves in them to keep the animals warm in cold weather. So they all started hunting for the place where the money was hidden.

Hank tapped with his hoof on the floor and the walls, to see if they sounded hollow, and Jinx, the cat, climbed up on all the shelves and peered into cupboards, and Eek and Quik and Eeny and Cousin Augustus went back down the old mouse hole in the corner and scurried around under the floor and explored every crack and crevice. Even Mr. and Mrs. Webb slipped into the many cracks in the walls and fire-place and looked round. But they didn't find any sign of the money.

"The only place we haven't looked is the chimney," said Freddy, the pig, at last.

"It is not in the chimney," said the oldest swallow. And all the other swallows said: "That's so."

"Well, I guess we'll have to give it up," said Freddy. "It isn't in the house, and if it's buried outside, we could never possibly find it."

And so they gave it up and came back and sat round the fire and told stories and played guessing games till bedtime.

VIII

EARLY

the

Next

morning Mr. Webb slipped out to get a breath of fresh air before breakfast. It was a bright clear morning. He took a long drink of fresh cold water from a raindrop, and then strolled along over the pine needles, humming to himself.

Oh, the winding road is long, is long.
      But never too long for me. . . .

Pretty soon he met an ant.

"Good morning," he said politely. "I am a stranger in these parts. I wonder if you can tell me if there is any good fly-catching in the vicinity?"

Now, almost always, if you speak to an ant, no matter how pleasantly, it will walk right by without answering. Ants do this because they are always busy, and they think conversation is a waste of time. But Mr. Webb was a fine-looking spider, and the ant was rather flattered at being spoken to by him. So she said:

"I'm sure I don't know, sir. But there aren't many spiders in our neighborhood, so I should think not."

"Ah, that's a pity," said Mr. Webb. "But it seems a very pleasant neighborhood."

"We like it," said the ant. "Although it's not as pleasant as it used to be before the robber ants came. They live in an old stump down in the woods, and they are all the time stealing our children and robbing our storehouses."

"Dear me!" said Mr. Webb. "That is very trying."

"Indeed you may say so!" she replied. "It's hard enough to bring up a family of fifty. children these days without having robbers about. We had to leave our old house and build a new one, deeper under the ground, so it wouldn't be so easy for them to break into it. Perhaps you'd like to see it?"

"I should be charmed," said the spider; and so she led him to where there was a little hole in the ground, out of which ants were carrying bits of dirt and sand, which they dropped outside before hurrying back for more. She led him down the hole and into a long tunnel. Part of the tunnel was so narrow that Mr. Webb had trouble squeezing through, but at last they came out in a large room which was really the ants' dining room. Here there were dozen of ants running to and fro, popping in and out of doorways; some of them bringing food which they fed to the ant children, and others carrying out dirt from the tunnels and corridors they were building. They were all much too busy to pay any attention to their visitor, and they merely nodded and said: "How do," and went on with their work.

"It is a very pleasant house," said Mr. Webb, when he had been shown through all the many rooms and passages.

"Ah, you should see our other house!" said the ant with a sigh. "Gold floors in the reception hall and the dining room, and a gold ceiling in the nursery! There wasn't a finer one in the woods."

Mr. Webb pricked up his ears. "I should think not!" he said. "Gold floors, eh? Now, may I ask how that happened?"

"Nobody knows," said the ant. "When my grandmother first moved into the house, some of them were there, and then later, when we enlarged the house and dug out more rooms, we found more of them."

"I should like to see that," said Mr. Webb.

"If I weren't so busy this morning, I would take you over and show them to you," said the ant.

"I am afraid I am keeping you from your work," said Mr. Webb; "so I'll just run along. But if you will show me where your old house is, I'll run in and look at it on my way back to join my friends."

So the ant went up to the door with him and showed him just which way to go, and then he thanked her politely for her hospitality and said good-bye.

Without much trouble he found the house that the ants had moved out of, and he crawled down the tunnel into the empty rooms that had once been a happy home, but were now empty and deserted. Soon he stood in the dining room. It wasn't very large. Even Mr. Webb, who was a very small spider, could walk across it in five or six steps. But sure enough the floor was of bright, shining, yellow gold. And there were raised letters on it, and the figure of an eagle.

Now before he was married to Mrs. Webb, Mr. Webb had travelled round a good deal. And once he had lived in a bank. So he knew what a twenty-dollar gold piece looks like. And now he knew that the floor of this ants' dining-room was a twenty-dollar gold piece.

He did not wait to look at the other rooms, but hurried back to the log house as fast as he could go. For he remembered what the swallow had told them about the bag of gold, and he knew that he had found it.

This was what had happened. The ants who had first built that house had happened to begin digging just where the bag of gold was buried. It had been buried a long, long time, and the cloth had rotted away. The ants had tunneled in and around the gold coins, and wherever one lay flat, they had made it the floor or ceiling of a room.

Mr. Webb got back just as the animals were ready to start. They gathered round him with their ears as close to him as they could get, so they could hear his tiny voice, and he told his story, and then they all rushed out to the ant house, and the two dogs and Freddy, the pig, started digging. Freddy dug with his long sharp nose, but the dogs dug with their forefeet. And in no time at all they had uncovered a great shining heap of gold coins.

Then they were all very glad, and Charles, the rooster, was so excited that he crowed and crowed.

But Henrietta said: "My goodness! Stop that noise! I don't see what you are all so happy about anyway. Now you've dug it up, what are you going to do with it?"

"Take it back to Mr. Bean, of course," said Robert.

"What are you going to do about going to Florida, then?" asked Henrietta. "Are you going to lug it all the way to Florida, and then back again? And what are you going to carry it in?"

"We hadn't thought about that," said the animals.

"Well, you'd better think about it now," said Henrietta. "The only thing you can do with the gold now is to bury it again, and get it when we come back from Florida. But I'm sure I don't know how we're ever going to take it to Mr. Bean."

"Oh, we can carry it in baskets or something," said Freddy. "Don't you worry about that, hen."

So they scraped the earth back into the hole and covered up the treasure, and then they started along.

IX

AS they

W ent on

southwest, the days grew hotter.

Away back up north, at the

other end of the road down which they were traveling, snowflakes

were flying, and Mr. Bean's breath was like smoke in the frosty air when Henrietta's sisters woke him in the morning and he put his head out of the window to see what the day was going to be like.

But down south the air was soft and warm, and the trees and the fields were green, and the animals tramped along merrily all day, and camped by the roadside at night. The only thing that worried them was how they were to get the gold coins back to Mr. Bean. There were about half a bushel of them, and even if they were in a sack or a basket, they would be much too heavy for one animal to carry, because gold is heavier than almost anything else in the world.

But Mrs. Wiggins, who always looked on the bright side of things, said: "We have got all winter in Florida to think about how to carry them. If we can't think of some scheme by spring, we aren't very bright animals. I for one don't intend to worry about it any more."

By this time the travelers had got used to being stared at by the people they met, and so almost always when they came to a village, they walked straight through it instead of going around. When they did this, Jack, the black dog, would go to the butcher shop and sit up on his hind legs and beg in the doorway, and usually the butcher would give him a piece of meat or a bone, which he shared with Robert.

A good many of the people had heard of them, too, and knew that they had come hundreds of miles down from the cold north to spend the winter in Florida, and these people would come out to meet them when they came to the edge of the town, and bring them things to eat, and make a great fuss over them. In one town a band came out to meet them, just as in Washington, and there were carriages for them, too, and all the animals but Hank and Mrs. Wiggins rode through the town in the carriages.

But, of course, there were bad people, too, who had heard about them, and thought it a good chance to get some fine animals without paying for them. One day, as they were going along by the bank of a muddy, sluggish river, two men with guns jumped out from behind some bushes. As soon as they saw the guns, the animals started to run, but they were not quick enough, and before they knew what had happened to them, Hank and Mrs. Wiggins had ropes around their necks and were being led off down the road.

The other animals knew that the men would shoot at them with the guns if they tried to help their friends; so they hid in the bushes, and then followed along, keeping out of sight.

Pretty soon the men came to a gate, and they led the cow and the horse through the gate and past a small, white house, and locked them up in a big, red barn. Then they walked back to the house, whistling, with their guns over their shoulders, to get their supper, for it was six o'clock.

"I guess there's *two* animals that won't do any more migratin'," said one.

And the other laughed a loud, coarse laugh and said: "They'll do a little work now, instead of loafing round the country."

And they opened the door and went into the house without wiping their muddy boots on the doormat.

As soon as they had gone in, Jinx, the cat, sneaked up to the barn through the long grass. He crept along so very carefully that the tops of the grass hardly moved. He climbed up and looked in through the little, dusty window, and saw Hank and Mrs. Wiggins standing on the barn floor. Their heads drooped, and they looked very miserable and unhappy. Then he tapped cautiously on the window with his claw, and called in a low voice: "Hey! Hank!"

The horse jumped and raised his head. "Is that you, Jinx?" he said.

"Yes," said the cat. "I came to see if you were all right. The others are hiding in the bushes down by the river. We're going to try to rescue you."

"Well, I don't see how you're going to do it," said Hank. "We are both tied up, and the barn-door is locked. It's very discouraging, to come all this distance and get almost to Florida, and then be stolen. I'm sure I don't know what Mr. Bean will say."

"Now don't talk like that," said Jinx. "You'll escape somehow. We won't desert you. Do you suppose you could kick a couple of boards out of the side of the barn if you could get loose?"

"I won't say I couldn't," said Hank. "I've got my heavy shoes on.

But it would take some time, and before I had made an opening big enough to get out of, the men would hear the racket and come out and tie me up again."

"We'll attend to that," said Jinx. "You just have patience, now, and I'll send the mice in to get you loose. They'll gnaw those ropes and straps off you in no time. Then I'll come and tell you when it's time to break out."

So Jinx went and told the mice, and they got into the barn through a crack in the floor, and gnawed at the ropes with their little, sharp teeth until they had cut them in two.

By this time it was dark, and Jinx and Freddy, the pig, and Charles and Henrietta and the two dogs and Alice and Emma came up to the house and peeked in the window. The two men had cleared off the supper table and were playing parchesi. They played four games, and between times they laughed and talked about how smart they were to have got two good animals without paying for them, and wondered how much money they would get for them when they sold them.

The big man was a very poor player, and he lost every game. He would study and study over his moves, but he always made them wrong. Now Freddy was a very good 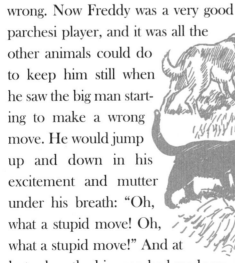 parchesi player, and it was all the other animals could do to keep him still when he saw the big man starting to make a wrong move. He would jump up and down in his excitement and mutter under his breath: "Oh, what a stupid move! Oh, what a stupid move!" And at last, when the big man had made an especially bad move and lost the fifth game, Freddy could stand it no longer, and he shouted out: "Oh, you big silly! Why didn't you move your *other man?* Now he's beat you again."

The men jumped up so quickly that they knocked over the parchesi board and spilled the men all over the floor.

"What was that?" said the big man.

"It sounded like a pig," said the other. "Up and after him!"

And they rushed out without even stopping to get their hats. But they grabbed up their guns as they went through the doorway.

The animals ran in all directions, but it was bright enough outside so that the men could see Freddy as he dashed out through the gate and down the road, and so they dashed after him. Now, Freddy was a very clever pig, but he wasn't much of a runner, and the smack, smack, smack of heavy boots on the hard road sounded louder and louder behind him, as the men caught up.

"They're going to catch me," he thought. "Oh dear! I do hope they don't like pork! The great stupid creatures! I could beat them at parchesi, and I could beat them at eating, and I'm ever so much brighter than they are. But they're going to catch me. And I've got more legs than they have, too!"

He didn't dare turn off the road because his legs were so short that he knew he would very quickly get tangled up in the bushes, but the road was close to the river at this place, and just as the big man reached out to grab him by the tail, Freddy dodged and jumped with a splash into the water. Most pigs don't like water any too well, but Freddy had been taught swimming by Emma, the duck, and he could do all sorts of fancy strokes, and could even swim on his back, which is something hardly any pigs ever learn to do. So he struck out bravely for the other shore.

The men stopped short, and the big one raised his gun to shoot. But the other said: "No, no! Don't shoot! We want to capture him alive and sell him." And he pulled off his coat and shoes and jumped in after Freddy.

The big man waited a minute; then he too laid down his gun and took off his coat and shoes and jumped in.

Freddy heard them puffing and blowing behind him like sea lions, but he put his snout down into the water and swam the Australian crawl, the way Emma had showed him, and pretty soon he came to the other bank. There was no use climbing out and trying to run away, because the men would catch him; so he turned around and swam back again.

For quite a long time the men chased him, up and down and across the river, and once or twice they nearly had him, but he was very wet and slippery, so that there was nothing for them to get hold of, and every time he got away. And then at last he heard a dog bark.

The sound came from the place on the bank where the men had left their guns, and Freddy swam toward it. And there, close down by the edge of the water, were all the animals, and Hank and Mrs. Wiggins were there too, because they had broken out of the barn while the men were chasing Freddy.

Robert and Jack helped the exhausted Freddy out of the water, but when the two men started to follow him, they growled and barked and showed their teeth. Then the men swam downstream a way, but the dogs followed along the bank and growled at them every time they tried to land. And at last they swam across the river and went home another way.

It was not a very pleasant way, because there was no road on the other side of the river, and to walk across fields in your stocking feet is very painful. The sticks and stones hurt like anything. And they were wet through, and had lost their guns, and when they got down opposite their house, they had to jump in and swim across the river again. And then they found the horse and the cow gone, and a big hole in the side of their barn.

And when they got in the house, they were angrier still, for there was the parchesi board on the floor, and the parchesi men had rolled off into corners and under the stove and behind things. If the floor had been clean, it wouldn't have been so bad, but it was terribly dirty because they never wiped their boots on the mat when they came in, and so it was almost impossible to find the men. Indeed, there were three that they never did find. And so they could never play parchesi any more at all.

X

NOW as They

went along, the weather got warmer and warmer, and so they got up very early in the mornings and did most of their traveling while it was still cool.

About eleven o'clock they would stop under the shade of a big tree by the roadside, and lie about in the grass and talk until late in the afternoon. And then they would go on for a while until they found a good camping-place. When they came to a river or a pond, they would all go in swimming. It was the pleasantest life you can imagine.

One day, about noon, they were all sitting in the shade beside the road at the top of a steep hill. On the other side of the road was a house, but nobody was in sight but a little girl, who was wheeling her dolls up and down in a dolls" baby carriage.

Most of the animals were asleep, because Jinx, the cat, had been talking, and nobody paid any attention when he talked. That didn't make any difference to Jinx, though. He went right on telling how smart he was and bragging about what he could do.

That was the worst of Jinx: he always talked about himself. If the animals talked about automobiles, he told how much *he* knew about them, and how well *he* could run one; and if they said: "Let's go in swimming," he told what a fine swimmer *he* was, although they all knew he hated the water and couldn't swim two strokes.

Today he was talking about bicycles.

"'Tisn't anything to ride a bicycle," he said. "I've ridden 'em—all kinds—bicycles and tricycles and velocipedes and—"

"Oh, you're a wonder!" said Freddy crossly, and all the other animals who were awake said: "Oh, *please* keep still, Jinx."

Alice and Emma, the two white ducks, didn't say anything, however, because they were  always very polite, and were afraid of hurting Jinx's feelings. They were almost too polite, if such a thing is possible. But they were just as tired of hearing Jinx talk as the others were; so Alice said: "Come on, Emma; let's go play with the little girl." And they got up and ruffled out their feathers and waddled sedately across the road and up the path to the house.

The little girl was delighted to have someone to play with, and she put the ducks in the carriage with the two dolls and pretended that they were the neighbor's children, and that she had to look after them while their mother was out shopping. And she pretended that they might catch cold and wrapped them up in a little blanket, and Alice and Emma were so polite that they let her do it, although it was so hot that they nearly boiled.

Then the little girl said: "Are you comfortable, darlings?"

And Emma said: "Quack, quack!"

"Oh!" said the little girl. "She can say: 'Mamma!'" And Emma had to keep on quacking for quite a long time while the little girl hopped up and down and clapped her hands.

By and by the little girl got tired of this and said she would take them for a ride, so she wheeled them down the path and out into the road. Then she saw a bright blue butterfly and ran off across the field after it, leaving the dolls' baby carriage standing in the road at the top of the hill, near where the animals were resting.

Jinx was still talking about bicycles.

"I can ride backwards, and with both paws off the handle bars, and I can ride up and down stairs—"

"Oh, stop talking such foolishness!" said Henrietta. "You couldn't ride a bicycle. Your legs aren't long enough to reach the pedals."

"They wouldn't have to be," said Jinx. "I could do all that going down hill. Just start at the top, and *whizzz!*—down you go at sixty miles an hour! And—"

"Oh, stop *talking!*" exclaimed Henrietta. "I never heard such an animal! Brag, brag, brag! That's all there is to you! You wouldn't dare ride down that hill in that doll carriage there!"

"Ho!" said Jinx. "That's nothing! That's so easy it isn't worth bothering about."

"All right," said Henrietta. "Let's see you do it, then."

"I suppose you think I can't?" said Jinx.

"I think you won't," said Henrietta bluntly.

Jinx got up and walked over to the doll carriage and climbed into it beside Alice and Emma and the two dolls.

"Why, it isn't anything," he said. "It isn't anything at *all!* Just slide down that hill? Pooh!" But he didn't seem very anxious to start.

"Please get out of the carriage, Jinx," said Emma. "There isn't room for all of us in here."

"Are you really going to slide down the hill, Jinx?" asked Alice. "Because if you are, I'm going to get out."

"Slide down that hill?" said Jinx. "And climb all the way back up again in the hot sun, just to prove I can do it? Huh! I should say not! If they don't believe me—well, they needn't, that's all!"

All the animals had waked up by now and had come out into the road.

"You don't dare slide down the hill," they shouted. "'Fraid cat! Coward!" And Freddy made up a verse and sang it while he danced around the carriage on his hind legs.

> "'Fraid cat Jinx,
> His tail's full of kinks!
>   He doesn't dare slide down the hill!
>   See how he shrinks!"

Now Jinx had no intention of sliding down the hill, which was a good mile long, with a curve at the bottom, and he was thinking hard for some good excuse. But while he was hesitating, Freddy bumped against the wheel of the carriage and gave it just enough of a push to start it slowly down the hill.

"Hey! What are you doing?" yelled Jinx, too frightened to jump.

The animals stopped shouting and stood with their mouths open as the doll carriage gathered speed and shot away from them down the steep hill. They heard the scared quacking of Alice and Emma, and saw their little white heads peering fearfully out; they saw Jinx

A very wet Jinx was crawling up onto the bank.

holding on for dear life with all his twenty claws as the carriage jumped and bounded from side to side of the road. And then it grew smaller and smaller and disappeared round the curve.

The animals were very much frightened, and they started down the hill as fast as they could go. Halfway down they heard a great noise behind them, and it was the little girl, who was coming after them, crying and sobbing at the loss of her dolls.

"That bad cat!" she wailed. "That bad, wicked cat! He stole my doll carriage and ran off with my dollies!"

The animals waited until she caught up, and Hank knelt down and let her climb up on his back. Then they went on.

Pretty soon they got to the curve at the foot of the hill. They went round it, and there was a bridge crossing a wide stream, and halfway across the bridge lay the doll carriage, upside down, and a very wet Jinx, with a bruise over one eye, was crawling up on to the bank out of the water. And out in the middle of the stream Alice and Emma were swimming about and quacking as if nothing had happened.

When the carriage had turned over, it had been going so fast that the ducks and the dolls and the cat had been thrown way up over the top of the bridge into the water. The dolls had sunk, and the cat had sunk, too, for a few minutes and had had a hard time getting ashore, for he wasn't much of a swimmer in spite of his bragging. But Alice and Emma hadn't minded a bit.

As soon as Jinx saw his friends, he tried to look as if he had done it on purpose.

"There!" he said. "I guess you won't dare *me* to do anything again! I guess I did it, didn't I? I guess *you* haven't got much to say!"

But the little girl jumped down from Hank's back and went over to him and began slapping him good and hard.

"You bad cat!" she cried. "You bad, *bad* cat! Where are my dollies?"

Jinx made himself as small as possible and put his head down between his paws and let her spank him. It didn't hurt as much as she thought it did, and as he said afterwards to Freddy—"it knocked all the water out of my fur."

But Alice and Emma dived for the dolls and brought them up and laid them on the bank to dry. And after a while, when the little girl was tired of spanking Jinx, she put them into the carriage again and Mrs. Wiggins pushed it back up the hill for her. But the little girl rode up on Hank's back.

After that, Jinx didn't talk so much. And if he did begin to boast, all the animals had to do was to say: "Kidnapper! Doll-stealer! Who got spanked by a girl?" And he would curl up and pretend to go to sleep.

VII

AND now

At last one day when the animals had been walking all morning through wild and swampy woods, they came out at the top of a long slope that went down to a wide valley in which were many green trees and comfortable-looking, white houses. A soft wind blew over the valley, and puffed into their faces a sweet delicious perfume, that none of them had ever smelled before. They sniffed the air delightedly.

"Mmmmmm!" said Mrs. Wiggins. "Isn't that good? It's better than clover. I wonder what it it."

"I know," said Jack. "I've smelled it at weddings. See all those little green trees down there? They're orange trees, and that smell is orange blossoms."

"Look! Look!" squealed Freddy. "There's a palm tree!"

"It's Florida!" shouted Jinx.

And all the animals shouted together: "Florida!" so that they could be heard for miles, and Alice and Emma hopped about and quacked and flapped their wings, and Charles crowed, and the dogs barked, and Mrs. Wiggins mooed, and Hank, the old, white horse, danced around like a young colt until his legs got all tangled up and he fell down and everybody laughed. Even the spiders raced around and around the web they had spun between Mrs. Wiggins's horns, and the mice capered and pranced.

"So this is Florida!" said Mrs. Wiggins. "Well, well!"

Then they started down the slope into Florida. And as they went, Freddy made up a song:

"The weather grew torrider and torrider,
And the orange-blossoms smelt horrider and horrider,
As we marched down into Florida."

"But the orange-blossoms *don't* smell horrid," said Robert.

"I know it," said Freddy. "But there isn't any other word that rhymes."

"Well, make up another song, then," said Robert.

So Freddy sang:

"Oh, the winding road to Florida
    Is a dusty road, and long,

But we animals gay have cheered the way
  With many a merry song.
Our hearts were bold—but our homes were cold.
  And that is why we've come
To Florida, to Florida,
  From our far-off northern home.

In Florida, in Florida,
  Where the orange blossom blows,
Where the alligator sings so sweet,
  And the sweet potato grows;
Oh, that is the place where I would be,
  And that is where I am—
In Florida, in Florida,
  As happy as a clam."

They all liked this song much better, and as they went along they sang lustily. They were so glad to have reached Florida at last that they forgot all about stopping to rest at noon, and they marched on until nearly three o'clock. Then Mrs. Wiggins sank down under a tree beside the road.

"I can't go another step!" she said. "I'm in a dripping perspiration. Charles, I'd take it kindly if you'd fan me with your wing for a few minutes."

So they all sat down and Charles very kindly fanned Mrs. Wiggins until she had cooled off. And as they were all pretty tired and hot, they decided to camp there that night and think about what they were going to do in Florida. And then in the morning they could go and begin doing it.

So they camped under the orange trees and discussed all the things they could do, and at last they decided to go to the seashore, as Freddy said he understood the sea-bathing was very fine there.

"But how can we find the seashore?" asked Robert. "You ought to have had that robin draw it on the map."

Freddy said it would be easy to find because Florida was a peninsula.

"What's a peninsula?" asked Jack, and Henrietta said: "Oh, don't ask him! He's just trying to show off."

But Freddy said: "A peninsula is a piece of land that is almost surrounded by water. That means that if you walk far enough in any direction but one, you will come to the ocean."

"Yes," said Robert, "but how do we know which direction is the one we ought *not* to walk in?"

"Why, the direction we came from, stupid," said Freddy. And he drew a little map on the ground and showed the animals what he meant.

So the next morning they started out to find the ocean. They travelled for four days before they saw it, away off in the distance, glittering and sparkling in the sunlight, and it was still another day before they came down to a broad beach of yellow sand and saw the great sheet of water stretching away before them for miles and miles. They just stood and looked at it for a long time, for none of them had ever seen anything like it before. And they rushed down the beach and swam out into the water.

So for a month they lived by the side of the ocean and rested from their long journey. They found an old barn not very far from the shore, and they cleaned it up and all lived there together happily. Every day at four o'clock they went in for a dip in the surf, and then they would lie round on the sand and talk until suppertime. It was a very lazy and pleasant life that they lived in Florida.

But after a while they got tired of doing nothing and began to long for new adventures. "Besides, we ought to travel around and see the country," said Charles. "When we get home, and everybody asks us what Florida is like, we want to be able to tell them."

So they said good-bye to the seashore, and to the horseshoe crabs and jellyfish, who had made things so pleasant for them during their stay, and set out for a tour of the state.

VII

DURING the Next

two months they visited all the principal points of interest in Florida, and saw all there was to see. They visited Palm Beach and the Everglades and Miami and the Big Cypress Swamp. And it was on the way across a corner of the swamp that they had a very exciting adventure.

It happened this way. When they first came to the swamp, most of the animals were afraid and did not want to go into it at all, for it stretched for miles and miles, and there were no roads or paths, and there was no firm ground to walk on, only water and mud and the great twisted, gnarly cypress roots. It was dark, too, because the trees grew so thick.

But Jinx said: "Oh, come on! Let's see what it's like. We don't have to go very far in. What are you afraid of?"

And so they started in.

At first it wasn't very hard walking, but soon the mud and water got deeper and the trees thicker together. And after a while longer there wasn't anything to walk on at all—only water and trees.

"I'm going back," said Mrs. Wiggins. And the other animals said they were too. Even Jinx agreed they couldn't go any farther.

But when they started to go back, they found that they hadn't the slightest idea which way to go. They had turned and twisted in and out among the trees so many times that they didn't know from which direction they had come. The water covered their footprints so they couldn't follow them. And over their heads the branches were so thick that they couldn't see the sun.

"Now we *are* in a mess!" said Henrietta, who had been riding on Hank's back. "I hope you're satisfied, Jinx!"

"It won't help any to call names," said Mrs. Wiggins. "Come along, let's try this direction. One way is as good as another, and this looks as if it might be right."

And so they went on, with Mrs. Wiggins in the lead. It was very dark and dismal. The water was black, and long beards of gray moss hung down from the branches of the trees. Again and again they had to swim, and the animals who could not swim climbed on the larger animals' backs.

At last it did seem as if they were coming out on dry land. Ahead of them they could see sunlight through the tree trunks, and they floundered and stumbled onward as fast as they could go. In a few minutes they came out on the bank of what seemed to be a small canal, and beyond the canal was a grassy meadow, green and pleasant in the bright sun.

"Well, this certainly isn't the way we came," said Mrs. Wiggins. "But, my word! that grass looks good! I guess we could get away with a few mouthfuls of that, eh, Hank? Come along, animals, let's swim over. It's something to stand on, at any rate."

"Look out! Don't bump your noses on those logs," said Jinx, pointing with one claw to what looked like a lot of tree trunks, lying half under water in the middle of the canal.

So they all swam over. But as they were climbing out on the farther bank, Henrietta began to cackle excitedly. "Look! Look! The logs are all coming to life!"

And sure enough, what they had thought were logs had suddenly started swimming after them. They were alligators!

"I certainly do *not* like this place!" said Mrs. Wiggins. But like most cows, she had a stout heart, and she turned round and lowered her horns and shook them threateningly at the alligators. "Keep away, now!" she said. "We won't stand any nonsense!"

But the alligators only laughed, and one of them said: "Oho! You won't, eh? Well, what did you come into our country for, then?"

"We're peaceable animals," said Mrs. Wiggins, "and all we ask is to be shown the shortest way out of your country. We are lost, and we shall be very much obliged to you if you will help us find ourselves again. But if you won't help us, we shall have to go on and find our own way out."

Then all the alligators laughed so hard that two of them choked, and their friends had to whack them on the backs with their tails. And they said: "Do you know where you are? You are on an island in the middle of the alligator country. You can't get away. And to-night we alligators are going to have you for supper."

The animals saw now that they were indeed in a bad fix. "This is even worse than being fricasseed," said Charles.

But Freddy, the clever pig, had an idea. And although he was very much scared, he said to the alligators: "Gentlemen, you will make a very great mistake if you eat us. We are not ordinary animals. We are the first animals in the world who ever migrated. We have come from far in the north; thousands of miles we have traveled, to visit your beautiful country, and to take back word of its loveliness to our people. Surely you would not be so inhospitable as to eat us for supper."

"He speaks very nicely," said one of the alligators, "but I am sure he would taste even better. He is so round and plump!"

But another one said: "There may be something in what you say, pig. We will take you to the Grandfather of All the Alligators, and you may tell him what you have told us. And perhaps he will let you go. And perhaps he will eat you for supper just the same. But that is for him to decide."

And so he led them across the island to where the water and the swamp began again on the other side. And he stood on the bank and called: "Oh, Grandfather of All the Alligators, there be strangers here who would have speech with thee."

Nothing happened for some time, and then there was a bubbling and a boiling of the water, and a huge head, as big as a barrel, appeared, and after the head a body as long as Mrs. Wiggins and Hank and Jack and Robert and Freddy together. It was the Grandfather of All the Alligators, and he was so old that there was green moss growing all over him.

He opened one wise old eye, and his deep grumbling voice said sleepily: "What do they want?"

"They don't want to be eaten for supper," said the other alligator.

"Eat them for lunch, then," said the Grandfather of All the Alligators, and began to sink out of sight again.

But Freddy rushed down to the edge of the water and shouted: "Oh, Grandfather of All the Alligators, we are strangers in your beautiful country and we have come thousands of miles to visit you and tell you of our own land, of which you have never heard."

The Grandfather of All the Alligators opened both eyes and stopped sinking.

"Why didn't you say so in the first place?" he asked. "That alters the case entirely. I hear very little news of the great world in this quiet spot. By all means tell me of your home."

"Oh, Grandfather of All the—" Freddy began. But the Grandfather of All the Alligators stopped him. "It will be better," he said, "if you call me simply grandfather." And he closed his eyes and sank till everything but his ears was under water, and prepared to listen.

Then Freddy told of the life they had lived up north on Mr. Bean's farm, and of how cold it was in winter, and of their trip to the South. Every time he stopped for breath, the alligators, who were sitting around him in a circle, would say: "Yes, yes; go on!" And Freddy went on until he was tired, and then Jinx took up the story until *he* was tired, and then Charles went on with it. And by the time Charles had finished, and they had told everything they could think of, it was almost sunset.

Then the Grandfather of All the Alligators came up to the top of the water again and opened his eyes and said: "I thank you for telling us of your wonderful country. It has been very interesting. And now, as it is almost suppertime, we will go on with the feast. I am sure you will all taste very much better for the entertainment you have given us."

At this the animals were very much alarmed. "You don't mean to say you meant to eat us all the time!" they cried.

"Why, of course," said the Grandfather of All the Alligators. "Nothing was ever said about our *not* eating you, was there?"

This made the animals very angry, and Jinx was so mad that he almost had a fit. "You mean to say," he screamed, "that you've gone and let us talk ourselves hoarse for nothing, you great big, muddy, long-nosed, leather-skinned hippopotamus, you? You ought to be ashamed of yourself! What do you suppose all the animals up north are going to think of you when they hear about it? Eating up visitors who come to make you a friendly call! A nice opinion they'll get of Florida!"

"My goodness, I should say so!" exclaimed Mrs. Wiggins. "And the President of the United States, too. He shook hands with us and wished us a pleasant journey. What'll *he* say?"

"He'll send his army down here and drive all you alligators into the ocean; that's what he'll do!" said Jinx.

The Grandfather of All the Alligators smiled, and his smile was eight feet broad. "What you say may be so," he remarked. "*But— who's* going to tell him? Answer me that. Who's going to tell him? You, madam?" he asked Mrs. Wiggins. "No-o-o, I think not. You'll be eaten up, horns, hoofs and tail. And so—"

But Henrietta interrupted. "*We're* going to tell him," she said. "My husband and I. You may eat the animals, but you can't eat us, because you can't catch us. *We* can fly."

"My dear," said the Grandfather of All the Alligators, "I am more than eight hundred years old. I was centuries old when Ponce de Leon came to Florida to look for the Fountain of Youth. I remember Balboa well—a tall man with a black beard and a shiny steel hat. He made the same mistake you did, my friends—he mistook me for a log. But he was more fortunate than you. He got away with merely the loss of one of his boots." The Grandfather of All the Alligators smiled at the memory. "A delicious boot that was, too—old Spanish leather. I chewed on it for half a day.

"Yes, as I was saying, I am very old. Yet in all my eight hundred years I have never seen or heard of a hen or a rooster who could fly like other birds."

Now it is true that hens and roosters cannot fly as well as most birds, but they don't like to be reminded of it. Henrietta became very angry.

"Is that so!" she exclaimed. "Well, if you've kept your eyes shut for eight hundred years, it's no wonder you don't know anything! Never saw a rooster who could fly, eh? Well, you're going to see one now. Charles," she said to her husband, "fly up in those trees on the other side of the water."

Now the trees were quite a long way off, and Charles had never in his life flown farther than from the ground to the top of a fence. "Good gracious, Henrietta," he whispered, "I can't fly up there. I won't be able to go half that distance, and I'll drop into the water and the alligators will eat me."

"They'll certainly eat you if you *don't* fly up there," she whispered back. "You've *got* to do it. It's our one chance of escaping. If they think you will go back and tell the President, they will let us."

"Well, I'll try it," said Charles. So he kissed Henrietta good-bye and squared his shoulders and flapped his wings and started, while all the animals cheered, and the alligators giggled and poked each other in the ribs with their elbows.

Charles flew up into the air—up, up, higher than he had ever been before, as high as the tops of the trees. And then he started across the water.

Down below, the animals held their breath as they watched him. They saw him flapping his wings so hard that feathers flew out of them and floated downward. But he could not get any higher; he was coming slowly down toward the water, and two of the alligators plunged in and swam out to be under him when he came down.

"He'll never make it," said Mrs. Wiggins sadly. "Never in the world!"

But suddenly they saw him stop moving his wings. He spread them out and held them motionless, and then, to the amazement of

"We alligators will have our little joke, you know."

all the onlookers, he went straight across the water—faster, faster, and landed with a flutter in the trees.

What had happened was this. There was a strong wind blowing across the swamp, but the island, shut in by walls of high trees, was like a room, and the wind did not come down there at all. It was this wind that had caught Charles and blown him safely across, but of course none of the onlookers knew this, and they thought that he had done it himself.

Then all the animals set up a great cheer, and the alligators had nothing to say at all, and the Grandfather of All the Alligators opened his eyes wider than he had opened them in six hundred years and exclaimed: "Well, upon my word! I never should have believed it! Never!"

But Henrietta said: "*Now* what are you going to do about eating us?"

"Why, that was all a joke, my dear," said the Grandfather of All the Alligators. "We alligators will have our little joke, you know. Do tell your accomplished husband to come back, so that we can thank him for this fine exhibition, and then he will show you the way out of the swamp, and part in peace and goodwill."

"Oh yes, you old fraud!" said Henrietta. "Ask him to come back so you can eat him? No, Charles will stay right where he is, in the top of that tree."

"Your suspicions are most unjust," said the Grandfather of All the Alligators with a sigh. "We wouldn't harm him for worlds. We respect and admire him greatly. However, I see you are anxious to be gone, and it is indeed getting late. My children," he said to the other alligators, "show these animals safely to the edge of the swamp, and see that no harm comes to them. Good-bye, my friends. I thank you one and all for your entertainment. I am sorry that you took our little joke in earnest. However, that is past now. No hard feelings, I trust?"

"Oh, none at all!" said Henrietta sarcastically. And the Grandfather of All the Alligators sank slowly out of sight.

The alligators showed the animals a dry and easy path to the edge of the swamp, and they were very happy when they were on dry land once more. Charles had not come down within reach of the alligators, but had fluttered along in the treetops. Then the alligators said good-bye and wished them a pleasant journey.

When the animals had gone on a little way, they looked back and saw the alligators sitting in a row and looking after them, and great tears were rolling from their eyes and dropping to the ground, and the sound of their sobbing could be heard for miles.

"Why, I believe they really are sorry to have us go," said Alice, the duck. "I suppose it *is* lonesome in that dreary swamp."

"Humph!" said Henrietta. "Of course they're sorry! But they're not crying because they like us. They're crying because they'll have to go to bed without their supper tonight."

XIII

NOW after The adventure with the alligators the animals rested for two days, and then they went on seeing the sights of Florida. They made a great many pleasant friends among the natives, and even Mr. and Mrs. Webb made the acquaintance of a number of very interesting and agreeable spiders, with whom they discussed fly-catching, and compared notes on weaving and other matters of interest.

But at last one morning when they awoke, the sky was full of flocks of birds—bluebirds and blackbirds and redwings and yellow-hammers and purple grackles—all flying steadily northward. And then they knew that spring had come and it was time for them to be starting back home.

"Well, I for one shall be glad to get back," said Mrs. Wiggins. "We've had a grand time traveling, but home's a pretty good place. The snow is all gone by this time, I expect, and Mr. Bean is getting ready to plant his potatoes and corn and cabbages."

"And the old elm by the barn is all covered with buds," said Charles.

"And the ice is gone out of the duck pond," said Alice and Emma.

"And Mr. Bean will need me to help with the spring plowing," said Hank.

"Come along, animals," said Freddy. "Let's start." And so they said good-bye to Florida and started home.

They had been traveling for about a week when they came one morning to a big field which was all heaped with tin cans and old shoes and ashes and rubbish of all kinds. There were prickly thistles growing in the field, and a goat was eating them.

"Good morning, goat," said Freddy.

"Good morning, pig," said the goat. "Have a thistle? They're delicious."

"No, thanks," said Freddy.

"Have you ever eaten one?" asked the goat.

"No," said Freddy. "They never looked very good to me."

"You'd be surprised," said the goat, "how tasty they are. Just take a nip of this big one here."

Freddy didn't want to try the thistle, but he was always very polite and didn't like to hurt the goat's feelings, so he took a large bite.

As soon as he had taken the bite, he wished he hadn't. The prickles tickled his mouth horribly and stuck into his tongue, and he coughed and sneezed and squealed and grunted and ran round and round in circles, while the other animals laughed and the goat looked at him in surprise. And at last he got it out of his mouth.

"I'm very sorry," said the goat. "Perhaps there was something the matter with that one. Now *here's* a nice one. Or perhaps you'd rather have a bit of old boot. There were two fine ones left here yesterday. I've eaten one, but—"

"No, thank you," said Freddy firmly. "Some people say a pig will eat anything, but really—one must draw the line somewhere, and I draw it at old boots."

"Well, well," said the goat with a sigh, "there's no accounting for tastes. I hoped that I might persuade you animals to settle down and live here with me. But of course if you don't like thistles, or boots—"

"We don't," said Mrs. Wiggins. "Any of us."

"Then that settles it," said the goat sorrowfully. "Because there's really nothing else here. I like it. But it's very lonesome. No one to talk to all day but the stupid cart-horses who bring the rubbish here to be dumped. And I do like good conversation."

He was so lonely that the animals spent the rest of the day with him and told him of their travels. Just as they were leaving, late in the afternoon, a farm wagon came along, piled high with rubbish. It belonged to a man who was moving into another house, and he had brought all the stuff that he didn't want to keep. He was going to throw it on the dump heap. On the very top of the load was a funny old-fashioned carriage.

The man threw the rubbish out of the wagon, carriage and all, and drove away.

"Must be some boots in that lot," said the goat, licking his lips, and began poking round in the heap.

But Jinx and Freddy had walked over and were looking at the funny old-fashioned carriage. They talked together in undertones for a few minutes, and then Jinx said: "Hey, Hank! Come here. Do you suppose you could draw this carriage?"

"Draw *that?*" said Hank indignantly. "I've drawn heavier wagons than that many's the time."

"Oh, I know you can draw it," said Jinx. "What I mean is—can you draw it the way it is, without any harness and straps and things?"

"No," said Hank. "I'd have to have a collar and traces and bridle and bit and surcingle and."

"Oh, we don't know what any of those things are," said Jinx, "and anyway we haven't got them. But here's an old piece of rope. Suppose we could tie that to the handles of the carriage and put it over your shoulders. Could you draw it then?"

"Why, I won't say I couldn't," said Hank. "But what do you want the carriage for anyway?"

"If you can draw it," said Jinx, "we can put the gold that we found in the ants' house in it and take it back to Mr. Bean."

Hank thought this was a fine plan, so Freddy got the rope and Jinx tied it to the handles of the carriage. All cats are good at tying knots. The stupidest cat can tie forty knots in a ball of yarn in two minutes— and if you don't believe it, ask your grandmother. So this was easy for Jinx. And then they looped the rope over Hank's shoulders and he pulled the carriage up on to the road.

The carriage had two seats and the top was like a square umbrella, with fringe around the edges. It was called a phaeton, and if you think that is a funny name, all I can say is that it was a very funny carriage. The animals laughed like anything when they saw Hank pulling it out of the dump heap, and Mrs. Wiggins laughed so hard that she had to lie down right in the middle of all the old tin cans.

But when Freddy told them what they could use it for, and how they could carry the gold back to Mr. Bean in it, they were very much pleased. The two dogs gathered together a number of things that they thought Mr. Bean would like and put them in the carriage. There was an old straw hat and an old overcoat, and two pails, one half full of red paint and one half full of green paint. "He can use them to paint the house," said Robert. And there was also a plaid shawl for Mrs. Bean. These were all things that people had thrown away on the dump heap, but the animals thought Mr. Bean could use them. And if he didn't use them, he could throw them away and nobody's feelings would be hurt.

Then they said good-bye to the goat. He didn't feel so bad about their going now, because he had a fresh wagon-load of rubbish to look over, and had already found a lot more old boots to chew on. Then all the small animals climbed into the phaeton and they started off. Robert and Emma and Jack sat on the front seat, and Freddy and Alice and Jinx and Henrietta sat on the back seat. The four mice played tag all over the carriage for a while, and then they curled up in the bottom and went to sleep. And Charles perched on top of the square umbrella.

When they had gone a little way, they looked back and waved good-bye to the goat, and he waved back at them. They could see him chewing away contentedly, and the ends of two old shoestrings were hanging out of his mouth.

XIV

UPHILL
and
Down-

hill the phaeton rolled along north-

ward. Sometimes Mrs. Wiggins drew it

and sometimes the two dogs drew it, but whenever they went through

a town, or were where they were meeting a good many people,

Hank drew it, because then the people didn't stare so. Once, when they went through quite a large town, Hank wasn't feeling very well, so Mrs. Wiggins put the rope over her shoulders and drew it for him. But the people all rushed to their doors and crowded round them and laughed so to see a cow harnessed to a carriage that Mrs. Wiggins got quite angry.

"I'm not going to have anybody laughing himself into a fit on *my* account," she said. And after that she would draw it only when they were on very lonely roads.

They were all so anxious to get home again that they traveled faster than they had on the way down, and it was not many days before they saw in the distance the white house and the red barn where Hank and Mrs. Wiggins had been taken prisoner by the two men with guns. And there were the two men standing by the gate and talking.

The animals stopped and looked at one another, and at first they didn't know what to do. Some of them thought they ought to wait until after dark and then sneak by when the men were asleep, but the others were in a hurry, and as the men didn't have their guns, they decided to disguise themselves and try to get past.

So Jinx got out the two pails of paint they had put in the carriage, and with a stick he painted Hank with red stripes up and down, and Robert with green stripes lengthwise, and Mrs. Wiggins he dotted all over with large red and green polka dots. He wanted to put some stripes on her horns, too, but she wouldn't let him on account of Mr. and Mrs. Webb.

Then Jack, the black dog, got up and sat on the front seat of the carriage, and he had on the straw hat and the overcoat, so that from a little way off he looked like a very small man. And Freddy sat on the back seat with the shawl over his head. Jinx painted circles around his eyes so that he looked as if he had spectacles on. His own mother wouldn't have known him.

All the small animals got into the carriage and hid under the seats. Mrs. Wiggins walked behind and Robert ran along underneath, and they went on toward where the men were. When the men caught sight of them, they opened their mouths wide and just stared. The big man had a pipe in his mouth and it fell out on to the road and broke, but he didn't even notice it. He just went on staring. Neither of the men had ever seen such queer-looking animals before.

"What is it?" said the big man at last, looking at Hank. "A zebra?"

"Maybe it's part of a traveling circus," said the little man. "I never see a horse with red stripes before."

"Who's the old lady in the back seat?" asked the big man. "She don't live around here, does she?"

"Never saw her before," said the other. "Why don't you ask the coachman?"

But before the big man could get up his nerve to call out to Jack, who did indeed look like a coachman in his straw hat and overcoat, the carriage went past him and he caught sight of Mrs. Wiggins.

"Great earth and seas!" he exclaimed, and both he and his friend jumped clean over the gate and crouched down behind it, shivering with fear.

"It's a leopard," said the big man. "Look at the spots! A leopard with horns!"

"Leopard nothing!" said the little man. "It's a cow. Look at the shape of it!"

"I never saw a cow all covered with red and green polka dots," said the big man. "It's a leopard."

"It's a cow," said his friend. "Maybe it's got some queer kind of measles."

"If it had the measles as bad as that, it would be sick in bed," said the other. "It's a leopard."

"Maybe it's got walking measles," said the little man. I've heard of that kind. But it certainly is a cow."

"It's not!" shouted the big man. "It's a leopard!"

"It's a cow," repeated the little man angrily.

"It's a leopard!" "It's a cow "A leopard!" "A cow!"

Mrs. Wiggins he dotted all over.

The little man was so enraged that he suddenly slapped the big man hard on the cheek, and the last the animals saw of them, the big man was chasing his friend across a field. "A cow, eh?" he was roaring angrily. "Don't you dare say that word again!" And they grew smaller and smaller and disappeared in the distance.

As soon as the animals had gone three or four miles farther they stopped and all went in swimming in the river that ran beside the road, to see if they could get the paint off. But it wouldn't come off, no matter how hard they scrubbed. Jinx sat on the bank and laughed and laughed.

"You'll laugh out of the other side of your mouth, young man, if *I* catch you," said Mrs. Wiggins. "You knew it wouldn't come off all the time."

"It'll come off if you rub hard enough," said Jinx.

"Yes, and so will my skin," snapped Mrs. Wiggins.

"Anyway," said Jinx, "*you* can't catch me. Who's afraid of an old cow? Who—" But Robert had sneaked out of the water and come up behind Jinx, and just then he grabbed him by the neck. "I can catch you, though," he said. "Freddy, get the pail of red paint. We'll just fix Jinx up so he'll look as funny as the rest of us. Then we'll have something to laugh at too."

So Freddy brought the pail of red paint, and Robert held Jinx over it and started to dip him down. He only intended to dip him in a little, so that he would have a bright red tail, but Jinx began to wriggle and twist so that Robert lost his hold, and splash! down went Jinx into the paint.

He jumped out at once and ran around like a crazy thing, rolling on the ground and scraping against trees, but the paint stuck to his thick fur and he couldn't get it off. For the paint wasn't very deep in the pail and he hadn't gone all the way in, so that the front part of him was black and the back part was red, and he was probably the funniest-looking cat that anybody ever saw.

From this time on the animals attracted a great deal more attention on the road than they ever had before, and if the people had stared at them when they were just regular animals, they stared twice as much now that they were all striped and spotted with red and green.

Some of the people were scared too. There was a tramp lying asleep one day by the road-side, and just as the animals were passing him, Alice sneezed. A duck doesn't sneeze very loud, but tramps don't sleep very soundly, and this tramp was wide awake in an instant. He stared at the animals, and then he looked up at the sky and down at the ground and back at the animals again, and then he pinched himself hard two or three times. And then, finding that he was really awake, he gave one more horrified look and with a dreadful yell turned and ran. He ran so fast his feet hardly seemed to touch the ground. They saw him go up one hill and disappear over the top, and then in a few minutes they saw him, very much smaller, going up another hill way beyond. And he was running just as fast as when he started. For all I know he may be running yet. I don't know that I blame him.

But the animals did not like to be stared at, and they did not like to scare people, so they did most of their travelling at night. They would sleep all day, and then along about sunset they would wake up and have a little something to eat and start out. They had some beautiful moonlit nights about this time, so that it was easier and pleasanter travelling by night than by day. The moon was like a great golden lantern hung in the sky to light them on their way, and now and then a watchdog in some farmhouse would wake up and bark sleepily as he heard them go by, laughing and singing and shouting to one another. They met very few animals or people on the road— only now and then a weasel or an owl, out hunting. And all the time they were getting nearer home.

XV

AT last, Late one night, they came down into the deep, dark pine woods where they had discovered the empty log house, and where they had found the bag of gold. Although the moon was shining brightly, it was very gloomy in the woods, and they were walking slowly and not talking very much, because they were thinking how they were going to carry the gold back in the carriage, and how glad Mr. Bean would be when he saw it. They had almost reached the log house when Robert and Jack both stopped at exactly the same moment and began sniffing the air.

"I smell tobacco," said Jack. "Not very good tobacco."

"It comes from the direction of the house," said Robert. "Somebody's smoking."

"All honest people are abed by this time of night," said Mrs. Wiggins. "Whoever it is is up to no good. Hank, you and I had better stay here, and the other animals can sneak up to the house and see what those people are up to."

So Freddy and Robert and Jack and Jinx went very quietly up to the house. As soon as they got near it, they saw that there was a light in the window.

"I don't like this," said Jinx. "I hope they haven't found our gold."

"I wish the swallows were awake," said Freddy. "We could ask them about it. But let's look in the window."

So they sneaked up and looked in the window, and there were three men sitting round the table and smoking claypipes. They were very rough-looking men, and they wore caps pulled down over their eyes, and they all had revolvers and dark lanterns, so the animals knew at once that they were burglars. On the table was a big heap of everything you can imagine—gold watches and pocketbooks and money and silver forks and spoons and earrings and bracelets and diamond rings. They were all the things that the burglars had stolen from the farmers who lived near the pine woods.

The biggest of the three burglars was dividing the heap of things into three parts. "One for you, and one for you, and one for me. One for you, and one for you, and one for me." But he wasn't dividing them very fairly. For each time he said: "One for you," he would pick up a small thing that wasn't worth very much, like a small spoon or a ten-cent piece, and put it in front of one of his companions. But when he said: "One for me," he would take out a gold watch or a ten-dollar bill or a jeweled bracelet all set with diamonds and put it in front of himself.

But the other burglars were very much smaller men and so they didn't dare say anything, although they looked very much discontented with their shares.

Now the window through which the animals were looking was rather high up, as windows go, and although the two dogs and Freddy, the pig, could see in by putting their forepaws on the windowsill and stretching their necks, Jinx was too short, and he had to climb up and hang on by his claws. He didn't mind this particularly, because his claws were sharp and strong, and he could have hung on like that for hours. But there was a big brown moth who was also trying to look in the window at what the burglars were doing, and it kept fluttering round on the pane right in front of Jinx's nose, so that half the time he couldn't see a thing.

At first he spoke to it politely, and asked it if it wouldn't please move up a little higher, where it could see just as well and wouldn't be in his way.

"Move up yourself!" growled the moth. "I was here first."

"Of course you were," said Jinx patiently. "But you must realize that I can't move up. And I should think common politeness—"

"Oh, shut *up*!" said the moth.

So Jinx didn't say any more, but he made up his mind to give that moth a lesson. So he let go for a minute with one forepaw, and made one slap at the moth and scooped it right off the window.

But Robert, who was standing next to Jinx, was doing something that all dogs and a good many people do. When anything surprised or interested him very much, he opened his eyes very wide, and when his eyes opened, his mouth seemed to come open too. So he was standing with his mouth wide open staring at the burglars, and when Jinx hit the big brown moth with his paw, he knocked it straight down Robert's throat.

"Arrrrrgh!" said Robert. "Woof!"

"What's that!" said all the burglars at once, and they jumped up and bent over the table to blow out the lamp. But as they all bent over at exactly the same time, their three heads came together in the middle, crack! And then the light was out and the animals couldn't see anything more, but they could hear the burglars rubbing their bumped heads and groaning.

For quite a long while the animals waited for something to happen, but nothing did. The burglars were evidently badly scared. They seemed to be whispering together, and at last Jinx said: "I'm going in to see what they're doing. I noticed when we came up to the house that the door was open a little way, and I think I can get in."

So he went round to the door, and sure enough it was open a crack, and he made himself narrow, as cats can, and slipped in. It was so dark inside that the burglars could not see anything at all, but Jinx could see them quite plainly. Cats can see in the dark. He jumped up on the mantelpiece to be out of the way, and sat down.

The two small burglars, whose names were Ed and Bill, were in a corner, trying to open one of the dark lanterns, so they could light it. But as they never used the lanterns, but only carried them to show that they were burglars, they didn't know how to open it. The big burglar, whose name was Percy, was standing by the table, on which were the three piles of stolen things that he had been dividing up, and he was feeling with his fingers in the other piles and taking out the biggest things and putting them on his own pile. But he couldn't see what he was doing, and pretty soon he knocked a watch and an emerald necklace off on the floor.

At the sound Ed and Bill started up. "What you doin' over there, Percy?" Bill whispered hoarsely.

And Ed said: "He's after them jools."

"Oh, I am *not*!" said Percy. "I was just feeling for the matches."

"Oh, you was, was you?" said Ed. "Well, you just come over here and give us a hand with this lantern."

So Percy hastily stuffed a handful of ten-dollar bills into his pocket and came over to them.

"Why don't you light the lamp?" he asked. "We're perfectly safe. That noise wasn't anything."

"Maybe so," said Bill. "But I'm going to have a look round with the lantern first. Here, see if you can get it open."

They were all standing close to the fireplace, and as Percy took the lantern, Jinx, who never could resist a joke, reached out and dug his claws into his shoulder.

"Ouch!" yelled Percy, dropping the lantern with a crash. "What d'ye mean, sticking pins in me like that?" And he struck out with his fist in the darkness and hit Bill on the nose.

Bill had just been going to say: "I didn't touch you, silly!" but when that hard fist hit him, he changed his mind and flew at Percy, and in a second they were rolling on the floor and clawing and kicking and pulling each other's hair like wildcats.

They rolled toward the table, and Ed, who was afraid that they would knock it over and spill all the money and jewelery on the floor, took a match from his pocket and scratched it on the mantelpiece just under where Jinx was sitting, doubled up with laughter at the commotion he had caused. The match flamed up, and by its light Ed saw Jinx.

Now, if you are a rather timid burglar, and you light a match in a dark room and see a cat that is half black and half red—for Jinx had been dipped in the paint pot, you remember—if you see such a cat grinning at you within an inch of your nose, you will probably do just as Ed did. He dropped his match and let out an awful yell.

When he yelled, Bill and Percy stopped fighting and sat up. "What's the matter?" they asked.

"There's a red and black cat sitting on the mantelpiece and grinning at me!" said Ed in a scared voice.

"Fiddlesticks!" said Percy, and Bill said: "Nonsense!" and then he too lit a match. He was near the window as he did so, and there was

Freddy, the pig, with his nose against the glass, staring in for all he was worth to see what was going on inside.

Then it was Bill's turn to drop his match and yell. "A pig with spectacles on is looking at us through the window!" For, of course, Freddy still had the circles around his eyes that Jinx had painted there.

"Fiddlesticks!" said Percy again, but he didn't say it quite as loud. And Bill and Ed didn't say anything.

There was silence for a few minutes, while the three scared burglars tried to get up enough courage to light another match. Then through the silence came the faint sound of wheels on the road outside.

"Listen!" whispered Percy. "Somebody coming. I'm going out to have a look. It won't be black and red cats, and pigs with glasses on, anyway." And he slipped silently out of the door.

The other two burglars tiptoed to the door and peered out after him, but although it was bright moonlight outside, the trees were so thick round the house that they could not see the road.

And then, as they waited, came a terrible yell, and it was three times as loud as Ed's yell and Bill's yell put together. And they heard footsteps running, and Percy dashed up to the door, his eyes nearly starting out of his head with fright.

"Run! Run for your lives!" he panted. "Out on the road there's a tiger harnessed to a carriage and behind the carriage there's a leopard with horns, as big as a cow. Run, or we shall all be eaten up!" And he dashed off into the woods and the two others rushed out of the door after him, and the animals could hear the crash of branches and the thump of heavy feet die away in the distance. And I may say here that they never saw either Ed or Bill or Percy again.

Of course what had happened was this. Mrs. Wiggins and Hank had got tired of waiting, and when they had heard the first two yells they had started down the road to see what was going on. They had not seen Percy come out of the door, and when he saw them and let out his terrible yell, they had been much more scared than he was. Indeed, Mrs. Wiggins was quite faint and had to lie down for a few minutes by the roadside while Charles and Henrietta fanned her with their wings.

"I'm all of a flutter!" she said. "Oh my, oh my! Just put your hoof on my side and feel how my heart beats, Hank. What a dreadful experience!"

But pretty soon she was able to get up and be helped into the house.

The burglars had left all the things they had stolen behind them in their flight, but as the animals had no matches, and as it was late, they decided not to do anything about them until morning. So they all curled up comfortably on the floor and went to sleep.

XVI

ALICE did Not

sleep very well that night. She had a stomachache. And she had a stomachache because she had eaten two chocolates and a caramel and a horehound drop that Robert had given her out of a bag of candy that he had found by the roadside. Robert had offered Emma some too, but she had very sensibly refused it. Candy doesn't agree with ducks.

So, as she couldn't sleep, no matter how hard she tried, Alice got up before daylight and went out into the woods. The cool morning air made her feel sleepy, so she thought she would try again, and, having found a sheltered spot under a big pine, she tucked her head under her wing and dozed off. When she woke up, the sun was shining and the swallows were pouring like smoke out of the chimney in search of their breakfast.

Alice called to one of them and asked him about the burglars.

"They've been here about a month," said the swallow. "They go out every night and rob the farmers' houses, and then come back and sleep all day. They usually get back about this time every morning, so you animals had better look out."

"I don't think they will be back *this* morning," said Alice. "But tell me, did they dig up the gold we found when we were here before?"

"No," said the swallow. "They haven't touched it."

"Thank you," said Alice. "That was all I wanted to know. Good morning." And she hurried back to tell the others that their treasure was safe.

But when she got back to the house, she stopped in amazement on the threshold. Her sister, Emma, was waddling importantly up and down with a bracelet set with big blue sapphires round her neck and a beautiful bag, all made of little links of pure gold, tucked under her wing. The four mice, with diamond rings round their necks like collars, were playing tag in a corner, and they sparkled and glittered like little streaks of fire as they chased one another. Henrietta looked very queenly with a hoop of rubies set on her head like a crown. She was bending down and trying to see herself in the little mirror set in the cover of a powder box, which she had snapped open with her claw. But Mrs. Wiggins was most gorgeous of all. There was a rope of pearls about her big neck, and a platinum wrist watch on her left ankle. She had hung an emerald necklace on each horn, and they hung down and bobbed and dangled beside her broad, pleasant face like enormous earrings. And she had powdered her wide, black nose until it was as white as flour. She looked truly reckless.

Alice, after a moment's astonishment, entered into the fun. She found a thin, gold chain with a diamond and pearl locket which she hung round her neck, and then she went over to where Henrietta was still admiring herself in the powder-box cover, and asked if she might have some powder for her bill.

"There isn't any left," said Henrietta.

"I'm sorry, Alice," said Mrs. Wiggins. "I'm afraid I used it all up. There's so much of me to powder, you know. I do wish I could see myself. Though I must say I don't believe I have improved my appearance much. I must look like an overdressed washerwoman. You can't do much with a cow," she added sadly.

Then Robert and Jack played a game. Each took six bracelets, and Mrs. Wiggins stood perfectly still, and they tried to throw them over her horns. But they weren't very good at it, and after Mrs. Wiggins had been hit on her nose several times, she said she guessed she wouldn't play any more, as they were knocking all the powder off.

Then Henrietta said: "What are we going to do with all this jewelry?"

"We ought to give it back to the people it was stolen from," said Hank.

"All very fine," said Henrietta. "But how do you propose to do that?"

Hank said he didn't exactly know. So they talked it over for a while and at last hit upon a plan. And after breakfast they loaded all the stolen things into the carriage and started out for the nearest farmhouse.

When they got there, there was nobody in sight, but Jack and Robert barked until at last a woman came to the door to see what was the matter. She was a large, fat woman, and looked quite a lot like Mrs. Wiggins. She was wiping soap-suds off her hands on her apron, because she had been washing her husband's other shirt.

"Land sakes alive!" she exclaimed when she saw the animals all grouped about the carriage. "What is this, a circus?"

It took quite a long time for the dogs to make her understand what they wanted her to do. They ran back and forth between her and the carriage, and at last she followed them. When she saw the heap of money and jewelry she gave a loud cry and seized the hoop of rubies that Henrietta had worn on her head.

"Land of love!" she cried. "Here's the ring that Cousin Eunice gave me last Christmas, the one the burglars stole when they broke into our house a month ago. And here's the emerald necklace I won as a prize at the pedro club last winter. And here's Hiram's gold cigarette case."

She ran to the corner of the house. "Hiram! Hiram!" she called. "Come here this minute."

So pretty soon Hiram, her husband, came from where he had been resting, up in the hay loft. And he found twenty dollars, beside the cigarette case, that the burglars had taken from him.

"Now, how do you suppose these animals got these things?" he said. "Do you suppose they found the place where the burglars hid them?"

"I don't know about that," said his wife. "But I do know that they brought them here so we could pick out what belonged to us. Such good, clever animals! I'm going to kiss every one of you!" Which she did, even the mice, who were scared to death. She looked very funny after she had kissed Mrs. Wiggins, because a lot of the powder came off on her face.

"Now," she said, "I'm going to go over to Aunt Etta' with these animals, because I saw her gold soup tureen among those things." And she climbed in the phaeton and they started off, while Hiram went back to do some more resting in the hay loft.

Aunt Etta was an educated woman. Every evening she sat on the porch and read the newspaper until it got so dark she couldn't see, and then she went in and lighted the lamp and finished reading it.

So when she had taken her soup tureen and one or two other things that the burglars had stolen, she said: "I know who these animals are. I saw a piece in the paper about them only last week. They're migrating. They came from way up north and went to Florida for the winter. They're very clever animals indeed. I expect they're on their way home now, as it's spring."

"Well," said her niece, "they won't get home until fall at this rate. They'll have to visit about a hundred farms to get all this stuff back to the people it belongs to. It's too bad they can't find a quicker way."

"A lot of the things have been advertised for in the paper," said Aunt Etta. "How would it be if we put an advertisement in, saying that all the things were here and the people could come here and get them? Then the animals wouldn't have to traipse all over the country, and they could go on home in a day or two."

The niece thought this was a good idea, and the animals looked at one another and nodded, and so Robert barked very loud to show that they thought it a good idea too. Then Aunt Etta got up. "I'll go in and telephone the newspaper office right away," she said, "and have the advertisement put in tonight. And then we'll give these animals something to eat and a place to be comfortable. They must be tired, having come such a long way."

So she telephoned the newspaper office, and then she went out in the barn and got some oats for Hank, and she showed Alice and Emma where the duck pond was, and introduced them to her own ducks, and she found two bones for the dogs, and a piece of cheese for the mice, and a saucer of cream for Jinx, and she cooked up some cornmeal mush for Charles and Henrietta, and led Mrs. Wiggins out into the pasture, where there was a very superior quality of grass. If she had noticed Mr. and Mrs. Webb she would probably have tried to catch some flies for them, she was such a kind and generous old lady, and so grateful for the return of her gold soup tureen.

Then, when the animals had all been given the things they liked best to eat, she sat down on the porch and told her niece everything she had read in the paper for the last six weeks.

XVII

SO for

Two days the animals stayed at Aunt Etta's, who, as Mrs. Wiggins said, was kindness itself. They sat on the front porch with her while she read the paper, and they ate the good things she prepared for them. A good many of the animals in the neighborhood who had heard about them came to call and to ask about their travels, and as there were so many who were interested in their adventures, Charles very kindly consented to give a lecture in the big barn on the second evening. The name of the lecture was *A Trip to the Sunny South*, and it was a great success.

Then on the third day all the farmers and their wives from far and near who had had things stolen by the burglars gathered in Aunt Etta's parlour, because that was the day the advertisement in the paper had told them to come, to get their things back. All the jewelry and money and watches and silverware were tastefully arranged on little tables covered with white doilies, and all the farmers had to do was to pick out the things that belonged to them. And when they had all got their property back, they made a great fuss over the animals, and one nice old lady, whose name was Mrs. Trigg, and who owned the rope of pearls that Mrs. Wiggins had dressed up in, said: "I wish there was something we could do for these good, kind animals to show them how much we appreciate what they have done for us. Can anyone think of anything?"

The farmers and their wives all clapped their hands and cheered at this, and made more of a fuss over the animals than ever, but no one could think of any way to reward them.

Then Robert had an idea, and he went up to Mrs. Trigg and barked three times.

"I believe that dog understood what you said," said Aunt Etta. "Just see the way he's looking at you."

Then Robert ran a little way toward the kitchen, and stopped and looked back; so Aunt Etta and Mrs. Trigg followed him, and he went straight to a shelf in the kitchen and stood on his hind legs and put his forepaws on the edge of it and looked over his shoulder at them and barked again.

There were a number of things on the shelf. There was a photograph of Aunt Etta, and a photograph of her married daughter who lived in Rochester, and a spool of black darning cotton, and an alarm clock, and a butcher's bill, and a picture postcard of Niagara Falls, and seven beans, and a box of matches, and quite a lot of dust. The dust was there because Aunt Etta, although she was a kindhearted woman, wasn't a very good housekeeper. She spent too much time reading the newspaper.

"Now, what do you suppose he wants up there?" said Mrs. Trigg.

"Why I do believe," said Aunt Etta, and I think she blushed a little." I do believe he wants that picture of me!" And she took the picture down and gave it to Robert.

Of course the picture wasn't what Robert wanted at all, but he was too polite to let her know it, and he thanked her by wagging his tail and smiling the way dogs do. And then he put his forepaws on the shelf and barked again.

"He wants something else, too," said Mrs. Trigg. "Now what can it be?" And she began touching all the things on the shelf and looking at Robert. And when she touched the alarm clock, he barked very loud, so she knew that was what he wanted. So Aunt Etta gave him the clock, and he carried it and the picture out on the porch and showed them to the other animals.

"Now," he said, "we've got an alarm clock for Mr. Bean, Charles. You won't have to get up early in the morning any more when we get back." And Charles was very much pleased.

It was getting along toward suppertime by now, and all the farmers were climbing into their buggies and automobiles and driving away. They were happy to have recovered their valuables, and when somebody started to sing, they all joined in. Many of them sang part-songs all the way home. It was very inspiring.

Soon there was nobody left on the porch but Aunt Etta and her niece and Mrs. Trigg and a stout lady who lived across the road and whose name was Mrs. Hackenbutt.

"It does seem to me," said Aunt Etta, "that a photograph and an alarm clock are a very small reward to give these animals for bringing back our things."

"It isn't very much," agreed her niece, "but I can't think of anything else. Can you?"

"*I* can think of something," said Mrs. Hackenbutt suddenly. "We

"Now we've got an alarm clock for Mr. Bean."

could help them to get all that dreadful paint off. I've been watching that cat and he's been licking himself for an hour. He wants to get it off. Now, if we could give them a good scrubbing—"

"That might do," said Aunt Etta. "I always say that there's nothing that good hot suds won't take out."

Now, if there is anything a cat hates more than cold water, it is hot water, and so Jinx immediately crawled under the porch and stayed there. Hank and Mrs. Wiggins would have liked to crawl under too, but of course they were too large. As for Robert and Freddy, they thought it was undignified to run away, so they sat nobly on the porch and waited while the women heated water in the washboiler and brought it out to them.

Then Mrs. Hackenbutt and Aunt Etta's niece rolled up their sleeves and set to work with scrubbing-brushes. They scrubbed and scrubbed, and pretty soon the thick paint began to loosen its hold on the animals' skins and peel off. "This isn't as bad as I thought it was going to be," said Mrs. Wiggins.

"It's fine," said Hank. "I used to wonder why Mr. Bean took a bath every Saturday night, but I know now why he likes it so much."

When they had got off as much paint as they could, the women led the animals round to the pump and rinsed them off with buckets of cool well-water. But Jinx didn't come out until it was all over, and then he took care to keep out of sight.

They stayed at Aunt Etta's house that night, and would have liked to stay longer, but they knew that Mr. Bean needed them and thought they ought to start along. They hurried back to the log house in the woods and dug up the gold and put it in the phaeton.

"And now," said Freddy, "our adventures are over. Soon we'll be back in our own comfortable home again, and I for one shall be glad to be there."

"Yes," said Mrs. Wiggins, "our adventures are over for this year at least."

But she was wrong. For the most exciting adventure of all was lying in wait for them up the long, homeward road.

XVIII

NOTHING
much
Happened

however, for the next few days. They plodded

along the road, doing a steady twenty-five

miles a day, for they were used to it now and could go much longer

without getting tired than when they first set out. Most of the people they met had heard about them by this time, and although they attracted a good deal of attention, nobody molested them. The heap of gold coins lay in the bottom of the phaeton, but they had covered it up with the old shawl, so that no one knew that anything was there.

At last one morning they came to the bridge where the animals had found Mr. and Mrs. Webb again after they had fallen into the river. The two spiders were much excited, and Mrs. Webb ran up to the tip of Mrs. Wiggins's left horn, and Mr. Webb ran up to the tip of her right horn, and they sat there and looked out across the landscape and shouted to each other: "Oh, do you remember this?" and "Oh, do you remember that?" until Mrs. Webb was so overcome by the recollection of their strange adventure that she burst into tears. Then Mr. Webb climbed hurriedly down from Mrs. Wiggins's right horn and climbed up her left horn and patted his wife clumsily on the back with one of his eight feet, which he could also use as hands, and said: "There, there, Emmeline! Don't cry!" And Mrs. Webb wiped her eyes with a tiny pocket-handkerchief which she had woven herself, and stopped crying.

The animals went on across the bridge and through the village, and when they were out in the country again, Jack said: "I think, if nobody minds, I'd better ride in the carriage for a while. We're getting near to where I used to live, and I don't want the man I used to live with to see me. It might cause trouble."

Mrs. Wiggins gave a chuckle. "I have to laugh every time I think of that man, and the way he bounced like a rubber ball on the top of his automobile when I tossed him up there. He was an awful coward, even if he did have a big, black moustache."

"Yes," said Jack, as he climbed into the phaeton and crouched down under the shawl, "but just the same I think we'd better hurry along. He has a bad disposition, and he would take a lot of trouble to get even with us for the things we did to him."

"We mustn't take any chances with all this money," said Henrietta. So they hurried along, and pretty soon they passed the road which led up to the farm where the man with the black moustache lived, and then a little later they passed the swimming-hole in the river, where Mrs. Wiggins had fallen in.

"We ought to be pretty safe now," said Jack, "because he doesn't often come up this way in his automobile. But I'll stay in here for a while, just the same."

In another mile or two the road, which had been running across a valley, began to climb a long hill. It was getting along into the afternoon now, and as the animals had been walking fast, they were hot and dusty; so they were all glad when they came to a stream that crossed the road part way up the hill. They decided to take a swim.

"I remember this place," said Robert. "We stopped here to take a swim the day we started out, just before we met the man with the black moustache the first time."

"Yes, yes, so we did!" exclaimed the other animals. "Why, we're almost home! If we go on now we can get back to Mr. Bean's before midnight."

Some of them were all for going on at once when they realized how close home was, but Charles said: "We don't want to get there at night, when Mr. and Mrs. Bean and all the other animals are asleep. That won't be any fun!"

And Freddy said: "We'll be so tired when we get there that we won't want to tell them about our travels, and they'll be so sleepy that they won't want to hear about them. I vote we camp here tonight, and go on in the morning. We'll get home about dinnertime."

"That sounds sensible," said Hank. "We've come a long way today. If you ask me, I've had about enough. It's all right for you other animals, but I have to pull this carriage, and all that gold is heavier than Mr. and Mrs. Bean put together."

So they pulled the carriage under a tree, and pretty soon they were all splashing about in the water, which was pretty cold, for it was still early in the spring. But animals, with the exception of cats, do not mind cold water as much as some people do.

Now they were so near home, and so sure that nothing could interfere with their getting there, that they did not keep a very good watch while they were in swimming. And they did not see a pair of sharp eyes that were watching them from the bushes, nor hear the rustle of leaves as the bushes parted and the dirty-faced boy, who was the son of the man with the black moustache, sneaked over to the carriage and, lifting a corner of the shawl that covered the heap of gold coins, peeked under it. When they came back out of the water and ran up and down the bank to dry themselves, the boy had gone.

They did not sit up very late that night, for they were all pretty tired. Before they went to bed, Robert and Charles and Jack wound and set the alarm clock. They had done this every night since Aunt Etta had given it to them. And this is the way they did it.

Jack held the clock in his mouth, and Robert took hold of the winder with his teeth, and they twisted. Sometimes it took them half an hour to do it, but they always did it. And when the clock part was wound up, they wound the alarm. But the thing you set the alarm with, to make it go off at a certain time in the morning, was so small that neither Robert nor Jack could get hold of it properly. And so when they had got it all wound, Charles would take hold of the thing with his beak and set it for whatever time they wanted to get up. This time they set it for five o'clock, because they wanted to get an early start.

They all took turns standing watch over the gold at night, and tonight it was Charles and Henrietta's turn. The other animals had found a warm and comfortable place to sleep under the little bridge, beside the stream, and when all good-nights had been said, the rooster and his wife made a final round of the camp to see that all was in order, and then flew up into the phaeton, perched on the back of the front seat, and tucked their heads under their wings.

They had not been asleep long when it began to rain. It rained gently at first, and Charles, half awakened, moved about a little on his perch, then dropped off again, lulled by the monotonous patter on the umbrella-like roof of the carriage. But the patter grew to a rattle, and then to a roar, and he awoke again to find his feathers getting wetter and wetter, and Henrietta tapping him crossly on the shoulder with her beak.

"Come come, Charles; wake up!" she was saying. "We'll get wet and catch our deaths, very likely."

"This will never do!" said Charles. "We can't stay here. I think, my dear, we had better join the others under the bridge."

"I think we had better do nothing of the kind," said Henrietta crossly. "We are here to watch the gold, and here we stay. We can get down under the shawl in the back seat and keep dry. Come along."

"But the mice are sleeping here tonight," Charles protested. "And you know how Eeny snores. I shouldn't sleep a wink."

But Henrietta was not listening; she had jumped down into the back seat, and Charles followed her, repeating: "I shan't sleep a wink! Not a wink!" But once they had got under the shawl, where it was dry and warm, and had pushed the sleepy mice over to make room, he did fall asleep again with great promptness. It is true that Eeny snored, although it was not a very loud snore, for Eeny was a very small mouse. And then Cousin Augustus had the nightmare, and dreamed that four tortoise-shell cats with red eyes were chasing him, baying like the bloodhounds in *Uncle Tom's Cabin*, which he had once seen when he had been on a visit to his aunt, who lived in the town hall at Joy Center, near Mr. Bean's farm. Cousin Augustus squeaked dreadfully when he had the nightmare, which was as often as he ate too much supper (and *that* was as often as he could)—and he jerked his legs and moaned and lashed his tail, so that Eek and Quik and Eeny had to get up and shake him awake. But even through all this Charles would have slept peacefully on if Henrietta had not pecked him on the neck and said: "Charles! Wake up! You'll have to do something about these mice. Keeping it up at all hours! I never heard such a racket! They don't seem to have any regard for anyone."

So Charles took his head out from under his wing. He couldn't see anything, because he was under the shawl, but he could hear Cousin Augustus waking up, and then saying: "Oh dear! Oh dear me! Such a dream! *Such* a dream!"

"Here, here!" said Charles sleepily, and trying to be stern. "What's all this? Do be still, can't you? Other people want to sleep if you don't!"

"Cousin Augustus had the nightmare," said Eek. "It's all over now."

Charles was satisfied with this and would have put his head back under his wing, but Henrietta pecked him again. So he said gruffly: "Well, we can't have that. Do you understand? We can't *have* it! We cannot have our rest broken in this way. I think you mice had better go and sleep somewhere else, as you don't seem able to do it quietly, like other animals."

The mice were a little afraid of Charles because he was so grand and talked so beautifully and strutted about the barnyard so nobly, and so they did not give him any back talk, but climbed down meekly out of the carriage and went to join the other animals under the bridge.

"Well, for once you had the gumption to stand up to somebody, even if it was only a mouse," said Henrietta. But Charles did not hear her, for he was again fast asleep.

There was now no sound under the shawl but the ticking of the alarm clock and Charles's gentle breathing, and so Henrietta went to sleep too. When she awoke again, it was still dark. For a few minutes she could not tell what it was that had roused her; then she heard a faint creak, and the carriage gave a lurch to one side. It was moving! Something or somebody was drawing the carriage down the road!

She pecked Charles sharply, and he awoke with a groan. "Oh, my *goodness*, Henrietta! What is it *now*? Can't you let me alone?"

"Hush!" she whispered. "Don't you feel the carriage moving? Someone is running away with it. Someone's stealing the gold!"

Charles was very wide awake in an instant. He poked his head out from underneath the shawl and looked about him. Two shadowy forms—men, they looked like, though they might be animals—were pulling the carriage down the hill, and they must have pulled it some distance from where Hank had left it, for the bridge was nowhere in sight.

"This comes of not keeping watch," whispered Henrietta, who had poked her head out beside him. "If you hadn't crawled under this shawl, you'd have been able to hear what was going on.

"You crawled under too," said Charles. "You're as much to blame as I am. But what shall we do? Even if I crow my loudest, they'll never hear me with the rain coming down the way it is."

"One of us must jump out and run back and give the alarm," said Henrietta. "And the other must stay here and find out where the carriage is being taken. You'd better go, Charles, and I'll stay."

Charles was too scared to complain at being ordered to go out in the heavy rain. The only thing he wanted was to get away from that carriage as quickly as possible. And being scared, he did what a scared rooster always does: he gave a loud squawk. And then he made a wild jump for the road. But his feet caught in the fringe of the shawl, and before he could get them free, and before Henrietta could get out herself, one of the dark figures dropped the handle of the carriage at which it was pulling, ran back, and caught them both. It was the dirty-faced boy.

"Hey! Pa!" he called. "Here's a couple nice chickens for Sunday dinner in here with the money."

They squawked and struggled, but he held on tight, and then the man with the black moustache came and tied their feet with string and shoved them roughly into the space under the front seat of the phaeton.

"I hope you're satisfied!" said Henrietta. "Of all the useless, good-for-nothing roosters, you're the worst! Why couldn't you keep your silly beak shut? My goodness, you certainly have got us in a nice mess now!" And she went on telling just what she thought of him. But Charles was not listening. "Sunday dinner," he was thinking, "Sunday dinner! Me, that's traveled hundreds and thousands of miles in my time—me, that's seen what I've seen and done what I've done, to end as a Sunday dinner! Fricasseed, probably, and eaten by perfect strangers!" And he burst into tears.

XIX

THE animals Slept very soundly that night under the bridge, without a suspicion of the loss of their gold, or of the terrible fate that had overtaken Charles and Henrietta. Robert was the first to awake in the morning. It had stopped raining, but a heavy mist hid everything from sight.

"My goodness!" said Robert. "It must be dreadfully late! I wonder why I didn't hear the alarm when it went off at five o'clock. Hey, Freddy!" he called. "Hank! Wake up! We ought to have been on our way two hours ago."

In two minutes all the animals were wide awake, and Freddy had gone out to see what was the matter with the alarm clock. Pretty soon he came running back. "The clock is gone," he panted, "and Charles and Henrietta are gone, and the phaeton is gone. Everything's gone. I bet Charles has run away with the treasure."

"Nonsense," said Mrs. Wiggins. "He couldn't if he wanted to. And besides, he isn't that kind of a rooster. I'm going out to see for myself."

The other animals followed her, and when they came to the place where the phaeton had been left, there was no phaeton there. But they found prints of muddy shoes all about the place, and the marks of the wheels in the muddy road were as plain as plain could be, so that they very soon knew what had happened.

"Charles and Henrietta were sleeping under the shawl," said Eek. "They made us get out. Probably they were captured in their sleep and didn't have a chance to call out to us."

"Here's one of Charles's tail feathers," cried Alice. "He wasn't captured without a struggle, you may be sure of that." She was a great admirer of Charles.

"We'd better start right away to follow these wheel marks," said Robert. "If we can find where the carriage has been taken to, maybe we can rescue them."

So they followed the marks on down the hill, and they led straight back the way the animals had come from Florida, until they came to the road that went down to the house where the man with the black moustache lived. And they turned down that road.

None of the animals said very much as they plodded along through the mist to the rescue of their friends. For they knew now that the man with the black moustache had stolen the carriage, and

"The clock is gone," he panted.

he was a dangerous and desperate character whom it would be hard to get the best of. Even Mr. Webb was worried. "He's a bad man," he said to his wife. "He'd squash a spider as soon as look at him." And Mrs. Webb shuddered.

Pretty soon they came near the house, and Jack said: "You'd better let me go ahead now, because I used to live here and I know my way round." So he led them by a back way round to where they could peek in the barn window, and sure enough, there was the phaeton, standing on the barn floor beside the rickety automobile. But the gold was not in it, and there was no sign of Charles and Henrietta.

Although the mist was so thick that they could not be seen from the house, they did not dare stay near the barn for fear that the man with the black moustache might come out and find them there. So the four mice said they would sneak up to the house and try to get in and find Charles and Henrietta, and the other animals went back and waited for them a little way down the road.

After quite a long time the mice came back, and the animals all crowded round them eagerly. "Did you see them?" they asked. "Are they all right? Did you find where the money is?"

"We didn't find out anything," said Eek. "We didn't even get into the house. I never saw such a house! Not a crack to get in by anywhere, and all the old mouse holes with pieces of tin nailed over them. We couldn't even get down the chimney, because there was a fire in the stove. He certainly is a mean man!"

"They're there, though," said Quik, "because we heard them talking. And Charles is there too, because we heard him crying."

"Poor thing" said Mrs. Wiggins. "But we'll get him out, if we have to tear the whole house down with our horns and claws and beaks and hoofs! Won't we, animals?"

"We will! We certainly will!" cried the determined travellers.

"But the first thing," she continued, "is to find out where Charles and Henrietta are, and the second thing is to find where the money is; then we can make a plan. Has anybody anything to suggest?"

"I want to suggest something," shouted Mr. Webb. But nobody heard him. So he crawled down into Mrs. Wiggins's ear and stamped around until he tickled her, and then told her, and she told the others. He had an idea that he could get into the house through a keyhole, if Robert would carry him up to the door.

This seemed a good idea to everyone except Mrs. Webb, who thought it too dangerous. Indeed, she burst into tears at the very thought. "No, no, Hubert," she sobbed. "I can't let you go. You said yourself he was a wicked man. Suppose he should see you and hit you with a newspaper or something. I should never forgive myself if I let you go."

Mr. Webb, however, was firm in his decision, as spiders are apt to be, and, having kissed his weeping wife tenderly on the forehead, he jumped down on to Robert's back and they started.

At the front door he got down, and while Robert hid behind a bush to wait for him, he crawled up and squeezed in through the keyhole. It was gloomy inside, because the windows were rather dirty, but that didn't bother Mr. Webb, and he walked up the wall as easily as you would walk up your own front steps, and then he walked across the ceiling to the front parlor, where he heard voices.

The reason he walked on the ceiling was because that was the safest place for him to be. He knew that on the walls or the floor he was much more likely to be seen, but people hardly ever look up at the ceiling except when they are in bed. And then, too, if you see a spider on the floor, it is easy to run over and step on him, but that is a pretty difficult thing to do if he is on the ceiling.

So Mr. Webb walked boldly into the front parlor on the ceiling. The man with the black moustache and the dirty-faced boy were sitting at a table counting the gold coins they had stolen from the animals. They would count twenty, and then they would wrap them up in a piece of newspaper and pack them away in a big canvas bag. But they didn't get on very fast because they both counted out loud, and they kept mixing each other up and having to start all over again. Mr.

Webb watched them for a while; then, hearing a noise in the far corner of the room, he walked over and saw Charles and Henrietta lying, with their feet tied, in a box beside the stove. Charles was lying on his back and staring gloomily at the ceiling, but Henrietta was picking busily with her beak at the knots in the string, and Mr. Webb saw that she had very nearly got herself loose.

All at once Charles caught sight of the spider. "Hey!" he shouted. "Mr. Webb! Oh, my golly, I'm glad to see you! How did you find us? Are the others all here?"

"What's the matter with those chickens?" said the boy. "Do you suppose one of 'em's laid an egg?"

"Eighteen, nineteen, twenty—it'll be the last egg it ever lays, then," said the man with a coarse laugh. "Day after tomorrow's Sunday," he added meaningly.

Mr. Webb hurried down the wall and climbed to the edge of the box. "For goodness' sake, Charles, keep still!" he whispered. "Henrietta, do you think you can get those strings off?"

Henrietta nodded without stopping her work.

"Very good, then," said Mr. Webb. "Get them loose enough so that you can get out of them quickly, but don't take them off, because it might be noticed. And I'll see what I can do. Cheer up, Charles," he added, slapping the unhappy rooster heartily on the back. "We won't desert you."

On the wall, in a gilt frame, was a large picture of a man with a gray moustache, who was the father of the man with the black moustache and the grandfather of the dirty-faced boy. Mr. Webb walked down into the darkness behind this picture, and sat down cross-legged on the dusty picture wire and tried to think of a plan. But though he thought of a good many, there was just one thing the matter with all of them—they wouldn't work.

"I'm wasting precious time here," he thought. "I'd better go back and tell the animals and let them try to think of something, since I can't." And he started up the wire toward the ceiling.

But just at the edge of the picture frame he caught sight of a fly. The fly was sound asleep. It had had a very hearty breakfast that morning of jelly and cream and egg that the man with the black moustache had spilled on the tablecloth at *his* breakfast, and it had flown up on to the picture frame to take a little nap before going down to lunch on more jelly and cream and egg.

Mr. Webb, however, had not had any breakfast, so he crept up quietly behind the fly and grabbed it by the leg. The fly buzzed and struggled, but Mr. Webb held on, and then it stopped struggling and said: "O, Mr. Spider—good, *kind* Mr. Spider, please let me go. Please don't eat me. If you won't eat me, I'll do anything you want me to."

Now most spiders would not have paid any attention, but would have gobbled the fly up then and there. But Mr. Webb had a very kind heart, and married life had further softened him, so that he paused. And while he was pausing, a thought came to him.

"If you'll give me your word to do exactly as I tell you," he said, "I'll let you go. What's more, I'll go away out of this house and won't come back again. But if you don't do it, then I and my wife and all my relations will come and live in this house and eat you all up."

The fly promised, and Mr. Webb let him go. "Now," he said, "you go out and get all your relations and neighbours and meet me in the hall, and I'll tell you what I want you to do."

So the fly slipped outdoors through the keyhole in the front door, and pretty soon he came back, and with him were all his family and neighbours. Young flies and stout, middle-aged flies and old grandfather flies with no teeth and old grandmother flies with the rheumatism in their wings—they came pouring in through the keyhole and formed in a wide circle around Mr. Webb on the hall ceiling. And Mr. Webb made a long speech and explained the situation and told them just what they were to do. And immediately they started in to do it.

First they flew into the front parlor and lit on the ceiling. Then when Mr. Webb saw that Henrietta had untied the last knot and had got Charles's feet as well as her own free, he said: "Go!" And the flies jumped into the air and began whirling round the room, buzzing as loud as they could. And the youngest and most active ones pestered the man and the boy. Two or three of them would light on the man's nose and dance round with all six feet so as to tickle as much as possible. And when he raised his hand to brush them off, they would fly over and tickle the back of the boy's neck. In a few minutes both the man and the boy were pretty nearly crazy. They stopped counting coins, and folded up newspapers and tried to slap the flies, but as soon as they did that, all the flies would go up to the ceiling. And then as soon as they laid the newspapers down, the flies would start in again.

"Phoo!" said the man. "Whoosh! Get away, you things! I don't see where they come from. There wasn't one here five minutes ago."

"It's no good trying to swat them," said the boy. "Poof! Get out of my ear! They seem to be trying to get out of the window. Let's open it, and maybe they'll go out."

The man looked at the window, where forty or fifty flies were walking around on the glass. "If it weren't for those animals, I'd open it," he said. "But I'm afraid they'll be around here somewhere after their gold. They're a pretty smart set of animals, and I won't feel safe until we have taken the gold into the village tomorrow morning, and put it in the bank. You remember what they did to us last fall."

"I'd rather have forty animals in here than all these flies," said the boy. "Besides, we can watch, and if we see them coming, we can slam the window down again." And he went and unlocked the window and threw it open, and stood beside it to put it down again when all the flies were out.

But although the flies streamed out by tens and dozens, as soon as they got outside, they went round to the front door and came in again through the keyhole, as Mr. Webb had instructed them to. So that although they had stopped bothering, there seemed to be just as many in the room as there were before. And for every dozen that flew out of the window, twelve came in through the keyhole.

FREDDY GOES TO FLORIDA / 131

"My goodness," said the boy, "there's no end to them."

"Well, we'll have to leave the window open, that's all," said the man. "Come, sit down and let's get these coins counted." And they started counting again, keeping a sharp lookout on the window.

Now, this was just what Mr. Webb had hoped they would do, and he motioned to Charles and Henrietta, who had been peering anxiously over the edge of the box. The man and the boy were watching the window, so that they did not see their two prisoners climb cautiously out of the box and tiptoe toward them. Charles was almost dead with fright, but he followed Henrietta until they stood just under the table. And then, at a signal from Mr. Webb, the flies all whirled down and began walking up and down the man's nose and buzzing in the boy's ears and generally plaguing them twice as much as they had before. And while they waved their arms to drive the flies off, and shut their eyes to keep the flies out of them, Charles and Henrietta bopped on the windowsill and down on the grass outside, and than ran for their lives.

Then Mr. Webb went out into the hall and the flies gathered round him, and he made them a little speech of thanks, and then dismissed them. As he followed the last fly out through the keyhole, he heard the parlor window go shut with a bang, and then the boy called: "Hey, pa! Pa! Look, pa! The chickens are gone!"

He chuckled to himself. "That's a good job done," he said. "But now how are we going to get the gold?"

XX

YOU may Believe

that Charles and Henrietta were glad to see their friends again, and that their friends were glad to see them. Charles shook hands with the dogs and Freddy and Hank and the mice, and Henrietta kissed the ducks and Mrs. Wiggins.

She almost put Mrs. Wiggins's eye out with her beak. Then she would have kissed Mrs. Webb, but Mrs. Webb begged to be excused.

"Now, animals," said Robert, "we've got to hold a council of war. We've got to get that gold, and we've got to get it before tomorrow morning, because Henrietta says they intend to take it into the village and put it in the bank tomorrow, and if they do that, we'll never see it again."

"We've got to get into the house somehow," said Jinx, "and it must be after dark, when they can't see us get in. So the flies can't help us any; they'll all be asleep. Now, how can we make them open a window or a door?"

"Mr. Bean always opens a window for fresh air when he goes to bed," said Hank.

"You can take my word for it, this man doesn't do that," said Henrietta. "1 never smelled such a stuffy house in my life."

"Mr. Bean spilt some grease on the stove once," said Robert, "and he opened the window to let the smoke out."

"Yes, but we can't get in to put anything on the stove," said Eek.

"Wait a minute," said Jinx suddenly. "That gives me an idea. Yes, I know how we can work it," he said excitedly. And he explained his plan, which, as you will see later, was a pretty clever one, even for a cat to think of.

Nothing could be done until late that night, so for the rest of the day the animals sat round in the woods, keeping well out of sight of the house. They tried to play games to pass away the time, but home was so near, and they were all so anxious to get there, and so impatient of the delay, that the games didn't seem much fun. But at last the sun went down and the long shadows crept out of the woods and hid the grass and trees, and the stars began to wink and twinkle in the dark-blue sky. Even then the animals did not start to carry out their plan, and it was not until about nine o'clock, when the light in the house had gone out and they knew that the man and the boy had gone to bed, that Jinx said it was time to go.

Then they all went into a field that was near the house, and Freddy with his sharp nose and Hank with the toes of his iron shoes tore up by the roots a good-sized heap of grass. This they carried up close to the house, and then Jinx took as much as he could carry and climbed up the back porch on to the roof and dropped it down the chimney. Then he went down and carried up another piece, and he kept on doing this until the chimney was all plugged up.

Inside the house the man and the boy were sound asleep, with the bag of gold by the head of their bed. Fortunately for the animals, they had made up a big fire in the stove so that they wouldn't have to build a new one in the morning, and pretty soon the smoke that couldn't get up through the chimney began to pour out into the front parlor. And from the front parlor it went into the hall and up the stairs, and at last into the bedroom. And then it got into the boy's throat and woke him up.

"Fire!" he yelled, jumping out of bed. "Fire! Wake up, pa! The house is on fire!"

In a minute they were both up and rushing down the stairs in their white nightshirts, dragging the heavy bag of gold after them. Bump, bump, clink, jingle it went. They unlocked the front door and rushed out into the yard, and there they dropped the bag and sat down on it, panting. Then they looked up at the house.

"Why, the house isn't afire!" said the man.

"Where does the smoke come from then?" asked the boy.

"I don't know," said his father. "Must be a fire somewhere. We'd better go back and see." So they dragged the bag of gold back into the house, but they left the front door open behind them in case the fire should break out suddenly.

The animals, who had been hiding behind trees and bushes, now crept up closer to the door, and as soon as they heard the man and the boy moving round in the front parlour, they tiptoed into the house. Jinx and the mice hurried upstairs into the bedroom, and while Jinx carried the two pairs of shoes into another room and hid them under a bureau, the mice gnawed all the buttons off the clothes. Freddy and Robert and Jack hid under the dining room table, and Hank hid most of himself behind the long velvet curtains at the dining-room window, although his head and tail showed. They made a good deal of noise getting in, but the man and the boy were talking excitedly and throwing up windows to let the smoke out, and didn't hear them. Even when Mrs. Wiggins knocked over the umbrella stand in the hall, they didn't notice it.

When the animals were all in the house and Mrs. Wiggins had lain down in a corner of the dining room with a red tablecloth thrown over her so as to look as much as possible like a piece of furniture, Jinx came to the head of the stairs and began to make noises. A cat can make terrible noises when he really tries, and Jinx was really trying. He moaned and groaned and howled and yowled, and in a minute the man and the boy came out into the hall. They were very much frightened, and the animals could see that their knees were shaking under the edges of their nightshirts.

"Oh, pa!" said the boy. "Wh-wh-what is that?"

"Here," said the man. "You take this bag of gold into the dining-room and watch it. I'm going up to see." And he started up the stairs.

The boy dragged the bag into the dining room and shut the door. All the animals stood perfectly still, and as there wasn't much light in the room, although it was bright moonlight outside, he didn't see them. But he did see Mrs. Wiggins.

"Why, where'd this red sofa come from?" he said aloud. "I never saw that before." And he went over and sat down on her.

Now Mrs. Wiggins had a sense of humor. That means that she always laughed at the wrong time. And she began to laugh now.

"Yow!" yelled the boy, and he jumped up, and, forgetting all about the bag of gold that he had been told to watch, he ran upstairs to tell his father that the sofa in the dining room was alive.

And at that moment Robert came out from underneath the table. "Now's our chance, animals," he said. And Mrs. Wiggins threw off the tablecloth, and Hank came out from behind the curtains, and Freddy and Jack came from under the table, and they all grabbed hold of the heavy bag with their teeth and heaved and dragged and pulled it out into the hall, and through the front door, and across the yard to the barn. As quickly as they could, they hoisted it into the phaeton, and Hank took the ropes over his shoulders and pulled the carriage out into the yard. Jinx and the mice had sneaked downstairs again while the man was looking through the bedrooms, and they climbed aboard with Charles and Henrietta and the ducks.

"All ready, Hank," said Robert. "We're all here. Next stop is Home. One, two, three—go!" And away they went out of the gate and up the road with a rattle of flying stones, as fast as Hank could gallop, with the dogs and Freddy running alongside, and Mrs. Wiggins thundering along behind, while all the smaller animals hung on for dear life with beaks and bills and claws.

Now, the man had not found anything upstairs, and he began to suspect that a trick had been played on him. When he heard the rattle of wheels and the thud of flying hoofs, he was sure of it. He didn't say anything then to the boy for leaving the gold unguarded; he would give him his licking for that later, he thought. He rushed downstairs to the dining room, and sure enough, the bag was gone. Then he ran to the door, just in time to see the last part of Mrs. Wiggins going through the gate.

"Get your clothes on!" he yelled to the boy, giving him a cuff on the ear. "It's the animals. I might have known it! But we can catch them if we hurry. They forgot that we had an automobile."

Now it was easy enough for them to get their clothes on, but it wasn't at all easy to keep them on, for the mice had gnawed all the buttons off. They worked and worked at them for a long time, and finally had to fasten them together with pins. And that didn't work very well either, for every time they moved, the pins stuck into them and made them yell. Then when they were all ready, they couldn't find their shoes at all, so they went out finally in their stocking feet, and cranked up their rickety old automobile and started in pursuit.

By this time the animals had got a pretty good start. But as they began to climb the hill on the other side of the valley, they looked over their shoulders, and far off down the road they could see the two little lights of the pursuing automobile growing bigger and bigger, and they could hear, plainer and plainer, the rattle and pop of the engine, as the man with the black moustache drove furiously on their trail.

"I don't know as we'll make it," panted Hank.

"We've *got* to make it," said Robert. "Keep going for all you're worth."

But as they went on, it grew plainer and plainer that they couldn't make it, for the automobile was traveling twice as fast as they were. And just as they got to the bridge where they had slept the night before, Hank slowed down to a walk.

"It's no use," he said. "I can't run up this hill. Can't we turn off and hide in the woods?"

"Not with a carriage," said Mrs. Wiggins. "But Hank, you go on, and I'll stay here on the bridge and keep them back. Go as fast as you can, and I'll overtake you if I can before you get home. And wait: I want the mice to stay, too. I think they can help."

At first the animals wouldn't consent to leave her behind. "We'll stay and fight it out beside you," they said. But she said no, she had a good plan, and they'd only spoil it if they stayed. So they said good-bye sorrowfully, and went on, leaving Mrs. Wiggins and the mice to hold the bridge.

As soon as they were gone, Mrs. Wiggins set to work. She pushed down the railings at the side of the bridge with her horns and tore up some of the boards and piled them all in the middle. Then she and the mice sat down behind a bush and waited. Pretty soon the automobile came bounding up the hill, rattling as if it would fall to pieces the next minute. And at every bound the man and the boy let out a great yell as the pins with which their clothes were fastened together stuck into them.

Just in time the man saw the pile of boards, and he slammed on the brakes and stopped so quickly that he and his son flew right out over the front and landed sitting down on the bridge. And at once they let out a piercing yell, for all the pins had stuck into them at the same time. Then they got up and began clearing away the boards.

"Now, mice," whispered Mrs. Wiggins, "out with you, and do as I told you." And the mice crept out, and each one of them climbed up on a tire, and they set to work with their sharp little teeth to nibble holes through the hard rubber.

"Pretty tough gnawing," squeaked Eeny.

"Keep at it, brothers," chirped Quik. "Everything depends on us now."

But the tires were very hard, and before any of them had made deep enough holes to let the air out, the boards were cleared away and me man started up his engine. Then the mice had to jump down, and Mrs. Wiggins got up and lowered her head and shook her horns and prepared to charge at the enemy. But just as the automobile started slowly across the bridge, and just as she was about to gallop out and fry to tumble it over into the water below—pingggg! went the left front tire, and fizz-wizz-wizz-wizz! went the right front tire, and the other two tires blew up with a bang, and the automobile wobbled and came to a standstill. For though the mice hadn't gnawed all the way through the tires, they had weakened them so that they gave way as soon as the automobile started.

Then the man with the black moustache knew that his chance was gone, and that he couldn't overtake the animals and get back the gold. For quite a little while he stood staring mournfully up the road. But he was a practical man, which means that he believed in doing *something* immediately, even if it wasn't anything very useful. So he picked up a piece of board and took the dirty-faced boy across his knee and gave him a good licking. And then he turned round and walked home in his stocking feet.

X

EARLY the Next

morning the head of Mr. Bean, the farmer, appeared at his bedroom window. The fresh morning breeze swung the red tassel of his white cotton nightcap and waved his bushy, gray whiskers. He was looking out to see what kind of a day it was going to be.

"My goodness!" said Mr. Bean. "It's nearly six o'clock! I certainly do miss that rooster! I haven't been up on time one single morning since he left."

He dressed quickly and went downstairs and out into the cow barn and gave Mrs. Wurzburger and Mrs. Wogus their breakfasts, and then he fed the chickens and the pigs and William, the horse, and the other animals. Jock, the wise old collie, went along with him.

Pretty soon Mrs. Bean rang the breakfast bell, and he went in and sat down at the table and tucked his napkin under his chin and had coffee and pancakes and hot biscuits and ham and eggs and oatmeal and two kinds of jam. And when he had had enough, he pushed back his chair and lit his pipe, taking care not to set fire to his whiskers with the match.

Then he said: "Mrs. Bean, I don't know how you feel about it, but I certainly should like to have those animals back again. It seems sort of lonesome here this nice spring weather without Robert and Hank and Mrs. Wiggins and all the rest of them."

"Mr. Bean," said his wife, "I have heard you say that every morning after breakfast since the animals went away. And I will reply as I always reply: I miss them too, especially Jinx. He was a nice cat."

"I've sometimes thought," said Mr. Bean, "that maybe they wouldn't have gone away if I had been nicer to them."

"You was always a kind man to your animals, Mr. Bean," his wife replied.

"Yes," he said. "I try to be. I gave them plenty to eat and didn't work them too hard, but after all I didn't make them as comfortable as I might. All their houses needed repairing, and they were pretty drafty and cold in the wintertime."

"Well, we didn't have the money to fix them up," said his wife.

"That's true. That's true," said Mr. Bean with a sigh. And for some time neither of them said anything.

Then all at once, out in the barnyard, Jock began to bark and the hens began to cackle and the cows mooed and the ducks quacked and the pigs squealed; and Mr. Bean jumped up and ran to the window. "What on earth is the matter?" he exclaimed, and then: "Wife! Wife!"

he cried. "Here they are! Here are the animals back! Come out! Come out into the yard!" And out they rushed to welcome the wanderers.

All the animals who had stayed at home lined up on either side of the gate to welcome them. First came Charles and Henrietta, wing in wing, and then came Jinx, proudly waving his red tail, and then Freddy and Jack and Robert. And behind them came the phaeton, drawn by Hank. And Mrs. Wiggins, with Alice and Emma and the four mice on her back, brought up the rear. They marched in the gate and went three times around the barnyard, while the animals and Mr. and Mrs. Bean cheered themselves hoarse. And then they stopped the phaeton directly in front of Mr. Bean, and Robert jumped into it and, with the help of Jack and Mrs. Wiggins, tumbled the bag of gold out on the ground.

"What on earth!" Mr. Bean exclaimed, and he bent down and untied the bag, and out rolled a stream of bright yellow coins. "Gold!" he cried. "Twenty-dollar gold pieces! Why, here's thousands of dollars! Enough to build twenty new barns if we want 'em! And you brought all this back to me!" He stood motionless for a minute, and then he snatched off his nightcap (which he still had on), and threw it up in the air and grabbed Mrs. Bean round the waist and waltzed her around the barnyard until they were both so dizzy they had to stop. And all the animals cheered and danced round too. Then Mr. and Mrs. Bean went round and hugged all the animals, even the mice, who were very happy, but scared all the same to be hugged so hard. And when the alarm clock and the shawl and the other things they had brought back with them had been admired, Mr. Bean made a speech.

"Animals and friends," he said, "I thank you a thousand times for this magnificent and munificent gift. Had you brought me back nothing but yourselves, I should have been more than happy, but since you have brought me wealth as well, I intend that you shall share in its benefits. You shall have new homes, fitted with all the modern conveniences. The workmen shall start on them tomorrow, and Mrs. Bean and I will draw the plans for them tonight. Those of you who work regularly shall work in the future no more than six hours a day, and when, as is sometimes necessary, either Hank or William works longer than that, he shall have an extra measure of oats, with sugar, for each hour of overtime. Since I have an alarm clock, Charles may sleep as late as he wishes in the morning. I will have electric lights strung up over the duck-pond, as well as in the various houses, and a small house will also be built for the mice. And perhaps next winter we can all go south together.

"And now, my friends, you are no doubt anxious to greet your relatives and talk over your adventures by flood and field; so today we will do no more work, but will celebrate it as a holiday in honor of your homecoming. No doubt, too, you are hungry, and Mrs. Bean will go in and prepare a feast for you, while I set to work on the plans for your new quarters. Again I thank you, my friends, from the bottom of my heart."

That night, when the celebration was over, and the animals had all gone to bed, Freddy, the pig, who had eaten a great deal more than was good for him and consequently did not feel like sleeping, walked out into the moonlight.

"After all," he said to himself, "it's exciting to travel and have adventures, but there's no place like home." And he looked affectionately at the old familiar pig pen, where so many happy hours had been spent. And then he made up this song:

> Oh, a life of adventure is gay and free,
>   And danger has its charm;
> And no pig of spirit will bound his life
>   By the fence on his master's farm.
>
> Yet there's no true pig but heaves a sigh
> At the pleasant thought of the old home sty.
>
> But one tires at last of wandering,
>   And the road grows steep and long,
> A treadmill round, where no peace is found,
>   If one follows it overlong.
>
> And however they wander, both pigs and men
> Are always glad to get home again.

"Is that someone singing?"

FREDDY GOES TO THE NORTH POLE

I
Freddy Has an Idea

JINX,
the
Cat was walking around in

the bushes behind the barn, looking for

excitement. Things had been very quiet

on the farm for a long time. Nothing really interesting had happened

since spring, when he and the other animals had come back from their trip to Florida. That had been a great trip! He purred whenever he thought of it.

Suddenly he crouched down and began to lash his tail. A little gray shape darted out from under the barn into the shadow of a bush. Noiselessly Jinx crept forward, inch by inch, until he was within jumping distance. But just as he was about to spring, a little squeaky voice came from under the bush:

"Hey, Jinx! Stop it! It's me—Eeny!"

Jinx stopped crouching and straightened up. He gave a disgusted sniff. "I might have known it!" he growled. "There's never anything new around this place! Since I made friends with you and your family and promised to leave you alone, I haven't seen hide nor hair, nor tooth nor tail of anything I could hunt. Friendship's all very well, but it spoils lots of good sport."

"I'm sorry," said the mouse. He came out from the shadow and sat down beside Jinx and began to clean his whiskers with his forepaws. "But you ought to be more careful, Jinx. You might have jumped on me and hurt me."

"How'd I know it was you?" said the cat. "You said your cousins were giving a party down in the pasture. I thought you'd be down there."

"I was," said Eeny. "But I came away early. It wasn't much of a party. Why, all they gave us to eat was grass roots and a little birch bark. Even if they are my cousins, I *must* say—"

"Oh, don't tell me anything about relatives! "said Jinx. "I've got a dozen brothers and sisters in this neighborhood, but if I was starving d'you think any of 'em would give me as much as a robin's claw or a mouse tail—excuse me, Eeny."

The mouse shuddered slightly and curled his tail tightly under him. "Don't mention it," he said.

Jinx gave a loud laugh. "I won't—again," he said. "Come on, let's go down to the pigpen and see what Freddy's doing."

As Jinx and Eeny walked side by side through the orchard, they met Mrs. Bean, the farmer's wife. Mrs. Bean had an empty bucket in her hand, because she had been feeding the pigs; and when she saw the two of them, she stared and stared. "Land sakes!" she exclaimed. "What this farm's coming to I don't know! When I was a girl, animals behaved the way you expected them to. Cats and mice didn't go out walking together and pigs didn't read newspapers and there weren't any of these animal parties given in the barn. It's more like a circus than a farm here ever since these animals got back from Florida last year. Here, Jinx! Come, kitty, kitty!"

Jinx walked over to her. He didn't want to, but Mrs. Bean liked him and was very good to him, so he was always polite to her. She petted him and scratched his head, and then she pointed to Eeny, who, while he waited for his friend, was nibbling at an apple that had fallen from one of the trees.

"Look, Jinx. Go chase the mouse. See? Nice fat mouse! M'm! Mice, Jinx, mice!"

Jinx crouched down and lashed his tail. "I'll have to chase you, Eeny," he said." Run over towards the fence, and I'll pretend to look for you, and then we can go on down and see Freddy."

Eeny scurried off, squeaking with pretended fright, and Jinx, looking as ferocious as possible, bounded after him. But as soon as they were out of sight of Mrs. Bean, they walked along again side by side.

"What did she mean about pigs reading newspapers?" asked Eeny.

"Oh," said Jinx," that's Freddy. I've been teaching him to read and he's crazy about it. He reads everything he can lay his hoofs on now."

"Good gracious!" squeaked the mouse. "I didn't know you could read, Jinx."

"Read!" Jinx waved his tail importantly. "That's nothing. I can do anything I set my mind to. I learned to read sitting on Mrs. Bean's lap when she read the newspaper out loud to Mr. Bean."

As they came in sight of the pigpen, they saw quite a group of animals sitting around in a circle outside, and in the middle of it was Freddy. He seemed to be reading aloud from a paper that lay on the ground in front of him, for whenever he said anything, all the others would either cheer or groan.

"Hurry up! He's reading the baseball news!" said Jinx, and started to run.

Eeny started to run too, but his legs were much too short to keep up with a cat. "Hey, Jinx, wait for me!" he shouted.

Jinx stopped. "Sorry," he said, and, picking up the mouse carefully in his mouth, bounded down into the middle of the circle, knocking over one or two of the smaller pigs as he did so. That was the way Jinx always did things. He had the best heart in the world, but he was apt to be rather rough and thoughtless.

"'Lo, Freddy, old scout," he said. "Who won yesterday?"

"The Giants," said the pig. "Very close game. Two and two at the end of the eighth inning, and then Whippenberger knocked a home run and brought two men in."

"Whippenberger?" said Jinx. "Who's he? That new shortstop? What's his batting average?"

"Oh my goodness!" said Freddy crossly. "You can read, Jinx. Why don't you look it up yourself? I'm sick of doing the reading for all the animals on the farm. I don't get a chance to do anything I want to any more. Always somebody coming down here to get me to read something. And I'm especially sick of reading all these long accounts of baseball games. Maybe you get some fun out of it, but I don't. What's the sense of getting all excited about a game played by somebody else—a game that we animals couldn't play ourselves if we wanted to? I think it's silly."

Freddy was usually so cheerful and good-natured that all the other animals were very much surprised at this outburst, and they just sat and stared at him without saying anything. But Jinx said:

"Maybe you're right, Freddy. I'd a lot rather go out and have adventures of my own than sit home and read about those somebody else had. Look at the fun we had going to Florida. Wasn't that better than reading a book about it?"

"Yes, yes. Oh my, I should say so!" exclaimed Freddy and Eeny and Robert, the dog. They and Jinx were the only ones there who had taken the Florida trip, and they naturally felt a little superior to the other animals on that account and were sometimes inclined to put on airs about it. And Ferdinand, the crow, who lived in the woods, had a very exasperating habit of sitting up in the big elm near the barn, where all the animals could hear him, and puffing out his chest and saying importantly: "Well, when I was in Florida —"And then he would burst into a loud derisive laugh.

So now, as soon as the subject of Florida was brought up, all the other animals groaned and walked away, leaving Freddy and Eeny and Jinx and Robert alone.

"I mean what I said, Jinx," said Freddy. "We ought to be doing something ourselves, instead of reading about what somebody else does. We ought to take another trip."

"We haven't been back from Florida very long," said Robert. "I don't think we ought to take another trip now. We all have our work to do on the farm, and we can't do it if we're always running off on pleasure trips. It wouldn't be fair to Mr. Bean. He feeds us and takes care of us, and we mustn't go back on him."

"That's right," said Freddy. "But I tell you what. I have an idea. Just wait till I run into my study for a minute. There's something I want to read to you."

Freddy had gathered together quite a library of old newspapers and printed advertising folders, which he kept in one corner of the pigpen. He also had *The Complete Works of Shakespeare in One Volume*, which for many years had been almost indispensable to Mr. and Mrs. Bean, since they had used it to prop up the corner of their bed that didn't have any leg on it. But when they could afford it, they bought a new bed, and then the book was thrown out and Freddy got it.

Freddy was very proud of his study, although it was so dark in the pigpen that nobody could possibly study there, or even read. But he knew all the different papers and pamphlets by their smell (the smell of *The Complete Works of Shakespeare in One Volume* differs from that of last week's newspaper more than you would believe), and so when he wanted to read anything, he just went in and got it and carried it outside.

Pretty soon he came back with a little booklet. On the cover it said: *Personally Conducted Tours to Europe.* And inside were pictures of some of the places people could be personally conducted to. Freddy read it aloud to them and explained how for a certain amount of money a person could join one of these tours, and then he didn't have to bother about buying his tickets or checking his baggage or anything. The company who ran the tour saw to everything, and it took him and all the other tourists round and showed them all the sights and got them back home safely. "And," said Freddy, "I don't see why we couldn't run such a company ourselves. Since we got back from Florida, lots of other animals, not only on this farm, but on other farms round here, have been wanting to take such a trip."

"I know a lot of mice that would like to go," said Eeny. "Only it's such a long way!"

"Oh, for animals that don't want to go far or can't get away for more than a day or two, we could get up short trips round here," said Freddy. "There are lots of interesting sights to see within just a short distance. Of course different animals are interested in different things. But we could have a tour of the ponds and rivers for ducks and geese, and a two-day trip to the cheese factory for mice, and so on."

"I choose to personally conduct the mouse tour," said Jinx, with a laugh.

Eeny frowned. Being a mouse, he didn't have any eyebrows, and so he had to do most of it with his ears, which made him look quite terrifying, even though he was so small. It quite terrified Freddy.

"Please, Eeny, don't do that!" he exclaimed. "I'm sure Jinx didn't mean anything. You didn't, did you, Jinx?"

"No, no, certainly not," replied the cat. "Don't be so touchy, Eeny."

"You'd be touchy if your father and six aunts and fourteen uncles and nine brothers and sisters had been eaten by cats."

"Give you my word," said Jinx solemnly, "I haven't eaten a mouse in over a year—worse luck!" he added under his breath.

"What did you say?" asked Eeny suspiciously.

"Nothing," said Jinx, "nothing. Just purring because I'm glad you mice don't hate me any more."

"H'm," said Eeny scornfully, and was about to make a sharp retort, but Robert said: "Come on, stop your quarrelling. I think that's a great idea of yours, Freddy. But I've got to go now; I just heard a buggy stop at the gate and I must go bark at it so Mr. Bean will know he's got company. Let's call a meeting in the cow barn tonight and talk it over."

"Right," said the pig. "And then we'll form a company and incorporate."

"Incorporate?" asked Robert. "What's that?"

"Oh, I ran across it in reading," said Freddy importantly. "It's what all companies do. You draw up rules and bylaws and then you pay the government a fee, and then you're incorporated. That means that whatever you do after that is legal."

"Then we ought to do it," said Robert. "Good-bye, you animals. See you later."

II
Barnyard Tours, Inc.

SO that Was how they started Barnyard Tours, Inc. The "Inc." stands for "Incorporated." Freddy was president, and Jinx was secretary, and Mrs. Wiggins was treasurer. Mrs. Wiggins was the cow who lived in the shed with Mrs. Wurzburger and Mrs. Wogus, her two sisters, and Mrs. Wogus's little girl, Marietta. Mrs. Wogus called Marietta her little girl, but of course she was a calf. Mrs. Wiggins was chosen treasurer because the cowshed made such a good treasury for the various things that the tourist animals paid the company. They brought all sorts of things, but mostly things to eat, because these were what the company wanted most. This was a very good arrangement for Mr. Bean, because by and by he didn't have to feed the animals on the farm at all, and yet they were getting fat on the delicacies the tourists brought to them.

The tours started in a very small way, of course. The first one was for mice. Mrs. Wiggins took thirty mice on her back and went down the river road for a mile or two and then crossed the canal and came back the other way, stopping at the cheese factory for lunch. The mice sat two by two, as you do in a sightseeing bus, and Eeny stood up in front, between Mrs. Wiggins's horns, and told them about the various points of interest they were passing, and pointed out bits of especially beautiful scenery and gave the names of the mice that lived in some of the finer residences. He was rather nervous at first, because he had never done any public speaking before, but after a while he began to enjoy it and grew quite poetic in the descriptive bits. Only he had to be careful not to make any jokes, because when he did, Mrs. Wiggins laughed heartily, and when she laughed, she shook so that the mice bounced about on her back, and once six of them fell off.

The mice were very much pleased with their trip and told all their friends, and gradually more and more animals came to the farm to inquire about tours. So many came finally that Mr. Bean was quite put out about it; he said he was sick and tired of seeing the barnyard crowded with strange animals, and he couldn't step foot outside the door without tripping over woodchucks and squirrels and rats or being bumped into by cows and horses. One night six skunks came, a father and mother and four children. One of the children wasn't very well, and they wanted to inquire about a place in the mountains to spend the summer where the water would be good and where the air would be bracing. The little skunks weren't very well brought up, and while the father and mother were in the barn talking to Jinx, they got to fighting, and they made so much noise that they woke up Mrs. Bean. She looked out the window and saw them, and of course she didn't know they had come on business, so she threw a pitcher of water on them. The mother skunk was quite mad, because she said the children might have caught their deaths of cold, being all wet through like that. Fortunately none of them took cold. But after that Robert said he thought they ought to open a regular office somewhere away from the house and near the road, where one animal could always be on hand to answer questions and give out information. Then they wouldn't bother Mr. and Mrs. Bean.

So they opened an office in an old shed that stood down in the corner of one of the fields quite a long way from the house. Most of the time Charles, the rooster, stayed in the office, because he was a very good talker, and he liked to tell other birds and animals things they didn't know. He was a good salesman. That means that he could often persuade animals to take trips that they really didn't care about taking at all. One time he talked so enthusiastically about the beautiful view you could get from the ten-acre lot, which was behind the house, on the hill, that he persuaded three horses from over near Centerboro to come up and plow it, just so they could see the view when they turned round at the end of each furrow. Mr. Bean was very much pleased when he found the field all plowed.

After a number of short one-day trips had been carried out successfully, they began to get up longer ones. Jinx took a mixed party of cats and rabbits and cows on a ten-day tour of the Adirondacks. He looked up all the routes beforehand on a map that was in Freddy's library. They had a fine time—climbed mountains and went swimming and were royally entertained by the woods animals they met.

Special trips were arranged too for each kind of animal. The smaller animals particularly, who never dared venture alone very far from home, were very glad to see something of the world under the protection of such a brave and loyal dog as Robert, or such a reckless swashbuckler as Jinx. Freddy even got up a trip for spiders from the barn and the house and they all worked together in the morning and built a big web and then spent a glorious afternoon catching flies, and came home, very tired but very happy, early in the evening. In return they wove a big mosquito net for Freddy to sleep under in the pigpen. Of course it wasn't very strong and tore quite easily, but they agreed to keep it in repair for a year.

The hardest animals to get up trips for were cows. Cows aren't much interested in what is going on in the world. "It's hot and dusty out on the road," they said, "and dogs chase us, and automobiles make us hurry in a very undignified way. We'd rather stand round in the shade and swish our tails and think."

"But if you take a trip and see strange sights, you'll have more interesting things to think about," Freddy objected. Of course he knew as well as you do that it is almost impossible to catch a cow thinking. They have very good brains and they can think when they want to, but usually it's just too much trouble. They said that simply because they felt they ought to have *some* excuse for not ever doing anything. But Freddy went round and made a lot of inquiries and finally found several places that would interest cows. One place was a meadow on an abandoned farm that had very thick sweet grass, and another had historic interest for cows because over a hundred years ago a very famous cow had fought and killed a bear there, and another was an especially good place for them to stand in and switch their tails and think. But it took so much talking to persuade any cows to take the trip that although several parties were got up, Freddy decided it didn't pay. "The overhead is too high," Freddy said.

One day Freddy and Jinx were sitting inside the shed. It was a very hot day and they had talked for a while, and then Jinx had curled up and gone to sleep, and Freddy had started to look at a map of the Arctic regions that a dog whose master kept a magazine stand had brought in and exchanged for a personally conducted tour through Scenic Centerboro. This was a very popular trip with dogs and cats, and would have been with other animals too, but the company didn't like to have its animal sightseers become too conspicuous. And so, of course, they couldn't go into towns and cities much. If people saw a party of dogs admiring the Centerboro Public Library—which was really very beautiful, built in the Gothic style—they wouldn't pay much attention to them. But if a party of rabbits or squirrels did the same thing, children would throw stones, and people would try to catch them, or at least would stare and make remarks, and it would be very unpleasant. And that would be bad for the company, because other animals would hear about it and wouldn't want to go on the tours.

While Freddy was poring sleepily over the map inside the shed, Charles, the rooster, was sitting on the fence outside, watching for customers. Charles liked the sound of his own voice pretty well, and when there wasn't anybody round to listen, he sometimes talked to himself. "Dear me," he was saying, "it *is* hot. Yes indeed, very hot. I do hope we'll get a shower to lay the dust." He kept saying this over and over. He was very economical and never wasted his best conversation on himself. Sometimes of course he said quite a good thing by mistake, but then he would save it up until someone came along and repeat it as if he had just thought of it.

By and by he saw something moving away off down the empty road. It got larger and larger, and pretty soon he saw it was a big gray farm horse. "Good gracious!" said Charles. "I wonder who that is. He walks very slowly, as if he were tired. He must have come a long way. Maybe he wants to take a tour."

"Good afternoon, horse," he said pleasantly when the animal had come near enough. "You a stranger in these parts?"

The horse did not answer, but came clumping stolidly along until he was opposite the shed.

Charles was naturally a little put out at being snubbed by a horse and he jumped down from the fence and walked out into the road. The horse saw him and stopped. "Excuse me, friend," he said. "Can you tell me if this is the place where there's a company that arranges trips for animals?"

"This is the place," said Charles, "and I'm part of the company. What can I do for you? We plan your vacations for you, tell you what to see and how to see it, conduct you to all points of greatest int—"

The horse shook his head slowly. "Ain't heard a word," he interrupted. "I know you're talkin' 'cause I can see your beak move, but I ain't as young as I was, and I'm gettin' a little deaf. Just hop up on my back like a good feller, and then we can talk comfortable."

As soon as Charles realized that the horse hadn't heard his first greeting and wasn't trying to snub him at all, he felt more agreeable, and he did as the other requested and repeated his remarks at greater length. But the horse still seemed doubtful.

"I understood there was a pig was president of this concern," he said. "I'd like to see him, I guess."

Charles glanced at the shed, from which came the mingled snores of one pig and one cat. "Our president is in conference just at present," he said importantly. "I'm afraid you couldn't see him without an appointment. But I am authorized to act for the company in these matters. If you tell me where you wish to go—"

"H'm," said the horse. "Well, I ain't ever got much information out of any rooster before—nor any information, for the matter of that, except maybe about what a smart feller he was, but maybe you're different. Anyway, I come a long way, and I don't want to go back empty-hoofed, so to speak. Ye see, I'm just a plain farm worker—have been all my life. I've worked hard. Now I'm gettin' old and

"This is the place," said Charles, "and I'm part of the company."

I can't work like I used to, but while I still got some of my faculties, I'd like to see a little of the world. That's reasonable, ain't it?"

"Very commendable," said Charles.

"And so here I am. Now what kind of trips have you got?"

"Well, from what you say, I suppose you want a long trip, and the only long trip we're planning just now is one to Florida this winter. Our president is going to take this party himself. He's a seasoned traveler and has had a great deal of experience in conducting tours, and he knows everything there is to know about Florida. Of course it is a long trip and therefore rather more expensive than some of the—"

"That's what I wanted to talk to you about," interrupted the horse. "I'm poor. I haven't got anything to pay for the trip with."

"Oh, surely we can arrange that," said Charles. "Our charges are not excessive. A small bag of oats, or a bale of hay—"

"The farmer where I live is poor, too," the horse replied. "And as I don't do as much work as I used to, I don't get any more oats and hay than just barely enough to get along on. I can't save any of it. But I thought maybe I could work it out. I'd be willing to come over either before or after the trip and do, say, ten good days' work. I'm still strong and hearty. I wouldn't skimp ye on my part of the bargain."

"Dear me," said Charles, "that's very awkward—very awkward indeed. No, I'm very sorry, but I'm afraid that wouldn't do. It wouldn't do at all. Our rules are very strict, and our terms are strictly cash in advance."

"Ah," said the horse thoughtfully. "Well, I guess that finishes it, then. I thought maybe we could strike a bargain. But if that's the case—"

"I'm sorry," said Charles firmly. "But we have to be businesslike, or where would we be? There's nothing personal in it, you understand—"

"Oh sure, I understand," said the horse impatiently. "Hop down now, I've got a long way to travel before night. Good day to ye. That's what I get for talking to a rooster, anyway." And he clumped off down the road.

Charles resumed his perch on the fence. "Stupid animal!" he said to himself. "Who ever heard of such a thing! Just like all of 'em: trying to get something for nothing. Oh, this being in business is not so easy. It takes lots of cleverness and tact and ability. It's a lucky day for the company when they got me to interview these animals. Why, suppose Freddy had been out here. For all his cleverness, he's not such a fine business man. Just between you and me, Charles, you handled that horse pretty well."

The longer Charles thought about it, the more pleased with himself he became, and finally he got so puffed up with pride that he went in and waked Freddy up and told him about it. But, to his amazement, Freddy was not at all pleased.

"What!" he exclaimed, "he offered to work his way on the trip, and you sent him away? Why, you ninny, that's the best idea I've heard since the company started. Why, you miserable fowl you, you oaf, you—you *umph*!"

"Umph "is a word that pigs use only when they are thoroughly disgusted with people. If a pig calls you an umph, you have a right to get mad about it—unless, of course, you happen to be one. Charles ruffled up the feathers in his neck and started to get mad, but before he could think of anything sarcastic to say, Freddy pushed him aside, crawled through the fence, and trotted off up the road in the direction the horse had taken.

Jinx hadn't waked up, and Charles tiptoed out of the shed, and walked dejectedly back to his home in the hen-coop. "That's gratitude for you!" he muttered. "Work and slave for these animals day in and day out, and what thanks do I get? Get called an umph. An umph—me! Well, I'm through, that's all. They can get somebody else to interview the tourists. We'll see how many they get when I'm not round."

But the next morning when Mrs. Wiggins told him that there was to be a meeting of the company at ten o'clock, his curiosity was too much for him, and he got to the office before anybody but Freddy had come. Freddy was again looking over the map of the Arctic regions. Charles, whose feelings were still hurt, would have gone out, but Freddy said:

"Don't go, Charles. I'm sorry I was rude to you yesterday. Please forgive me, will you?"

Of course there was nothing for Charles to do but to accept the apology, which he did, very handsomely. "Certainly, Freddy," he said. "Pray don't mention it again." He was going on to say more, because no matter how long he had talked, he could always find more to say on any subject, and he had hardly said anything yet, but the other animals began to arrive, and pretty soon Freddy called the meeting to order.

"Ladies and gentlemen, friends and fellow stockholders," he said, "I have the great pleasure to announce to you that at the end of the first three months of business, your company finds itself in a very strong position. Although no very long trips have been organized, twenty-eight short trips have been successfully completed without loss or damage to any client, with the exception of one spider, who lost three legs on the third Flycatching Expedition in a fight with a wasp, and one mouse who had indigestion as a result of eating too much cheese at the cheese factory on Scenic Tour No. 3 for Mice. Both of these unfortunates, I am happy to say, have stated of their own free will that the company is not to blame. In addition to such profits of the business as have already been divided up, there is in the treasury a substantial surplus of nuts, grain, and various kinds of food, as well as of odds and ends which we have accepted in payment, and which we shall undoubtedly find use for later."

There were loud cheers at this very favourable report, and then Freddy went on:

"But the principal reason for calling this meeting is that something happened which showed me a new way in which the company can benefit both us and our friend and owner, Mr. Bean."

"Three cheers for Mr. Bean," called Hank, the old white horse, and the animals cheered lustily, for Mr. Bean was well liked. Even Mr. and Mrs. Webb, the spiders, who had come to the meeting on Mrs. Wiggins's back, cheered heartily, but of course nobody heard them.

Then Freddy told them about the horse. "He wants to take a long trip, but he hasn't anything to pay for it with, so he has offered to give two weeks' work. Do you see what that means, animals? That means that Hank, here, can take two weeks' vacation whenever he wants to. Now, suppose for every animal, bird, and insect here we can get a substitute in this way. Two weeks' vacation for us all. And there is no need to limit it to two weeks. Up to today there has been one great difficulty in getting up tours. Most animals haven't anything to pay with. But there are hundreds who will be willing to work their way. I see no reason why Mr. Bean should not have twice as many animals at work on the farm as he has now. And at the same time I see no reason why any of us should ever have to work again."

At this there was a perfectly tremendous burst of cheering, and then all the animals came up and shook hands with Freddy and congratulated him on having such a fine idea. Mrs. Wiggins was so enthusiastic that she slapped him on the back, and as she was a large cow and Freddy was a rather small pig, she knocked him clean through the side of the shed. He took two boards out with him as he went and this weakened the shed so that the roof fell right down on top of the meeting. But nobody was hurt, and all the animals scrambled out except Mrs. Wiggins who was so ashamed of what she had done that she just stayed right there until they got worried about her and pulled her out. And then when she saw Freddy's black eye, and the awful damage she had done to the office of the company, she broke down and cried and wanted to go home, and it was quite a long time before Freddy could comfort her and persuade her that nobody thought it was her fault.

The animals went to work on the new scheme right away. It was really quite a good scheme. You see, on a farm every bird and animal gets food and lodging from the farmer. In return he is supposed to do certain work. A horse's duty is to draw plows and wagons and buggies; and a dog's duty is to bark at strangers and do tricks and keep an eye on the children and look intelligent when his master talks to him; and a cat's duty is to chase mice, and purr when he's petted and sleep in ladies' laps and sit on the fence nights and sing. Some animals don't have any special duties. A pig's duty is just to be a pig, which isn't very hard if you have a good appetite.

Most of the work is done in the summer, and that is why it was so easy for the animals to get off and go to Florida as they had the previous winter. But now, if they could get substitutes, it would be easy for them to get off at any time of the year. So they went around and saw all the animals on the nearby farms and told them about the new scheme. And they found cows and horses and sheep and pigs and goats and cats and dogs—ninety-four animals in all, not counting birds and insects and wild animals like chipmunks and skunks and rabbits—who each agreed to do two weeks' work the following summer if they could be taken on the Florida trip. For the next two months Barnyard Tours, Inc., was a pretty busy company. Hundreds of animals who had never before been able to afford even the short sightseeing trips came to the farm and offered one or two hours' work if they could take a one- or two-day tour. Freddy and Jinx and Robert and Charles and Hank and even Mrs. Wiggins were almost never home. They were off every day personally conducting groups of animal tourists. The mice—Eek and Quik and Eeny and Cousin Augustus—took so many parties of rats and mice and chipmunks to the cheese factory that they began to get very fat, and they had to have all the mouse holes in the barn enlarged so they could get through them. Of course they got the tourists to do all the heavy gnawing.

Mr. Bean was delighted with the way the work on the farm was getting done. The day he plowed the twenty-acre field, thirty-five horses came and helped him, and it didn't take more than half an hour. Then one day he started to paint the barn. He painted one side of it before supper, and he was going to paint the rest the next day. But that night Freddy got a lot of squirrels down from the woods, and they finished the job before morning. They dipped their tails in the paint and used them as brushes, and then, when they were through, they cleaned them off with turpentine. There wasn't enough turpentine, and three of the squirrels had to go round with white tails all the following winter, till the paint wore off.

One evening Jinx heard Mr. Bean say to his wife: "Mrs. B., if the stumps were cleared out of that lot down back of the pond and it was planted with potatoes next year, we'd make a lot of money."

"You've often said, Mr. B.," replied his wife, "that there was money to be made out of that lot. Many and many's the time I've heard you say it. But it would take an awful lot of work."

"Yes," said Mr. Bean, "And I'm not as young as I was. Not by a whole lot, I ain't. And I've come to the time of life when I want to sit back and not work so hard. We've got plenty to get along on. What's the use making more money when we ain't got any children to leave it to? I guess we'll leave them stumps alone." And he leaned back and puffed hard on his pipe, and the smoke trickled out of his bushy whiskers so that he looked like a haystack about to burst into flames.

And Mrs. Bean sighed and said: "This is a nice farm. But it's lonesome for just us two. I do wish we had some children to leave it to."

But Jinx jumped up and ran out into the barn and called a meeting, and the next night nearly two hundred animals gathered down in the lot beyond the pond and set to work to clean out the stumps. They went at it with paws and claws and snouts—dogs and pigs and woodchucks and squirrels and rabbits and even mice—and the dirt simply flew out of the holes. Then when they had dug all around one stump, and the roots had been gnawed through, the horses would put a rope around it and pull it down to the end of the field. By morning there wasn't a stump left and when Mr. Bean leaned out of his window just after sunrise to see what kind of day it was going to be, he noticed a big pile of stumps away down across the pond that hadn't been there the night before. At first he didn't know what had happened, but when he had got out his telescope and had a good look, he hurried into his clothes and hurried downstairs and "Hurry up my breakfast, Mrs. B.," he called. "There's queer goings-on on this farm, and I've got to find out about 'em." But he didn't take time for much breakfast. He ate only three eggs and four sausages and two stacks of buckwheat cakes and a cup of coffee and five slices of toast, and then he hurried to the lot beyond the pond. And when he saw that the stumps were all cleaned out and piled up neatly in a corner of the lot, he stared and stared. And then he said very slowly two or three times: "Peter grieve us!" And then he went back to the house and told Mrs. Bean.

"All we've got to do now is plow that field and plant it next spring," he said. "Bushels and bushels of potatoes just for a little work. I want to tell you, Mrs. B.," he said, "that hereafter these animals can do what they please around here. I've farmed this place, man and boy, for fifty-two years, but those animals are better farmers than I am."

Mrs. Bean looked at him in surprise. "I never thought I'd live to see the day, Mr. B., when you'd admit that any human being, let alone an animal, knew more about farming than you did. And, whatever you say, I'll never believe it. But I think the least thing we can do, Mr. B., is to give the animals a party."

III
The Explorers Set Out

NOW there **I**sn't room to tell about the party the Beans gave, nor how they invited all the animals and people for miles around, nor of the eating and drinking and dancing and merrymaking, nor of how the barns and pens and coops were illuminated with colored lights, and fireworks were set off, and everybody had a perfectly grand time and didn't get home until after midnight. A little while after, the ninety-four tourist animals started off for Florida. They divided into four parties, and Freddy and Jinx and Robert and Hank were each put in charge of one party. The trip was a complete success in every way. When they came back in the spring, Hank's party brought back a wagonload of coconuts, which Mr. Bean sold to his neighbors for ten cents apiece, and Freddy's party brought back a lot of very handsome picture postcards of all the places they had visited, which Mrs. Bean was much pleased with and tacked up on the wall in the living room. The others didn't bring anything, but two young alligators, named Armando and Juanita, came back with Robert. He had rescued them from a man who had caught them in the Everglades and was taking them to be sold into captivity. They were very grateful to Robert and cried so bitterly when they heard he was going back home and wasn't going to take them along that he decided to let them come. They followed him about everywhere. "Just like dogs," said Mrs. Wiggins, and shook with laughter at the thought of a faithful pet like Robert having faithful pets of his own.

All that spring Barnyard Tours, Inc., was very busy. The roads were so full of traveling animals that automobile traffic was seriously interfered with and the Rome and Utica and Syracuse automobile clubs complained to the Mayor of Centerboro, and the Mayor of Centerboro called up Mr. Bean on the telephone and said that something would have to be done. Mr. Bean promised to do something, but before he could decide what to do, Freddy saw an editorial complaining about it in the Centerboro paper, and he told the other animals. So they were more careful after that and took back roads or went cross-country whenever possible.

The work on the farm was done as if by magic. Whatever Mr. Bean said he was going to do got done before he had time to do it. If he said in the evening: "Tomorrow I'm going to plow the lower pasture," in the morning when he went out to plow it, the work would all be done. Even most of Mrs. Bean's work was done for her by the animals. At first when she came into the kitchen and found a dozen squirrels busily sweeping the floor with their tails, she shooed them out quickly. But after she found out that they were helping her, she let them alone. She would sit comfortably in her rocking chair and doze while dozens of little animals ran all over the house, picking up and dusting and sweeping. Now and then she would smile and lean down and pat a mouse on the head who was hurrying out with a mouthful of threads he had picked off the floor, and now and then one of the squirrels or rabbits or cats would jump up in her lap to have his head scratched. Of course the animals couldn't cook and sew and make beds, but they were a great help and they kept the house as neat as a pin.

But Freddy and Jinx and the other members of the firm were growing restless. They had no regular work to do on the farm any more, for with so many animals paying for trips with work, there were more workers than work to be done. And after they had personally conducted tour after tour over the same ground, they began to get tired of it.

"Personally," said Freddy, "I'm fed up. I'm sick to death of that Scenic Centerboro tour, of explaining over and over again to groups of silly animals about the Public Library and the Presbyterian Church and the fine view from the hill behind the Trumbull place. And the foolish questions they ask! And the complaints!"

"You said a snoutful, pig," said Jinx, who was inclined to be a little vulgar in his speech, but was otherwise a very estimable animal. "And the smaller they are, the more complaints they have. A cow or a horse, now, will take things good-naturedly and won't expect too much. But there were a couple of beetles on that last trip—my word, but they were unpleasant people! I carried 'em all the way on my back, and first they couldn't see, and then the dust got in their noses, and then when it began to rain and there wasn't any more dust, they complained about that and tried to crawl into my ears to get out of the wet. Can you beat that?"

"We don't have to beat it," said Freddy seriously. Freddy had become very serious during the past year, and rather dignified. Once he had been a carefree, lighthearted young pig, always playing jokes or writing poetry or inventing new games, but the cares of business had weighed him down, and nowadays he almost never even smiled. Which was too bad, since a pig's face is built for smiling, and Freddy never looked so handsome as when he was squealing with laughter. "You see," he went on, "I've been figuring up and we've got enough work coming to us for the trips we've been taking animals on so that we could all go away for two years if we wanted to, and all the farm work would be done while we were away. We don't have to have any more trips for two years. Now I've got a plan. What do you say we go find the North Pole?"

Jinx didn't want to let on that he had never heard of the north pole, so he just said: "Fine! That's a great idea, Freddy. How do we get there?"

So Freddy explained that the North Pole was at the top of the world—that if you went straight north, you'd reach it, and that if you kept right on going in the same direction after you had passed the Pole, you'd be going south again. Jinx didn't understand this very well; in fact, he didn't really believe it at all; but he was so tired of the life he had been leading for the past few months that he didn't care much what he did as long as it was something different. And so he was very enthusiastic about it and went with Freddy down to the study, where they got out maps and spent the whole afternoon laying out routes and deciding whom they would ask to go with them.

For this wasn't a trip that just any animal could go on. "We want only hard seasoned travelers," said Freddy, "animals who can put up with danger and hardship, who are willing to be cold and uncomfortable and hungry and weary for days on end. This won't be like going to Florida. But who wants to go to Florida?—a soft trip like that! This will be a real adventure. And if we make it, think of the honor of being the first animals to visit the North Pole! Why, I bet we get our pictures in the New York papers!"

This was enough for Jinx. He was rather vain of his good looks, and thought how fine it would be to see his picture on the front page of all the papers and to have hundreds of people all over the country saying: "Look! Look! Here's that wonderful cat that went to the North Pole! Isn't he a beauty?" But all he said was: "Well, when do we start?"

"No reason to wait," said Freddy. "We'll go talk to the others right now." And by bedtime Robert, the dog, and Hank, the old white horse, and Mrs. Wogus, who was Mrs. Wiggins's sister, and Ferdinand, the sarcastic old crow, had all agreed to go. Some of the other animals they asked refused. Mrs. Wiggins said no, she was too old and she liked her comfort too much to go traipsing off into the wilds. Charles, the rooster, wanted very much to go, but his wife Henrietta wouldn't hear of it. The general feeling in the barnyard seemed to be that it was very foolish to leave comfortable homes to explore a country that consisted of nothing but snow and ice, that was certainly uncomfortable and probably dangerous.

But none of these sensible arguments could persuade the six adventurers, who, like all the brave spirits who have made history and sailed unknown seas and charted unknown continents in the past, cared less for ease than for glory and laughed at danger and hardship.

And so on a bright morning a week later they set out on their perilous journey. First came Hank, the old white horse, harnessed to the rickety phaeton that they had brought back from their trip to Florida. Inside the phaeton rode Freddy and Jinx, but there wasn't much room even for them, for most of the space was taken up with piles of cast-off blankets and old overcoats that they had gathered, with the help of their friends, from all the neighboring farms and with which they planned to keep warm in the polar regions. Behind the phaeton walked Mrs. Wogus, and when it went up a hill, she helped Hank by putting her forehead against the back of the vehicle and pushing. Robert ran alongside, and Ferdinand, who had rather a sour disposition, sat on the dashboard, with his eyes shut, looking very bored and weary, as they drove out of the yard.

The Beans, of course, knew nothing about the trip, but when they heard the commotion outside, they jumped up from their breakfast and ran out on the porch.

"Why, I do believe," said Mrs. Bean, " that they're starting out on another trip! Well, well, will wonders never cease?"

"So they are, Mrs. B.," replied her husband. "Now I wonder where they're off to this time. Consarn it, I wish we could talk animal talk; then we'd know. But hey, Hank!" he called. "Wait a minute! Whoa! Back up there!" And as Hank stopped obediently, Mr. Bean dashed into the house and presently returned with his second-best nightcap, a white one with a red tassel, which he tied to the top of the phaeton. "There," he said, "now you've got a flag. Good-bye, animals! Have a good time, and remember there's a good home and a warm welcome waiting for you when you get tired of the road."

"Good-bye!" called Mrs. Bean. "Be careful about automobiles and don't sit in drafts or get under trees in thunderstorms or stay up too late nights or—" But the rest of her advice was drowned in the cheers of the animals who were staying behind, as the little procession marched out of the gate, with the standard of the house of Bean waving above them.

But, for all the cheering and waving of paws and claws and hoofs and handkerchiefs, Ferdinand, perched on the dashboard, never even opened his eyes.

IV
Ferdinand Returns

LIFE on **The** farm went along quietly all that summer. As the fame of Barnyard Tours, Inc., increased, more and more animals kept coming to inquire about trips, and Charles, the rooster, was kept very busy in the office from early morning till late at night, answering questions and making up parties. After the first week nothing was heard of the explorers until fall, when the birds began to fly past on their way south for the winter. Then an occasional woodpecker or white-throat would swoop down into the big elm and deliver a message. The animals learned that everything was going well; that Freddy had had a bad cold, but was better; that Ferdinand had had a fight with a gang of thieving blue jays and had beaten them badly; that the expedition had high hopes of reaching the Pole before Christmas, in which case they would be back home by midsummer.

The winter came and passed without more news. In the spring two chickadees who had been living in the elm since October announced that they were starting for the north, and agreed, in return for the grain and bits of suet with which Charles had fed them all winter, to come back if they learned anything of the wanderers and give their report before going ahead with the house that they planned to build that spring in Labrador. But the chickadees did not come back. They might, of course, have been caught and eaten by hawks or cats. They might have decided that it was too far to come all the way back to the farm, just to tell the animals that their friends were well. But still they hadn't come back, and the animals worried. Every day Charles sent one of his eight daughters, who were growing up now into long-legged noisy chickens, with manners that were the despair of Henrietta, their mother, to perch on the gatepost and watch the road for the first sign of the returning travelers. But July passed, August passed, and no one came.

And then at last the animals decided that something must be done. It was Mrs. Wiggins who really got things going. "I just can't sleep nights," she complained, "for thinking of those dear friends away off up there in the cold and the snow, maybe without anything to eat, and my own dear sister, Mrs. Wogus, with them; and her little girl, Marietta, sobbing herself to sleep every night because she wants her mother back. We've got to do something, and we're *going*

to do something. Even if I have to go alone, I'm going to start out and find them. If anyone else wants to come along, he can, but I'm going anyway."

"A very laudable resolve, Mrs. Wiggins," said Charles." A very brave and noble resolution. I've been thinking myself for some time that a rescue party should be formed."

"Then why didn't you say something about it? "Mrs. Wiggins demanded. She knew perfectly well that the idea had never occurred to the rooster.

"I thought it best to wait," replied Charles with dignity, "until we were really sure that something hadn't gone wrong. We'd look rather foolish starting out to rescue them and then meeting them half a mile down the road, wouldn't we?"

"There are some things worse than looking foolish," snapped Mrs. Wiggins, "though no selfish, stuck-up rooster would ever know it."

"I take no offence at your words," said Charles, "since I realize the anxiety that you must be feeling, and that, after all, I share with you. Certainly, though, you won't be permitted to go on this quest alone. I'm sure that every animal in the barnyard will want to take part. Personally—"

"They can do as they please," Mrs. Wiggins interrupted." I start tomorrow morning." And she turned her back on Charles and went on moodily chewing her cud.

But the next morning when she came out of the cowshed, firm in her resolve to start for the north without delay, she was surprised to find a great crowd of animals of all kinds waiting for her. The afternoon before, Charles had sent his eight daughters and his seven sons round to all the farms in the neighborhood to call for volunteers for the rescue party, and as all the adventurers except Ferdinand were very popular, nearly every animal who could get away had agreed to go. There they were, waiting, and as Mrs. Wiggins came out they gave a cheer that brought the nightcapped heads of Mr. and Mrs. Bean to the window.

"What's all this?" asked Mrs. Wiggins.

"What's all this?" asked Mrs. Wiggins as the animals crowded around her.

Charles stepped forward and explained. "Of course," he said, "we can't all go, for there are nearly a hundred of us volunteers here, and the rescue party shouldn't consist of more than ten or fifteen. Some of us, therefore, will have to resign the privilege of engaging in this glorious venture and remain at home, disappointed, but happy in the knowledge that in volunteering we have done our manifest duty. In order to avoid the embarrassment which any of you may feel in dropping out now," he went on, turning to the crowd of animals, "I will set the example by voluntarily withdrawing from the rescue party. Much as my heart has been set on it, eagerly as I have looked forward to this venture, I shall yet be able with dry eyes to watch the departure of the devoted band among whom I had hoped to number myself, since I shall—"

But the speech was never finished, for with an angry clucking Henrietta, his wife, pushed her way through the circle of curious animals. "What's all this I hear?" she demanded. "Not going, did you say? Well, just let me see you try to stay at home! You'll wish you'd never been hatched, that's all I've got to say! To desert your friends when they're in want and danger—I never heard such cowardly nonsense! You're going, and, what's more, I'm going with you, to see there's no shirking."

"Tut, tut, my dear," said Charles in a whisper. "You don't understand. Of course I'm going. But all these animals can't go, and I was merely—"

But Henrietta cuffed him aside with her wing. "You be quiet, young man, if you know what's good for you. And now, Mrs. Wiggins," she went on, "I take it what you want is to get started as soon as possible. If we let my husband do any more talking, we won't get started for a week. What I suggest is that you select the animals you want to have with you on this trip yourself. Isn't that fair, animals?"

They all agreed and formed a long line, which went twice around the barnyard and out into the road, and Mrs. Wiggins walked up and down and tried to make her choice, but all the animals wanted to go so badly that she didn't have the heart to dismiss any of them, and finally she got so mixed up and confused that she just sat down in the middle of the barnyard and cried.

Mrs. Wiggins didn't have much of an education, but she had a good heart, and all the animals were very fond of her, so they all crowded around to try to cheer her up. But there were so many of them that those on the outside of the crowd who couldn't get near her began to push, and then the ones they had pushed got angry and pushed back, and pretty soon the whole barnyard was a mob of angry animals, growling and pushing and shoving, and in the middle, almost smothered, was Mrs. Wiggins.

Goodness knows what might have happened if at that moment Charles's eldest daughter, Leah, whose turn it was to sit on the fence and watch the road, hadn't come dashing into the yard with the news that she thought she had seen Ferdinand away off up the road. At once all the animals disentangled themselves and rushed out the gate, and, sure enough, a quarter of a mile up the road they saw a small black figure coming slowly towards them. It limped, and one wing hung down and trailed in the dust, but it was certainly a crow, and as it came nearer, they saw that it was indeed Ferdinand.

The animals surrounded him and nearly deafened him with questions. Since he couldn't have been heard if he had tried to answer, he simply trudged along through the gate, across the yard, and into the barn, where he took a long drink from the watering-trough, then came outside and raised his claw for silence.

"My friends," he said when his audience had stopped whispering and shuffling and trying to edge themselves into a better position, "I have been on the road for nearly two months, walking all the time, for, as you see, my wing is broken. To tell you all that has happened is too long a story, for I have come back to get help, and we must

start at once. But three months ago we had reached the Arctic Ocean. We had camped on the shore while Freddy worked out with his map the route we were to follow in our dash for the Pole. Everything had gone well so far; we were very happy and comfortable in the tent we made with the blankets, and with few exceptions all the animals of the North had been very friendly and helpful. It was warmer that night than it had been in some time, and all around us we heard the ice cracking and booming as it split and melted. We thought we had camped far enough back from the shore to be safe, but in the morning when we stepped outside the tent door, there was water all around us. The piece of ice we had been camping on had split off during the night and we were on an iceberg in the middle of the Arctic Ocean."

A buzz of excitement went up from the animals and they crowded closer to listen. Mrs. Wiggins was sobbing softly. "My poor sister," she gulped.

"You needn't be alarmed, madam," said Ferdinand impatiently. "Your sister is quite safe. Whether you will ever see her again, however, is another matter. To continue: we had plenty to eat, and our fur coats and the tent kept us warm. But as we drifted, day after day, the iceberg slowly melted and large chunks split off and fell into the water. It was only a matter of time when there would no longer be room for us all to stand on it. As the only member of the party who could fly, I had gone on a number of scouting expeditions to see if we could get help. But although a number of animals were willing to do anything they could, there was really nothing they could do. A school of whales came by one day, and they all put their heads against the berg and tried to push it towards land, but it was so slippery that they kept slipping off and bumping into one another, and finally they gave up.

"On one of my flights I had seen that we were approaching land, and I figured that we should pass within half a mile of it in about two days. We had decided that our only chance of escape was for the animals to try to swim that half-mile to shore. There was little hope of their reaching it, for even Freddy, who, as you know, is a champion swimmer and has won several prizes, could not hope to stay long afloat in that icy water. But there was no other way, and we had made up our minds to it, when on the very morning we had fixed for the attempt, on coming out of the ice cave in which we had been camping, we saw that a ship had come alongside the berg, and the sailors were climbing up its steep sides. They had seen the phaeton, which stood outside the cave on a ledge, and had come to find out how it got there.

"The sailors were greatly surprised to find a cow and a cat and a dog and a pig and a horse and a crow on an iceberg in the open sea, and they took us all on board and made quite a fuss over us. They were particularly delighted with Mrs. Wogus, for the only milk they had had for the past six months had been condensed milk out of a can. Just before we all went aboard, Freddy took me aside. 'Don't let them catch you, Ferdinand,' he said. 'These sailors won't let us go if they can help it, but there's still hope while you're free.' So I flew up on top of the berg where they couldn't reach me. I stayed round for two days, and I must say those sailors treated the animals like kings and queens. They took turns riding Hank round the deck, and they made leather collars for Jinx and Robert, and they were so pleased with Mrs. Wogus that they gave her a cabin all to herself with lace curtains at the windows, and the captain took off his hat to her whenever she came on deck. They treated Freddy well, too, but I didn't just like the greedy way some of them looked at him, and once when Freddy went by, I saw the mate nudge the captain in the ribs, and heard him say: 'A nice dish of pig's knuckles and sauerkraut now, eh, Mr. Hooker?' And the captain said: 'Chops, Mr. Pomeroy; chops is my choice—with a bit of apple.' And they both licked their lips and grinned.

"Well, that can't be helped, and what's happened now, nobody knows. For my part, I think they were just fooling and said those things because they wanted to see Freddy get pale. Pigs look so funny when they are scared. But, to make a long story short, on the third day Freddy said to me: 'You'd better go now. I've found out that this ship is a whaling ship, but they've had a bad year and haven't caught a single whale, so they've decided to take a vacation from whaling and see if they can't find Santa Claus's house. You know he lives up round the North Pole somewhere. They're going to sail north as far as they can, and then when they get stuck in the ice, they'll go on foot. You'd better fly home as fast as you can and bring help for us.' Then he said good-bye to me. 'You may never see me again, Ferdinand,' he said mournfully. 'These sailors are nice and friendly to me, but they're big fat men, all pork-eaters—I can tell a pork-eater just by the way he looks at me, so greedy it makes me fairly blush sometimes—and what's friendship to a hungry man?" 'Oh, cheer up,' I said. 'A little pig like you wouldn't make more'n a breakfast for the cabin boy. They'll try to fatten you up first, and if you're careful of your diet and watch the calories and keep off starchy foods, you'll stay thin, and I'll round up some of your friends and have them back here to rescue you before anything serious happens.' Well, that didn't seem to comfort him much, for Freddy likes to eat almost better than he likes to make up poetry, but we said good-bye and I started flying home. I'd have been here long before this, for I was flying day and night, if I hadn't run into a telegraph wire on the fourth night and broken my wing. It's mending all right and I'll be able to fly in another week, but meanwhile I've had to walk.

"And now I've talked enough. I call for volunteers to rescue our friends and—neighbors from captivity in the Far North. Who'll go?"

V
The Rescue Party

OF course All the animals wanted to go, but Ferdinand wouldn't stand for any nonsense, and he lined them up and very soon had picked five and dismissed the others. Those he had chosen grouped themselves around him, looking very important. There were Mrs.

Wiggins, and Jack, the big black dog, and a wise old gray horse who lived over near Centerboro and had once been in a circus. He was Hank's uncle, and everybody called him Uncle William. And there was a porcupine named Cecil, who lived back in the woods and was very slow and lazy and rather stupid, but Ferdinand thought he would be a good one to have along, since a porcupine can go anywhere and no other animal will molest him. And lastly there was a close friend of Ferdinand's, a wicked-looking billy-goat (his name really was Bill), whom none of the animals liked because he was so malicious and bad-tempered. The only nice thing about him was that he was so fond of Ferdinand. They used to spend hours together down in the far pasture, their heads together, and the other animals, hearing the crow's harsh laughter and the goat's wicked giggle, used to wonder what mischief they were hatching. But, whatever it was, none of them ever found out.

At Mrs. Wiggins's request, Charles and Henrietta were allowed to join the party, although Ferdinand grumbled that he didn't see what they wanted to take a lot of poultry along for. But when the four mice who had been on the first trip to Florida came boldly forward and said they were going too, he burst into harsh laughter. "Mice!" he exclaimed. "Who ever heard of mice on an Arctic expedition? What good could you do, I'd like to know? Could you fight a walrus or lick a polar bear? Listen to this, Bill. Look what wants to join the rescue party. Why, you can't hardly *see* 'em!"

Now nothing makes a mouse madder than to be made fun of on account of his size, and when Eek and Quik and Eeny and Cousin Augustus heard the loud laughter of Bill and Ferdinand and the suppressed snickers of the other animals, they were wild with rage. "What could we do, eh?" shouted Eeny, and his voice was about as loud as the whistle on a peanut stand. "We'll *show* you what! You big black imitation of a stuffed mantelpiece ornament! Come on, boys!" And with that he and Eek made a rush for the crow, while Quik and Cousin Augustus dashed at Bill and, swarming up his legs before he could shake them off, ran up along his back and began chewing at his ears. Ferdinand tried to hold off the mice by jabbing at them with his beak, but they managed to keep behind him and dash in and nip his ankles whenever they saw an opening, until he cawed with pain. Meanwhile Bill was shaking his head and dancing and bucking frantically to get rid of the other two mice, but they just dug their sharp little teeth in deeper and hung on.

"Stop!" yelled Ferdinand. "Oh—ouch! Stop it, I say! I take it all back; you're worse'n lions and tigers. I'll let you go if you'll—ow yow!—if you'll only *quit*!"

So Eek and Eeny quit and sat down on the doorsill and didn't say anything at all, which was very sensible of them, because it is very silly, when you've won an argument, to keep on arguing. And the other two mice jumped off Bill's back and sat down beside them, and then Ferdinand made a speech. It was rather a good speech, but it was also rather too long, as most speeches are, so it is not set down here. He told the animals that he was going to be captain of the expedition, since he had had some Arctic experience and knew what roads they would have to travel, and he said that any animal who wasn't willing to agree to take orders from him had better drop out right now at the start. He said that it was a long, hard, perilous trip they were starting on, as he knew personally, and that he expected every animal to do his duty. And when the speech was over, the mice climbed aboard Mrs. Wiggins, and Charles and Henrietta climbed aboard Uncle William, and Ferdinand perched on one of Bill's horns, and the party set out amid the prolonged cheering of the stay-at-homes.

For the first few days they traveled steadily northward through a pleasant farming country. The people here had become accustomed to seeing a great many animals on the roads and paid little attention to them. But as they got farther north, and the farms began to give way to woodland, the people were more curious about them, and they had one or two narrow escapes from being captured, so they did most of their traveling by night. They had a good deal of trouble with Cecil. Porcupines can't walk very fast, and Cecil was always lagging behind and making them wait for him. They tried having him ride on Uncle William's back, but they only tried it once, for his quills were as sharp as needles, and every time he moved, a dozen or so of them would stick into Uncle William. He was awfully sorry and apologetic about it, but, as Uncle William said, apologies make poor poultices. So after that Cecil walked again, and the others just had to put up with his slowness.

As they went on, the woods grew thicker and wilder, and the roads grew narrower and ruttier, and the houses fewer and farther between. By the end of the first week Ferdinand's wing was all right again, so that he could fly on ahead and spy out the land, and this enabled them to take a good many short cuts. One night they crossed the Saint Lawrence River by a long bridge, and then they were in Canada. They had some trouble crossing the bridge because customs men lie in wait at each end and make travelers pay a tax on certain articles. These articles that can't be brought into a country without paying are called dutiable. Of course the animals didn't have any luggage with them, but the Canadian customs man thought some of the animals themselves were dutiable, so he held them up. "Let's see," he said. "Milk and feathers and beef and hides—I dunno but there's a duty on all of 'em." And he took out a little book and licked his thumb and began looking through the pages to see if he could find out what the duty would be on Mrs. Wiggins and Charles and

Henrietta. Things looked bad for a minute, but Ferdinand whispered in the goat's ear and then flew straight at the man and knocked the book out of his hand. The latter stooped to pick it up, and as he did so, Bill put his head down and charged at him. The goat's hard head with the strong curving horns hit the seat of the customs man's trousers with a smack and shot him into the ditch at the side of the road, and before he had even begun to pick himself up, the animals had galloped off into the night.

Soon after this the roads disappeared altogether and they plodded along through the deep forest. The woods animals were very kind to them and showed them paths and gave them directions how to avoid swamps and lakes. Sometimes a deer would guide them for a day or more over the forest trails, just for the sake of hearing a little gossip about what was going on in the outside world. Deer lead very secluded lives, and although they are curious, they are too timid ever to venture into the more cultivated regions where important things are going on. A quite small bit of gossip will last a deer for a month, and he'll tell it over and over to all his friends, and they hurry to tell it to their friends, until it is known all over the north country. But they are very honest animals and never gossip maliciously.

One afternoon the animals came out of the gloomy forest on to the shore of a shining lake. At their feet—which were hot and dusty, for they had walked fast and far—a beach of fine white sand sloped down into the cool water. With a whoop they dashed down and were soon splashing and shouting and playing the kind of tricks on each other that are lots of fun when you play them on someone else, but not so funny when they're played on you. Even the mice found a little pool between two stones, about half an inch deep, where Eeny, who had taken lessons in swimming from Freddy, showed them how to swim the breast stroke. But of course mice never make good swimmers.

Mrs. Wiggins wasn't a very good swimmer either. She had practised a good deal in the pond at home, and maybe she would have learned, but she was so clumsy in the water and looked so frightened that the other animals all laughed at her, and then she would begin to laugh at herself and would swallow water and choke and have to be towed ashore practically helpless. Today she was just paddling round when Bill decided that it would be fun to duck her. He climbed up on her back in the water, and down she went. When she came up, she looked so bewildered that they all went into fits of laughter, and Bill did it again. Then he did it again. Then Mrs. Wiggins waded ashore and sat down in the sand. "I like a joke as well as the next one," she said, "but enough's enough."

The late afternoon sun wasn't very hot and she felt a little chilly, so she decided to take a walk along the shore to get warm. When she got down to the end of the beach, she went round a point, and there on the other side was another little beach, and behind it a tumble-down house in a clearing. Corn was growing in the clearing, and Mrs. Wiggins was very fond of corn. There were no people in sight, and the house looked deserted, but "It's better to be safe than sorry," said Mrs. Wiggins to herself, and so she crouched down and tried to sneak up through the underbrush as she had seen Jinx do when he was stalking a bird. She wasn't very good at it. She made an awful lot of noise, and she must have looked very funny. But it didn't matter, for there wasn't anyone to hear her; and pretty soon she was in among the corn and munching the ears with her big teeth.

When she had eaten a peck or two, she thought she'd explore a little. "Funny," she said—she had a great habit of talking to herself when she was alone—"funny there's no one around. The house looks lived in. There's a washtub outside, and that ax can't have been there long—it isn't rusty. Folks must be away." She walked round the house at some distance, then she walked round it a little closer, then she walked up to the kitchen window and looked in—and got the surprise of her life. For there was a little girl with a very dirty face sitting in the middle of the floor and crying. Her dress was ragged, and her tears had washed little white streaks through the grime on her cheeks, making her face look even dirtier than it was, which was almost impossible. But what surprised and horrified Mrs. Wiggins was to see that there was a long rope in the kitchen, and one end of it was around the little girl's waist, and the other was tied to a pipe under the kitchen sink.

"Good gracious sakes alive!" Mrs. Wiggins exclaimed (very strong language for a cow). "Who on *earth* has tied that poor child up like that? Perhaps an ogre has captured her and is fattening her up to eat." For Mrs. Wiggins, though only a cow, knew about ogres. There were stories about them in Grimm's *Fairy Tales,* which was one of the nicest books in Freddy's library, and Freddy had often read them aloud to the animals during the long winter evenings in the warm cow-barn.

But it couldn't be that. The little girl was too thin. Anyway, the first thing to do was to rescue her. And so Mrs. Wiggins tapped gently on the glass with the tip of her left horn.

The little girl sobbed twice, gulped, sniffed, and looked up. Mrs. Wiggins was not handsome, and the window was so dirty and had so many cracks in it that from the inside of the room she looked like a funny picture of a cow that somebody had partly erased with a very smeary eraser; but her eyes were so big and brown and kind and sympathetic that the little girl wasn't afraid at all, and she jumped up and ran as close to the window as the rope would let her, which was about two feet, and said: "Hello, cow! What's your name? Have you come to take us away?"

Mrs. Wiggins nodded her head and then, without waiting to hear what the little girl was saying, went around to the kitchen door and put her head against it and gave it a big push, and the door fell in with a bang and Mrs. Wiggins walked over it into the kitchen. But when she got in, she found that she couldn't do anything. She took the rope in her teeth and pulled, but it wouldn't break, and she tried to break the pipe that it was tied to with her horns, but she couldn't get at it properly, and all the while the little girl was jumping up and down in her excitement, laughing and crying, and saying: "Oh, hurry, hurry! They'll be back pretty soon, and they won't let you take us away. Please hurry!"

"Well," said Mrs. Wiggins to herself, "we're not getting anywhere this way. Not anywhere at *all*!" She thought a minute; then she went to the door and gave three long moos. This was the signal the animals had agreed on as a call for help. And, sure enough, in less than three minutes Jack and Bill and Uncle William and Charles and Henrietta came tearing across the clearing. The mice were on Bill's back, and Cecil was coming along behind as fast as he could. And Ferdinand was flying in circles overhead and acting as scout.

They all crowded into the kitchen, and while the other animals sat around and made sympathetic noises at the little girl, who was a little overpowered by seeing so many of them all at once, the mice got to work on the rope and in a few minutes had gnawed it apart. Then the little girl threw her arms around Mrs. Wiggins's neck and kissed her, which affected the cow so much that she cried. And then they went outside, where Ferdinand was on guard.

"There's a man and a woman coming across the lake in a boat," said the crow. "The man's got a gun. We've got to get out of here *quick*!"

"We're not going without that child," said Mrs. Wiggins stoutly. "She can't stay here, to be mistreated by those scoundrels. Tying her up like that! And you ought to see the bruises on her arms where they've struck her."

"Well, go get her, then," said Ferdinand irritably—for the little girl had stayed in the house—"Though what you want with her on a rescue party I don't know. She'll just be a hindrance."

"We've just rescued *her*," said Uncle William. "We can't leave her to be beaten and tied up and mistreated any more. I agree with Mrs. Wiggins."

"Well, we can't rescue everybody in the north woods," said the crow, "or we'll never find our friends. But have it your own way. Only hurry."

So Mrs. Wiggins went into the house again. The little girl was not in the kitchen, but there were voices upstairs, and, listening, she heard a boy's voice say: "That's all foolishness. A cow couldn't come in the house and—" "But she did," the little girl interrupted. "She brought some mice and they chewed the rope apart, and they're coming to get you loose too, and then we'll go into the woods with them and live on berries and nuts and never be tied up any more."

"Good gracious me!" said Mrs. Wiggins to herself. "There's another of them! What ever will Ferdinand say to that! Well, it can't be helped. He's only a crow, anyway." And she went through into the front hall and started up the stairs.

The stairs were very narrow, so that she almost got stuck where they turned going up, and they creaked and cracked ominously, but she climbed on and presently found herself in a room with a big bay window, and in it were the little girl and a boy a few years older, who was tied up with a long rope to the foot of the bed.

Mrs. Wiggins didn't waste time. She grabbed the rope with her teeth and pulled, and the bed—which was a very handsome old Colonial piece, but rather rickety—fell apart with a clatter. The little girl wanted to hug her again, but all the animals downstairs were shouting: "Hurry! Hurry!" so she pushed them through the door and, as they hurried downstairs, started to follow them. Halfway down she stuck. She pushed and heaved and panted and grunted, but only succeeded in wedging herself more firmly between wall and banisters. All the other animals had left and run off into the woods with the children to hide from the man and woman, who had pulled their boat up on the beach and were coming towards the house. Only Ferdinand had remained behind, and he was hopping about at the foot of the stairs, almost wild with exasperation, and cawing angrily at her: "Shove, can't you? Oh, I might have known it! I might have known better than to bring a cow on this expedition! Darn you, why don't you shove?"

"I *am* shoving!" panted Mrs. Wiggins. "But it's no use. Hurry, Ferdinand, or you'll be caught too. I hear them coming up the path."

With a caw of disgust Ferdinand hopped towards the door. He was only just in time, for as he spread his wings to take flight from the doorstep, the woman was just coming up on the porch with the man close behind her. She jumped as the crow swished by her face, and the man exclaimed: "Well, the nerve of that crow! " and threw his gun up to his shoulder and pulled the trigger. Bang! But he had been too startled to aim carefully and he missed.

Inside the house Mrs. Wiggins was very much afraid. And when she was afraid, she was afraid all over. She shook and trembled so that the banisters rattled.

"What's that noise?" said the woman.

"I expect it's Everett," the man replied. "Tryin' to get loose from the bed."

A vindictive look came over the woman's face, and she seized a broom that stood by the door. "I'll learn him!" she shouted. "I'll learn him to—"

"'Teach,' sister," interrupted the man. "You 'learn' to do things, but you 'teach' other people to—Ouch!" he broke off, for she had struck him angrily over the head with the broomstick.

"Teach or learn," she yelled, "I'll fix him! I'll tan that white skin of his'n!"

"'His,' sister," corrected the man as he rubbed his head, but she had dashed into the house.

She was so blind with rage as she ran up the stairs that she didn't see Mrs. Wiggins until she bumped into her. Then she backed down a couple of steps and stared until it seemed to the cow as if her eyes would jump right out of her head and roll downstairs like marbles if she opened them any wider. And then with a yell of rage and fear— for of course it was rather surprising to find a cow on her front stairs—she swung up the broomstick and began beating Mrs. Wiggins over the head with it.

In her effort to escape the flying broom Mrs. Wiggins did just what she should have done before—she backed up—and at once found that she wasn't stuck any longer. She backed clumsily up the stairs with her eyes shut and her horns lowered to protect herself as well as she could, and backed into the room where the little boy had been tied, and managed to get the door shut before the woman could get in. Then she sat down against the door, so it couldn't be pushed open, and heaved a deep sigh." Safe for a minute anyway," she said to herself. "My, what an awful woman!"

The woman pushed against the door for a while; then she ran downstairs and got her brother and they both pushed. But even the strongest brother and sister can't push open a door if a cow wants to keep it shut. So pretty soon they went back downstairs and evidently discovered that the children had escaped, for from the big bay window—which was really the nicest thing about their house and had an excellent view of the lake—the cow could see them walking about the clearing calling: "Ella! Everett! Where are you, children dear?" and promising all sorts of good things for supper if they'd only come back. "But of course," said Mrs. Wiggins to herself, "Ella and Everett know perfectly well what they'll get for supper if they really do come back. Broomstick pudding—that's what they'll get. Well, well! And how ever am I to get out of *this* mess, I'd like to know."

VI
Three Join the Party

THE man And woman—as the animals found out later—were brother and sister, and in this little house in the clearing they had been born, and in it they had lived ever since.

They had very little money. They ate what they raised in the scraggly garden, and sometimes the man made a little money by acting as guide to a party of hunters from the city. The man's name was Pete, and the woman's name was Kate. Kate had never gone to school, but Pete's father had sent him to school for a year in the nearest village, and that was why Pete was always correcting Kate's grammar. He was very fond of grammar, and he had a book with all the grammatical rules in it that he had kept from his schooldays, and every night after supper he would sit down at the table with a pencil and a piece of wrapping paper and would parse sentences he found in an old newspaper. He probably knew more about syntax than anybody else in the United States.

He was always correcting Kate's grammar, which was really pretty bad, but Kate didn't like it. She thought he was showing off and being superior—which he was—and it made her mad. She would have beaten him with the broomstick when she was mad, for she was stronger than he was, but after she had beaten him, his bones ached so that he had to go to bed and couldn't work in the garden, and she had to wait on him and do the weeding and hoeing herself. So, as she had to beat somebody when she got mad, she beat the children.

The children were not their children. Their mother was Kate's sister. When she died, Kate took the children. She wanted them because she thought she could make them work for her. Pete wanted them too. They were somebody for him to teach grammar to. So the children, small as they were, had to work and learn grammar all day long. When they were good, they were spanked; and when they were bad, they were beaten. They had tried to run away several times, and that was why Kate had tied them up. She always tied them up when both she and Pete were away from the house at the same time. If the animals hadn't come along, they would probably still be living in the little house in the clearing, working and learning grammar and being spanked when they were good, and beaten when they were bad.

Of course the animals didn't learn all this until much later. But they had seen that the children were unhappy and ill-treated, and they were agreed that they must be helped to escape. Meanwhile Mrs. Wiggins must be rescued.

They had taken the children back into a dense thicket of spruce some distance from the clearing. Kate and Pete were still calling in honey-sweet tones: "Come, Everett! Come, Ella, darling! Supper's on the table, dear little ones!" While they held their council of war, the children—who of course didn't know what was being said—sat contentedly on Uncle William's back and giggled at the mice, who were trying to amuse them by dancing on their hind legs between Uncle William's ears. Ferdinand had reported that Mrs. Wiggins was back in the upstairs room with the big window and it wasn't long before they had thought up a plan for setting her free. Bill galloped off to the other side of the lake. When he got there, he came out on the shore and danced around on his hind legs until Pete caught sight of him. Bill was about the same size as Everett, and as Pete couldn't see him very clearly from that distance, he thought he was the little boy. So he jumped into the boat and started rowing across after him. Kate wanted to go too, but Pete said: "You stay and look after the cow. She's worth more to us than the children."

"But she can't get away," shouted Kate. "And those children have got a good lickin' comin' to them. Wait till I lay my hands on that there Everett!"

"How often must I tell you," said Pete wearily, pausing in his rowing, "not to say 'that there'?"

He was too far away to be hit with the broomstick Kate still had in her hand, so she picked up a stone and threw it at him, as he began pulling on the oars again. But she was a bad shot—so bad a shot indeed, that the stone flew backward over her shoulder and crashed through the big bay window in the upper room and hit Mrs. Wiggins on the left horn.

The cow jumped and let out a bellow of surprise at this unexpected attack; then she looked up and saw Ferdinand perched on the windowsill. At first she thought he had thrown the stone and she started to give him a piece of her mind, and it took some time for him to persuade her that he hadn't done it. Then he said: "We're going to rescue you. But first you have to knock all the glass out of that window with your horns.

"What's that for?" exclaimed Mrs. Wiggins. "I can't jump out of this—"

"Don't ask questions," snapped the crow angrily. "Do as you're told."

So Mrs. Wiggins did as she was told as hard as she could, and pretty soon all the glass was out of the window.

Meanwhile Kate had heard the crash of smashing windowpanes and came rushing up towards the house, broomstick in hand. But while she had been arguing with Pete down on the beach, Uncle William and Jack and Cecil had sneaked into the house through the kitchen door, and they were busy pulling the feather beds and pillows and mattresses off the upstairs bedsteads and throwing them out the big window, so there would be a soft pile of things for Mrs. Wiggins to jump out on. They had worked so fast that by the time Kate reached the head of the stairs, everything was all ready, and Uncle William could hold the door so she couldn't get in.

But Mrs. Wiggins didn't want to jump. She got her forefeet on the sill and looked down and shuddered. "Oh my!" she groaned. "I can't do it! It makes me dizzy just to look." And she put one hoof in front of her eyes.

Kate was banging steadily on the door with her broom-handle, and Ferdinand let out a caw of disgust. But Uncle William shook his head. "No use arguing," he said in a low voice. "All ready, Cecil?"

The porcupine nodded.

Uncle William went over and stood beside the cow. "'Tisn't much of a jump, really," he said. "Lean 'way out and look down. Like this, see? Why, you could almost climb down! See that window-ledge under us?" And as Mrs. Wiggins leaned out farther, he said: "All right, Cecil," and the porcupine jumped on the cow's back.

With a roar of pain and surprise, Mrs. Wiggins leaped through the window and landed on her back on the pile of mattresses, with all four legs in the air.

You never can tell how anything is going to strike a cow. All the animals thought she'd be very mad. But when she had scrambled to her feet and shaken herself and found that she was safe and sound and not really hurt at all, she laughed and laughed and laughed. And when Cecil and Uncle William and Jack jumped out after her, she laughed so loud that you could hear her for six miles. She made so much noise that she frightened even Kate, who stopped banging on the door, although all she had to do now was turn the knob and walk in.

But Kate didn't stay frightened very long. She hurried downstairs and got outside just as the animals were making off towards the woods, with the feather beds piled on Mrs. Wiggins's back. Ferdinand had insisted on taking them. They'd need them, he said, in the Far North.

"Ha!" snorted Mrs. Wiggins as, at a warning caw from the crow, she looked round to see Kate running towards her, broomstick swinging threateningly. "I've had about enough of this!" And she turned round to face the enemy, lowered her horns, and pawed the ground angrily. The feather beds fell off her back, and the other animals scuttled out of the way. And then as Kate came closer, she charged.

The next thing Kate knew she was hanging in the fork of a tree about twelve feet above the ground, and the animals were disappearing into the thick woods. She shouted and called for Pete to come and help her down, but Pete was still hunting for the children on the other side of the lake. There was nothing for her to do but wait until he came back. So she made herself as comfortable as she could and tried to pass the time by inventing new punishments for the children. She had just thought up a new and more painful method of spanking and was just beginning to enjoy herself when a big black dog galloped up, stopped under her tree, and began to bark.

The dog was Jack, whom the animals had sent back as rearguard to cover their retreat with the children. But Kate didn't know this, and as she hadn't noticed Jack particularly when the animals had run away from the house, she thought he was just a stray dog. At first his barking and jumping and tail-wagging annoyed her. Kate was one of those unfortunate persons who almost never feel anything but annoyance. When things happened, things that would please or excite or interest you or me, Kate was just annoyed. So she was annoyed now at Jack and shook her fist at him and called him names. But it's not much fun to call names or shake fists at people who don't pay any attention to it, and Jack didn't pay any attention, but sat down under the tree and looked up and smiled pleasantly and wagged his tail. So Kate stopped. And pretty soon she said: "Oh dear, I wish Pete would hurry up."

At that Jack jumped up and ran down to the beach and barked and barked, and pretty soon Pete heard him, and as he hadn't been able to find any trace of the children, he got into the boat and rowed back to see what was going on. Jack led him to the tree, and Pete got a ladder and helped Kate down.

As soon as her feet touched the ground, she got down on her knees beside Jack and hugged him and petted him. "Nice doggy," she said. "Good doggy. Ain't he a nice doggy, Pete? Why, he understands everything I say! And ain't he handsome? I never seen a handsomer dog."

Kate had never in her life said anything nice to anybody before, much less petted anybody, and Pete was so amazed that his jaw fell open and he put his hands to his head and grabbed two large handfuls of hair and pulled them right out, which was his way of expressing amazement. He even forgot to correct her grammar. But Kate took Jack back to the house and gave him a leg of venison and two roast partridges and a big dish of potatoes and gravy. In fact, she gave him everything there was in the icebox, so that all Pete got for supper that night was four gingersnaps and a bowl of cornflakes with a little sugar on them.

But after supper she said: "Pete, we got to get them children back."

Pete had his grammar open and was reading the "Rules Governing the Use of the Subjunctive." He held the book in one hand while the fingers of the other felt round the inside of the bowl to pick out the last crumbs of cornflakes. "Those," he said absently, and went on reading.

Kate pulled the book away from him. "Listen to me," she said. "We got to follow them children. Tomorrow'll be too late."

"We can't follow them tonight," said Pete. "We can't see the trail."

"We don't need to see it," she replied. "What's this dog for, I'd like to know? Let him smell one of Everett's shoes; he'll follow 'em all right."

"H'm, that's an idea," said Pete. "They can't have got far. And maybe we can find the cow, too."

"We've got to find all of 'em," said Kate. "With the children to do the work, and the cow to give milk and cream and butter, we'll be settin' pretty. But we'll set mighty uncomfortable if we don't find 'em."

"Sit," said Pete. But the idea of having a little milk on his cornflakes occasionally was pleasant, so he got up and lit a lantern while Kate went after one of Everett's shoes.

As soon as Jack had smelled the shoe, he started off, nose to ground, like a bloodhound. Kate and Pete were delighted. They wouldn't have been so happy if they had known that they were being led in exactly the opposite direction from the one the children had taken. Jack had intended to make the chase as difficult as possible for them—to lead them through swamps and briers and up steep hills; but he was kind-hearted, like most dogs, and after they had fed him and treated him so well, he couldn't bear to be meaner than he had to. So after they had followed him steadily for two hours, he decided to put an end to the game and get back to his friends.

They were going along the side of a hill when he noticed by the light of Pete's lantern a heap of big boulders and under them a hole that might have been the mouth of a cave. He gave a sharp yelp, as if the scent was getting very hot, and dashed off towards the opening; then he stopped a yard or two short of it, barking short eager barks, as if he knew the children were inside.

But to his surprise and disappointment neither Pete nor Kate showed any desire to go into the cave. He had hoped that they would, and then he could run away and rejoin his friends. There was a queer smell about the cave, too, now that he was close to it—a strong smell that he had never smelled before. He went a little nearer to investigate, and then gave a sharp yelp of surprise, for out of the hole came lumbering a huge black shape with long white teeth in a snarling mouth and eyes that glowed red in the lantern-light.

Right there Jack decided that he had done enough for one evening, and he turned round and started home. His first jump took him three yards past his companions, who were both trying to climb the same tree, and his second jump took him over the branches of a fallen hemlock, and his third jump scared into fits an old grandfather rabbit who had come out to forage for a late supper, and who reached home trembling and shaking an hour later and took to his bed for three weeks. By his fourth jump Jack had got into his stride, and he raced on over fallen trees and through bushes and briers and along deer paths, *as* fast as he could go, for by the thumping and swishing and crackling behind him he knew that that terrible animal was close on his heels.

Pretty soon he heard a hoarse voice behind him: "Hey, wait a minute."

"Yes, I will!" the dog jeered over his shoulder, without slackening his pace.

"Wait a minute," repeated the other animal. "I want to talk to you."

"Well, go on," barked Jack. "I'm listening."

"Don't be funny," replied the other crossly. "How can I talk this way?"

"You seem to be doing pretty well," said Jack.

"Oh, you make me tired!" returned the pursuer.

"Just what I'm trying to do," snapped Jack. Then he laughed. "That was a pretty good one, eh what?" he inquired.

"Oh, you're a wit all right," grunted the other. "But what's the sense of all this running? I'm not chasing you. I'm running away too."

"Running away from an empty cupboard," said Jack. "I know. You aren't chasing me. You're taking your supper out for a little exercise."

"Nonsense," grumbled the pursuer. "Bears don't eat dogs."

"Hey!" barked Jack in surprise. "Are you a bear?" But still he didn't slow up.

"Sure I am," came the reply. "But I can't talk like this. Stop and sit down a minute."

"You stop first," said Jack, leaping over a little stream.

"Yes, and you'll go on running," objected the bear as he splashed through the shallow water.

"No, I won't. I'll take two more jumps after you stop, and then I'll stop. And then we can talk if you want to so bad."

So they worked it that way.

Pretty soon he heard a oarse voice behind him, "Hey, wait a minute."

"Now," said the bear, when they had got their breath back and were sitting facing each other some distance apart in the dark woods, "what I wanted to say to you was this: I don't suppose you're any friend to that man and woman you came to my cave with or you'd have stayed with them when I came out. Is that so?"

"They're no friends of mine," said Jack.

"Good. They're no friends of mine either. They've been hunting me with a gun ever since I came into these parts, three years ago. It's got so I can hardly stick my nose outside my cave nowadays without hearing that gun go bang and feeling a bullet whiz through my fur. Up to now I've been safe in the cave, but now they know where it is, I shan't be able to live there any longer. And being as you're the one that brought 'em there—"

"Gosh, I'm sorry," said Jack. "I didn't know—"

"I know you didn't," said the bear. "But you brought 'em, anyway. I don't bear any grudge, but it seems to me you have a certain responsibility, and for that reason maybe you'd be willing to help me."

"Sure," said Jack heartily, "anything I can do."

"Well, then," said the bear, " I'm a peaceable animal. What I want is a nice quiet home and three square meals a day—nothing fancy, you understand, just a comfortable den and good plain food. But the woods are no place for bears nowadays—haven't been since my grandfather was a cub. There's too much talk in the cities nowadays about back to nature. I don't object to men going back to nature, but I don't see why they have to take a gun with them. This time of year there are more hunters in the woods than there are animals. What I want is peace and quiet. And I thought maybe you could help me find it."

"Why, so I can," said Jack, "or could if I weren't going in the opposite direction. There's just the place on the farm where I live— a big wood lot that nobody ever goes into, and I'm sure Mr. Bean would let you live there. Only you see . . ." And he explained about the rescue party.

The bear was greatly interested. "I'd like to meet your friends," he said. "They sound like a fine lot of animals."

"Oh, they're all right," said Jack. "They're a good lot of fellows. I'd like to have you meet them if you want to come along with me."

"Sure," said the bear. "Sure, I'd like to. And maybe—well, I've been thinking that maybe I could go along with you on this trip. I'm strong, and I don't mind the cold, and my knowledge of the woods might be of use to you. At least I'd be more of a help than a hindrance. What do you think?"

"Why, it's all right with me," said Jack. "Of course Ferdinand's the leader; he'd have to decide. If you went, you could come back home with us, too."

"That's what I was thinking," said the bear. "And, to tell you the truth, if I don't go with you, I don't know what I will do."

"Well, come along then," said the dog. "We've got some distance to go. Ha ha!" He laughed in two or three short little barks." To think I thought you were chasing me, and all the time you were just running away too! But you certainly gave me a scare."

"I'm sorry for that," said the bear. "But I'll try to make it up to you some time."

VII
A Lecture Tour in the North Woods

EVEN Ferdinand Was pleased at the addition of the bear to their party, and indeed he was very useful, for he knew all the edible berries and roots that the woods animals live on, and that they, as farm-bred animals, had never learned anything about. He was very nervous for a day or two, until he was sure that Kate and Pete were not pursuing them, but then he brightened up and made himself quite agreeable.

Ella and Everett were very happy. They had got so accustomed to being spanked at least three times a day that they thought it was a regular part of living, like getting up and going to bed, and at first they missed it. So for the first few days they spanked each other every morning before breakfast. But there were so many other things to do and to see that pretty soon they forgot all about it. They rode on Mrs. Wiggins's back and on Uncle William's back and on the bear's back, and they raced through the woods with Jack after imaginary rabbits and tigers and played tag with Charles and Henrietta. All the animals grew very fond of them; even Ferdinand, who liked himself so well that he couldn't like anybody else very much, occasionally flew down and perched on their shoulders, although he said he only did it to get his feet warm.

Poor Cecil was the only one who couldn't play with them. He wanted to awfully, but he was too prickly. It made him very sad, and he used to cry sometimes at night thinking about it. But he was a sensible porcupine and very soon decided that it was silly to cry about something he couldn't help; and then, as usually happens, he found that he could have a perfectly good time with them even though he did have to be careful not to let them touch him.

As they went on north, the winter came down to meet them. It grew colder and colder. Finally one morning Charles stuck his head out from under the feather bed where he had been sleeping all snug and warm, in order to crow and wake the others up. He kept his eyes shut, for he was very sleepy, but when he opened his beak to crow, no sound came out and his mouth was full of something soft and cold. That woke him wide awake at once, and his eyes flew open. And then he really was scared for a minute, for there was only a grayish whiteness everywhere; he could see nothing, not even the feather bed.

With a muffled squawk he wriggled out and jumped and flapped his wings agitatedly, and the whiteness broke up into flakes and dust and whirled about his head, and when it at last settled, he saw what had really happened: he had been sleeping under a blanket of snow, six inches thick, that had fallen during the night.

Charles grinned sheepishly and shivered and hopped up on to a low branch. Of course! They had been snowed under. Those two big white mounds with smaller mounds between them were Uncle William and the bear, who slept one on each side of the children to keep them warm. That other big mound was Mrs. Wiggins; he could hear her snoring gently and see a little whirl of snow fly up with every breath from where her nose was; and one horn was sticking out. And beyond were lower mounds where the other animals were snoozing away in their feather beds. Yes, and up on that spruce limb was Ferdinand, his head under his wing, and a little heap of snow piled up between his shoulders. Charles threw back his head and flapped his wings and gave a loud, shrill crow.

At once the snow blanket began to heave and bulge and heads and legs and horns stuck out through it, and presently all the animals were on their feet, shaking snow out of their fur, their noses steaming like so many teakettles in the cold morning air.

"My gracious!" said Mrs. Wiggins. "This is winter with a vengeance!"

Ferdinand cawed derisively. "Winter!" he exclaimed. "Why this is nothing—*nothing* to what's coming. Maybe you animals'll wake up to the fact some time that this isn't any picnic we're going on."

"Oh my goodness!" said the cow. "Who said it was? Can't I make a single remark about the weather without your jumping all over me?"

"Oh, who's jumping all over you?" snapped the crow. "I just get sick of hearing you complain when there isn't anything to complain about."

"I'm complaining about you," retorted Mrs. Wiggins, "and I guess anyone here will bear me out that there's something to complain about."

"He, he!" snickered the goat. "Laugh that one off, Ferd. That's a hot one, that is."

Bill's laughter made the crow mad. He hopped down to the ground. "Look here," he said, "if there's any dissatisfaction with me as leader of this expedition, I want to know about it now."

"No, no!" said all the animals. "We're perfectly satisfied. You're a fine leader. Mrs. Wiggins didn't mean anything." But Ferdinand walked straight up to the cow. "And how about you?" he asked, looking her straight in the eye.

"My goodness!" she said again. "This has all come up very suddenly. I didn't really mean anything against you, Ferdinand."

"Then you've no complaint to make?" he demanded.

Now, Mrs. Wiggins was very good-natured, and she didn't want to hurt anybody's feelings, but she didn't see why she should have to back down when she hadn't really done anything. So she said boldly: "Yes, I have."

"All right," said Ferdinand grimly. "Out with it."

The cow hesitated. She couldn't really think of anything she had against the crow, except that he was bad-tempered and bossy and disagreeable, and she didn't want to use any of those words because she was afraid they might make him feel bad. If she could only think of one that didn't mean quite so much; even one that didn't mean anything at all would be better. . . . And then she suddenly remembered a word that she had heard in a story that Freddy had been reading out loud one night in the cow-barn. She didn't know what it meant, but it sounded like the right kind of word. So she said: "Well, if you want to know, I think you're too sophisticated."

At this unexpected word Ferdinand gave a little jump. Then he opened his beak to say something, but as he didn't know what the word meant, he couldn't think of any way to argue against it, and he just stood there with his beak open, looking very foolish.

Mrs. Wiggins turned to the other animals. "Isn't he too sophisticated?" she asked, and as none of them wanted to admit that he didn't know what the word meant, they all nodded and said yes.

Poor Ferdinand managed to pull his wits together somewhat. "I am *not* sophisticated!" he exclaimed. "I've been perfectly open and aboveboard about everything, and—"

"Oh, that isn't what I mean at all," said the cow; and as she didn't know what she did mean, it was perfectly true.

"Well, what do you mean, then?" asked the harassed crow.

"Just what I say," returned Mrs. Wiggins. She appealed to the others. " Isn't it perfectly plain?" And they all nodded emphatically and said: "Yes, yes. Perfectly."

"Well, it isn't what *I* mean by sophisticated," said Ferdinand, now thoroughly mixed up.

"Just what *do* you mean by it?" asked the cow coldly.

And at that the crow just turned round and walked off with his shoulders hunched up and didn't come near the others for the rest of the day. But it had done him some good, as Mrs. Wiggins observed with satisfaction, for from that time on he treated her with marked respect.

They went on through the snowy woods for several days, and the snow came down in thick flakes and got deeper and deeper and harder and harder to walk through. The big animals didn't mind it much, but the smaller animals and Charles and Henrietta and the children had to ride most of the time; and the children in particular were cold because they didn't have warm enough clothing. They were only warm at night when they snuggled down under a feather bed between Uncle William and the bear. Moreover, it was a good deal harder to find enough food, now that the country was all covered with snow.

So pretty soon the animals began to grumble. If Ferdinand was such a good leader, they said, he ought to be able to keep them from starving or freezing. They wouldn't be much good to the animals they had come to rescue if they starved or froze stiff. And if the snow got much deeper, how were they going to travel at all? They asked Ferdinand these questions. "You've been here before," they said. "How did you get food?"

"We took it with us in the old phaeton," said the crow.

"How did you keep warm?"

"We took blankets with us and wrapped them around us."

"And how did you walk over the deep snow?"

"We made snowshoes," said the crow. "I can show you how to do that."

"H'm," said Jack thoughtfully. "That takes care of one thing. But what are we going to do for food and clothing?"

"Yes," said Henrietta. "Why didn't you tell us all this in the first place, when we started out? You didn't think about anybody but yourself. You don't mind the cold the way we do, and you can fly through the air and live on nuts and things that you steal from squirrels and chipmunks. It's very easy for *you*. But why didn't you think about *us*? A fine leader you are!"

Ferdinand looked round out of the corners of his eyes at his comrades. It was perfectly true. When he had come back to organize the rescue party, he had been so full of his own importance that he had forgotten all about such little matters as proper food and clothing. He'd have to think of something pretty quickly, or they'd reduce him to the ranks and elect a new leader. He could see them looking meaningly at one another—even his bosom friend, Bill, was shaking his head very seriously and avoided his eye—and he could hear a *buzz-buzz* as they whispered to each other: "Too sophisticated. Yes, yes; too sophisticated." Then suddenly an idea came to him. He ruffled out his feathers.

"My friends," he said importantly, "on the face of it, what you allege against me seems to be true. I did *not* see fit to burden us with large stores of food and clothing, which would seriously have hampered us. There is a better way to get what we need. There are reasons why I did not tell you about it before—"

Bill giggled audibly. "I'll say there were!" he muttered coarsely; but Ferdinand gave him a hard look and he subsided, though his beard continued to tremble with subdued laughter.

"The time, however," continued the crow, "has now come. As you have seen, these woods are full of birds and animals—creatures of little experience, who have never known much about anything but their small woodland affairs and are intensely curious about the outside world. What's the one thing we can give them that they haven't got? Why, our experience of the outside world, of course. We've travelled; we've been everywhere and done everything; we know life. We can sell that knowledge for the things we need."

At this point Bill snickered again. "You mean you're going to trade your good advice for food?" he asked. "Well, if these animals are anything like me, you won't get many customers. My experience is that you can get all the good advice you want from your relatives. You don't have to go outside the family. And you don't have to pay for it, either. Sell advice indeed! Huh! Might as well try to sell Cecil here a quill toothpick!"

"That was *not* what I meant," said Ferdinand coldly, "and now that this unseemly interruption is over, I will tell you that my idea was simply this: to give a series of lectures of various kinds, admission to which will be paid in articles of food or clothing."

"That's a good idea all right," said Uncle William, "as far as food goes. But how do you expect to get blankets and clothing for the children? These woods animals haven't got such things."

"They'll find them," said the crow confidently. "Why, suppose you wanted to find an old coat for this boy to wear. I mean if you were at home, in your own stable. Couldn't you do it?"

"Why, yes, as a matter of fact, I could," replied the horse.

"There's a couple of old overcoats down in the toolshed. But that's different. Up here in the woods—"

"Up here in the woods it's just the same, said Ferdinand. "There are hunters and campers and trappers and lumbermen, and they're always throwing away things."

"But how can you find them, in all these square miles of trees? "

"*You* couldn't. That's just the point. But take one of these deer. He knows every square inch of ground for miles. If there's an old coat within five miles of here, he'll know it. If there isn't, he'll have a friend over the hill who'll know where there is one. And so on."

"Why not have a lecture tonight?" said Charles. "I have one, you know, that I prepared after our trip to Florida. 'A Trip to the Sunny Southland.' And that one about Washington: 'How Our Legislators Live.' That was very well received. And—"

"Oh, be still!" said Henrietta. "Nobody wants to hear you lecture If they'd heard you talk as much as I have, they'd pay to stay away."

"But that's the point: they haven't!" said Charles triumphantly.

"Well, they will!" said his wife sarcastically. "Believe me, if there's an animal between here and the pole that doesn't know your life-history by the time the winter's over, I'll be surprised."

Charles hung his head, but Ferdinand came to his rescue. "I think it's a good idea for Charles to deliver his Florida talk tonight," he said. "We'll stay here today and make snowshoes. I'll go notify those chickadees over in that pine there, and they'll tell all the other birds and animals. I bet we have a big attendance."

For the rest of the day under the crow's supervision the travelers gnawed down small saplings and tore off strips of bark, which they bent and tied into rough snowshoes. Charles alone was absent. He had retired into a thicket where he could rehearse his speech privately, and every now and then phrases would float out to the workers and they would smile at each other. "I have been asked. . . . A very unpretentious task, my friends. . . . Undaunted I flew at the alligator and pecked him so that he winced. 'Sir,' I said. . . .

With my skill in debate, I of course won the prize without difficulty. . . ." And so on.

The lecture that evening, however, was a great success. A large and enthusiastic audience of deer, coons, foxes, rabbits, porcupines, and skunks hung breathlessly on Charles's words, rocked with laughter at his sallies, and cheered wildly at the stories of hairbreadth escapes—which, as he said afterwards, while not strictly true, were founded on fact. The other members of the rescue party, with the exception of the children, Henrietta, and the bear, acted as ushers at the beginning, but sneaked off when he began to talk and played twenty questions until the meeting broke up. They had heard it all so many times that they felt they just couldn't stand it again, and, as Ferdinand said: "We're all fond of Charles, but he *is* tiresome when he gets to talking about himself, and if we stay, we'll get so irritated we'll throw things, and that wouldn't do."

The children stayed, and at first they were so delighted to have so many animals around them that they were a little noisy, but although they didn't understand what Charles was saying, they understood pretty soon that he was making a speech, and, being considerate children, they sat quietly and applauded when the others applauded, and at the end when some of the animals went up to shake hands with the lecturer, they went up too.

The bear stayed, partly because he hadn't heard Charles talk before, and partly because two of his cousins whom he hadn't seen in a long time came to the lecture. He sat with them in the front row, but he was so glad to see them again that he talked a good deal and had to be shushed by the other animals several times before he would keep still.

As for Henrietta, although in private she scolded her husband soundly at every opportunity, she was really very proud of him and would fly at anyone else who ventured even the slightest criticism of him, and so tonight she perched quite close beside him on the low branch from which he spoke, and admired him so openly and applauded so enthusiastically that it embarrassed even Charles a little.

"Not so loud!" he whispered to her once when she continued stamping and shouting "Bravo!" long after the audience had stopped. "They'll think it's funny."

"They don't know I'm your wife," she muttered.

"They'll think I hired you to applaud," he replied.

"Oh, shut up and go on with your talk," she whispered angrily. Then she shouted "Bravo!" again and looked him defiantly in the eye. And Charles went hastily on with the lecture.

The box office, presided over by Ferdinand, took in enough food to feed them for a week, a heavy flannel shirt checkered in big red and black squares, two old sweaters, four pairs of lumbermen's heavy socks, a knitted bed jacket with pink ribbons, a whisk broom, two boxes of matches, a bottle of hair tonic, and a postage-stamp album containing a complete collection of the stamps of the British colonies. The woods animals had found these various articles at different times and had hidden them away for no particular reason, as animals do. Everett put on the flannel shirt, which came down to his heels, and Ella wore one of the sweaters, which she had to hold up so she wouldn't trip over it, and they both put on the heavy socks, which were much too large, so that they looked very funny. But they didn't care, for they were warm.

From that day on, the trip became more of a lecture tour than a rescue expedition. The news of their coming ran ahead of them, and every ten miles or so they would be met by a committee of animals who wanted to engage them to give a series of lectures in their territory. But of course they were in a hurry, so they decided that they could give only one lecture in each place, and if the animals wanted to hear a different talk, they would have to travel along with them to the next stop. Many animals did this, and the result was that although the snow soon got very deep, they seldom had to use their snowshoes, for in order to pay their admission to the next lecture, the animals who traveled with them would go on ahead and break trail for them. When fifty to a hundred moose and deer and bear had tramped over a trail, it was almost as hard and smooth as a state road.

Of course Charles couldn't do all the lecturing. He always talked so loud that he was hoarse for a week after one lecture." He gives himself too much," said Henrietta. So Uncle William talked on "Life under the Big Top," which was recollections of his year with a circus, and Bill had a humorous talk," Here and There in Rural New York," which was very well received, and Jack spoke on "Our Civilization: Whither Bound?" which was rather philosophical and not so popular among the younger woods animals. After a time he gave that up and talked on "How to Live with Human Beings," a good many of the facts for which he got from the mice. Ferdinand talked on" Life in a Southern Treetop," and Mrs. Wiggins had two topics: "The Inside of the Dairy Business" and "From Cow-barn to White House," which told of her trip to Washington, where she shook hands with the President. She had a homey humor which always went well with the crowd, and always spoke extempore, which means that she never knew what she was going to say until after she had said it. Her lectures were always well attended, partly, of course, because many of the woods animals had never seen a cow before. Later, too, they got up some debates, the most popular of which was one between the bear and Uncle William called "Farm vs. Forest." Uncle William argued that life on the farm was best, and the bear took the opposite view. But to please the woods audience it was arranged beforehand that the bear should win.

And so the gallant little band went on northward, traveling swiftly on the road that the woods animals made for them. They were always on the alert for news of their friends, and at the end of each lecture the speaker would explain the purpose of the expedition and appeal to his audience for news of the whaling ship and the lost animals. But although among the birds and the deer there were many rumours of a party of strange animals who had been seen here and there in the Arctic regions, there was no real news.

All these rumors seemed to come from the north, however, so they knew they were still traveling in the right direction.

VIII
Jack and Charles Get in Trouble

And now The winter came down upon them in earnest. The snow was like powdered ice, the trees snapped and cracked in the cold, and though at night under their feather beds they were snug and comfortable, during the day they had to keep moving briskly to keep warm. And as it got colder, it got more and more difficult to get the bear up in the morning, because he was accustomed to crawling into his hole and sleeping all winter, and no matter how loud Charles crowed, he just went on snoring comfortably, and if they pulled the covers all off him, he just curled up tighter and grunted and went on sleeping. They tried shaking him, but he was so big and heavy and they had to shake so long before he woke up that they were all tired out afterwards and had to rest for an hour before they could start the day's march. Then one morning when she was helping to shake him awake, Mrs. Wiggins happened to stick one horn into his ribs. And immediately the bear's eyes flew open and he gave a wriggle and a silly laugh and shouted: "Ugh! Stop that tickling!

Mrs. Wiggins sat back on her haunches and bellowed with laughter. "Hey! Animals!" she gasped. "He's ticklish! Can you imagine that—a ticklish bear?" But while she was laughing, he had gone back to sleep. So she tickled him again, until he rolled around, giggling and pawing the air and begging her to stop. And this time she woke him up thoroughly. After that it was Mrs. Wiggins's job to get the bear up every morning.

The animals slept very soundly at night, and, with the feather beds over their ears, they couldn't hear anything that went on in the forest around them. But very early one morning Jack and Charles, who were sleeping next to Uncle William, woke up, feeling cold, to find that the horse had dragged the covers off them in his sleep.

Jack got one corner in his teeth and tried to drag them back, but Uncle William was lying on them.

"We'll have to wake him up," said Charles. "We'll disturb everybody if we do," replied the dog. "You know how he snorts when he wakes up."

"Well, it can't be helped," said the rooster sharply." It won't be time to get up for nearly two hours yet, and I don't propose to lie here and freeze just because that big lump has—"

"Listen!" said Jack.

From the dark forest came a long-drawn howl.

"Sounds like a dog," said Charles. "But dogs always live with people, don't they? And there aren't any people for miles."

"Maybe he's lost," said Jack. "I tell you what we'll do. You aren't sleepy any more, are you?"

"Not after all this row," said Charles grumpily.

"Well then, let's take a little walk and see if we can find him. If he's lost, maybe we can put him on the road home.

Charles grumbled a little, but he was just as curious to know about the strange dog as Jack was, so presently they set out, leaving their friends snoring comfortably away in their beds. The snow was packed so hard that even the rooster could walk on it without sinking in, but as it made his feet cold, he preferred to ride on Jack's back. As soon as they were a little way from the camp, Jack gave a few barks, to let the other dog know they were coming, and was answered after a minute with some sharp yelps.

"Maybe he's caught in a trap," said Charles. "Anyway, he didn't sound very far away. But what are those funny noises in the bushes?"

"I don't know," Jack replied. "I've noticed them on both sides of us. It's as if somebody were going along beside us, keeping out of sight. But of course that's impossible. It must be the snow. There's a funny smell, though. D'you notice it?"

"Yes. I've been wondering what it was," said Charles. This wasn't true, for roosters can't smell at all. Even the very finest perfume would be wasted on them. But they're so vain that they never want to admit that there's anything they can't do, and that was why Charles said yes.

"Smells like bear a little, and like dog a little," said Jack reflectively, "yet it isn't either. I wonder—Hello! Here he is! "For they had come out into an open glade, in the middle of which a very big shaggy dog was lying in the snow.

"How do you do? "said Jack politely." We thought we heard you howl, and we wondered if there was anything we could do for you. We thought perhaps you were lost, and although we're strangers in this part of the country ourselves, we can perhaps help to put you on the right road."

"Thank you, thank you. Very kind, I'm sure," said the other. He got up and shook the snow from his coat, which was thick and shaggy, and grayish tan in color. He smiled as he spoke, but his eyes, which were slanting and sly, did not smile, and his teeth were long and white. Charles shifted his feet uneasily on Jack's back and whispered: "I don't like this fellow. I don't like the way he looks at me. He makes me feel as if I didn't have any feathers on."

"Yes, yes," the other continued as he came closer to them. "Very kind indeed. You're a farm dog, I expect?"

"Yes," said Jack. "We're traveling with a party of friends—bound for the North Pole. My friend and I were just wondering what kind of dog you were. A very rare species, no doubt. We've never seen a dog like you before."

"Never seen—No, I dare say you haven't," said the stranger absently. "The North Pole! Well, well! How interesting!" He came very close and, putting up his nose, sniffed at Charles so intently that the rooster felt the gooseflesh prickling on his back between his wings. "And your friend is a rooster? Yes, yes; I know the smell"—he licked his chops—"though it's a long time since—" He broke off. "Ah, well; we'll speak of that later. I must tell you how much I appreciate your thoughtfulness in coming out to find me. I had scarcely hoped—" He broke off again and smiled as if very much pleased with himself.

"Well," said Jack bluntly, "I see you're not in trouble, and you're evidently not lost, so I guess there isn't anything we can do for you, and we'd better be getting back to our friends. If you'd care to come back and have a bite of breakfast with us, I know our friends would be pleased."

"Thanks so much," replied the other; "you're too kind. But I can't permit your generosity to go unrewarded. I really must insist on your staying and having breakfast with me and *my* friends. I'm sure

they'll be ever so much more pleased to see *you* than *your* friends would be to see *me*." And he laughed outright.

"*Your* friends?" exclaimed Jack. "But I thought you—"

"Forgive me," said the stranger. "In the pleasure of meeting you I had forgotten that I was neglecting to present them to you." He raised his nose and sent forth a long, doleful howl, and immediately there was a rustling in the bushes all about them, and the two travellers found themselves the centre of a ring of huge shaggy grey dogs, all sitting on their haunches and smiling at them with very hungry-looking jaws.

Too late Jack realized that he had walked straight into a trap, although what kind of a trap it was, and what sort of animals these were, he had no idea. He could feel Charles trembling violently, but he managed to keep his presence of mind.

"Well, well," he said, "I'm very glad to meet them, I'm sure. But I don't think I've seen any of them at any of our lectures, have I?"

The other laughed, a little less politely this time. "No," he said, "I don't think you have. And you won't see them at any lectures in the future. In fact, you're not likely to attend any future lectures yourself, unless you do exactly as we tell you to. Eh, boys?" And he looked round at his friends, who all grinned and licked their chops expectantly.

In spite of his danger, Jack began to get mad. It was beginning to get light now, and he could see that these animals were really a very ferocious-looking crew. But although it was high time his own friends were up and about the business of getting breakfast, he knew that without Charles to wake them they would probably sleep late, and it would be an hour or more before they would become alarmed at his absence and set out to look for him. He must gain as much time as he could. "I don't know what you're talking about," he said, "but I suppose it's some sort of a joke, for I don't believe for a minute that you intend to try to keep us here against our will. We've never done you any harm—" But he got no further, for the leader suddenly lifted his muzzle and barked a sharp command. Immediately the other animals got to their feet and closed in around their prisoners.

"Come," said the leader. "We've stayed here long enough. You come with us."

Jack looked round at the ring of sharp teeth and menacing eyes. "All right," he said. "But if any harm comes to us, you'll be sorry."

Two or three of the captors laughed at this as they moved off, but the leader said: "You'll come to no harm if you go quietly and do as we say. Forward, march!" And the animals wheeled like a squad of soldiers and marched their prisoners off into the forest.

As Jack walked along over the frozen snow, listening to the laughter and coarse jokes of his guards, an idea came to him. "Get up on my head, Charles," he said in a low voice.

Charles was so frightened that at first he paid no attention, but kept on shivering and muttering: "Oh dear! Oh dear me! Whatever will Henrietta do without me? And my eighteen little ones at home; shall I never see them again? Oh, what a sad and untimely end to a useful and glorious life!" But presently, after Jack had repeated his order several times, Charles obeyed. Most of the trees in this part of the forest were tall and had no branches for twenty or thirty feet up, but pretty soon they passed through a clump of spruces whose low boughs were just over their heads. "Now, Charles! Jump when I tell you," whispered Jack. Before the other animals realized what he was doing, he stopped, shouted: "Jump!" and, rearing up on his hind

"Is that someone singing?"

legs, fairly tossed the fluttering rooster up on to one of the limbs. "Now crow for all you're worth!" he cried.

And Charles crowed as he had never crowed before. His feet slipping and sliding on the ice-covered limb, his tail feathers snapped at by the mob of infuriated animals, who were leaping up beneath him and trying to pull him down, he crowed until the woods echoed for miles, and elk and bears and beaver and foxes and weasels, going about their morning business in distant parts of the forest, paused and lifted their heads and said: "Is that someone singing? What a beautiful voice!"

But it did not last for long. The limb was so slippery that Charles could not hop higher up on it and so get out of reach of his pursuers, and presently one of them caught him by the wing and pulled him roughly down. Jack had had no chance to escape, for two of the largest of the animals had stood on each side of him while the others were trying to recapture Charles, and he knew that if he tried to run, they would stop him. Now one of them picked up Charles carefully and replaced him on Jack's back, and the leader came up and spoke to him.

"Another little trick like that," he said, "and there won't be enough of you left in five minutes to make soup of. I shan't warn you again."

But the prisoners did not need the warning. They were thoroughly discouraged.

In about two hours they came to a cave, which was evidently the headquarters of their captors. Charles shuddered violently as he saw the bones lying about the outside of the cave. "Those are rooster bones, some of them," he groaned. "Oh, I feel in my own bones that I shall never see my eighteen little ones again."

There were several large rooms in the cave and they were led through a narrow doorway into one of these, and a guard was posted outside. After a while the leader of the animals came in." Now," he said, "we can have a little talk, and I'll tell you what I want you to do. If you agree to do it, we'll let you go. If you don't, we'll eat you. You can take your choice."

"We don't want to be eaten," said Jack.

"All right, then. Now listen to me. We've been following you for several days. There are a little boy and a little girl in your party. We want them. If you will promise to bring them to us, we'll let you go right away. If you won't promise—" He smiled politely, but unpleasantly. "Well, in that case, my dear dog, I'm afraid that you and your young feathered friend here—"

"Oh, please!" interrupted Charles. "Don't say it again."

"Very well. But make up your minds quickly. My friends are impatient—and hungry."

"But," said Jack, "suppose we promise and then just go away and don't bring them to you."

"Oh, you won't do that," said the other. "I fancy that I am a better judge of animal nature than to think that of you. Your friend might do it, but no dog would. No dog will tell a lie, even to save his own skin."

This was perfectly true. No dog in the history of the world has ever been known to tell a lie, and that is why man has selected the dog as his chief friend among the animals.

"What do you want the children for?" asked Jack. "Are you going to eat *them*?"

"Oh, my dear fellow!" exclaimed the other. "How could you dream of such a thing? Certainly not! W—ah—well, it's a little difficult to explain. You see—"

"We see perfectly well," interrupted Jack. "And we're not going to do it. You can eat us if you want to. But wait till our friends find out about it. Eh, Charles?"

"You bet!" said Charles. Like all roosters, he had plenty of courage when he was angry, and the suggestion that they should betray their friends had made him good and mad. "You great big bully, you! You cheap, sneaky baby-eater! When they get through with you, there won't be enough left to stop up a keyhole with. You get out of here!" And he flew at the astonished animal, clawing and pecking at his eyes, and drove him out of the room into the other part of the cave.

"There, Jack," he said as he smoothed down his ruffled feathers, "I guess I fixed him! Now all we've got to do is stand at the doorway. It's narrow and only one of them can get at us at a time. Let's see 'em try to eat us up!"

But Jack was gloomy. "That's all right for a while," he said, "but by and by we'll have to get some sleep, and then they can sneak in and overpower us."

"Well, anyway," said the rooster, "we can hold them off for a while, and maybe Uncle William and Mrs. Wiggins and the rest of them will get here by then."

"Maybe," said Jack hopelessly. "Well, it's all we can do."

At that moment the sharp muzzle of their enemy appeared again in the doorway. "Keep back!" Charles warned him. But he did not try to come in.

"Oh sure, I'll keep back," he snarled, glaring at them with his wicked yellow eyes. "We can wait. We'll have a better appetite tomorrow than we've got today. Huh! We wouldn't let you go now anyway. No rooster can play tricks on a wolf and get away with it." And he disappeared.

"Wolf!" exclaimed Jack. "Whew! We *are* in a mess if these are wolves. I've never seen one before, but I've heard about them. They're the worst animals in the woods. They hunt in packs, and they'll attack and eat any animal that isn't strong enough to defend himself. They even eat people sometimes."

"Eat people!" exclaimed Charles. "I never heard of such a thing! Why, I can't believe it, Jack; it just isn't done! Haven't they any sense of decency?"

"What do you suppose they want the children for?" asked Jack.

"Well, perhaps you're right," replied the rooster. "The only wolf

I ever heard of was the one in the story Freddy read us once, the one that pretended he was the little girl's grandmother and ate her up. But I thought that was just a fairy story."

"Red Ridinghood," said Jack. "Well, they'll eat *us* up all right, and don't you forget it."

"I'd like to forget it, for a while anyway," said Charles. "Are you sleepy?"

"Beginning to be," said Jack. "It's so quiet here, and I didn't have my sleep out this morning. Suppose you tell a story to while away the time and keep us awake. They'll surely come to rescue us before long."

"All right," replied the rooster. "Keep your eye on the door."

"Once upon a time there was a very handsome dog named John, and he lived. . ."

IX
A Fight in the Forest

WHEN Charles Had crowed so loud

and long and despairingly for help,

the animals had all been asleep, and

Mrs. Wiggins was snoring so loudly that none of them heard

him. None, that is, except Henrietta. But Charles was Henrietta's husband, and somehow that familiar voice, raised in fear and entreaty, had penetrated her dreams. She woke and poked her head out from under the feather bed just in time to hear the last "Help!" he uttered before the wolves pulled him down. In an instant she was out of bed, clucking excitedly, and pecking sharply at Mrs. Wiggins's nose.

"Wake up!" she cried. "Charles is in trouble! Something awful is going on; I know it! Oh, wake up, animals! Wake up and help me!"

"Wha's 'at?" murmured Mrs. Wiggins sleepily. "Trouble? Wha's a trouble? Fly on my nose, tha's a trouble. Go 'way, fly." And she shook her head, sighed, and went to sleep again.

But Henrietta kept right on squawking and pecking, and before long all the animals were on their feet and listening to her story.

"No time to waste," said Uncle William. "I've warned Charles not to wander away from the camp. He could easily get lost, and there are wildcats in these woods, who'd like nothing better than a fat rooster for breakfast."

"Don't you call my husband fat!" exclaimed the hen. "Poking fun at him when he's in trouble, and—"

"I beg your pardon," said the horse. "I mis-spoke myself. Charles has a very handsome and elegant figure; I've often commented upon it. But look, here are his tracks, and here are Jack's with him. They can't come to much harm together. Still, we'd better follow them and see what's up."

So they hurried along and presently came to the clearing where the wolf had been waiting.

"H'm," said Mrs. Wiggins, "more dogs, a lot of dogs. And they've all gone off together."

"Pretty big for dogs," said Eek, who was riding on Mrs. Wiggins's back.

The bear had been looking carefully at the tracks, and he put his nose down and smelt of them. "They're not dogs," he said quietly. "Wish they were. They're wolves. And if we want to see Jack and Charles again, we've got to hurry. Come along, and be ready for trouble." And he lumbered off rapidly on the trail the wolves had left behind them.

Only a few of the travellers had even heard of the existence of such animals as wolves, but it was no time for asking questions, and the bear looked so worried that they knew something really serious had happened. They swung along at a good round pace and by and by came to where the tracks disappeared into the cave. No one was in sight, but as they approached, a wolf walked out and stood facing them.

"Ah, good morning, friends," he said politely.

The animals stopped, all but Henrietta, who ruffled up her feathers and advanced upon the wolf, her head held low, ready to fly at him if he made a move in her direction. She looked really dangerous, though only a hen.

"I'll good-morning you, you disreputable varmint!" she clucked furiously. "Where's my husband?"

"My dear madam!" exclaimed the wolf. "Really, I assure you it's unnecessary to take such a tone. Your husband and his friend are quite safe. There's just a little matter to be adjusted between us, and then—"

"Come, come," put in the bear, "not so many words, wolf. We want our friends." And he gave a low, deep, grumbling growl that made the wolf, for all his sarcastic grin, back a little way into the shelter of the cave mouth. "Come on; bring them out."

But the wolf shook his head. "Just a little 'formality to be observed first," he said. "Just hand those nice plump children over to us, and you shall have your friends at once."

His words seemed to drive Henrietta into a fury. "Formality, eh!" she screamed. "We'll teach you to put on airs with us! You let my husband out or we'll chew your heads off and make your moth-eaten hides up into a rug for Mr. Bean's kitchen!" And as the wolf started to laugh, she suddenly flew at him and, fixing her claws firmly into his shaggy head, pecked at his eyes until he howled with pain and had to roll on the ground to get rid of her. He was up in an instant, however, and darted at her with open jaws, all his sarcastic politeness forgotten. If he had caught her, it would have been the last of Henrietta, but the bear had stepped forward, and with a sudden blow of his enormous paw he sent the wolf sprawling over a log, where he lay for a moment before he picked himself up and limped back without a word into the cave.

"I guess that'll teach 'em!" said Henrietta. "Come on, animals. Let's go in and bring out Charles and Jack."

But the bear shook his head. "Not so fast," he said. "I know these wolves. Get ready for trouble; there's going to be plenty of it in a minute."

Almost before he had finished speaking, eight or nine long, lean bodies shot out of the cave opening, and in an instant the animals were fighting for their lives. The woods seemed to be full of wolves. They darted, wheeled, and snapped with their long, wicked jaws, seeking for a hold with which to pull their enemies down. At first the travellers were off their guard, and if the bear had not been ready, the rescue expedition would have come to an end right there. But, standing on his hind legs like a boxer, he knocked over two with a quick right and left at the first rush and, catching a third one by the tail in his big mouth, whirled him with a jerk of his head up into a pinetree, where he hung, howling.

By this time the other animals had got into the fight. One of the wolves had caught hold of Everett and was dragging him towards the cave, but Cecil caught sight of him and, remembering how he had persuaded Mrs. Wiggins to jump out of the window, simply walked under the wolf and then gave a little jump, and the wolf yelped, let go, and ran off squealing into the cave to pull the sharp quills out of his stomach. Each animal had a different method of fighting. Bill dashed about in short rushes like a small battering-ram, knocking over wolf after wolf, but not hurting them much. Mrs. Wiggins fought back to back with the bear, scooping up the wolves and tossing them high in the air. But she was such a kindhearted animal that even in all the excitement and danger she tried not to wound them seriously with the points of her long, sharp horns. Uncle William reared and plunged, kicked and bit and trampled, and it was he who really turned the tide of battle, for when he turned round and lashed out with his hind legs, any wolf who was struck by those huge iron-shod hoofs was unlikely to take further interest in the fighting.

And presently the signal of recall was given, a long howl, and the wolves retreated into the cave, leaving three of their number helpless outside. The travellers took stock of their injuries. No one was hurt much, though the trampled snow was strewn with feathers and bits of fur. Ferdinand had sprained his beak slightly, and Mrs. Wiggins' tail was a little sore because one wolf had caught hold of it and tried to pull it off, and one of the mice was lost, having been shaken off the cow's back. But he turned up presently from a drift into which he had burrowed to be out of the way.

"My goodness!" said Mrs. Wiggins. "I didn't know fighting was so much fun! Strenuous, of course. But I don't know when I've enjoyed myself so much."

"It's fun when you win," said Uncle William. "But what do we do now? We can't follow up our victory, because the cave mouth is too small for us larger animals to get into."

At that moment the muzzle of the wolf leader appeared in the doorway. One eye was half closed as a result of Henrietta's attentions, but he could still grin.

"Well," he said, "now you've had your fun, I suppose you know who'll pay for it?"

"If you dare so much as touch a feather of my husband's head—" Henrietta began.

"Oh, we'll give you the feathers," said the wolf. "No use for them. But I trust it won't come to that. Our offer still holds. Give us the children, and you can have your friends."

"I suppose you realize," said Ferdinand, "that we can stay here and starve you out?"

"Oh sure," admitted the wolf. "But you know we shan't starve until we've eaten you know whom." And he winked villainously. "Well," he added, "think it over. I'll be back for your answer in a little while." And he vanished.

Meanwhile inside the cave the two prisoners had been left undisturbed, although two guards were kept stationed just outside the door of their room. Jack lay down by the door, and Charles, who was getting hungry, wandered up and down, scratching now and then at the dirt floor in the hope of finding something to eat. Presently he uncovered half a dozen small black objects and, looking at them closely, discovered that they were large ants, which, after the manner of ants, were enjoying their winter's sleep. "H'm," said the rooster, "never liked ants much. Too spicy for my taste. But beggars can't be choosers." And with half a dozen quick pecks he swallowed the unsuspecting insects and then began scratching for more.

He had uncovered quite a colony of them and was making a meal of them when an idea struck him. He stopped eating and, catching hold of one of the ants by a leg, shook him roughly. "Hey," he shouted, "wake up!"

The ant stretched, yawned, then sat up and began washing his face with his forelegs.

"What's the idea?" he said crossly. "Can't you let a fellow sleep?"

"I beg your pardon," said Charles politely. "But it's a big piece of luck finding you here—"

"Luck for you or luck for me?" inquired the ant sarcastically.

"Both of us, I hope," said the rooster. "See here; how many of you ants are there in this anthill that I seem to have stumbled on?"

"Oh, about four thousand, last census," said the ant. "Four thousand soldiers, that is. We're the permanent garrison. I suppose there'd be as many more workers, but I don't know about that. Say, is that all you waked me up for—to ask silly questions? What are you, a newspaper reporter or something?"

"No, no," said Charles. "The fact is, I've got a little military job I want done, and I'd like to hire about four thousand soldiers to do it. Of course I realize it means waking you all up in the winter when you want to sleep, but it isn't much of a job, really; won't take over an hour; and I'll pay well."

"Well, you've come to the right ant," said the other." I'm captain of the Queen's Guard. But what's your idea of pay?"

"Honey," said Charles. "I've got about twenty pounds of honey that some bears brought in to pay for their seats at one of my lectures. I'm doing a lecture tour of the North, you see."

"No, I don't," said the ant. "I can't abide lectures. And why anybody should pay good honey to hear 'em—however, that's your business. H'm. Honey, eh? The boys haven't had any honey in a long time. I guess they wouldn't mind waking up for that. Well, that's O.K. Twenty pounds divided by four thousand soldiers—how much is that per ant?"

"Oh, figure it out afterwards," said Charles. "I'm in a hurry. My life's in danger; I haven't time to do arithmetic. How soon can you mobilize?"

"Have the whole army awake and in line in twenty minutes," said the captain. He looked about him. "Hey, Ed!" he shouted. "Why, where's Ed? And old Three Legs? See him anywhere? He lost the other three in a skirmish with some slave-hunting ants last fall. They were both sleeping right beside me."

Charles looked away and blushed slightly, for he was sure that both the captain's comrades were at that moment in his gizzard. But the ant didn't notice. "That's funny," he said. "Well, can't bother now." He seized a neighboring sleeper by the feeler and shook him. "Hey! Get up, Johnny! To arms, the Queen's Guard! Wake up, boys; here's a job for you." And he rushed about, kicking and punching and shaking his friends until half a dozen yawning, sleepy-eyed ants were grumbling and asking what was the matter.

"Run down to the citadel," said the captain," and wake up General Formicularis and tell him to rouse the garrison and bring 'em up right away, all four regiments. Tell him to send through the barracks and turn 'em all out. Tell him there's good rich booty in it for everyone. Honey! That'll bring him."

The ants, old campaigners all, were by this time alert and wide awake, and they dashed down into the narrow passageways leading to the citadel. For a time there was no sound but a faint rustling underfoot, from where, deep down in the underground barracks and corridors and guardrooms, the call to arms was being sounded.

Suddenly Charles cocked his ear towards the door. "Isn't that Henrietta's voice?" he asked.

"Sounds like her," said Jack. "There's something going on outside. Perhaps they have come to rescue us."

"I thought I heard her voice," said Charles with what seemed to his friend a strange lack of enthusiasm. " She's angry at something."

"Probably at the wolves," said Jack. "Yes, probably. But you know, Jack, I—I almost begin to like it here. It's quiet and peaceful and—"

"Nonsense! "said Jack. "You're afraid of Henrietta because she's angry. But she isn't angry at you. She wants to rescue you. Think how glad she'll be to see you—"

"She'll hide it pretty well," said Charles mournfully. "Oh yes, I suppose she'll be glad. But she'll give me an awful raking over for getting in such a mess. I shan't hear the last of it for months. Ah, here we are!" he exclaimed as the head of a long procession of ant soldiers emerged from a small hole at his feet.

The soldiers came up at the double, and in a few minutes the entire army, four thousand strong, was spread out over the floor of the room, each of the regiments divided into companies with its captain at its head, and the general, a stout, puffy ant, a little in front, surrounded by his staff. Charles gave them a military salute with his right claw and then delivered a short address, telling them what he wanted them to do and ending with a stirring appeal to their patriotism, to the well-known fighting reputation of the famous First Division, which they comprised, and a promise of much honey.

Orders were quickly given. The first regiment, deployed as skirmishers, marched out along the roof of the cave; the others followed in columns of four. For perhaps five minutes after they had gone, there was silence, then a most terrific howling broke out among the wolves. "Hurray!" shouted Charles. "The attack has begun!" And he and Jack in their delight fell into each other's arms.

Outside the cave their friends, who had been holding a conference and trying to decide upon some method of rescue, were suddenly amazed to see a dozen wolves dash out of the dark opening, howling and snapping at their flanks and pawing madly at their heads. The wolves took no notice of their late enemies, but dashed off in different directions and were soon lost to sight. And before the watchers could recover from their surprise, out of the cave came Charles and Jack.

The animals rushed towards them and surrounded them. "What is it?" they exclaimed. "What did you do to them? They're gone, every last wolf. How in the world did you ever manage it?"

Charles puffed out his chest grandly. "Manage it?" he said. "Pooh! Nothing to it; nothing to it at all! Have any of you ever been bitten by an ant?"

"I have," said Bill. "I sat down in an anthill once by mistake, and my word! how those beasts can sting!"

"Well, that's all there was to it," said Charles. "I hired an ant army to attack them. Promised them honey. Somebody better go get that honey, by the way. And so here we are again, safe and sound. Ha! Ask old General Charles if you want to get anything done! I guess I showed those wolves a thing or two! I guess they won't try any tricks on this rooster again!"

But Henrietta pushed herself through his ring of admirers and caught him by the ear with her beak. "That's enough! " she said furiously. "You think you can cause me all this grief and then get away with it, do you? You think you can just stand around and tell how smart you are, eh? Well, I want a word with you, my lad! "And under the amused glances of his friends, she led him round behind a bush, from which he presently emerged, much crestfallen. Nothing further was heard of his cleverness. Indeed he did not dare open his beak again in Henrietta's hearing for two days.

X
The Dash for the Pole

WORD of The brave fight that the travelers had put up had evidently gone around among the animals of the North, for they saw no more wolves after this, though they crossed the tracks of these animals every day. It grew colder and colder; the days were very short and the nights correspondingly long, so much of their travelling had to be done before sunrise and after sunset, by the wavering, drifting light of the aurora borealis. Soon they left the forest behind and travelled over endless snow plains, and the audiences of their lectures were composed mostly of reindeer. And at last they came to the Polar Sea.

"If I'm not mistaken," said Ferdinand, "this is about where we went adrift on the iceberg. Of course the sea is frozen over now, and the whaling ship must be frozen in the ice somewhere to the north of us. But we don't want to find the ship. My guess is that the crew, and probably our friends with them, will have reached Santa Claus's house long before this. That's at the North Pole—straight north from here. See, here's a map of how we'll go." And he drew it in the snow. He made a mark and said: "That's where we are," and then he made another mark and said: "That's the North Pole," and then he drew a straight line connecting them and said: "That's the route we take."

"H'm," said Mrs. Wiggins. "I don't see that that tells us much. I could have drawn that map myself."

"You're smarter than I thought you were," remarked Ferdinand, and Mrs. Wiggins didn't know whether to be angry or not. But the other animals all agreed that that was the only course to take, so they set out due north over the frozen sea.

And in two days they heard news of their friends. Just before dusk—which came at two in the afternoon—Ferdinand, who had gone for a short flight to stretch his wings, which were apt to get a little stiff with disuse when he rode on Bill's head and didn't use them all day, spied a black speck in the northern sky. It grew larger and larger, and presently he saw that it was a huge eagle. Ferdinand climbed to meet him, since he knew that only a very hungry eagle will condescend to eat a crow. And soon they were flying side by side.

"Hail, crow," said the eagle. "Whither away so far from home?" Eagles always speak in very high-flown language and are very touchy of their dignity, because they are the national bird.

"Good evening, your honor," said Ferdinand. "I'm with a party who have come to rescue a number of friends. They were captured by the crew of a whaling ship, and the last we heard of them, they were bound for the Pole to visit Santa Claus. Have you seen anything of them?"

"These eyes beheld them only yesterday," said the eagle over his shoulder, for he was flying much faster than Ferdinand, who had a hard time to keep up.

"Hey!" said the crow. "What's that? Would you slow up a little and circle around a bit? It's very important to me."

The eagle shrugged his shoulders. "Is a crow's business as important as an eagle's?" he demanded. "And he the messenger of Santa Claus? I have no time for your petty affairs, crow. And yet—" He paused in his flight, banked, and soared in a wide circle. "Perchance at this juncture even the aid of the lowly crow is not to be despised. So listen and heed well, for I have little time to spare. Things have gone very ill with my master since the arrival of those seafaring men and their pets—"

"They're there, then?" interrupted Ferdinand.

"I bade you *listen*," said the eagle sharply. "Did I not speak of their arrival? You are wasting with your idle words time that is far more precious than your own—more precious even than mine, for it is the time of my master, Santa Claus, and it lacks but a short space of time to Christmas." He said considerably more about wasting time, but Ferdinand had sense enough not to point out that if time was being wasted, it was not he who was wasting it. And presently the eagle went on.

"You have left me little time to inform you how affairs stand, and indeed it is a long story. You are eager, I take it, to rescue your friends and return them to the country of their birth. In this you may be assured of my help—for I shall return in a week—and of the help of others whose acquaintance you will soon make. But those sailors must also be persuaded to return to their pursuit of whales, and this will be no easy matter. It is a problem on which we will consult together upon my return. Farewell, crow, and convey to that excellent pig, your friend, my kindest remembrances."

"But," said Ferdinand hastily, as the eagle began to flap his huge wings, "just what *is* the matter? You haven't told—"

"He is indeed a most talented member of the porcine race," went on the eagle. "Never to my knowledge have I been paid so delicate and tactful a compliment as in the poem which he wrote about me. Let me see; how did it go?

> *O eagle, mightiest of all living things,*
> *Nor Death nor Destiny spreads stronger wings.*
> *Thy claws of brass, thy beak of burnished steel,*
> *Make malefactor pigs in terror squeal.*

And so on. Very beautiful words. Request him to sing it for you."

"Yes, I will; but you haven't—" Ferdinand began. The eagle by this time, however, was under way. "Good-bye," he shouted, and drew away from the disappointed crow at a speed which made pursuit useless.

"Well, he was a lot of help," grumbled Ferdinand as he swooped earthward. "However, we know where they are, and Freddy's all right. That's something."

The animals had watched the meeting with the eagle with great interest and continued the day's march in the highest spirits when they learned that they were really within so short a distance of their friends. But a day's flight to an eagle may be a week's hard going for an animal, and it was several days before there was any indication that they were nearing the Pole. Meanwhile they racked their brains to guess what the eagle had meant when he had hinted that things were not all as they should be at Santa Claus's house. Indeed, they had several quarrels about it, some holding one view, some another, until it was decided that the only sensible plan was to give up talking and speculating about it until they got there.

On the second day after meeting the eagle they climbed up through a low range of ice hills, and Ferdinand said that they were again on land, though it made no difference to them, since both earth and water were frozen, and covered with ice and snow. North from the hills stretched an empty, snowy plain, but they had not gone far over this when they came to something very strange: a gate.

It was a very neat gate, with strong posts set solidly into the snow, and made of pickets freshly painted green, so that it could be seen for a long distance. And tacked to one side of it was a piece of plank with the following legend painted on it:

KEEP OUT
This means YOU!!
By order of the Board

The animals gathered round it. "What are we to keep out *of?*" they asked each other.

"It looks so silly, without any fence," said Mrs. Wiggins. "I never heard of such a thing. A gate without a fence is like a roof without any barn under it."

"And what's the board?" asked Jack. "The only board is the one the sign's painted on," said Ferdinand. " I expect that's what it means."

"Well, I don't take any orders from any old board," said Bill. And he went back a little way and put his head down and ran at the sign and butted it flat on the snow.

So the animals went on, and in an hour or two they came to another sign.

TRESPASSERS WILL BE PROSECUTED
S. C., Inc.
Hooker, G. M.

Again the animals were puzzled, but Uncle William said: "There are signs like that on some of the farms down our way. I think trespassers are people that shoot and fish. And prosecuting is what the farmer does to them if he catches them."

"Well, we haven't got guns or fishing poles," said Jack, "and if we had, there's nothing to use them on. I wonder who S. C., Inc., is."

"What are we to keep out of?"

"Probably the farmer," said the horse. "And Hooker, G. M., is his address. Like the letters Mrs. Bean sends to her sister, addressed: Elizabeth, N. J., you know."

"But there isn't any state called G. M.," said Ferdinand." N. J. is New Jersey, but who ever heard—"

"Well, we're in Canada," interrupted Cecil. "Perhaps that's the state of Canada we're in."

"Oh, come on," said the bear. "All these signs mean we're getting somewhere, at least." And he started on.

"I don't want to be prosecuted," said Mrs. Wiggins doubtfully. But she followed the others as they trailed on past the sign.

They were getting so near the Pole now that they had no sunlight at all to travel by. They were in the region where the sun shines day and night all summer long, but where in winter it never lifts its bright head above the horizon. The continuous darkness made the bear even more sleepy, so that he had to have Cecil ride on his back and jump up and down occasionally when he began to get too drowsy. And they could only tell what time of day it was by the position of the stars.

Just after passing the second sign they noticed a glow on the northern horizon which was neither stars nor northern lights, and as they went on, the glow spread and began to twinkle with little points of light. More and more sparkling lights appeared, and in a little while they saw what it was—a long hedge of Christmas trees, all trimmed with tinsel streamers and gold and silver stars and shiny blue and green and red balls and lighted up with hundreds and thousands of little candles. And behind the hedge they could just make out the gleaming walls and pinnacles and towers and turrets of a tremendous ice palace.

They gave a cheer and hurried forward. They pushed through the hedge and saw before them a high gateway in a wall of ice. High above them in the wall were windows in which lights twinkled. Here they hesitated for a moment, and Ferdinand looked round for the door-bell, but Uncle William said: "The gate's ajar. It must be all right to go in." He pushed with his shoulder, and the gate swung open.

They followed him a little doubtfully into a big courtyard, tastefully planted with holly bushes, interspersed with Christmas trees in tubs, and with a frozen fountain in the middle. They were wondering what they should do next when they heard someone singing. The voice was a light pleasing tenor; it had a familiar ring to their ears. And these were the words:

O Pole, O Pole, O glorious Pole!
To you I sing this song,
Where bedtime comes but once a year,
Since the nights are six months long.

Yes, the nights are six months long, my dears,
And the days are the same, you see,
So breakfast and supper each last a week.
And dinner sometimes three.

Then there's tea and lunch, and we sometimes munch
Occasional snacks between—
Such mountains of candies and cakes and pies
Have never before been seen.

Let the wild winds howl about the Pole,
Let the snowflakes swirl and swoop;
We're snug and warm and safe from harm
And they're bringing in the soup.

We'll sit at the table as long as we're able,
We'll rise and stretch, and then,
Since there's nothing to do but gobble and chew,
We'll sit right down again.

We'll tuck our napkins under our chins
To keep our waistcoats neat,
And then we'll eat and eat and eat
And eat and eat and eat.

"Nobody but a greedy pig would sing a song like that," muttered Ferdinand disgustedly.

"It's piggish, all right," said Jack, "but I'm glad to hear that voice." And he shouted: "Freddy!" and all the others shouted with him.

A small round startled face appeared at one of the upper windows and vanished again, and in a few moments a door was flung open and Freddy himself came dashing out. "Ferdinand!" he shouted. "You brought 'em! Good old Ferdy! And Jack! And Mrs. Wiggins! Gosh, but I'm glad to see you! And Uncle William and Charles and Henrietta, and even the mice! Golly, this is *great*!" He rushed round hugging them one after the other. "And these two children! Now where in the world did you pick them up? But come in, come in! Mustn't stay out in the cold, and we've a lot to say to each other."

He led them into a large hall, at the far end of which was a fireplace as big as a barn door, in which huge logs were burning brightly. "Take off your things and sit down," said Freddy, throwing off the handsome fur coat he had been wearing.

"My goodness, Freddy, you're fat as butter," said Mrs. Wiggins.

Freddy had indeed grown dreadfully stout. He was almost perfectly round, and his cheeks were so fat that his eyes were almost invisible. He looked slightly displeased at the cow's remark, but then he smiled and his eyes disappeared entirely. "High living," he explained. "We live well here on the top of the world."

As they approached the fire, a big man with a bushy white beard and sharp black eyes, twinkling with fun and kindliness, rose from a deep chair and came towards them. He had on a fur-trimmed red coat, belted at the waist, and green trousers tucked into high black boots, and there were bells at his wrists and knees that jingled when he moved. The animals stopped self-consciously. They knew it was no one but Santa Claus himself.

"He looks enough like Mr. Bean to be his brother!" said Mrs. Wiggins.

"Ssssh!" Freddy warned her. "He understands our talk."

But Santa Claus had heard the remark, and he smiled. "I know of your Mr. Bean," he said." He is a fine man; I am proud to resemble him in any way."

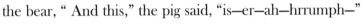

Then Freddy presented his friends, and Santa Claus shook hands warmly with each of them. When he came to the bear, " And this," the pig said, "is—er—ah—hrrumph—"

"I beg your pardon," said the saint. "I didn't catch your name."

The bear shifted awkwardly from one foot to another and blushed—at least he blushed inside, but it couldn't be seen through his fur. "I—er—I—Well, I haven't any name," he said finally.

"No name?" said Santa Claus. "Well, now, how did that happen? You're the first animal I ever knew who hadn't one."

The bear hesitated a moment; then he said: "Well, sir, I really have got a name, but I never liked it, so I never used it. It's—no, I can't say it. It's so silly."

"H'm," said Santa Claus thoughtfully. "If you don't like your name, there's no reason why you shouldn't change it. Isn't there any name you like?"

The bear brightened. "Really?" he asked. "I always thought you had to keep your name, whether you liked it or not. But if you say so—"

"I do," said Santa Claus.

"Well, then, the name I choose is Peter," said the bear.

"That's a fine name," said Santa Claus. "I'm glad to make your acquaintance, Peter. And now, animals, come up round the fire and make yourselves comfortable. You must be cold after such a long trip. Get warm first, and then Freddy will show you your rooms and you can wash up, and then we'll have some supper."

"There's one thing we'd like to ask you, sir," said Ferdinand, and he repeated what the eagle had told him. " Is it true that these sailors have caused trouble?"

A worried look came into the saint's eyes. "Trouble?" he said. "Oh, I wouldn't say that. They've changed things certainly. They—"

He stopped, for at that moment a door flew open and a man came into the room—a tall thin man, with drooping black moustaches and hard, sharp black eyes. He had sea boots on, and a red sash about his waist, in which a pistol was stuck. "Ah, Mr. Claus," he said in a harsh voice, "talkin' to the animals again, eh? I thought I heard you." He swept a contemptuous glance over the group about the fire. "Well, I'm sorry to disturb you, but there's this here matter of the workmen in the mechanical-toy department; they don't seem to want to adopt the suggestions of Mr. Pomeroy, and we think you'd better talk to 'em. Then the *New York Times* just came in on the last mail, and there's an editorial there about you we think you should answer. We've got the answer all drafted, but we want your signature."

Santa Claus got up wearily. "All right, all right; I'll come," he said. Then turning to his new guests, "Freddy will entertain you until I'm at liberty," he said. "And he can answer the question you just asked me." He stooped suddenly and caught up Ella and swung her to his shoulder, then held out a hand to Everett. "You children come along with me," he said.

The children giggled delightedly, but the man with the harsh voice said: "Surely, Mr. Claus, you don't intend to bring these children to a business conference? They'll only be in the way. They—"

"Surely I do," boomed Santa Claus in his deep bass voice." This business is run for children and don't you forget it. When you leave the children out, you leave Santa Claus out, Mr. Hooker. Let's have that perfectly clear."

Hooker shrugged and turned on his heel, and before he followed him, Santa Claus paused and whispered to the children: "Don't mind him. He isn't as unpleasant as he tries to make out. And, anyway, I'll tell you stories all the time he's talking." And the door closed behind them.

XI
Santa and the Sailors

THE animals, Who had stood up politely when Santa Claus left the room, gathered again round the fire and began asking Freddy questions.

The pig settled back comfortably in his chair.

"Well, I'll tell you all about it," he said. "But don't sit on the floor. What are all these chairs for?"

"Animals don't use chairs," said Uncle William. "Chairs are for human beings. When I was with the circus, one of my acts had to be done sitting in a chair, and I was never so uncomfortable in my life."

"Once you get used to 'em," said Freddy, "you'll never go back to the floor. Try that big one there, Mrs. Wiggins." The cow looked at it doubtfully. "Don't be afraid," he continued. "All this furniture is made in Santa Claus's workshop; it's none of your flimsy factory-made stuff that falls apart if you breathe on it."

So Mrs. Wiggins sat down gingerly; then, as nothing happened, leaned back with a sigh. "My goodness, it *is* comfortable as all get-out," she said.

"Of course it is. Well, I'll get on with my story. You know what happened up to the time that Ferdinand left us. After that we sailed north for a time, and then the ice-pack closed in on the ship, so we left it and went on across the ice. We reached here without any trouble, except for Jinx's head; he had a row with a polar bear. Jinx said something fresh to the bear—you know how Jinx is—and the bear hit him a clip with his paw and took all the hair off Jinx's head—snatched him bald-headed. It'll grow again all right, Santa Claus says, but he certainly does look funny."

"But where *is* Jinx?" asked Jack. "And all the rest of them? Why don't they come say hello to us?"

"Yes," said Ferdinand. "After all, we did come to rescue you animals. And now there's nobody but you to welcome us."

"Oh, I forgot to tell you—they're all out skiing. They'll be back by dinnertime. All except Jinx. He spends all his time down in the gymnasium. We'll go down in a few minutes and find him. Well, as I was saying, when we got here, Santa Claus was kindness itself. He gave a big dinner party for us that night, and the next day showed us over his whole place. That's how the trouble started. While he was showing us the workrooms where the toys are made, and explaining how he finds out what children want and sees that they get the right toys in their stockings and on their Christmas trees, I heard Mr. Pomeroy, the mate of the ship, say to the captain: 'This place wants systematizing, Mr. Hooker.'

"'You're right, as you nearly always are, Mr. Pomeroy,' said the captain. 'Efficiency, that's what's needed. I never see a place run as inefficient as this is.'

"They went on talking in the same way, and I didn't think much about it then; but next day they came into this room and asked if they could talk to Santa Claus about his business—said they had some suggestions to make. Santa Claus said he was always glad to get suggestions, and then they began. I was here and heard all of it. The captain said that they had been greatly interested in going over the plant, but that both he and his friends had been surprised and even alarmed at the old-fashioned way in which things were run.

"'Why, what's the matter with them?' asked Santa.

"'Pretty near everything,' said Hooker solemnly, and Mr. Pomeroy nodded gloomily. 'Yes, sir,' the captain went on, 'our expert opinion is that in five years, if you keep on runnin' like this, you'll have to close down.'

"'Suppose you tell me exactly what you think is wrong,' said Santa.

"'Well, sir,' said the captain, 'things in America have changed a good deal in the past twenty-five years. Your methods of manufacture and distribution is as out of date as your grandmother's lace cap—with all due respect. Take the matter of chimneys. You take the toys down the chimney Christmas Eve. You've always done it that way, and you're still doing it that way, in spite of the fact that in modern houses the chimney doesn't go down to a fireplace where the children hang up their stockings—it goes straight down to the furnace in the cellar. And in big apartment houses you can't get to some of the children at all.'

"'We have our ways of getting round that,' said Santa Claus.

"'Sure you do,' said the captain. ' But it's a lot of trouble. No, sir, Mr. Claus, that's only one thing, and there's dozens. Suppose, for instance, you had a hundred per cent efficient factory here; what good is that if you can't get rid of your product? What are you doing to make the children of America toy-conscious? Where in this great land of ours will you find another firm which doesn't spend one penny for advertising? No advertising appropriation at *all*! Think of it, Mr. Pomeroy!'

"'I am,' said the mate with a groan. 'It's suicidal, Mr. Hooker; that's what it is: suicidal!'

"Santa Claus tried to say something, but the captain went right on. 'Take the matter of publicity, now, Mr. Claus. I admit you get a lot of free publicity every year at Christmas time. Your picture's in all the magazines. Yes, but it's all in other people's advertisements. And you're wearin' the same old suit and drivin' the same old reindeer you were drivin' when my dear old grandpa was a dirty-faced kid. You're too far away, Mr. Claus; you ain't got your finger on the pulse of the nation.'

"Well, there was a lot more of it, and every time Santa Claus tried to say something, one or other of 'em would interrupt him and go on. And then they made what they called their proposition to him. They would come in and reorganize his business for him. It wouldn't cost him a cent, they said—'And in two months, Mr. Claus,' said the mate, 'you won't know the place.'

"It surprised us all a lot when we found out he had agreed to do it. I think he did it partly because he was tired of hearing them talk, and partly because they really thought they were doing him a favor. He's very kind-hearted, and he thought their feelings would be hurt if he wouldn't let them help him. So what they did was this: they organized a company: Santa Claus, Incorporated—"

"Why," exclaimed Jack, "that's what the 'S. C., Inc.,' meant on the sign we saw."

"Yes," said Freddy. "It was incorporated just like our Barnyard Tours at home."

"But it said: 'Hooker, G. M.,' on the sign, too," said Charles. "What did that mean? And that other sign that said: 'By order of the Board'?"

"'Hooker, G. M.,' means 'Hooker, General Manager,'" said Freddy. "And the Board is the Board of Governors. That consists of Santa Claus and the captain and Mr. Pomeroy and Mr. Bashwater. He was the chief harpooner of the whaling ship, and he's now the efficiency expert."

"Good grief!" exclaimed Mrs. Wiggins. "What a lot of big words about nothing! It's all a pack of nonsense, if you ask me."

"That's what we all think," said Freddy. "But Santa Claus is worried about it. They're changing everything, and he doesn't know what to do. We've got to help him get rid of them."

"Just what have they done?" asked Ferdinand.

"Well, they put all those signs around, warning people away. Of course that doesn't matter, because nobody pays any attention to them. But they've started an eight-hour day in the workshops—everybody has to be there at eight and work until five, with an hour out for lunch. You see, these people that make the toys come from all over the United States. They're people who used to work in offices and factories, and who have got too old, or are not well enough, to work so hard. When Santa Claus hears about anybody like that, he sends for him and brings him up here. He used to let these people work when they wanted to. If they wanted to stop for a while and play games or read or rest, why, they just did it, and then by and by went back and worked some more. But that's all changed now, and they don't like it very much. That kind of hard work is just the thing Santa Claus wanted to help them to get away from.

"Then the people in the workshops used to make the toys any way they wanted to. If they wanted to paint a toy rabbit pink and give him a tail like a squirrel's, they did it. But now each kind of toy has to be made in just one way, and one workman cuts it out, and the next paints the body and passes it on to the third, who paints in the eyes, and so on. Each workmen does just one thing. Santa didn't like it, but Mr. Bashwater said that it was mass production, whatever that means. He said that that was how Mr. Henry Ford managed to turn out so many automobiles. But Santa Claus said: 'Mr. Henry Ford makes toys for grown-ups. Every grown-up likes to have his toys just like every other grown-up's. But children like their toys different.'"

"That's so," put in Bill. "When Mrs. Bean got that sewing-machine, I heard her tell the man who sold it to her that she wanted it just like the one Mrs. Swazy had."

"You'd think she'd want it a little different, wouldn't you?" said Mrs. Wiggins.

"People are funny," said Uncle William.

Freddy told them some more about the changes that the sailors were making, and then took them upstairs. "This is my room," he said, throwing open a door. It was a bright and cozy little room. The furniture was painted bright blue with red trimmings, and the chintz window-curtains showed a pattern of small red pigs playing tag in a blue clover field, and over the fireplace was a painting of three very handsome pigs with blue silk bows around their necks, sitting in a row on a sofa and looking very self-conscious, as anyone does when he is having his picture painted.

"You don't mean to say you sleep in that bed?" said Bill.

"Sure, I do," replied the pig. "You don't know how comfortable it is until you've tried it. Did you ever sleep in one?"

"Me?" exclaimed the goat disgustedly. "I should say not!"

"Well," said Freddy, "I used to think that human beings were softies because they didn't sleep on bare boards with a little straw, the way most animals do. But I've changed my mind. Why shouldn't we be as comfortable as we can? You wait till you've tried that nice soft bed in your room, Bill."

The goat snorted and was about to make a sarcastic reply, when Cecil, who had been looking out of the window, shouted: "Oh, look! There come the others!"

Sure enough, through an opening in the Christmas-tree hedge shot a fur-muffled figure on skis, to be followed by another and then another. The first two, leaning sideways, made a graceful turn and brought up in a flurry of snow close to the palace wall, but the third, who seemed very large and clumsy, turned too sharply and went head over heels in a double somersault, while the skis flew high in the air. The fur cap had fallen off, revealing the kind face and mild brown eyes of Mrs. Wogus, who gazed about with a somewhat dazed and surprised look, and then, catching sight of the grins on the faces of her companions, broke into a loud laugh.

Freddy threw up the window and called out the news to them, and they tumbled upstairs and greeted their friends with delight. They made a great hubbub with their laughter and questions and answers; and Mrs. Wogus insisted on kissing all the newcomers, which none of them liked very much, for she had a very large wet nose anyway, and now her face was covered with melting snow. The mice were drenched and shivering after she had kissed them, and Freddy had to take them into the bathroom and give them a rub-down with a towel so they wouldn't catch cold.

Then he showed them all their rooms. Each one had furniture just the right size for the animal who was to use it. The mice shared a room together, and it looked like a room in a doll house, with its three tiny beds covered with little patchwork quilts, the small rocking-chairs, and the framed photograph of an Edam cheese over the mantel. Each room had its private bath, and although some of them were on different sides of the palace, Freddy assured them that they all had a southern exposure. "It's the only house in the world," he said, "in which all the rooms face south."

It took some time for the animals to understand this. "Don't be silly, Freddy," said Mrs. Wiggins. "How can windows on all sides of a house face in the same direction?"

"Because this house is built on the North Pole. There isn't any direction but south here."

"But suppose I leave here and want to go west," said Charles.

"You can't," said Freddy. "Because any direction you go from here is straight towards the South Pole."

The cow thought a minute. "Yes, I see that," she said." But it seems funny to me. If we start somewhere, and both go in the same direction, we're together, aren't we?"

Freddy agreed that this must be so.

"Well, then, if I start out of the back door of this house, and you start out of the front door, and Hank starts out of the side door, we're all going in the same direction. And yet we aren't going together at all, and the farther we go, the farther apart we are."

"Yes," said Freddy, "but if we keep on long enough, we'll all meet in the same place, the South Pole, so we must be *really* getting nearer together all the time." And he went on with a long explanation, which interested him so much that he never noticed that the others had gradually left the room. Then he looked up and saw that there was no one with him. "Well, well," he sighed, "that's what it is to be a poet." And he went back to his own room, sat down at the little writing-desk by the window, on the wall above which were pinned various sets of verses he was working on, and started another poem. He wrote:

> *Oh east is east, and west is west,*
> *And never the twain shall meet—*

Then he stopped and frowned. "Reminiscent, somehow," he muttered: "Wonder if it's too metaphysical. It's darned good, though." He went on.

> *Until they come to the end of the earth,*
> *To Santa Claus's retreat.*

He stopped again. "Oh, yes, I remember," he said, and grinned. "It'll make Kipling pretty sore—gives him the lie direct." Then he continued.

> *Where east is south, and west is south*
> *And north is south also;*
> *Where all directions are the same,*
> *Whichever way you go.*

"Hey, Freddy," came Hank's voice from the hall. "We're going down to the gym."

Freddy sighed, put in a comma and two exclamation points, then after pinning the paper up beside the others, hurried downstairs to the gymnasium, through the glass door of which the new arrivals were peering with many nudgings and suppressed giggles. For inside, Jinx, as yet unaware of their gaze, was looking at himself in a long mirror. Beside him was a small jar of ointment, and every now and then he would scoop a little out on his paw and rub it carefully into the bald spot on the top of his head, and then he would turn and twist his neck in the effort to see better. He looked very discontented with his appearance while doing this, but pretty soon he backed away from the glass a little and, keeping his chin up so he couldn't see the bald spot, tried the effect of various expressions. He tried looking dignified, and he tried smiling graciously, and he tried looking nonchalant, and superior, and arch, and imposing, and unconcerned in a thunderstorm. But he was so pleased with all these expressions that gradually they all came to be one expression, and whatever he tried he just succeeded in smirking in a self-satisfied way. And at that moment the pressure against the gymnasium door, against which all the animals were pushing in order to see, got so strong that it flew suddenly open, and they all fell in on the floor.

At the crash Jinx jumped three feet in the air, and his tail got as big as a whisk broom, but when he saw who it was, he was so delighted that he forgot to be angry, and when he had greeted them all, he showed them over the gymnasium.

"I spend most of my time here," he said. "I don't care much for outdoor sports this winter."

"What do you do, mostly?" asked Jack.

"Oh, I've been doing some high trapeze work," replied the cat. "It's said to be rather dangerous—jumping from trapeze to trapeze in mid air, and so on—but, goodness, what of that! I always say, what's life without a little spice of danger—"

"Show us some of your stunts," said Bill.

"Eh?" said Jinx. "Oh yes, I will some time. Let me show you what Santa Claus gave me yesterday." And he brought out a mechanical mouse, which he wound up and set on the floor, and it ran about just like a real one. "I practise hunting with it. See? "He made a pounce and caught the toy between his forepaws.

But at this exhibition Cousin Augustus shuddered, covering his eyes with his paw, and the three other mice squeaked violently.

Jinx turned and looked at them. "Hey!" he said. "What's the matter? Why good gosh, that doesn't mean anything! Any more than when children play war, with toy swords and pistols, it means they're going to shoot each other. Don't be so silly, mice."

But the mice didn't like it and said so." Suppose we came in here some time and you got us mixed up," said Eeny. "Where'd we be then?" So Jinx had to apologize and put the mechanical mouse away.

Pretty soon they all went down to supper. The animals all sat at one end of the huge banquet hall at small tables, four at a table according to size. The horses and cows were together, and in front of them were big bowls containing oats, and a big heap of fragrant hay in the centre of the table. At another table were the two dogs and the cat and the pig, and even the mice had a tiny table, which fairly groaned under the weight of an assortment of cheeses—Cousin Augustus counted fourteen kinds. The animals were a little nervous at first about eating at a table, since none of them were used to it, but of course they didn't have to use knives and forks, and they got on pretty well, though they didn't know what to do with the napkins they found at their places. Mrs. Wiggins thought you were supposed to eat them, and she had actually started to chew hers, when her sister stopped her and explained what they were for. Then she said: "Good gracious, I hope I can eat my supper without getting it all over my chin! Fine manners Santa Claus must think we have, to give us these things!

After supper they went down to a room that was even bigger than the banquet hall. It was called the Present Room, and each of them was given a present, because at Santa Claus's house it was Christmas all the time, so everybody gets a present every day. The presents were very nice. Freddy got a ten-pound box of candied fruit, and Jinx got a red and white striped gymnasium suit, and Mrs. Wogus got a book on skiing, and Hank, who was learning to read, got a copy of *Black Beauty,* and Robert got a collar with his name on it in rhinestones, and so on. Even the mice each got a tiny wristwatch, and Ella got a big doll, and Everett got an electric train.

Besides the presents that were given to them, there were hundreds and thousands of toys and books and doll houses and presents of all kinds in the Present Room, and they could play with any they wanted to. They spent a very happy evening there, but it had been a busy day, and by nine o'clock they were all tucked up in bed and the lights were out—all except Freddy's. He was sitting at his desk, and in front of him was a sheet of paper on which was written in big capitals: "ODE TO SANTA CLAUS." And under it was written: "O Santa Claus—" And under that on the paper was Freddy's head, for when he had got that far in the poem, he had fallen asleep.

XII
In the Polar Palace

THERE were **So** many pleasant things to do in Santa Claus's palace that it seemed to the animals that they had hardly finished breakfast before it was time to go to bed. Outdoors they skated and skied and tobogganed, and when they slid down hill, there were always some of Santa Claus's reindeer who were glad to pull them up to the top of the hill in exchange for a ride down. They built magnificent snow forts and had pitched battles: animals against sailors. The animals couldn't throw snowballs so straight as the sailors, but they were better strategists; that is, they didn't just give a loud shout and charge the enemy; they retreated and avoided battle until the enemy was in a bad position. Some of these battles lasted all day. Near the palace there was a little depression in the snow surrounded by low ice cliffs, and it was here almost always that the sailors met defeat. They couldn't seem to learn how it was done. Yet it was very simple. As soon as the battle started near the palace, Freddy would lead half the animal army quietly away and station them on the top of these cliffs. Then the rest of the animals would pretend to run away, and the sailors would follow them, shouting and cheering, with Hooker in the lead, waving a wooden sword and yelling: "Forward, my hearties! On to victory! Hew them down! Let not a man escape!" and so on. He loved to lead these charges.

The retreating animals would rush helter-skelter down into the depression in the snow and up the other side, the sailors hot on their heels. But as soon as the animals had reached the top of the cliffs, they would turn and begin heaving down masses of snow on the sailors, and the other animals, who had remained hidden until then, would start rolling down huge snowballs that they had prepared, and pretty soon the sailors would be completely buried in snow, and the animals would have to come down and dig them out.

And then they'd all trudge home together to supper, tired and happy, Mr. Hooker riding on the back of Uncle William or Mrs. Wiggins, and shouting to his mate: "That was a fine fight, Mr. Pomeroy. We'd 'a won, too, if there hadn't been so much snow come tumblin' down on us. Well, we'll try it again tomorrow."

Sometimes they stayed indoors and played games in the Present Room, or dressed up and did charades, or worked the electric railroads, or had yacht races in the swimming pool. There was every kind of game or toy you could think of in the Present Room, so that they could do something different every day for a year if they wanted to. They played with Ella and Everett too. Everett drilled them like soldiers, and Ella had them sit on benches and pretended to teach school. When they were bad and shuffled their feet and whispered and pinched each other, she spanked them. She knew how to spank, too, because she had been spanked so many times herself by Kate. But of course she didn't spank very hard. It was funny to see her trying to spank Mrs. Wiggins or Hank. Sometimes she played school with the sailors, and they really learned a good deal, for their grammar wasn't very good, and Ella had learned a lot of grammar from Pete.

"What is the subject of the sentence 'I saw the cat,' Mr. Pomeroy?" she would ask.

"Hey, Mr. Hooker," the mate would mutter behind his hand, "give me a little help, will you?"

The captain would look very virtuous. "Can't do it, Mr. Pomeroy," he would answer in a hoarse whisper. "'Tain't fair. If you don't know, say so." Mr. Hooker had no more idea what the answer was than the mate did.

Then Mr. Bashwater, the harpooner, who knew the answers to practically every question because he had had a college education, would whisper: "'I' is the answer."

And Mr. Pomeroy would think that Mr. Bashwater was making fun of him and would turn round, forgetting he was in school, and say angrily: "What d'ye mean—'I is the answer'! You trying to be funny? You can't say: 'I is.' It's' 'I am.'"

"I mean 'I' is the subject," Mr. Bashwater would try to explain, but that would only make it worse, and it would end by both Mr. Bashwater and Mr. Pomeroy being sent to stand in the corner with their faces to the wall, for quarrelling.

The animals and the sailors were really very fond of one another, and so although the animals were trying as hard as they could to think of some way of getting the sailors to go away and let Santa Claus alone, they wanted to do it without hurting them or making them unhappy. They talked about it a good deal among themselves.

One day Jack was out watching Mr. Bashwater practising throwing his harpoon at a snowman to keep his hand in. The captain and the mate and the boatswain, a very untidy sailor named Joel, were looking on, applauding the good shots and groaning at the bad ones, and sometimes pretending that the snowman was really a whale. "Thar she blows!" Joel would shout. "Two p'ints off the port bow!" And Mr. Pomeroy would squint under the flat of his hand and sing out: "Eighty barrels, if she's a pint!" meaning that they would get that much oil from the whale. And then Mr. Bashwater would throw the harpoon and bellow: "All aboard for a Nantucket sleighride!" which is a term whalers use for being towed by a whale to which they have made fast.

"I tell you what, Mr. Pomeroy," said the captain; "I sometimes get homesick for the old ship. Yes, sir, homesick ain't the word for what I feel sometimes, thinkin' o' them moonlit nights with the canvas a-creakin' and the riggin' a-singin' in the wind and the black water a-foamin' past."

"And them other nights, Mr. Hooker," replied the mate, "with the fire from the try works lightin' up the sea around us, and the blubber a-boilin' and a-sputterin' in the kettles, and the thick oily smoke a-chokin' us so we can't hardly breathe."

"Ain't no sweeter smell than whale-oil," put in the harpooner. "But where all the whales is gone to I dunno."

"Ah, that's just it," said Hooker, thoughtfully pulling his long black moustache. "If I thought we'd have any luck, I wouldn't stay here another day. Still an' all, it's a good life—easier'n shipboard—and once this business is put on a real efficiency basis—"

"Yes," said Mr. Bashwater as he hurled his harpoon again at the snowman," and the men is contented, ain't they, Joel?

"Ay, that they are," said the boatswain. "Happy as larks, they are. And why, sir? Well, if you ask me—"

"We didn't ask you, Joel," said Mr. Hooker quietly. "Don't forget that."

"No, sir, now I come to think, you didn't. But I'll tell you anyway. They're happy because they get lots to eat and presents every day, and because they can lie abed o' mornin's, but mostly on account o' the ice cream."

"The ice cream!" exclaimed the mate.

"Ay, sir. Y' see, our cookie is a good cook; I ain't breathin' a whisper against him. But he ain't no hand with a freezer; you know it yourself, sir. While Mr. Claus's ice cream—well, sir, I never tasted nothin' like it. It's grand, and that's the gospel truth."

Jack did not wait to hear any more, but went up into the Present Room, where his friends were playing games. He told them what Joel had said. "And," he added, "if we could do something to the ice cream so it wouldn't be so good, maybe the sailors would get homesick, and then they would leave of their own accord."

The animals didn't think it was a very bright idea, but as it was the only one they had, they decided to try it out. Freddy, who spent a good deal of time in the kitchen and could come and go there without being noticed, went downstairs and presently returned with the inside part of the freezer under his fur coat. They put it on Mrs. Wiggins's left horn, and after several tries she managed to punch a hole through it. Then Freddy took it back. And that day at dinner the ice cream was so salty that no one could eat it.

The animals were greatly pleased when they looked down the long dining room and saw the sailors waving their arms angrily and beating on the table with their spoons and heard the shouts of anger. "That'll fix 'em," said Freddy. "If we can just keep them good and discontented, the captain'll have to take them back to the ship." But unfortunately for their plot, Santa Claus, having found out the cause of the trouble, had an enormous bowl of caramel custard brought in to take the place of the ice cream. The animals, knowing that the ice cream would be bad, had all said they didn't want any dessert, so of course the caramel custard wasn't passed to them, and the sailors got it all.

"Well," said Uncle William, "I guess we bit off our nose to spite our face that time."

The animals all looked very glum—all but Ferdinand, who didn't care for sweets. He laughed. But Jinx said: "Well, we mustn't stop trying to think of something just because this failed. We've *got* to make them go away."

All this time it was getting closer to Christmas. Every day the eagle came with a big sack of mail in his claws containing letters that children had written to Santa Claus. They had been forwarded by the post-masters in different cities to the Postmaster General in Washington, who kept a special sack for them. Letters that didn't go through the mail, but were put up chimneys and into fireplaces by their writers, were collected by birds and passed on from claw to claw until they reached some point on the eagle's route, where he stopped and picked them up. The toy-makers in the workshops were carving and whittling and sawing and hammering and gluing and painting for dear life; and the sailors worked all day in the wrapping room, surrounded by piles of colored paper and bales of ribbon and big boxes of stickers, wrap-ping up presents. Santa Claus got his sleigh out and gave it a fresh coat of red paint and greased the runners and shined up the harness. He was a little worried about one of his reindeer, who had gone lame as the result of a fall, but the reindeer himself wasn't worried. "I'll be all right Christmas Eve," he said. "Sound as a dollar! Don't you fret, sir."

The captain had become very fond of the mice. He carried them round in his pocket and petted them all the time, and as he was very handy at carving things with a jackknife, he had made them a little merry-go-round that they never got tired riding on. In the evening he would take them up to his room, which was fitted up like the cabin of a ship, and put them on the table, and then he would play old-fashioned waltzes and polkas and mazurkas and schot-tisches on his flute, and they would dance for him. Then when it was ten o'clock, he would take them to their own room and tuck them up in bed. This was a little difficult for him, as the room was so small that he could only get his head and one arm through the door, but he enjoyed doing it very much.

They particularly liked it when he took them to the meetings of the board, because then he and Mr. Pomeroy and Mr. Bashwater all made long speeches at Santa Claus. They liked Mr. Bashwater's speeches best, because he made a great many gestures and banged on the table and was so eloquent that he was always bathed in perspiration when he finally sat down. They were a little sorry for Santa Claus, who always seemed to want to know what the speeches were about. They themselves, like most people, just enjoyed the speeches, without caring what they were about.

They were a little embarrassed when the other animals asked them what had been going on. "Oh, Mr. Bashwater made a fine long speech," they'd answer.

"But what did he *say?*" Jinx would ask impatiently.

They'd think and think, and by and by Eeny would say: "We—e—ell, let me see; I guess it was about the advertising appropriation for 1931, wasn't it, Eek? Mr. Hooker wanted to use some of the big magazines, and Mr. Pomeroy said they were trying to reach children and not just people with childish minds, and then Mr. Bashwater made a long speech, and—well, I don't know, but it was a swell speech, anyway." And so the animals knew just as much as they did before they had asked.

But sometimes the captain took the mice down into the smoking-room where the sailors went to have what they called a nightcap before going to bed, and here they learned two very important things. The sailors sat in a big half-circle before the roaring fire, each with a cup of tea or a glass of hot milk in his hand, smoking and telling stories and munching on cookies and little sweet crackers. But all the stories were of three kinds: they were about whales, or about ghosts, or about buried treasure. When Ferdinand heard of this, he said: "H'm" several times very thoughtfully, and then he flew up on to the big chandelier in the Present Room and stood on one leg and put his head under his wing and meditated for nearly an hour.

The mice didn't think very much about it, because Ferdinand always said he was meditating when he did this, but they knew that usually it was only another way of saying that he was taking a nap. But that evening the crow called them together in a corner of the Present Room.

"I want you to tell me," he said, "just what kind of ghost stories the sailors tell."

"Scary ones," said Eeny; and Quik said: "Awful scary ones." And Eeny said: "Mostly they're about figures in long white sheets that wail, and sometimes they're about voices that come out of the darkness, or about things that creep up behind and jump."

"H'm," said Ferdinand. "All these things take place at night, I suppose?"

"Oh, yes; late at night," said Cousin Augustus. "Goodness, I wish they wouldn't tell so many of them. I used to like to run round at night; all mice do. But now whenever I'm up after twelve, I hear footsteps coming after me and at every corner see giant cats with phosphorescent eyes."

"H'm," said Ferdinand again. "That certainly gives me an idea." So he went back and meditated again for a while, and then he called a meeting and told the animals about his plan and what he wanted each of them to do. "Go to your rooms at the usual time," he said, "just as you always do. But don't go to bed. And on the stroke of midnight we'll all meet here, and if those sailors stay here after tonight—well, my name isn't Ferdinand."

XIII
The Animals
Play Ghosts

EVERYONE in The

big palace was sound asleep when the animals came one by one into the Present Room. The midnight adventure was so exciting and so funny that they laughed and whispered together until Ferdinand's "Ssssh!" quieted them. "Now no giggling," he said severely.

"You know this is a serious business. It may seem like a joke, but it isn't. All ready?"

They stole down a long corridor, through an archway and across a wide court, and then up a winding stair towards the sailors' wing. Halfway up the stair they became aware of a continuous steady murmur, which rose and fell rather like the distant roar of surf on a rocky coast. It was the sailors snoring.

"My goodness," said Mrs. Wiggins, "we don't have to be very quiet."

"We'll have to do a little groaning first, to wake them up," said Ferdinand. "Mrs. W., you and the bear can do that better than the rest of us. Go up and groan outside the doors. And the rest of you be getting your costumes on and your things ready."

So the cow and the bear went up into the long hall with its many doors, behind each of which two sailors were asleep, and began to groan. They groaned low at first, but they couldn't even hear themselves above the snoring. Then they groaned louder, and louder still. And still the snoring went on uninterrupted. Even when Mrs. Wiggins let out a good full-throated bellow, it made no impression at all.

The animals didn't know what to do. "We can't scare 'em if we can't wake 'em up," said Bill.

"I can wake 'em up," said Charles. "If I crow, they'll think it's morning." So Charles crowed, and the snoring died down like the sound an airplane makes when it leaves the earth and disappears slowly in the sky, and the sound of sleepy voices came from the rooms: "Hey, Bill, time to get up." "Wake up, Ed." "Why, it's only half past twelve." "What's that noise?" "'Tain't morning yet." And so on.

Then the six largest animals, who had dressed themselves in sheets and had false faces on, each opened one of the doors and stood on their hind legs and walked into the bedrooms, while the other animals in the hall made all the frightening noises they could think of, only not so loud that their voices would be recognized.

As soon as the sailors heard the noises and looked towards the doors and saw the tall sheeted figures with their ferocious goblin faces coming slowly towards them, they all let out terrific yells and pulled the bedclothes up over their heads. They pulled them up so hard that their bare feet were uncovered, and the animals came up to the beds and gently nipped the sailor's toes with their teeth. Then the sailors all yelled again and tumbled out of the beds and tried to get under them. But as the beds weren't very wide, there wasn't quite room for two underneath, so the sailors fought each other and tried to push each other out into the rooms. And while they were doing that, the animals went back into the hall and closed the doors softly behind them.

Mr. Pomeroy slept in a room at the head of the stairs with Mr. Bashwater. Now, each of the animals had scared two sailors, and as each sailor yelled twice, you will see that there were twenty-four yells in all. And twenty-four yells, from sailors whose throats have been toughened by the gales of the seven seas, are loud enough to wake up the soundest sleepers. So they woke Mr. Pomeroy and Mr. Bashwater.

Mr. Pomeroy came to the door and opened it. Directly in front of him he saw a huge white form whose wildly grinning face was topped by two horns. He didn't know that the form was his old friend Hank, or that the two horns were Hank's ears, for which holes had been cut in the sheet. He fell backward with a scream into the arms of Mr. Bashwater, who, as soon as Mr. Pomeroy's fall gave him an unobstructed view of the door, also fell backward, and there they lay on their backs inside the door, Mr. Pomeroy's head on Mr. Bashwater's chest.

But these two were of sterner stuff than the other sailors, and as soon as they had mustered up courage to open their eyes and saw that the door was closed and the dreadful apparition had vanished, they got up, and Mr. Pomeroy went to the speaking tube that connected his room with Mr. Hooker's, and blew in it.

Mr. Hooker and the boatswain, Joel, slept on the floor above, and Mr. Hooker had had the speaking tube put in so that, if any orders that he wanted to give the men occurred to him in the night,

They pulled them up so hard that their bare feet were uncovered.

he could tell Mr. Pomeroy and have them carried out right away. So in a moment the captain's sleepy voice said hello.

"Hello, captain," gasped the mate. "Guess you'd better come down here. There's a demon or an ogre or something out in the hall; he's about ten feet high and he's got teeth as long as your hand, and I think he's et up about half the crew accordin' to the noise they been makin'."

"Eh?" said the captain incredulously. "Come, come, Mr. Pomeroy, this is no hour for jesting."

"Jesting!" exclaimed the indignant mate. "You come down and look at him and you'll see how much jest there is to it."

It took some time to convince Mr. Hooker that there was really something wrong, but when he had talked to Mr. Bashwater and found that his description of the demon agreed with the mate's, he said: "All right, all right, my men. Just wait till I get my cutlass and pistols. I'll soon settle his hash for him. Demon indeed! Cuttin' up didoes with my crew! I'll show him."

The animals were rather scared themselves now, and they retreated into the stairway. Pretty soon they heard the clump, clump of the captain's heavy sea boots coming along the corridor. "Where is he?" roared the valiant captain. "Show me your ogre! Bring on your demons! What's a demon to me? What's ten demons? Me that's fought a galleyful o' Barbary pirates to a standstill single-handed! Me that's been a mate o' Blackbeard an' Teach! Me that's tamed the wild rhinoceros till he'd eat sugar out o' my hand, an' strode into the dens o' the Bengal tiger with no weapons but my fingers and my teeth! Trot out your terrors; let's see your ten-foot-high man-eaters! Let old Hooker git his hands on 'em once, and he won't leave nothin' of 'em but a couple o' teenty weenty grease spots on the floor that ye can mop up with a lady's pocket-handkercher."

So roared the captain as he clumped down the hall, and the animals, thoroughly frightened, crowded in the stairway, not daring to move. He came to the head of the stairs and peered down. "Are you down there, demon?" he shouted. "Come up an' rassle; come up an' git a taste o' old Doc Hooker's demon-medicine. Ye won't, hey? Well, I spose I'll have to come down to you, then."

Now, among the false faces the animals had found in the Present Room was a particularly villainous-looking Chinese mask, and Freddy had touched it up with some radium paint so that it glowed fearsomely in the dark. Cowering with the other animals in the stairway, he had kept it hidden until the captain threatened to come down. But at that threat fear overcame all the animals, and with one accord they turned to run. Someone pushed Freddy, and to keep his balance he threw up the hand that held the mask. At the same moment Cousin Augustus's nerve gave way and he had hysterics.

Hooker, peering down the dark stairs, heard a strange tiny voice, a sort of whimpering squeak, and at the same moment was confronted by the baleful ferocity of the Chinese mask. He gave a yell— a louder yell than had yet been heard that night—dropped his cutlass, and, turning quickly, dashed back towards his room at top speed. What he did when he got there nobody knew, for he was not seen again that night, but there was a lot of dust on his coat at breakfast next morning—the kind of dust that is seldom found anywhere but under beds.

For a moment the animals were silent. Then they burst into a roar of laughter. "Good old captain!" they shouted. "'Trot out your terrors,' eh? 'Me that's tamed the wild rhinoceros!' It's 'Me that's run from a mouse squeak,' I guess. Can you beat that? He was scareder than any of 'em."

"That's all right," said Ferdinand. "We've done fine. But there's something still to do. There's one we haven't scared, and that's Joel. We've got to scare 'em all, you see. If there's one that hasn't been scared, he'll be brave, and he'll shame all the others into being brave and staying too. But if they're all scared, they'll all want to leave."

So they went upstairs to Joel's room. The captain's yell had awakened Joel and he was sitting up in bed. Mrs. Wiggins got up on her hind legs, pulled her sheet around her, opened the door, and groaned. But the boatswain didn't yell and pull the covers over his head. He just said pleasantly: "Ah! A ghost. Come in, ghost. I've always wanted to see a ghost. Come in and sit down." And he got up out of bed and politely offered her a chair.

Mrs. Wiggins didn't know what to do. The boatswain wasn't scared at all, but she thought that if she walked slowly towards him, it might scare him, so she tried that. Unfortunately the sheet that she wore was so long that it trailed on the ground, and as she moved towards the bed, she tripped on it and fell across the chair, smashing it into kindling wood.

Joel just smiled. "That's queer," he said. "I thought ghosts didn't weigh anything." Mrs. Wiggins scrambled to her feet and dashed out of the room, slamming the door behind her.

Out in the hall, Ferdinand was very angry. "You must have done something wrong," he said. "It ought to be easy to scare him; he isn't half so brave as the captain."

But Mrs. Wiggins was angry too. She had heard the other animals snicker when she fell over the chair. She tore off her sheet. "All right," she said. "I'm going to bed. You can scare him yourself if you're so set on it. I've had enough monkeyshines for one evening."

She was just starting for the stairs when the door opened again and Joel, in a long white nightshirt, appeared on the threshold with a candle in one hand and a pistol in the other.

"Well, upon my soul!" he exclaimed, looking from the crumpled sheet on the floor to Mrs. Wiggins. "It was the cow all the time, and not a ghost at all! Dear, dear! I have no luck at all! I did so want to see a ghost!" Then he looked round at the other animals, who still had their costumes on, and his face brightened. "But perhaps these are really ghosts," he went on. "Well, there's one sure way to find out. All the storybooks say that when you shoot at a ghost, the bullet goes right through him and he doesn't even notice it." And he pointed the pistol straight at the bear.

The animals weren't sure whether he really meant to shoot or not, but they weren't taking any chances, so immediately they began pulling off their sheets and throwing aside their false faces. Then, looking very much crestfallen, they filed off down the hall to the stairs. Joel watched until the last of them had disappeared; then he went back to bed.

The animals did not blame Mrs. Wiggins for the failure of their plan. After all, she had done the best she could, and it was not her fault that Joel was not afraid of ghosts. But they knew that it wasn't any use trying to scare the sailors anymore. Joel would tell his story, and the sailors would be ready for them the next time, and they would get the worst of it. They would just have to think up something else.

The sailors, fortunately, took the joke in good part. They thought the animals had been very clever to play such a trick on them. Mr. Pomeroy and Mr. Bashwater were a little ashamed of having been so frightened, and they tried to get even by hiding in dark corners and jumping out and shouting "Boo!" when any of the animals went past. As for the captain, he explained a dozen times a day that he had known all along that the ghosts were just animals dressed up, and that when he had run away he had only been entering into the spirit of the thing. "I just pretended to be scared," he said. "That's what you should have done, Joel. Trouble with you is you don't know how to play. If somebody put a jack-o'-lantern on your porch Halloween night, you'd just go out and kick it to pieces. That's no way to act. Let 'em have their fun, I say."

XIV
The Flight of Hooker

FREDDY had Taken

very little interest in the schemes for get-

ting rid of the sailors. He seemed to care

for nothing but eating and sleeping and writing poetry. He had grown

very fat, and as soon as a meal was over, he would go up to his room and lie down on the couch and take a nap. Then he would get up and lounge about and work at his verses or read until time for the next meal. His friends could seldom get him to go out skiing or coasting.

"You *ought* to get some exercise, Freddy," they would say. "All that fat can't be healthy." And they would tell him stories of pigs they had known who got so fat they burst.

But Freddy would just laugh. "Never felt better in my life," he would reply. "Being fat's no disgrace. Look at all the famous men who have been fat."

"But you used to be so slim and elegant and handsome," they would protest.

"Handsome is as handsome does," Freddy would say. "And if it's a choice between being handsome and a second helping of chocolate layer cake, I'll take the cake every time." And to clinch the point he would take a chocolate bar from the drawer of his desk and bite off a big piece.

One day he was sitting at his desk when Jinx pushed open the door and walked in. Any other animal would have knocked first, but Jinx's manners were never very good, for he had been badly brought up. His mother had been a handsome but very vain tabby, who spent hours keeping her fur soft and sleek, but let her kittens, of whom there were seven besides Jinx, grow up just any way. So he really couldn't be blamed for his rudeness.

Freddy frowned. "Tut, tut, Jinx," he said. "I'm glad to see you, of course, but you *must* learn to respect people's privacy. Don't you ever knock on doors?"

"Ho!" exclaimed the cat. "If I'm in the way—"

"Nonsense!" put in Freddy. "Don't be so touchy. It's all right with me. But others might not understand, and—"

"Oh, lay off, old boy," said Jinx, throwing himself down upon the sofa. "And tell us the news. I haven't seen you, except at the dinner-table, for a cat's age."

"Oh, I've been busy," said Freddy. "I tell you, Jinx, it's no easy thing being a poet. You fellows think I just dash these things off, but I tell you there's hours and hours of solid work behind every verse I turn out. Take this little thing here," and he handed a sheet of paper to his friend. "I've slaved over it until the perspiration has fairly dripped off my face."

"You could do with a little sweating," said the cat, eyeing the stout figure that filled the easy chair from arm to arm.

"That's as may be," said Freddy. "But read it out to me, will you? I'd like to hear how it sounds."

Jinx read the poem aloud.

> Contented with my earthly lot,
>   My soul rejoicing sings
> Until I gaze into the sky—
>   Then through my mind there rings
> That saddest of all earthly thoughts:
>   Why do not pigs have wings?
>
> When unimportant birds and bugs
>   And bats and other things
> Can soar and wheel and flit, and know
>   The joy that flying brings—
> Why is the pig denied the air?
>   Why do not pigs have wings?
>
> My feet must stay upon the ground
>   In all my wanderings.
> Yet still desire fills all my heart
>   With anxious questionings—
> If even men have learned to fly,
>   Why can't this pig have wings?

"Do you like it?" asked Freddy anxiously.

"Very pretty," said the cat. "How in the world you think of all these things I don't know."

"'Things,'" repeated Freddy absently. "That's a rhyme I didn't use—Eh? Oh, you asked how I think of them. Why, they just come to me," he added modestly.

"But do you really want to fly?" asked the cat.

"Fly? Goodness, no! Why should I?"

"But that's what your poem was about."

"Oh, you don't understand," said Freddy. "That's just something I wanted in the poem, not something I really wanted. I just made myself think I wanted it so I could have something to write about."

Jinx stretched and yawned. "Well, that's beyond me. But I don't understand poetry anyway. Give me good old prose every time. Take that book I was reading yesterday, *Treasure Island.* All about pirates and buried treasure and fighting. That's some book, Freddy."

"I don't get time to read as much as I ought to," said the pig. "What's the book about?"

"I'm just telling you. There was a map—it's printed in the front of the book—that showed where some pirate treasure was buried, and a lot of these sailors were after it. Men like Hooker they were, old pirates. And then some people got it—"

But Freddy was not listening any more. Jinx went on telling the story, but the pig had picked up a pencil and was drawing something on a piece of paper.

Presently Jinx broke off and said: "Hey, you aren't listening!"

"Eh?" said Freddy, looking up. "Oh no, I'm sorry, Jinx. But what you said gave me an idea. Look here: if we draw a map like the one in that book and leave it where the sailors will find it, we'll get rid of them for good."

"Get rid of them?" said Jinx, who was sometimes rather slow. "How?"

"Why, we'll make a map of one of those islands off the coast of Florida, and we'll mark on it 'Gold here' or 'Treasure buried here' or something like that. You know the mice say that buried treasure is the one thing they're always interested in. If they find such a map, ten to one they'll go off to find the treasure."

As soon as Jinx got the idea, he became very enthusiastic. He went down and got the copy of *Treasure Island* he had been reading, and he and Freddy carefully drew a map something like the one in the book. They put a red cross in the middle of the island, and under it they wrote: "Dig here." They decorated the map with pictures of ships and sea serpents, and at the bottom they wrote: "This is my private map of the island where my treasure is buried. There are 400 lbs. gold, 2 qts. pigeon-blood rubies, I pt. diamonds, $1\frac{1}{2}$ gals. emeralds, 3 bushels mixed jewels. Packed in neat canvas containers, convenient for handling. (Signed) Capt. Kidd."

"That ought to fix 'em," said Jinx, and he and Freddy sneaked up to Hooker's room and put the map where they were sure he would find it, between the leaves of the copy of *Alice in Wonderland* that was on his bedside table. He had a mark in at page six, and they put the map in at page eight, because although Mr. Hooker was a very slow reader, they felt sure he would at least turn the page that night.

They said nothing about their plan to the other animals, so that if it didn't come off as they expected it to, nobody but themselves would be disappointed. But they told the mice, so that if the map dropped out of the book without being noticed, they could draw the captain's attention to it.

At a quarter of twelve that night Quik came rushing down to Freddy's room. He called frantically to the gently snoring pig and even tried to shake him, but it was rather as if a man should attempt to shake the Woolworth Building. Freddy just snored on. But the mouse was desperate, so he climbed up on the bed and bit his friend sharply in the ear.

The snore ended in a squeal and a kick and a flop that brought the terrified pig out into the middle of the floor, all wrapped up in the bedclothes. Quik was thrown into the wastebasket, and he stayed there until Freddy had stopped fighting with the bedclothes and shouting: "Help! Murder! Somebody's stabbed me! " Then he crawled out and turned on the light and apologized for having been so brutal.

"But I had to wake you, Freddy," he said. The captain's going away."

"Going away?" said Freddy. "That's what we wanted him to do. But couldn't you tell me in the morning instead of—"

"He's going away alone, secretly," said Quik. "After he put us to bed, we followed him back to his room. He got into bed and opened the book to read, and the map fell out. He picked it up and looked at it carefully and said 'Oho!' several times, and then he got up and started towards the speaking tube that goes to Mr. Pomeroy's room. He was evidently going to tell Mr. Pomeroy about the map, but then he changed his mind and began dressing. He went to the speaking tube several times, but each time he shook his head and went back to his dressing. Then he buckled on his pistols and cutlass and put the map and his toothbrush and shaving things and flute and bottle of hair-dye and a couple of fairy-tale books in a little suitcase and took his boots in his hand and tiptoed downstairs."

"Good heavens!" said Freddy. "I never thought he'd go alone! He's going to try to sneak off and get the treasure all for himself! That isn't what we want at all! Go find which way he's gone, Quik, and I'll wake the others. We'll meet in the Present Room."

It took some time to wake the other animals and explain to them what had happened, and by the time they were dressed and had gathered in the Present Room, it was nearly one o'clock, and Quik had come back and reported that Mr. Hooker had harnessed up four of the reindeer to Santa Claus's sleigh and had driven off.

Ferdinand looked very grave when he heard this. "We can't possibly catch him," he said. "Those are Santa Claus's special reindeer— the ones he uses Christmas Eve to deliver presents. They're specially trained and they're faster than anything on earth, even a fast automobile or an airplane. I'm sure I don't know what Santa Claus will say, and Christmas is only two days off."

"How could we stop him even if we did catch him?" asked Hank. "He's got his pistols. He wouldn't stop for a few animals."

"Oh, we could tell the reindeer that Santa Claus wanted them to come back," said Freddy. "They'd turn round and come back then whether Mr. Hooker wanted them to or not."

"Won't they know enough to come back anyway before Christmas Eve?" asked Robert. "They know Santa Claus can't deliver his presents without them.

"I doubt it," said Ferdinand. "Reindeer aren't over-bright, and if they think about it at all, they'll just decide that if Santa Claus hadn't wanted them to go, he wouldn't have let Mr. Hooker take them."

"Well," said Jinx at last, after they had all argued for some time without coming to any conclusion, "maybe we haven't any chance of catching up with him. I'm going to do *something*."

"So am I," said Freddy. "Go get into your furs, Jinx. Meet you in the yard."

The two animals bundled up warmly and hurried out to the stable where the rest of the reindeer were kept. With some difficulty they managed to hitch up one of the reindeer to a small sleigh that was sometimes used for racing, and started out.

They had explained to the reindeer what had happened, and had promised him an extra slab of moss—which is what reindeer eat—for his dinner, and he galloped along at a good speed, although they knew that far ahead of them Mr. Hooker must be going three times as far with every stride. The tracks of his sleigh disappeared in the darkness ahead of them, lying as straight on the smooth snow as if drawn with a ruler, and the only sound was the light thudding of the reindeer's feet and the hiss of the runners gliding over the frozen surface.

"There's one chance I count on," said Jinx. "From what the mice said, the captain didn't take any food with him. He was probably afraid of waking somebody up and having to explain if he went down to the pantry. But if I know Mr. Hooker, he won't go far without stopping for food. Never saw such a man for food. He'll stop at the first igloo he comes to."

"Igloo?" said Freddy sleepily.

"Yes, one of those huts the Eskimos make out of snow and live in. You've seen 'em time and time again."

"Oh yes, of course," said the pig. The warmth of his robes and the silence had made him sleepy, and as they went along, he murmured drowsily:

> *"Oh, kindly give a mew*
> *When you see the first igloo.*
> *I'm awfully sleepy, it's true,*
> *But I'll wake up when you do,*
> *And the captain we pursue*
> *We'll take back to his crew,*
> *And as heroes then we two*
> *Will drive up the avenue*
> *And be greeted—"*

"Oh, for goodness' sake, shut up!" said Jinx. But Freddy's head had fallen forward on his chest and he was asleep.

They drove on for a long time without seeing anything but snow, and the tracks of the captain's sleigh stretching across it, and at last even Jinx was beginning to nod, when the reindeer said: "Hey! Wake up! I see something ahead."

Their four eyes opened with a jerk, and, sure enough, ahead of them was a dark mass which they made out to be a sleigh, and as they approached and drew up abreast of it, they saw that one of the reindeer was lying on the snow, and the captain was vainly endeavoring to get him to his feet.

Hooker stood up and stared at them. "Hey," he said. "What's this—cats and pigs? You animals certainly do beat all, riding around in cutters just like folks! But tatter my tops'ls if you ain't come at just the right minute! " He stepped over to the side of their sleigh." Out you go," he shouted, and, seizing Jinx in his right hand and Freddy in his left, he pulled them out, dropped them in a heap on the snow, then tossed in his suitcase, leaped in, and, smacking the reindeer on the back with the flat of his cutlass, drove off in a whirl of snow.

"He'll beat me if I don't go," called back the reindeer over his shoulder. "But I'll go as slow as I dare."

"Well," said Jinx, when they had got to their feet and brushed off the snow, "we aren't much better off than we were, but at least we've got Santa's sleigh back for him." He went over to the reindeer who was lying on the ground. "What's the matter?" he asked.

"I was lame when we started out," said the reindeer. "My leg just gave out. Santa was trying to get it cured up by Christmas, but I guess I can't go out with him now. I can't walk on it."

"H'm," said Jinx thoughtfully. "We've got to catch the captain if we can. No use trying to unhitch you four and then hitch up three of you. The harness is too complicated for us. Tell you what we can do, though, Freddy. I think I can manage to get the harness off, and then if you're game to ride bareback, we can take two of the reindeer and follow Hooker. We can leave you here for a while, can't we?" he asked the lame reindeer. "We'll come back for you."

"Oh, sure," said the other. "I'm perfectly comfortable. Go ahead. Hope you can catch him. We'd never have taken him in the first place if we'd guessed he wasn't going on Santa Claus's business."

With a good deal of trouble they managed to get the harness off, for Jinx's claws were cold, once he took his gloves off, and Freddy's trotters were of little use. Then the reindeer had to kneel down so they could get on their backs, and off they started.

In the first mile Freddy fell off eight times, and Jinx five. Then Freddy had the idea of getting the reindeer to hold their heads back so their antlers came close to their backs. This gave something to hold on to, and after that they made good speed. It was great fun.

The reindeer went like the wind; their hoofs made no noise on the snow; and in a short time Hooker was again in sight ahead of them.

"Better slow up," said Freddy. " It's no use catching up. We can't do anything yet."

So the reindeer slowed down to an easy trot, and after another hour or so they saw a little group of conical snow houses in the distance.

"Eskimos," said Freddy. "Bet you he stops to eat." And, sure enough, Hooker pulled up at the door of the largest igloo, and soon his sleigh was surrounded by a crowd of fur-clad men, women, and children.

They had hoped that he would get out and go into the igloo, but pretty soon they saw the Eskimos bringing out things for him to eat. "We'd better get up close," said Jinx. "We've got to do something now, or we'll never stop him."

Freddy slipped down from his reindeer. "I've got an idea," he said. "Edge up as close as you can, and if you see that he has caught sight of me, drive right up close to the sleigh and distract his attention."

The pig, looking in his fur coat for all the world like just another fat, roly-poly little Eskimo girl, slipped unnoticed into the crowd and worked his way forward until he was close to the captain, who at that moment was reaching out the other side of the sleigh to take a large frozen fish that one of the men was handing him. Quickly Freddy reached in behind Hooker's legs under the seat and dragged out the small suitcase. If he had had hands to carry it with, he would have got away without attracting attention. But he had to take it in his mouth, and he had only wormed his way to the edge of the crowd when several of the women caught sight of him and set up a high shrill screaming. Of course they had never seen a pig before, much less a pig in a fur coat and cap, walking on his hind legs, so it is no wonder they were frightened.

Freddy ran as fast as he could to where his reindeer was kneeling down so he could get aboard. But Hooker had seen him too and had leaped from the sleigh and was pounding after him. Then Freddy tripped and fell, and the suitcase was flung several yards in front of him. He picked himself up, but it was too late to recover the case—Hooker was bending to take it up. Freddy swung himself up on the reindeer, who got up at once and started off.

But Jinx had been watching. He had moved in closer, and now he leaned forward and whispered something in his reindeer's ear. Just as Hooker bent over and reached out his hand, the reindeer, with Jinx on his back, trotted up and with a swoop of his head snatched up the suitcase on the prong of his horn and galloped triumphantly away. At the same moment, at a shout from Freddy, the reindeer that was hitched to the sleigh also galloped off, and Hooker was left alone in the Eskimo village. As they headed back north at top speed, Jinx looked over his shoulder. The captain, surrounded by a crowd of wondering Eskimos, was dancing up and down in fury, shaking his fists after the vanishing animals. Then, just before the distance got too great for Jinx to see what was going on, Hooker snatched off his hat, flung it on the ground, and jumped on it with both feet.

XV
Christmas Eve at Santa's

IT was Late in the afternoon when Jinx and Freddy finally got back to the palace. Santa Claus laughed until the tears ran down his fat red cheeks when he heard their story.

"I don't know what I'll do when you animals leave me and go

back to your homes," he said. "We've always had a good time up here on the top of the world, but since you've been here, it has been twice as much fun. Well, well, the poor old captain! I should like to have seen his face! But I'm afraid it serves him right for taking the reindeer without my permission. I must send out and bring Blixen in, I suppose. I'm sorry his leg has given out, for tomorrow night is Christmas Eve, and there isn't another reindeer I can put in his place on the sleigh. They're fairly fast, some of them, but they're not sure-footed enough, and a reindeer has to be sure-footed to keep from falling when he gets on some of those steep, snow-covered roofs."

"Why couldn't you put Uncle William in his place, sir?" asked Freddy. "He's fairly fast for a horse—of course nothing like your reindeer, but he used to be in a circus, and from what he's told us about the tricks he had to do, I'm sure he'd have no trouble in keeping his feet on the steepest roof."

"Why, that's a fine idea, Freddy," said Santa Claus. "I never thought of it. I did think Bill might do, because a goat is used to climbing; but he's so much smaller than the reindeer that I'm afraid he'd look funny hitched up with them. The children wouldn't like it if Santa Claus came with three reindeer and a goat. Well, now, why didn't I ever think of that? You two go in and get something to eat; you must be pretty hungry. And ask Uncle William to come out and see me."

Freddy and Jinx went in and ate a huge lunch, and then they took Mr. Hooker's suitcase up to his room. But before they left it, they took out the map. "We mustn't leave that here," said Jinx. "He'll just try to get away with it again if we do."

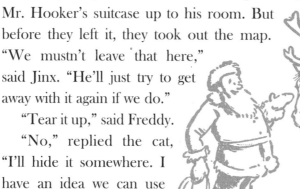

"Tear it up," said Freddy.

"No," replied the cat, "I'll hide it somewhere. I have an idea we can use it yet."

Freddy and Jinx went in and ate a huge lunch.

Late that evening an Eskimo brought the captain back to the palace on a dogsled. Mr. Hooker seemed very grumpy, and he went straight to his room without speaking to anybody. He came down to breakfast the next morning, but only answered with grunts when spoken to, and between courses sat and twirled his moustaches and glared down the long dining room at the animals. When the mice had finished their breakfast, they went over to his table, but instead of picking them up he merely glowered angrily at them, then jumped to his feet, shook his fist at them, shouted: "Traitors!" in a loud voice, and went back to his room, where he remained until lunch, playing strange wild music on his flute.

But as it was the day before Christmas, everybody in the palace was very busy, and nobody had time to wonder about the captain. The thousands and thousands of presents were stacked up in the courtyard, ready to be loaded into the sleigh and the pack that Santa Claus carries on his back. A lot of last-minute letters were being hastily opened and presents wrapped and addressed for the children who had written them. And the animals and the sailors and all the workmen in the toy factory were hanging up their own stockings and decorating trees and getting presents ready for each other. And in the midst of all this hurry and bustle, Santa Claus had found time to hitch up Uncle William with the three reindeer and give him a try-out round the yard and over the palace roofs.

"I don't see how he manages to deliver all these presents," said Mrs. Wiggins. She and Mrs. Wogus were wrapping up some dog-biscuits in red paper to put in Robert's stocking.

"It isn't really as much work as it looks," said Mrs. Wogus, "though it's enough, land knows! I've had it all explained to me. You see, he tries to deliver all the presents as near twelve o'clock as he can. When it's twelve o'clock in New England, it's only eleven in Ohio, and out on the Pacific coast it's still early in the evening, and in Japan it is still noon of the day before."

"Eh?" exclaimed Mrs. Wiggins. "What are you talking about, sister! If it's twelve o'clock, it's twelve o'clock. I never heard—"

"Oh, you don't understand," said Mrs. Wogus. "I could show you if I had a globe. What I mean is, the earth goes round, and the sun comes up on New England before it does on California, doesn't it? And when it's shining on Mr. Bean's farm, it's dark in Japan, isn't it?"

"I guess so," said Mrs. Wiggins doubtfully. "It sounds all right when you say it, but when I begin to think about it, it makes my head feel funny."

"You don't want to think about it," said her sister. "You just see how it is, and then it's perfectly simple. Santa Claus delivers his presents in New England at twelve o'clock. An hour later he gets to Ohio. But it isn't one o'clock there, it's only twelve. He goes round the whole world the same way. He delivers all his presents at midnight, but he has twenty-four hours to do it in."

"Oh dear!" said Mrs. Wiggins. "Don't tell me any more. You've got me all confused now. See here, are we going to give Henrietta this china egg with the forget-me-nots on it, or the bottle of Jockey Club perfume?"

"I think she'd like the perfume best. Wrap it up and I'll get a card ready. Where are the stickers?"

Mrs. Wogus didn't try to explain any more. and it is doubtful if Mrs. Wiggins ever really understood about the change of time, although she was not to blame for that, as she had never been to school and had lived all her life on a very small farm. Nor did it really matter, for she understood so many things that were more important, such as how to be nice to animals who were in trouble, and what to say to stop animals' being angry at each other.

As soon as everything was ready, Santa Claus set out. He had fastened a pair of antlers to Uncle William's head so that the horse would look as much as possible like a reindeer. Uncle William was very proud to be going with Santa Claus. It was the most wonderful thing that had ever happened to him. He had raced a good deal when he was younger, but he had never even imagined such speed as he made that night. He never knew afterwards quite how it happened, whether the reindeer pulled him along or whether there was some magic about it. His hoofs seemed to skim the snow. They sped through the forest so fast that the trees fairly whizzed backward past them, like the pickets on a fence that you pass in a swift automobile. Soon the forest was behind, and houses began to appear. A leap, and they were on a roof; Santa was out of the sleigh and down the chimney and back again in the sleigh almost before they had come to a stop—and then another leap, and in a swirl of snow they were off again. Through towns and villages and cities, up narrow mountain roads, across bridges, over cultivated valleys, along beaches where the surf broke white in the starlight, they raced, faster and faster; passing lighted trains that seemed to be standing still, though they were making their fifty miles an hour; passing speeding automobiles whose occupants caught but a glimpse of them as they hurried by and were never sure afterwards of the reality of what they had seen. After a little it was all like a dream to Uncle William; he galloped and galloped, and lights and buildings and woods and fields whizzed by in a confused mass; and he could hear Santa Claus humming a little tune to himself as he pulled the reins gently, now to the left, now to the right, to guide their flight. The horse didn't seem to get tired, either, for all the swiftness of the pace. It was too exciting, he was too proud of his part in it, to feel fatigue. And when at last he was back in the stable, and his harness was taken off and a good feed of oats was brought to him, he was sorry that it was all over.

"Splendid work!" said Santa Claus, patting him on the shoulder. "If it weren't for you, there'd be a lot of unhappy children tomorrow morning who'd be wondering why I'd forgotten them. And you never slipped once. Even I lost my footing on that steep slate roof in Minneapolis, and if I hadn't caught hold of the chimney, you'd have had to dig me out of the snowdrift at the side of the house." He shook with laughter. "That's happened to me more than once, I can tell you. You'd be surprised at some of the things that have happened. Once I fell through a skylight right into a bed where four children were trying to keep awake so they could see me when I came down the chimney. They saw me all right, and felt me. I nearly squashed them."

"You must have had lots of funny experiences," said the horse.

"I have. I'll tell you about them some time. But now I think we both want to get to bed. There'll be lots of eating and excitement tomorrow, and we want to be rested."

Christmas at Santa Claus's palace was, as you may imagine, nothing but fun and happiness for all the animals and people under that generous roof. It would take much too long to tell of the presents they exchanged, and the turkeys and plum puddings and mince pies and candy they ate, and the games they played. Even Mr. Hooker recovered from his anger and disappointment sufficiently to eat an enormous dinner—for which he dressed in full pirate costume—cocked hat, gold-laced coat, earrings, red sash, and all—and to play for them afterwards on his flute while they all danced.

The dancing was really worth seeing. The sailors danced hornpipes and jigs; the ship's carpenter, Mr. McTavish, put on kilts and danced a Highland fling; Mr. Bashwater did the harpooner's jig, which is something like the gimpus dance, with many complicated figures; and even the captain finally consented to do his famous and very graceful dance to Mendelssohn's *Spring Song,* for which he wore a leopard-skin and a green wreath, and carried a basket of artificial crocuses. The animals danced too, mostly old-fashioned round dances. Mrs. Wogus in particular turned out to be a really fine dancer. Her polka was quite astonishing.

Late in the evening, when the merriment was at its height, there was one unpleasant incident. One of the sailors, a greedy and ill-tempered man named Pell, was complaining about the present his roommate, Mr. Osnip, had given him. "It's all very well to talk about the Christmas spirit," he was saying. "But Jim Osnip hasn't got it. He just simply hasn't got it, that's all! Why I gave him a swell ivory manicure set, and what did he give me? A couple of miserable little guest-towels.

Why, they're not even linen! And look, here's the price tag—he didn't even take it off—nineteen cents! What kind of a present is that to give your mate?"

Some of the sailors had gathered round, and Mr. Bashwater said: "Why, Pell, I think those are very nice towels. Jim hasn't got very much money, you know, and he's spent a lot of time embroidering your monogram on them. See here—"

"I don't care about that at all," said Pell crossly. "What I say is—"

But just then Mr. Osnip himself pushed through the ring. "You don't like 'em, eh?" he said." All right, give 'em back. Here's your old manicure set. Give me those towels!" And he started to pull them away from his friend.

But Mr. Pell didn't really want to give up the towels, so he hung on to them, and they tugged and pulled until at last one of the towels gave way and tore down the middle, leaving Mr. Pell lying on his back with half a towel in his hand, and Mr. Osnip lying on *his* back with a towel and a half in *his* hand.

The disturbance had brought everyone together in that corner of the Present Room. Freddy had been upstairs fixing up something on his typewriter, and now, as he came down with a sealed envelope in his mouth, Jinx came up to him and said: "You're just in time. Now's the time to give it to him."

Freddy nodded and pushed his way through the crowd. Mr. Hooker had just taken matters in hand and was scolding the two sailors, who stood before him blushing and with downcast and shamefaced looks. The pig stood on his hind legs and offered the envelope to the captain.

"What's this?" said Mr. Hooker.

The sailors all looked over his shoulder as he turned the envelope over in his hands. "It says something on it," said one of them.

"Eh? So it does. 'The contents of this letter are of interest to the officers and crew of the *Mary Ann*.' H'm, wonder what can be in it."

"Why don't you open it and find out?" suggested someone.

"That's an idea," said Hooker, and tore open the envelope. Out dropped a folded paper.

Hooker had recognized it immediately as the treasure map, and he stooped to snatch it up before anyone else should see what it was. But Mr. Osnip was quicker, and in a few moments every sailor in the room knew what it was and they all crowded closer about the captain, who, realizing now that it was useless to try to keep it for himself, and knowing that the animals could not give him away, pretended that he had known what it was all the time.

"It's a little surprise I've had in store for you for some time, men," he said. "I found this several days ago, but I knew if I told you about it then, you'd want to start right away to hunt for the treasure, so I thought I'd wait until Christmas was over. Santa Claus would have been hurt if we'd left before Christmas. And then I thought it would make a nice Christmas surprise for you. It's my Christmas present to all of you."

At this there was a burst of prolonged cheering. "Hurray! Hurray! Three cheers for Mr. Hooker! And for Captain Kidd's treasure!"

"Now what I think we ought to do," went on the captain, "is to pack our suitcases and set out tonight. We don't want anybody else to get to the treasure ahead of us, and although it has been where it is for over a hundred years, you never can tell how much longer it may stay there. We don't know how many other maps like this are in existence. So get your stuff ready, and then say good-bye to Santa Claus, and don't forget to thank him for the nice time you've had and for all the nice presents, and we'll get on our way."

After another fit of cheering the sailors scattered to their rooms to pack.

"Well, I guess we fixed that all right," said Freddy.

"I'll say we did," replied the cat. "They've forgotten all about reorganizing Santa Claus's business already. He'll be pretty glad, I bet."

"Yes," said Freddy, "but I expect we'd better tell him about the map."

"I suppose we ought to," replied Jinx.

So they went into Santa Claus's study and told him the whole story.

Santa Claus was not at all angry with them, and he was amused at their cleverness, but he looked at the same time rather worried. "I'm pleased that you've taken so much trouble for me," he said, "and it's true that I'd be glad to have the sailors go. They are nice men and I like them, but their ideas about business are very upsetting. I thought at first that their way of doing things might make my work here easier, and in some ways it did, but I think, after all, I prefer the old-fashioned way of doing things. Everybody was happy, and, after all, that's the main thing.

"Nevertheless I don't see how we can let them go like this. It isn't really quite honest, is it, to let them take a long, hard journey, and spend months of their time hunting for something that we know doesn't exist?"

"No—o—o," said Freddy slowly. "I don't suppose it is. But—"

"There isn't really any 'but' about it," said Santa Claus. "You agree with me, you see. I think we'll have to tell them."

"Oh, but, gosh!" protested Jinx. "Excuse me, sir, but I mean, isn't there anything else we can do? Don't you know of any real treasure they could hunt for? If we could only—"

"Wait!" exclaimed Santa Claus. "That gives me an idea, Jinx. It certainly gives me an idea! Our objection is that there isn't any treasure on the island you drew the map of, isn't it? But suppose we put a treasure there, eh? Suppose I harnessed up the reindeer and drove down there and planted a treasure for them to dig up? That would fix it, wouldn't it?

The animals were delighted with this scheme. But when it came to carrying it out there were some difficulties. On the maps they had made a list of the treasure: four hundred pounds of gold and several bushels of precious stones. "I'm a pretty rich man," said Santa Claus, "but even I couldn't get together as big a treasure as that. Still,

I guess we could arrange that. The main thing is that they shan't be disappointed with what they find. I'll get together enough valuables so they'll all have plenty of money to live on comfortably for the rest of their lives. And then I'll drive down there and bury it in a day or two. Ah, here they come to say good-bye to me," he said, as the thump of heavy sea boots was heard outside in the hall.

"We oughtn't to be staying much longer ourselves," said Robert as the animals stood in the courtyard and waved good-bye to the sailors, who straggled out of the gate, each with a suitcase bulging with the presents he had received in one hand, and a handkerchief in the other which he turned to wave every few steps, for they were all sorry to go.

"I suppose you're right," said Hank. "Mr. Bean is probably pretty worried about us, although Santa Claus told me the other day that he'd sent him a letter to say that we were all right."

"Well, for my part," said Henrietta, "I'll be glad to get back. I've got my children to bring up, and my work to do—goodness knows what state that coop is in now, for Leah's a good girl, but she's no housekeeper. And all this traipsing round the country and having a good time is all very well, but I was brought up to think that work was of some use in the world too. And I expect you were too, Hank."

"Yes, I expect I was," replied the horse, "though I don't think a little fun ever hurt anybody."

"A *little* fun—certainly. But there's been nothing but fun and games and cuttin' loose for months. Now I say it's time we sobered down and did some work."

"Oh, you and your work, Henrietta," said Jinx, who was the only one of the animals who ever dared talk back to the hen. "You make me tired. Loosen up and shake a leg once in a while. Do a little dance or sing a song or turn a somersault or something. It'd do you good. And what work are you going to do here?"

"There's work enough waiting for all of us at home," she said crossly.

"Sure, but home's a long way off. In the mean time why not have what fun you can? Not just be an old sour face."

"Humph!" grunted the hen. "Who cares what an old bald-headed cat says! If you'd—"

"Oh, come," said Hank, "let's not quarrel. Listen! The sailors have stopped and they're singing *Good night, Ladies*."

The sound of the song floated to them through the cold air from where, far off now on the broad snow-field, the sailors were grouped about their captain, who was leading them with his flute. They sang the song, gave a final cheer, waved their handkerchiefs once more, then turned and plodded on out of sight.

But Freddy took up the tune. "Good-bye, sailors," he sang,

"Good-bye, sailors,
Good-bye, sailors,
We're glad to have you go.
Merrily you slide along, slide along, glide along,
Merrily you glide along
O'er the deep white snow."

XVI
The Ride Home

I'LL tell **You** what I'm going to

do," said Santa Claus. They were sitting

around the fire after dinner, two days

after the sailors had gone. "I know you animals feel you ought to

be getting back home, so I'm not going to try to keep you. But it's a long trip on foot back to Mr. Bean's farm. Now, out in the stable is a big sleigh that we use sometimes for sleighride parties. It will hold twenty-five people, so I guess it's big enough for you all to be comfortable. I'll hitch up a dozen or so of the racing reindeer to it and take you all back home. Of course we won't go so fast as I can go with the little sleigh on Christmas Eve, but we'll make better time than an automobile could, or even a train. And you'll be home to celebrate New Year's with the Beans."

The animals said at first oh no, they couldn't think of having him go to all that trouble, and it was asking too much, and so on; but he had made up his mind. So the next morning they packed up and went out into the courtyard, where the sleigh was waiting. Santa Claus sat on the driver's seat with the twenty-four reins of red leather in his hands, and Ella and Everett, one on each side of him; and the animals packed themselves in and burrowed down in the warm straw in the body of the sleigh, and they set off.

For the first hour or so nobody said much of anything. They all felt rather sad at leaving the pleasant little bedrooms and all the come forts they had enjoyed, and they had already begun to miss the jolly meals in the big dining room and the long, happy days playing games outdoors and in the Present Room, and the cosy evenings about the fire, when they talked quietly and Santa Claus told stories. But after a while their spirits revived and they laughed and sang and joked as the winter landscape raced past them, and the steel runners whined over the snow.

At the end of the first day they camped by the little lake on which stood the house where Ella and Everett had once lived. When supper was over and they were all gathered about the big fire of

wood that they had collected in the forest, Santa Claus walked across the frozen lake to the house and rapped on the door.

"Come in, come!" called a harsh, impatient voice.

He opened the door and walked in. There beside the table sat Kate and Pete, Kate busy with some sewing, Pete studying his grammar. They both looked up and scowled.

"Good evening," said Santa Claus pleasantly. "You're Kate and Pete, I suppose?"

"Yeah," said Kate, "just for the sake of the argument, I suppose we are, and I suppose you're Santy Claus."

"That's just who I am, as a matter of fact," replied the saint.

"Oh, sure," said Kate, "and I'm Cinderella, and this is my friend the King of the Cannibal Island, and—"

"Suppose we see what the gentleman wants," interrupted Pete.

Kate scowled more deeply than ever, but she stopped talking, and Santa Claus said: "I came to speak to you about Ella and Everett, who used to live here."

They both jumped up at that, and Kate said eagerly: "You seen 'em? You know where they are?"

"Yes," Santa replied, "they're safe and comfortable. But they're not coming back here. You're not fit to look after those children, and so—"

"Oh, we aren't, hey?" demanded Kate furiously, looking round for her broom. "Well, let me tell you something, Mr. Whatever-your-name-is. If you've got them children, you bring 'em back here quick, if you want to keep out of trouble. There's a law in this country against kidnappers, and if you don't watch out, you'll find yourself in jail." She turned quickly on Pete. "Why don't *you* do somethin'? You're a man, ain't you? Tell him he's got to bring them children back. Don't just stand there and take all his sass."

"'Sass' is not in Webster," remarked Pete. "And I suggested before that we listen to what he has to say. Then if it is necessary, I shall do something."

"Very sensible," said Santa Claus. "I think you will be satisfied with what I have to say." He fumbled under his coat and drew out a fat pocketbook, from which he counted down on the table a number of bills.

"This money," he said, "is yours if you give up all claim to the children."

Kate put her hand over the money before she had counted it. "'Tain't enough!" she shouted. "Tryin' to buy my dear children from me that I cherish like the apple of my eye! You old varmint!"

"'Varmint,'" said Pete, "is a colloquialism not generally used in polite circles. And suppose we count the money." He proceeded to do so. "Very generous, I think," he said.

But Kate was not satisfied. "'Tain't enough!" she repeated. "Double it! Double it or get out!"

"Oh, very well," said Santa, reaching for the money.

But at this Kate backed down. "Well," she said, "perhaps I was a mite hasty. I love them children like the—"

"Like the apple of your eye," said Santa Claus. "Quite so. And now that that is settled, I wish you a very good evening."

As he closed the door, he heard Kate shout: "Gimme them bills!" and Pete replied: "'Those' would be more correct usage." And then there was a sound of whacking. Kate was using her broomstick.

They slept by the lake that night, and the next morning, bright and early, they were off again. Pretty soon the woods gave way to farming country, and then larger and larger villages appeared. At noon they whizzed across the long bridge over the Saint Lawrence River so fast that the customs men never even saw them go by, and then they were in the United States again. By four o'clock they were nearly home, and they were all leaning out excitedly and pointing out to each other familiar landmarks.

"Here's Centerboro," they shouted, as the snowy road plunged down a hill and between a long double line of big elm trees that bordered the main street.

Nobody paid any attention to the shrill whistle that was repeated several times as they passed the Town Hall, but a block or two farther on a tall man with a silver star on the breast of his overcoat sprang out into the path of the swiftly approaching sleigh. "Stop!" he shouted. "Stop, I tell ye!"

Santa Claus sawed on the reins and brought the reindeer prancing and snorting to a stop in a smother of flying snow.

"It's a speed trap," said Hank. "They catch a lot of autos going too fast in the summertime, I've heard."

"But they can't stop Santa Claus!" exclaimed the other animals.

The man, who had a very red face and a little beard that waggled when he talked, came up to the side of the sleigh. "You stop when I tell ye to!" he shouted angrily. "You fellers seem to think ye own the county, so ye do. But I'll show ye! I arrest ye for breakin' the speed limit, and ye're comm' with me to the Jestice of the Peace."

"The speed limit is for automobiles," said Santa Claus. "This isn't an automobile."

"Is that so!" replied the constable. "Goin' to give me an argument, be ye? Come along here all dressed up in a red suit with the out-landishest rig I ever see in my born days, and give me an argument, me, Henry Snedeker, that's been constable in this town since before you was in long clothes. Well, I arrest ye fer exceedin' the speed limit, and fer disturbin' the peace, and fer—"

He stopped suddenly and his mouth fell open, and he began edging away in alarm. He had been standing close to the side of the sleigh, but had paid no attention to its occupants. The animals were all getting angry, and at last the bear leaned over the side and put his nose close to the constable's face and gave a deep bass growl.

"What ye got in there, animals?" demanded the constable. "A menagerie, eh? A circus! Ye can't operate a circus in this town with-out a licence. I arrest ye for operatin' a circus without a licence, too."

The anger in his voice was somewhat mixed with fear now, but he still stood his ground, and began lugging an old-fashioned horse-pistol out of his pocket.

"I'll go to the Justice of the Peace with you," said Santa Claus, "if you'll tell me where he is. If you only want to make a speech, I'm going on, for I'm in a hurry."

"You'll go on when I tell ye to," replied Mr. Snedeker. He tried to cock the ancient pistol, but it had rusted so badly that even when he put the butt on the ground and held the barrel in both hands and tried to force back the hammer with his foot, he had no success. And while he was still struggling with it, the bear jumped out of the sleigh, seized him about the waist in his powerful grip, and tossed him in among the other animals, who promptly sat upon him.

Santa Claus laughed heartily. "Now," he said, "if you'll tell me where the Justice of the Peace lives, I'll drive there, and we'll have this settled."

"An' I arrest ye for assault an' battery," the muffled voice went on from the bottom of the sleigh, "an' fer unprovoked attack, an'—"

"The Justice of the Peace is three doors down, on the right," said Hank. "But why don't you just let us throw him out in the snow and go on, sir? They'll probably fine you and delay you half a day."

"No," said Santa Claus, "that would be breaking the law. We don't want to do that. I can fix it all right." And so he drove on and was presently ringing the Justice's doorbell.

The door was opened by a little old woman in black, and Santa entered and the animals trooped after him, the bear carrying the still protesting constable.

The Justice of the Peace was a small dried-up little man in black, with steel spectacles pushed up on his forehead. He rose from behind a black-walnut desk where he had been taking a nap. "What's this—what's this?" he spluttered as the strangely assorted crowd pushed into the room. "What's the meaning of this, sir?"

The constable, released by the bear, told his story. "They were going at least fifty miles an hour," he said.

"We were going at least a hundred," put in Santa Claus.

"What, what, what?" exclaimed the magistrate. "You *admit* going at such a dangerous rate of speed?"

"Certainly," said Santa Claus.

"Twenty-five dollars," said the magistrate. "Now as to these other charges—assault and battery, obstructing the public highway, operating a menagerie without a licence, illegal entry, arson—"

"Wait a minute," said the saint. "I haven't had time to commit all these offences. I've only been in your town about three minutes."

"That will have to be proved," said the Justice of the Peace. "Your name?"

"Santa Claus."

The magistrate stared at him. "You are choosing a poor time to joke," he said severely.

"Perjury and contempt of court," said the constable.

"Nevertheless, that *is* my name," said Santa Claus.

"Well, well," said the Justice of the Peace, "it's possible, of course. Let it pass. Somebody else *might* have that name. Age?"

"Eight hundred years, roughly," replied the saint.

"Eight hun—Say, look here, mister," burst out the constable, "you'll get eight hundred years in jail—'roughly' too—if there's any more of this. Your honor—"

"Yes, yes, yes," said the magistrate testily, "take him off to jail, Henry. Maybe a night in the town cooler will make him see sense."

"One moment," said Santa Claus. "I have given you my right name and my right age. I can prove it to you in three minutes."

The constable and the magistrate looked at each other with raised eyebrows, and the constable winked. There was a silence through which the voice of the little old woman could be heard complaining. "All these nasty animals traipsing through my clean front hall and tracking up the floor with their great muddy feet!"

"All right," said the Justice of the Peace. "I'll give you three minutes."

"Good," said the saint with a smile. "We'll take you first, Constable Henry Snedeker. You're about sixty-five years old. On the 23rd of December fifty-six years ago you wrote a letter to Santa Claus asking for a jackknife. You got the jackknife in your stocking, along with two oranges, a jumping jack, two Jackson balls, and a stick of peppermint candy. Am I right?"

The constable fell back against the wall. "Consarn ye!" he exclaimed in angry amazement, "ye are Santa Claus after all! And to think of all the things ye've stuffed in my stocking when I was a little shaver, and I go and arrest ye fer speedin'! Well, sir, I'll be dosh heckled!"

But the Justice of the Peace was not convinced. "Come, brace up, Henry," he said. "You know your memory ain't what it was. How do *you* know what you had in your stocking fifty-six years ago? Every boy has had a knife and those other things given him at some time. Your memory's playing you tricks."

"No," said Santa Claus, "Mr. Snedeker's memory is remarkably clear. Now, your honor, I will refresh yours. Your name is Philemon Prendegast. You're sixty-eight years old. When you were fourteen, your sister, who let us in and is now standing there in the doorway, was ashamed of you because you still played with dolls. On Christmas Eve 1876 I put in your stocking, as you had requested, a French doll with long yellow—"

"Stop, stop!" shouted the magistrate, jumping to his feet with a very red face. "You're crazy! Get out of here, all of you! Out, out! Your fine is remitted—"

The constable had doubled up with laughter in a chair. "Dolls!" he roared. "Ho! That's a good one, that is! Wait till the boys down to the store get hold of that one! Old Squire Prendegast playin' with—" He choked on a howl of merriment, and the bear had to slap him on the back before he could get his breath back.

The little old lady in black had come forward and bobbed an old-fashioned curtsy to Santa Claus. "I'm very pleased to meet you," she said. "To think of all the Christmas Eves I sat up and held my eyelids open with my fingers so I could get a glimpse of you, and now I see you for the first time. You always came after I had dropped off to sleep. But, sir, please don't say anything about Philemon and the dolls to anybody else. 'Twan't his fault he played with 'em, and anyway—"

"Anyway it wasn't any harm," interrupted Santa Claus. "You're quite right. I shan't say anything about it to anybody. And Mr. Snedeker," he added, turning to the constable, who was wiping his eyes, "I think, if I were you, I wouldn't say anything about it either. I never threaten, but I know you're pretty fond of peace and quiet in your home, and it would be too bad if those active little grandchildren of yours should get a lot of drums and whistles and tin horns next Christmas, wouldn't it?"

The constable looked somewhat crestfallen. "I s'pose 'twould," he said. "Gosh, there's little enough happens in this town, and then a good story comes along and I can't tell it. But I won't. I promise you, sir."

So Santa Claus said good-bye to the Prendegasts and Mr. Snedeker, and they went out and got into the sleigh and drove on. And in fifteen minutes the sleigh was the center of a shouting, happy mob of animals in the Beans' driveway, and Mr. and Mrs. Bean had shaken hands with Santa Claus and hugged all the animals and kissed the children and patted the reindeer and accepted Santa Claus's invitation to come up to the North Pole and spend next Christmas with him. And Mr. Bean had made a short speech.

It wasn't a very good speech, for Mr. Bean was not a practised public speaker; indeed, he wasn't much of a private speaker either, and sometimes a whole day would go by without his having said anything but" Please pass the potatoes," or something like that. But his speech was very much appreciated. First he thanked Santa Claus for having taken such good care of the animals, who, he said, were the finest lot of animals on any farm, in any county, in any state, in the whole country. There weren't any words, he said, to express how glad he was to have them back. And they'd brought back with them, he said, the one thing he and Mrs. Bean had always wanted—the two children. Now, he said, they had something to work for and bring up and leave the farm to.

And then he took off his hat and threw it up in the frosty air and gave three cheers for everybody, in which Santa Claus and the children and the animals all joined, and then he lit his pipe and hoisted Everett on his shoulder and stumped off into the house to show the little boy a model of a windmill that he had once carved with his jackknife. And Mrs. Bean showed Santa Claus into the parlor and gave him yesterday's Centerboro *Gazette* to read while she was getting supper ready. And the animals showed the bear his new home, and then all went into the cow barn for a good long gossip. And everybody was thoroughly and completely happy.

And as there is very little to write about either people or animals when they are thoroughly and completely happy (except to say that they *are* thoroughly and completely happy), this is the end of the story.

—but at that moment Freddy came to grief

FREDDY THE DETECTIVE

I
Freddy's First Case

IT was **H**ot. When Alice and

Emma, the two white ducks, got tired of

diving and swimming about in the pond,

they climbed out on the bank and looked over toward the house where

Mr. Bean, the farmer, lived, and: "Oh!" said Emma, "the house looks as if it was melting. All the straight lines—the roof and the door and the walls—are wiggling. Look, Alice."

"It always looks like that when it's hot," said Alice.

"Well, I don't like it," said Emma. "It makes me feel funny in my stomach. I think things ought to stay what they are, even if they *are* hot. Let's jump in again and cool off."

Alice looked at the water without much interest. It wasn't a very large pond, and in it were three cows and two horses and a dog and on the bank were half a dozen other animals who were resting after their clip. "Too much company," she said crossly, or as crossly as she could, for she was really a very mild duck. "I don't know why they call it a *duck*-pond. Just as soon as warm weather comes, every animal on the farm seems to think he has a perfect right to use it as a swimming pool without so much as saying please. And just look at that, Emma!" she exclaimed. "What chance would you and I have in there now?"

Two of the cows, Mrs. Wiggins and Mrs. Wurzburger, were having a race across the pond and back. They splashed and floundered and snorted, making waves that would have upset the stoutest duck, while the animals on the bank cheered and shouted encouragement.

"Come on, let's take a walk," said Emma. "Let's find a place in the shade where there's a breeze. That water's just as hot as the air is, anyway."

They waddled up the lane toward the house, and in a corner of the fence they came upon Jinx, the black cat, who was lying on his back with all four paws in the air, trying to keep cool.

"Hello, ducks!" he hailed them. "Gosh, you look nice and cool!"

"Well, you don't," said Alice. "I should think you'd stifle, lying in that breathless corner. Why don't you come with us? We're going to look for a breeze.

"Whoops!" shouted Jinx, jumping up with a bound. "I'm with you, girls. Tell you what: we'll go find Freddy. That pig'll be in a cool spot, you bet. He knows how to be comfortable better than any other animal on this farm."

Freddy was indeed a very clever pig. It was he who had organized the animals on Mr. Bean's farm into a company, known as Barnyard Tours, Inc., which took parties of other animals on sightseeing trips. He knew how to read, and he had gathered together quite a library of the books and magazines and newspapers that different animals had brought in to pay for their trips with. He kept them in a corner of the pigpen which he called his study.

The ducks knew that even if Freddy wasn't in a cool spot, he would have a new bit of interesting gossip, or some story he had just read, to tell them about, so they started out to find him.

"Have you heard about Everett's train of cars?" asked Jinx as they walked along.

"No," said the ducks. Everett and his sister, Ella, were the two adopted children of Mr. and Mrs. Bean, whom the animals had rescued the year before from a dreadful place where they had been living in the North Woods. Because they had rescued them, the animals all felt a great interest in Ella and Everett, and they were fond of them too, so no two children ever had a better time. The ducks taught them to swim and the horses taught them to ride and the cat taught them how to climb and to move through the woods without making a sound, and Ferdinand, the crow, had even wanted to teach them how to fly, but of course that wasn't much use, because they didn't have any wings. But there were always animals to play games and do things with, and they certainly had as good a time as any children who ever lived.

"Well," said Jinx, "it's the funniest thing I ever heard of. When Everett went to sleep last night, the train was beside him on the bed. When he woke up this morning, it was gone. Mrs. Bean has looked all over the house, and I've done some looking on my own account. But it's gone; there's no doubt about that."

"Well, that *is* queer," said Emma. "You don't suppose he hid it himself, as a joke?"

"Oh no, not a chance. He's been looking everywhere all morning.

He's very fond of that train. I'd like to get my claws on the one that took it!" the cat exclaimed fiercely.

"Mercy!" exclaimed Emma with a slight shudder. "I wish you wouldn't glare like that, Jinx. Alice and I didn't have anything to do with it."

"No, no; of course you didn't," replied the cat soothingly. "Imagine a duck being a burglar!" He laughed heartily.

But the ducks turned on him indignantly. "Well, I guess we could be burglars if we wanted to!" said Emma. "I guess we're not as poor-spirited as you seem to think!"

"I guess not, indeed!" put in Alice. "Look at our Uncle Wesley! I guess you know what he did, that time when that big old elephant escaped from the circus at Centerboro and tried to take a bath in our pond. He chased him off the place!"

"Oh sure!" said the cat. "Sure I remember." Jinx remembered how the elephant had laughed, too, when pompous little Uncle Wesley had ordered him out of the pond. But he didn't say anything to the ducks about that. "Well, anyway," he went on, "I think it's a shame, and we ought to do something about it—though it's too hot to do anything about anything today," he added, and stopped to wipe the perspiration from his whiskers with a forepaw.

They walked round the house and down the road to the fence where the farm ended; then they walked back along the fence to the woods and across the back pasture, but saw no sign of Freddy.

"It's funny," said Jinx. "I felt sure we'd run into him. Let's sit down under this tree and rest awhile."

"You can if you want to," said Emma, "but I started out to find Freddy, and now I'm going to find him." Like all ducks, she was very stubborn, and when she had made up her mind to anything, nothing could stop her.

"Oh, all right," said the cat good-naturedly. "Only it's so hot. Let's try the pigpen. Maybe he's in his study."

But he wasn't in the pigpen, and he wasn't in the stable or the cow-barn.

"He must be puttering round in the woods somewhere, then," said Alice. "Maybe he's calling on Peter." Peter was the bear whom the animals had brought back from the north the year before, and who now lived in a cave in Mr. Bean's woods.

"It'll be cooler in the woods, anyway," said Jinx. So they went back across the pasture and plunged into the green silence of the trees.

It was very still in the woods, and  very dark after the glaring sunshine outside. They walked slowly along, calling:

"Freddy! Hey, Freddy!" every now and then. Jinx liked the woods, but the ducks began to get a little nervous. "I don't like this," said Emma. "It's so dim and still, and I feel as if something were following us. There! Did you hear that?" She stopped, and they all looked back over their shoulders, for somewhere behind them a twig had snapped.

"Nonsense!" said Jinx. "There's nothing here to hurt you. Come along."

"Mmmmm," said Emma doubtfully, "I don't like noises behind me. Uncle Wesley always said: 'When you're out walking and hear noises behind you, it is better to go right home.'"

"But you're with *me*!" said Jinx.

"Oh, all right," said Emma. "We know you won't let anything catch us"; and they went on.

But the ducks were very nervous, and they walked with their heads turned round so far backwards that they were continually tripping over roots and stones, and even Jinx began to feel a little uneasy, particularly as his ears, which were sharper than the ducks', told him that someone really was following them. He wasn't afraid for himself, for there was no animal in these woods that could hurt him, but he thought it might be a fox, and there's nothing a fox likes better for supper than a nice plump duck.

He was about to suggest that they turn back when Alice suddenly gave a terrified quack and tumbled over in a faint.

"Good gracious!" exclaimed Emma. "She must have seen something that frightened her terribly. She hasn't done that in I don't know when. No, no; there isn't anything you can do. She'll be all right in a minute. Just keep her head low. Dear me, I wish we were out of here!"

"We'll go right back," said Jinx, who was supporting the swooning duck in his paws. "There! She's coming round now. Well, Alice, you did give us a fright! What was it you saw?"

Alice's eyes opened slowly. "Where am I?" she murmured; then as she remembered, she scrambled to her feet. "There!" She pointed with her bill. "Right behind that clump of bushes. There was a face, with a long pointed white nose—" She broke off and shuddered violently. "It gave me such a turn!"

"You wait here," said Jinx. "I'll show him!" And he crouched low on the ground and crept noiselessly toward the bushes.

As he came close to them, the ducks saw him gather himself together, then spring clean over the bushes. There was a commotion among the leaves, a snarl, a shrill squeal of fright, and out into the open dashed Freddy with Jinx on his back. The cat was cuffing the

pig soundly about the head, but as they came near the ducks, he jumped down, and Freddy stopped, shook himself, and looked about him ruefully.

"You didn't have to be so rough, Jinx," he complained. "I wasn't doing any harm."

"You scared Alice, here, into a faint," said the cat angrily. "What on earth were you trying to do—play Indian?"

"I'm sorry, Alice," said Freddy. "I really didn't mean to scare you. I didn't think you saw me. I was just shadowing you."

"Shadowing!" said Jinx. "What's that?"

"Oh," said Freddy importantly; "it's a term used by detectives. It means following you to see what you're up to. I'm going to be a detective, and I was practicing."

"Well, I don't know what a detective is, said Emma, "but you can just try it on somebody else next time. I think it's mean of you to scare us like that. You even scared Jinx."

"You did *not!*" said the cat quickly. "But you were trying to, and I'm going to get even with you for it, Freddy. I'm—"

"I wasn't; honestly I wasn't, Jinx," protested the pig. "Look here; I wasn't going to tell anybody about it, but I'll let you three in on it to make up for giving you such a scare. I got the idea from a book I found in the barn, *The Adventures of Sherlock Holmes.* It's the best book I've come across in a long time, and you'll admit I know something about literature. I'll venture to say that there isn't a pig in the country has a finer library or a wider knowledge of—"

"Oh, cut out the hot air, interrupted Jinx rudely, "and let's have the story."

"Well, it's this way," said Freddy. "This Sherlock Holmes was a great detective. Whenever a crime was committed, and nobody knew who committed it, they'd call in Sherlock Holmes, and he'd find the criminal."

"But how did he find him if nobody knew who he was?" asked Alice.

"Because he was so clever," Freddy replied. "Maybe the criminal would leave footprints behind, and then Holmes would find out who made them. Oh, he was a wonder! He saw little things about people that nobody else would notice, for one thing. He could look at you and tell about where you'd been and what you'd been doing, just by noticing these things. Why, I'll show you how it's done; it's easy when you know how. Look at Jinx, here. Look on his back. There are a lot of little pieces of grass and leaves in his fur. This is a piece of a leaf off a raspberry bush. The only raspberry bushes on the farm are around the fence up by the house, so we know he's been there. Then—how did they get on his back? Well, it's a hot day, and cats sometimes lie on their backs to get cool, so we can be pretty sure he has been sleeping on his back in the corner of the fence up by the house."

"Gosh, that's pretty good, Freddy," said Jinx.

"It really isn't so good," said Freddy modestly, "because I saw you sleeping there. But of course I could have told that you had been there anyway, as soon as I saw the leaves in your fur."

"But what were you following us for?" asked Alice.

"Why, just what I've been telling you. I was shadowing you. I was practicing being a detective. I followed you all around the farm. I didn't mean you to see me, of course. If I'd been a good detective, you wouldn't have known anything about it. I was trying to see what you were up to."

"Why didn't you ask, then?" said Emma.

"Detectives don't *ask*!" said Freddy impatiently. "*Can't* you understand?"

"No, I can't. You were taking such a lot of bother to find out something we'd have told you right off. We were just looking for you!"

"He means that he was pretending that we were criminals," Jinx explained. "Of course if we had been, and we'd been going to steal something, we wouldn't have told him. It wouldn't be any use to ask then. See?"

"Oh," said Emma, and Alice said: "Oh," in just the same tone. And then they both said in their little flat voices: "Let's go back."

Jinx winked at Freddy. They were very fond of the ducks. Alice and Emma were the kindest-hearted little creatures in the world, but it was useless to try to explain anything to them that they didn't already know about, and even with things they knew about they sometimes got terribly mixed up.

They waddled along happily together, their fright entirely forgotten, and Jinx and Freddy followed them, talking about detectives. Freddy told one or two of Sherlock Holmes's adventures out of the book, and Jinx was greatly interested. By and by he said: "Look here, Freddy, I forgot all about it in the excitement, but there's a job for a detective on this farm now." And he told about the missing train.

Freddy was all enthusiasm. "I'll get on the job right away," he said. "I'll find that train, you bet! There are a lot of mysteries on a farm like this and I'll solve 'em all. Maybe I can write them up in a book: 'The Adventures of Freddy the Detective.' And this'll be the first one. Freddy's First Case."

"If you find the train," said Jinx.

"Oh dear," said Freddy mournfully, "I like you, Jinx, but why do you always have to say things like that? Of course I'll find it."

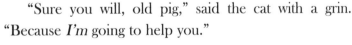
"Sure you will, old pig," said the cat with a grin. "Because *I'm* going to help you."

II
The Rats Defy the Law

"THE first Thing to do," said Freddy, "is to Visit the Scene of the Crime."

The smaller animals always helped Mrs. Bean with the house-

work, and were in and out of the house a good deal all day, so when

Jinx and Freddy went in the kitchen door and up the back stairs, Mrs. Bean merely glanced up from the peas that two rabbits were helping her shell and said: "Be careful of those stairs, animals. They're pretty steep. I don't want you should hurt yourselves."

The children's room was the front bedroom over the porch, next to Mr. and Mrs. Bean's. Jinx started to walk across the floor, but Freddy stopped him. "Please don't disturb anything," he said, "until I have finished my investigation."

"Oh, I'm not disturbing anything. What's the matter with you?" demanded the cat.

"You're disturbing the clues," replied the pig testily. "All crimes have clues, and if you follow the clues, you find the criminal."

"If I knew what clues were, I'd know better what you were talking about," said Jinx.

But Freddy did not answer. He was being a detective for all he was worth. He went very carefully over the floor, and then he examined the bed and the window-sill, and finally he got a tapemeasure out of Ella's little sewing-basket and measured the height of the sill and the distance from the bed to the window and several other things. Jinx sat down by the door and watched, trying hard to look superior and sarcastic. But it's hard to look superior and sarcastic all by yourself when nobody's paying any attention to you, so after a while he gave it up and went to sleep.

A little later he woke up again. Freddy was standing looking out of the window, wrapped in thought. "Well," said Jinx, "found any of those—what do you call 'em?—clues you were looking for?"

"I have," said Freddy importantly. "What's more, I know who stole the train.

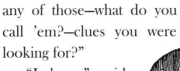

The cat jumped up. "Gosh, Freddy, do you really? Who was it?"

"I'll tell you in a minute. Let me ask you a few questions, first. I want to get my case complete. Now, was this window open last night?"

"I suppose so," replied Jinx. "They all sleep with their windows open. Mighty unhealthy habit, I call it, but—"

"And the door was shut, I suppose," interrupted Freddy.

"Sure. I was around the house on and off all night. I know it was shut."

"Did you hear any noises last night?"

"That's a foolish question," said the cat. "I always hear noises, every night. There are some noises that go on all night, like the clock ticking and Mr. Bean snoring, and then I heard the wind going around the house, and the furniture creaking, and—"

"No, no," interrupted Freddy impatiently, "I mean unusual noises. Think carefully now."

"H'm," said Jinx thoughtfully, "why, let's see. I heard one thing I don't usually hear. Those four flies that sleep on the kitchen ceiling— I caught one of them this morning, by the way—they woke up and got quarreling about something in the night. Of course that's not exactly what you'd call a noise; even I could hardly hear it. And then, there *was* something, it seems to me. What was it? I just faintly remember—Oh, I know! It was a couple of thumps."

"Thumps?"

"Yes. Outside somewhere."

"What kind of thumps?"

"Oh, I don't know. Just thumps. I thought maybe it was some of those coons from over in the woods. They're always playing monkeyshines at night. But I was too sleepy to go look."

"Ah," said Freddy, "I thought so. Well, my case is complete without that, but it all hangs together very nicely. A very nice piece of detective work. See here, Jinx. I'll show you just how I solved the case. Here's the first clue I discovered. We'll call it Exhibit A. What do you make of that?"

There were some scratches on the white paint of the windowsill, and in several of them were traces of green paint. Jinx looked at them, sniffed of them, and said: "Ah! Just so!" because he couldn't think of anything else to say.

"That doesn't mean anything to you?" asked Freddy.

"Yes, yes. Quite!" said Jinx hastily. "Green paint. Very significant."

"I'm glad you follow me," said Freddy. "Now for Exhibit B." And he took Jinx over to the bed and showed him half a dozen very fine, very short, dark gray hairs on the pillow.

Jinx looked at the hairs, but when he sniffed at them, he sniffed so hard that he blew them on to the floor.

"Hey!" shouted Freddy. "Be a little careful, can't you? You're destroying the evidence! We need those for our case."

"Case of what—measles?" said the cat contemptuously. "Say, look here, Freddy; are you trying to kid me, or are you just plain silly? You talk about those little old gray hairs and that green paint as if you'd found a pitcher of cream. If this is all there is to your detective business, I'm going. I know lots of better ways of having fun than—"

"Oh, wait a minute!" exclaimed the pig. "Gosh, Jinx, I thought you *understood* what it meant. You *said* you did. Look here. Those cars in the train are painted green, aren't they? Well, what does that paint mean, then? It means that the cars rubbed on the windowsill when the thief was taking them out of the window last night, doesn't it?"

"H'm. I see what you're getting at," said Jinx.

"All right," went on Freddy. "Now, what kind of hairs were those I showed you?"

"Those hairs? I don't know. Just hairs."

"Oh, use a little sense! Were they Ella's? Or Mrs. Bean's?"

"No, of course not. Hairs like that—why, I suppose they might be cat hairs."

"Where is there a gray cat in this neighborhood?" asked Freddy.

"H'm. Mice, then," said Jinx. "No," he added, "they're too coarse for mouse hairs. But—rats!" he exclaimed suddenly. "By George, they're rat hairs, Freddy! Well, of all the nerve!"

Jinx was really very much upset, for the presence of a rat in the house was against all the rules. When Jinx had first come to the farm, several years earlier, there had been a family of rats living in the house, and several of them in the barn. When Jinx had ordered them out, they had just laughed at him, but Jinx was a brave and stalwart cat and a fierce fighter, and after several battles in which the rats had got much the worst of it, they had met him one night under a flag of truce and had agreed that if he would let them alone, they would all move down into the woods and would not enter either house or barn again. Until now they had kept the agreement.

"I can't believe it," said Jinx. "Those are rat hairs, all right, but there's only one way a rat could get into this room. He couldn't climb up the porch. He'd have to come in the door. And the door was shut all night. I don't believe any rat would dare come in during the daytime and hide."

"He wouldn't have to," said Freddy. "Look under the bed, Jinx."

The cat went under the bed and came out in a moment looking more worried than ever. "A fresh rat-hole!" he exclaimed. "Yes, there's no doubt about it. But it must have been a job to get that train of cars out of the window. I suppose they pushed them out and then got out on the porch roof and pushed them over the edge."

"And those were the thumps you heard," said Freddy. "Now come outside. They couldn't have carried the cars off. Each car is as big as a rat, as there were four of them and a tender, all fastened together. They must have dragged them, and we can probably find where they dragged them to."

In the big flower-bed in front of the porch six or seven squirrels were hard at work, pulling out weeds and raking with their claws and then sweeping the dirt smooth with their tails.

"Hey, Bill," called Freddy to the largest squirrel, who seemed to be the foreman, "come here a minute. I want to ask you something."

Bill dusted off his paws, growled to the other workmen to "keep busy, now, and no loafing while my back's turned," and came over to the pig.

"I suppose, Bill, you've heard about this train of cars that's missing, haven't you?" asked Freddy.

"Couldn't very well help it, sir," said the squirrel. "Everybody's talking about it."

"Well," said the pig, "we have reason to believe that the thief took it out of the window and pushed it off the roof. Now, I wonder if when you started work here this morning, you noticed any traces of where it fell into the flower-bed?"

"That I did, sir," replied the foreman.

"That's what it must have been, though I didn't think of it at the time. A leaf was broken off one of those big cannas, and there was a big dent in the dirt, just where—" He broke off to shout angrily at one of the workmen. "Hey, Caspar! Don't pull that up! It's not a weed! Can't I ever teach you fellows the difference between chickweed and nasturtiums? You've got no more brains than a chipmunk! Excuse me, sir," he apologized to Freddy. "You can't trust these fellows a minute. They know the difference all right, but they pretend they think the nasturtiums are weeds so they can pull 'em up and eat 'em. They like the taste."

"Quite so, quite so," said Freddy hastily. "But you were saying—?"

"Dear, dear, what was I saying?" The squirrel scratched his ear thoughtfully. "Oh, yes—right to the left, there, was where the dent was. And I remember that you could see where something had been dragged off in the direction of the barn. You can't see it now, since the dew has dried off the grass, but 'twas plain as plain. Straight down toward the barn, sir."

Freddy thanked the squirrel, and he and Jinx went to the barn, to see Hank, the old white horse.

"Ah, Freddy," said Hank, "we don't see you round here nowadays as much as we might. But I suppose you're busy with your books, reading and writing poetry."

"Oh, poetry's all right," said Freddy, "but I've got something really important to do now. I'm a detective."

"Think of that!" said Hank admiringly. "And what do you—er, well—what are you detecting today?"

"I'm on the trail of a gang of thieves," replied the pig. "They stole Everett's train of cars last night, and I believe they've brought it down here. At least, they came by here with it, and I wondered if you heard or saw anything of them."

Hank chewed thoughtfully on a mouthful of hay. "No," he said. "I don't recollect anything. Who stole it?"

Freddy said they had reason to believe it was rats.

"Rats in the house!" exclaimed Hank. "Why, that's bad for you, Jinx. What'll Mr. Bean say when he finds out?"

"I guess it *is* bad for me!" said the cat. "Darn those rats anyway! I never yet knew a rat who could keep his word! Now I'll have to begin all over again."

"Now you speak of it," said Hank thoughtfully, "I remember that I've been hearing some funny noises lately. Little rustlings and squeakings under the floor. I never thought of rats, because they'd promised not to come in here, but I ain't so sure now. Maybe they've moved back into their old quarters, where they used to live before you came."

This piece of news upset Jinx even more, for the rats had had a large establishment under the barn, a maze of tunnels and passages and underground rooms. He jumped down from the manger where he had been sitting, and went outside, followed by Freddy. "Their main entrance used to be under the foundations at the back," he said. "We'll see if it shows any signs of having been used lately."

But just as they came out the door a gray shape darted across an open space and into the shelter of a clump of weeds that grew close to the barn wall.

Jinx leaped after it. "Hey, you!" he shouted angrily. "Come out of there!" But the rat had dived down a hole and disappeared.

Jinx turned to Freddy, trembling with rage. "Can you beat it?" he demanded. "They're here all right. That was old Simon. He was their leader in all the fights I had with them. The sly old wretch! I wonder what they're up to. They wouldn't dare come back if they didn't have some pretty good scheme in their heads."

"Let's have a talk with them," suggested Freddy. "Send one of the mice down with a flag of truce. Maybe we can find out something."

So Eeny, one of the mice who lived in the barn, was sent down with a flag of truce, and pretty soon up came old Simon with two of his sons, Zeke and Ezra.

"Hello, Jinx," said Simon with an oily smile. "Long time since I've had the pleasure of seeing you. You're looking well, remarkably well for a cat. Though a little worried. Something on your mind?"

"Come, cut out the soft soap!" said Jinx roughly. "Look here, Simon; what's the big idea? I want to know what you're doing in this barn."

Simon looked surprised. "Why, Jinx—it's our old home. Our old family mansion. Why shouldn't we be here?"

"You know blame well," said Jinx angrily. "You agreed two years ago—"

"Oh yes, that agreement." Simon waved a paw airily. "You didn't really take that seriously, did you? It seemed the best way, at the time, to settle our little misunderstanding. But of course this is our home; you couldn't expect us to go live down in those damp, musty woods forever. Could you, now?"

"You certainly won't live forever if you come back to the barn," said Jinx dryly.

"Ha, ha!" laughed Simon; and his two sons laughed "Ha, ha, ha!" and smoothed their whiskers with their paws. "You will have your joke, Jinx. But come, let's be serious. It seems to us that every animal has a right to live where he wants to. We've talked it all over. All you other animals—cows and pigs and dogs and horses—have warm comfortable houses to live in. Why should the rats be the only ones to live in gloomy, unhealthy burrows in the ground?"

"Because you're thieves, that's why!" exclaimed Jinx. "I wouldn't have any objection to your living in the barn, and neither would Mr. Bean, but you steal the grain and everything else you can lay your paws on, and you gnaw holes in everything and destroy property. That's why."

The old gray rat spread out his paws.

"But we have to live! Even the humble rats have to live."

Jinx laughed a harsh laugh. "Oh, no, you don't!" he said. "Not while I've got my claws and teeth. Well," he added, "I see you've made up your minds, so I suppose it's war again, eh?"

But Simon did not seem disturbed. "War?" he said. "Why war? There won't be any war. We don't have to fight you, Jinx, to live in the barn." He grinned wickedly. "You may think we do, but we don't. Things have changed, Jinx."

"Is that so?" said the cat. "Well, I don't know what you're up to, but take my word for it, it won't last long. I give you warning—the next time I see a rat in the barn, it's good-bye, rat. And that means you, and you, and you," and he glared at each of them in turn so fiercely that they moved away a little uncomfortably.

"Well," said Simon, "if that's all you got us up here for, we might as well be going, pleasant as it is to see you again. Boys—"

""Wait a minute," interrupted Freddy. "Simon, what about the train of toy cars you stole last night?"

Zeke and Ezra looked startled, but Simon merely grinned. "So-o-o!" he said slowly, "you found out about that, did you?" There was a faint gleam of admiration in his beady black eyes. "Very clever of you, Freddy. Not that it will be any advantage to you. You'd have found out we had it soon enough."

"We expect you to give it back," said the pig. "Every animal on the farm will be sore at you if you don't. They're all very fond of Everett, and—"

"Oh, sure; they're all fond of Everett!" interrupted Zeke angrily. "He pets 'em and feeds 'em. But what has he ever done for us? And what has Mr. Bean ever done for us? Set traps and mixed poison— that's what he's done for us! Driven us out of our comfortable homes! And you think we should be nice and kind and do things for him and say 'pretty please' just because he's a man and owns this farm. Well, we're sick of men. Men are all alike, selfish know-it-alls, an. if you don't do as they say—out you go! But you just wait! You and the rest of the stuck-up animals on this farm that think you're so smart! We've got a few tricks up our sleeve yet. You wait till you see that train of cars the next time; you'll laugh out of the other side of your mouths! Just wait till—"

But here Simon interrupted him. "Come, come, son; there's nothing to be gained by violence. You must excuse him, gentlemen. My son is so impetuous. Dear, dear! I suppose we were all that way once. Ah, youth, youth! Even you were once young, I suppose, Freddy, though now you've become so stupid and fat and stodgy that no doubt you've forgotten those far-off days when you were a gay squealing piglet, and the whole world was your trough."

"I'm not old and I'm not stodgy," snapped Freddy; but Jinx said: "You're impudent, Simon. And no rat is ever impudent to me twice. I'll give you till tonight to clear out of the barn and to return that train. If by eight o'clock it's not done, then it's war! And understand me: when I say war, I mean *war*! Now, git!" And he bared his teeth in such a ferocious grin that the three rats, with a snarl, dived down the hole and disappeared.

"You know," said Freddy, as they walked back to the house, "there's really something in what they say. It must be rather hard to be driven out of your home and hunted from pillar to post."

"You have a sympathetic nature, Freddy," replied his friend. "It does you credit, but your sympathy is wasted on these rats. Nobody'd hunt 'em if they'd behave themselves. And, anyway, if all animals behaved themselves, how could you go on being a detective? There wouldn't be any crimes for you to detect."

"I suppose that's so," sighed the pig. "Perhaps I shouldn't be a detective after all, Jinx. I shall always feel so sorry for the criminals when I find them that I'll probably let them go."

"Huh, that's silly!" said the cat. "I feel sorry for those rats—yes, I do! But what'll you bet they bring back the train and leave the barn tonight?"

"I bet they don't," replied Freddy promptly. "They've got something up their sleeve, all right. Did you see how Simon stopped Zeke when he was afraid he'd say too much? No, sir! They're going to start something, and they're going to start it right away or I miss my guess. You're going to watch the barn tonight, I suppose?"

"Sure, I'll have to."

"Well, I'm going to watch with you, then," said Freddy. "You see, a detective's job isn't finished when he's found out who the criminal is. He has to put him in jail. I'm going home now to think this case over. Meet you in Hank's stall at eight o'clock." And he trotted off, stopping now and then to peer intently at the ground as if searching for further clues.

III
The Armored Train

THUNDER
rumbled
Distantly,

and the orchard trees stood out black

against the flickering western sky as Freddy

stole into the barn and made his way silently to Hank's stall.

"Hello," whispered Hank. "Jinx has gone up to take a turn around the hay-mow. We'll be getting some rain presently, I expect. I guess Mr. Bean will be glad; everything's got pretty well burned up this long dry spell. But I've known for two days we'd get a storm. I always feel it in that off hind leg of mine. Stiffened up something dreadful today."

"Sh-h-h!" hissed Freddy. "Mustn't talk. Rats'll hear."

Hank grunted something under his breath and then was silent. Freddy could hear the crisp dry swish as hay was pulled from the rack, and the slow comfortable munching that followed. The flicker of lightning was almost continuous now in the square of the open doorway, and the approaching drums of the thunder shook the windless air. Then something furry brushed against Freddy's shoulder and he jumped violently and let out a startled squeal.

"Shut up, you idiot," came Jinx's whisper. "It's only me."

Freddy was so ashamed that he couldn't think of anything to say. What would Sherlock Holmes think of a detective who jumped almost out of his skin when his friend touched him?

"I thought I heard some gnawing going on," murmured Jinx, "but I can't find anything. We'll just wait awhile."

Freddy wondered what good he would be if they did find the rats in the hay-mow. Pigs are stout fighters, but they like to fight in the open; and up there in the pitch-dark, floundering about in the hay— well, the idea didn't appeal to him much. Then he reflected that after all both he and Jinx wanted first of all to find out just what the rats were up to and where they had hidden the train of cars. There probably wouldn't be any fighting tonight.

The storm came nearer. A puff of cool air came through the doorway and blew chaff in Freddy's eyes. Between the thunder claps he could hear the *thump* of windows being put down in the house. And then with a sharp rattle, and then with a roar that was louder than the thunder, the rain came down upon the barn.

Jinx put his mouth close to Freddy's ear. "They can't hear us now," he shouted. "Let's get upstairs. I have an idea that if

anything happens, it will be up there, because that's where the big feed-box is. They'll go after those oats, and then—Wham-o!" And the cat gave his friend a joyous whack on the back.

As they reached the top of the stairs, the rain stopped suddenly. There was a moment of silence, and through it the friends heard a queer rattling noise, as if someone was dragging empty tin cans across the floor. A distant flicker of lightning lit the loft dimly, and Freddy saw something that made queer prickles travel up his spine. A long low shape was moving slowly across from the hay-mow toward the feed-box.

If it was an animal, it was the strangest animal Freddy had ever seen. It was nearly four feet long, but not more than four or five inches high. It seemed to glide along like a snake, and as it moved it rattled and squeaked, as if its insides were full of machinery.

"I'm going," said Freddy firmly, but as he backed toward the stairs, there came a sharper flash of lightning, and he saw what the strange animal was. It was the train of cars.

A train of toy cars that moves all by itself in an empty loft during a thunderstorm would make even a policeman a little uneasy. But though Freddy was scared, like all true detectives he was more curious than frightened, and he stood his ground. For a minute it was dark and they could hear nothing through the crashing thunder. Then came another flash, and as the train of cars was swallowed up again in the darkness, Jinx sprang.

Freddy waited. As the thunder died away again, he heard a rattling and banging in the middle of the floor, and then the loft seemed to be full of the squeaking laughter of rats. "He-he-he!" they giggled. "Smarty-cat Jinx! He can't catch us now!" Lightning danced over the landscape outside, and for what seemed quite a long time Freddy watched a strange battle between the cat and the train. Jinx leaped upon it, bit it, pounded and slashed at it with his paws, tried to knock it over; and all the time it moved jerkily on toward the feed-box, accompanied by the shouts and jeers of rats. Then as darkness poured into the barn again, Jinx gave up and bounded back to Freddy's side. "Back downstairs," he panted. "It's no use. We'll have to try something else."

Back in Hank's stall again, Jinx stretched out on the floor to rest, and Freddy said: "I'd have tried to help you, Jinx, but I didn't understand what it was all about or what you were trying to do. And, frankly, that train of cars, moving all by itself, had me scared."

"It had me scared at first, too," admitted Jinx. "But my eyes are pretty good in the dark, you know, and I saw what was inside the cars."

"Inside them! You mean—" A light suddenly burst on Freddy. "The rats!" He saw it all. Those four cars had wheels, but there were no floors in them, and each was big enough to hold a good-sized rat. Easy enough for the rat to get in, and then he was as safe as a turtle inside his shell.

"Of course," said Jinx. "And you see what it means. They can get from their holes to the feed-box and back, and I can't stop 'em. Of course if Mr. Bean sweeps up all the grain that's around on the floor, and stops up that hole in the side of the box, it will be harder for them. Then they'll have to get out of their armored train. But I don't want Mr. Bean to find out about it. He won't know anything about the train, you see, and he'll just think I'm no good at my job."

"But what can we do?" asked Freddy.

"Well, you're the detective, aren't you?" asked Jinx irritably. "You've done a lot of big talk about how you were in charge of the case, and so on. Oh, I admit you did a good job finding out who stole the train—you mustn't think I'm cross at you. I'm just sore about the whole business. But if you're going in for being a detective, this is your chance to get a reputation. You've got as much at stake as I have."

Freddy didn't sleep much that night. He knew what Jinx had said was so. Sherlock Holmes would have rounded up those rats and had them behind the bars in a couple of days. But he couldn't think of anything to do. He was up early the next morning, reading the stories in the Sherlock Holmes book, but the cases were all so different from his that he found nothing to help him. He went down to the barn.

"They're up there," said Hank. "Hard at it since before daylight." And indeed from where he was, Freddy could hear the rattle of the train being drawn across the floor by its crew of rats. He climbed the stairs cautiously. There it was, moving away from the feed-box. He could see the rats' feet moving as they pushed it along, and the tender was piled full of yellow oats.

"There's *one* thing I can do," said Freddy to himself, and he made a dash for the train, knocked over the tender, and spilled the grain out on the floor. But the rats only laughed. "Pooh, pooh for Freddy!" they shouted derisively. "We'll get more than that the next trip. Do you want to know how we work it, silly pig? Four of us go over and eat all we can hold. The next trip, four others go and eat all they can hold. Then, the next trip, four others go and—"

But Freddy was tearing mad. To be mocked at by rats is more than any self-respecting pig can stand. He jumped at the train and tried to get his snout under it and fling it in the air, but it was too low. He did manage, however, to push two cars over on their sides, and while the rats lay there kicking, he tried to bite them. But he only succeeded in breaking one of his front teeth on a car wheel, and before he gave up, one of the rats had nipped him sharply in the ear. Then he went back downstairs, followed by more uncomplimentary remarks than he had ever heard before at one time in his life.

Freddy felt pretty low.

IV
The Mystery of Egbert

FREDDY'S
failure
Bothered

him a good deal. The rats soon spread the news

of it far and wide, and Freddy couldn't go outside

the pigpen without meeting animals who asked him how the case was

getting on and whether he had got the train of cars back yet. "They're all very kind and sympathetic," he said to Jinx, "because nobody likes Simon and his family. But I won't get any other cases if I don't solve this one pretty quick. And from the way it looks now, it's going to take some time.

"Yes, and I'll be out of a job if Mr. Bean finds out," replied the cat. "We've got to do something, and do it now. I suppose you've heard the song the rats are singing about you?"

Freddy grunted angrily. Yes, he had heard it all right. Every time he went near the barn, the rats began shouting it out at the top of their lungs, and they used it as a sort of marching song when they trundled the train back and forth between their hole and the feed-box.

Freddy,
The sleuth,
He busted a tooth,
He's a silly old bonehead, and that is the truth.

Freddy the pig,
He talks very big,
But all that he's good for's to guzzle and swig.

Freddy the fat,
He's never learned that
It takes forty-nine pigs to equal one rat.

And there were many more verses. It was not very good, just as a song, but it irritated Freddy frightfully, and that was what the rats wanted. It would irritate anyone to have a song like that yelled at him morning, noon, and night.

"Well," said Jinx, "I'm counting

on you. There's nothing much I can do but hang round the barn and try to get a crack at Simon when he's not inside that train. Haven't you got any ideas at all?"

"Sure, I've got ideas," Freddy replied. "I'm working on the thing all the time. But you know how detectives work. They wouldn't be any good if they told everything they were doing. Everything is going satisfactorily, though a little slower than I had hoped. But I'm making as good progress as could be expected."

"Humph!" said the cat. "As good progress as I could expect from you—and that's just none at all." But he said it under his breath, for perhaps Freddy *did* have an idea—he was really a very clever pig—and it was no good offending him. Jinx needed his help too badly for that.

But Freddy really had no ideas at all. There was no good using force; he had tried that, and all he had got out of it was a broken tooth that sent his family into fits of laughter whenever he smiled. Anyway, detectives seldom used force; they used guile. He went back to his library and got comfortable and tried to think up some guile to use on the rats. And as usual when he lay perfectly still and concentrated for a short time, he fell asleep.

He was awakened by a timid but persistent tapping at the door. "Come in," he said sleepily, and then as a white nose and two white ears appeared round the edge of the door, he jumped up. "Ah, Mrs. Winnick," he said as the rest of an elderly rabbit followed the ears into the room; "long time since I have seen you. What can I do for you today?"

Mrs. Winnick was a widow who lived down by the edge of the woods. In her day she had been as pretty a young rabbit as you could wish to see, but since the loss of her husband the cares of providing for a large family had taken every bit of her time and energy. She took no part in the gay social life of the other animals in the neighborhood, and they seldom saw her, though they were good to her, and one or other of them was always taking a fresh head of lettuce or a couple of carrots down to her, for they suspected that she and the children did not always get enough food.

"Oh, Mr. Freddy," she burst out, "it's about Egbert. He's disappeared,

and whatever I shall do I don't know. He was always such a good boy, too—kind and helpful, and willing to look after the baby. With the other children it's play, play, play all day long, but Egbert—" And she began to cry.

Freddy was not greatly disturbed by her tears. Most animals don't like to cry because it makes their eyes red, but white rabbits have red eyes anyway, so crying doesn't make them look any different. And as they are very sentimental and tender-hearted little animals, and easily upset, they cry a good deal.

"Come, come," said Freddy briskly. "Just tell me all about it, and we'll see what can be done. I'm sure it's not as bad as you think. Now, do you want me to help you find Egbert?" And as she nodded tearful assent, "Well," he continued, "let's get at the facts. Let's see—Egbert. He's your eighth oldest, isn't he? Or ninth?"

"Twelfth," she replied, "and always such a good—"

"Yes," said Freddy quickly. "And when did you last see him?"

After asking a good many questions Freddy got Mrs. Winnick's story. The night before Egbert had taken several of the children up through the woods to Jones's Creek to get some watercress. At nine o'clock the children had come home without him. They had not found any good watercress, and Egbert had said that he would go farther down the creek to a place he knew where there was sure to be some, but that they must go home, as it was their bedtime, and their mother would worry. Mrs. Winnick had put the children to bed and had presently gone to bed herself. But this morning Egbert's bed was empty. He had not come home, and nothing had been seen or heard of him since.

Freddy consoled the weeping widow as best he could. "I'll get to work on it right away," he said, "and meanwhile don't worry. I'll soon have Egbert back for you. By the way, who sent you to me?"

"It was the children," said the rabbit. "They'd heard about your setting up to be a detective, and they wanted me to come and see you. Not that I have any faith in it—excuse me, sir. But you haven't been at it very long, have you?"

"No," Freddy admitted, "but there always has to be a first time, doesn't there? Even Sherlock Holmes made a start once, didn't he? Don't you worry, ma "am. I've made a deep study of the subject, and there isn't an animal in the country that knows more about detecting than I do. Why, I've read a whole book about it."

Mrs. Winnick seemed satisfied with this and went off home, stopping after every three or four hops to cry a little and blow her nose. Freddy wasted no time, but set out at once for the creek. He found the watercress bed which Egbert had visited with his little brothers and sisters, then went slowly on downstream, keeping a sharp lookout for any signs of the missing rabbit. Once he saw where some wintergreen leaves had been nibbled, and once, in a sandy place, he saw the plain imprint of a rabbit's foot, so he knew he was on the right track. And then where the stream widened out, just before it took a bend round to the right to join the river, he found another big bed of cress, and in the swampy shore a large number of rabbit's footprints.

Freddy had been very happy when he started out. Although he had failed to get back Everett's train of cars, Mrs. Winnick's visit had cheered him up a lot. Here was a new problem. He would solve it and prove to his friends that he was a real detective after all. But now this problem was just as bad as the other one. What was he going to do? These were Egbert's footprints all right, but what good did they do him? There ought to be some clue that he could follow up. There always was in the Sherlock Holmes stories. "You can't solve a case without clues," he muttered unhappily. "These might be clues to Sherlock Holmes, but to me they're just a lot of footprints." And he sat down on the bank to think.

He was thinking so hard that for some time he did not see a small rabbit who hopped down out of the woods to the cress bed, picked a few stalks, then hopped back up among the trees. The rabbit had made several trips before Freddy suddenly caught sight of him.

The rabbit hadn't seen Freddy either, and when the pig started up suddenly, he dodged quickly behind a bush.

"So *you're* the one who made all those footprints in the mud here, are you?" said Freddy.

"Yes, sir," came a small anxious voice from behind the bush. "Isn't it all right, sir?"

"Sure it's all right," said the pig. "Come out; I won't hurt you. I'm looking for a rabbit about your size. Haven't seen one around, have you?"

The rabbit hopped timidly out. "No, sir, he said. "Who was he, sir?"

"Ah," said Freddy mysteriously, *"I'm* the one to be asking the questions. I'm a detective. Just you answer up briskly, young fellow. Haven't seen any other rabbits around, eh?"

"No, sir—"

"No other footprints in the mud when you came here?"

"I don't think so, sir. You see, I—"

"How long have you been here?"

"Since last night, sir. You see, I came to get some watercress, and as I was—"

Freddy stopped him. "That's enough," he said severely. "Please just answer the questions I ask you, without adding anything of your own. Just answer yes or no. You heard no unusual noises?"

"Yes, sir—I mean no, sir," said the rabbit, who was getting confused.

"What do you mean—'yes, sir, no, sir'?" said Freddy. "Please give me a straight answer. Did you or did you not hear any unusual noises?"

"No, sir—I mean—" The rabbit gulped. "—no, sir."

"Good," said the pig. "That's the stuff; a straight answer to a straight question. And—ha, h'm—let me see—" He hadn't found out anything, and yet he couldn't think of any more questions to ask. "Well, ah—what are you doing here anyway?"

But the rabbit didn't answer. "Come, come," said Freddy sharply. "Answer me! What are you—"

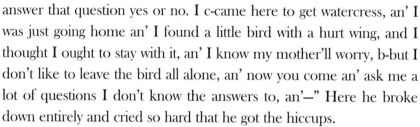

But the rabbit interrupted him by bursting into tears. "You told me to answer yes or no," he sobbed, "and you can't answer that question yes or no. I c-came here to get watercress, an' I was just going home an' I found a little bird with a hurt wing, and I thought I ought to stay with it, an' I know my mother'll worry, b-but I don't like to leave the bird all alone, an' now you come an' ask me a lot of questions I don't know the answers to, an'—" Here he broke down entirely and cried so hard that he got the hiccups.

Freddy was a kind-hearted animal, but he had been so absorbed in asking questions in a thoroughly detective-like manner that he hadn't really noticed that he was frightening the rabbit so badly that the poor little creature couldn't give him any information even if he had it to give. In this Freddy was more like a real detective than he realized. Some detectives will ask a simple question like "What is your name?" in so frightening a voice that the person he asks can't even remember whether he has a name or not.

"There, there," said Freddy, patting the rabbit on the back, "I'm sorry I scared you. It's all right. Where is this bird?"

"Up in a hollow behind that tree," hiccuped the little animal.

"All right," said Freddy. "I'll look after him for you. You run along home. I've got to find this other rabbit I was telling you about, but first I'll see that the bird is taken care of. Run along and tell your mother not to worry any more."

The rabbit wasted no time, but trotted off, still crying, and hiccuping occasionally through his tears, and Freddy went in search of the bird. He found it presently—a fledgling wood thrush, too young to talk yet. Beside it was a small heap of watercress which the rabbit had evidently been trying to feed it.

"Tut, tut," said Freddy. "Feeding an infant like that watercress! He'll be sick. And he's hidden here so that his mother couldn't possibly find him. That rabbit has a kind heart, but he certainly isn't very bright." He picked up the little thrush carefully in his mouth and carried it, fluttering feebly, out into an open space, then went back into the bushes and sat down. In five minutes there was a rush of wings and the mother thrush alighted beside the hungry fledgling and began consoling him with little chirps. Freddy slipped away without waiting to be thanked.

"Now," he said to himself, "for Egbert. Though how in the world I'm to find him I don't know. But I've *got* to or I'll never dare to show my face in the farmyard again. I wish I'd never tried to be a detective, that's what I wish!"

On a chance he decided to go a little farther down the creek, at least as far as the hermit's house, a deserted cabin which stood on the other side of the stream. Perhaps some of the waterside animals might have seen the missing rabbit.

But he had not gone far before something drove all thought of Egbert from his mind. There were sounds coming from the hermit's house. Shouts and rough laughter and occasional pistol-shots. What a chance for a detective! Freddy crept forward; then, finding that the bushes on the opposite bank were too high to permit him to see what was going on, he plunged into the water, swam quietly across, and worked his way up toward the house. And this is what he saw:

Hanging from the limb of a tall tree in front of the house was a swing made of two ropes and a board for a seat. A big man with a cap pulled down over his eyes, and his coat collar turned up, was swinging in long, dizzy swoops. He had a revolver in his hand, and at the top of his swing, when he was level with the top of the house, he would shoot the revolver and try to hit the chimney. A smaller man was sitting in a rocking chair on the porch. He wore a black mask over his face, and no cap, and was knitting busily away at a woolen muffler.

Pretty soon the big man stopped swinging. "Come now, Looey," he shouted. "It's your turn now."

The small man shook his head. "No, Red, I must get this muffler done. We'll both want to wrap up warm tomorrow night; we'll be out late."

"Oh, come on," said Red. "Take a couple of shots anyway. Bet you can't beat me. I got two out of seven."

The other got up rather unwillingly. "Well, all right. But you have got to promise to be more careful. I worry about you all the time. You remember that last bank we robbed; it was a rainy night and you didn't wear your rubbers, and you caught a bad cold."

"Yes, yes, Looey," Red replied. "I'll be careful. Come on, now. Into the swing."

"You'll have to push me, Red," said Looey, taking a large revolver from the pocket of his coat. He seated himself in the swing, and the big man started him swinging. Higher and higher he went, until at each push Red was running right under him. Then when he was high enough, he aimed the revolver, and bang! a brick flew from the chimney.

"Hooray for Looey!" shouted Red. "A bull's-eye! Shoot again!" Freddy, peering out from his hiding-place, was so excited he could hardly breathe. Here was real work for a detective, and no mistake. For these men were certainly robbers. And if he could capture them, his name as a detective was made.

But just then, as Looey was whizzing for the tenth time up into the treetops, one of the ropes broke; he let go his hold and went up in a great curve like a rocket, then came hurtling down through the foliage and into the very bush behind which Freddy was hiding.

He wasn't hurt, for the bush had broken his fall, and he picked himself up immediately, and his eye fell on the amazed pig. Freddy did not wait to see what would happen. With a squeal of fright he bolted.

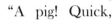

"A pig! Quick, Red, a nice fat pig!" shouted Looey, and started after him, the other robber close behind. There was much shouting and a great banging of revolvers, and two or three bullets whizzed past Freddy's head, but he was a good runner and in a very few minutes had left them far behind.

He ran on for a while, then sat down to rest under a beech tree— and realized suddenly that he didn't know where he was. The woods on this side of the creek extended for many miles. If he could find the creek, he would be all right—but he did not know where the creek was. And the day was cloudy; he could not tell his direction from the position of the sun. "Well, I suppose the best thing to do is to keep on going," he said to himself. "May meet a squirrel or a jay who can tell me where I am." And he started on.

But though he walked and walked, he met no one, and there was no sign of the creek. He had just about decided that he would have to stay out all night when he noticed some footprints. "H'm, someone been along here not many minutes ago," he said. "Looks like a pig, too. Wonder what another pig is doing in these woods. I guess I'll follow them and see if I can catch up."

So he went on, following the footprints, until he came to a place where the other pig had sat down to rest before going on. There was the plain print of a curly tail in the leaf mould under a beech tree. Freddy sat down too, and then suddenly something about the place seemed familiar to him. This beech tree, those bushes over there— "Why, this is where I sat down to rest myself a long time ago! Those are my own footprints I've been following!"

This realization made him feel very foolish, as well it might, for it *is* rather silly for a detective to try to shadow himself. Still, he realized that all he had to do was to follow those footprints *backward* instead of forward, and he would come out by the hermit's house. Which he did, and presently he heard the sound of voices.

But this time he did not stop to see what the robbers were doing. He gave the house a wide berth, jumped into the creek, swam across, and in a few minutes more was back on familiar ground.

"I'll just stop in and see if anything has been heard of Egbert," he said to himself. So he turned down toward the Widow Winnick's home. Half a dozen small rabbits were playing about on the edge of the woods as he came up, and one of them called down the rabbit-hole: "Mother! Mr. Freddy's here!"

Almost at once Mrs. Winnick's head popped up through the opening. But it was a changed Mrs. Winnick that beamed happily at him.

"Oh, Mr. Freddy!" she cried. "How can I ever thank you? My Egbert! You found him for me

"But," stammered the bewildered Freddy, "I didn't—" And then he stopped. For one of the little rabbits who were standing around him in a respectful and admiring circle hiccuped, and said politely: "Excuse me." And Freddy saw it all. Of course! That rabbit had been Egbert all the time!

He recovered himself just in time. "Oh, don't thank me, Mrs. Winnick. Don't thank me," he said rather grandly. "It was nothing, I assure you—nothing at all. Indeed, I am very grateful to you for having sent me down in that direction, for I have made some very important discoveries. However, I am glad Egbert got back safely. All the other children are well, I hope. Good, good; I am very glad to hear it. Good evening." And he went on homeward.

"Well," he said to himself, "I guess as a detective I'm not so bad after all. Restored a lost child to his mother and discovered a band of robbers, all in one day! Huh, Sherlock Holmes never did more than that, I bet. And now for those rats!"

V
The Case of
Prinny's Dinner

FREDDY

was

A pretty busy pig for the next few weeks. Mrs. Winnick told all her friends about how quickly he had found Egbert, and her friends told other animals, and they all praised him very highly.

At first Freddy tried to explain. He said that he really hadn't done anything at all, and that he didn't even know that the rabbit he had sent home was Egbert. But everyone said:

"Oh, you just talk that way because you are so modest," and they praised him more highly than ever.

And they brought him detective work to do. Most of them were simple cases, like Egbert's, of young animals that had run away from home or got lost. But a number of them were quite important. There was, for instance, the strange case of Prinny's dinner. Prinny was a little white woolly dog who lived with Miss Mary McMinnickle in a little house a mile or so down the road. Prinny was a nice dog, in spite of his name, of which he was very much ashamed. His whole name was Prince Charming, but Miss McMinnickle called him Prinny for short. Now Prinny's dinner was always put out for him on the back porch in a big white bowl. Sometimes Prinny was there when it was put out, and then he ate it and everything was all right. But sometimes he would be away from home when Miss McMinnickle put it out, and he would come back an hour or two later and the bowl would be empty.

"The funny part of it is," he said to Freddy, "that there isn't ever a sign of any animal having been near it. I wish you'd see what you can do about it."

So Freddy took the case. First he got some flour and sprinkled it around on the porch, but though the food was gone from the bowl when he and Prinny came back later, there were no footprints to be seen. Then he watched for two afternoons, hidden behind the back fence with his eye at a knothole. But on these days the dinner was not touched.

"Have you any idea who it is?" asked Prinny anxiously. The poor little dog was getting quite thin.

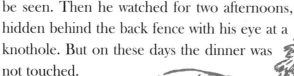

"H'm," said Freddy; "yes. It's narrowing down, it's narrowing down. Give me another day or two and I think we'll have him."

Now, this time Freddy wasn't just looking wise and pretending, for he really did have an idea. The next day, before the sun had come up, he went down to Miss McMinnickle's. He took with him Eeny and Quik, two of the mice who lived in the barn, and they hid under the back porch. The mice were very proud that Freddy had asked them to help him, so they didn't mind the long wait, and they all played "twenty questions" and other guessing games until finally, late in the afternoon, they heard Miss McMinnickle come out on the porch and set down the bowl containing Prinny's dinner.

"Quiet now, boys," said Freddy. "I told Prinny to stay up at the farm until after dark, so the thief will think that there's no one here."

For half an hour they waited. Then, without any warning, without any sound of cautious footsteps on the floor of the porch close over their heads, there was a rattling sound, as if someone were tapping the bowl with a stick. The mice looked at Freddy in alarm, but he winked reassuringly at them. "They're there," he said. "Wait here till I call you." And he crawled quickly out from under the porch.

Three crows were perched on the edge of the big bowl, gobbling down Prinny's dinner as fast as they could. At sight of Freddy they flew with a startled squawk up into the branches of a tree, from which they glared down at him angrily.

"Aha!" said the detective. "Caught you at it, didn't I? Ferdy, I didn't think it of you, stealing a poor little dog's dinner! I knew it was some kind of bird when we didn't find any footprints and when hiding behind the fence wasn't any good. I suppose you saw me from the air, eh? But I thought it would be some of those thieving jays from the woods. I didn't expect to find *you* here, Ferdy."

Ferdinand, the oldest of the crows, who had been Freddy's companion on the trip to the north pole the year before, merely grinned at his friend. "Aw, you can't prove anything, pig," he said. "Who's going to believe you? It's just your word against mine."

"Is that so!" exclaimed Freddy. "Well, I've got witnesses, smarty. Come out, boys," he called, and the two mice came out and sat on the edge of the porch.

Ferdinand looked a little worried at this. He was caught, and all the animals would soon know about it. Of course, they couldn't do anything to him. But they would be angry at him, and it isn't much fun living with people who don't approve of your actions, even if they can't punish you for them. In fact, it is often much pleasanter, when you have done something you shouldn't, to be punished and get it over with. Ferdinand thought of this, and he also thought of his dignity. He had always been a very dignified crow, and it certainly wasn't very dignified to be caught stealing a little dog's dinner.

So he flew down beside the pig. "Oh, come, Freddy," he said; "it was just a joke. Can't we settle this out of court? We'll promise not to do it again if you won't say anything about it."

"Well, that's up to Prinny," said the pig. "It doesn't seem like a very good joke to him. But I'll talk to him about it. You three crows had better not be here when he gets back, though."

"All right," said Ferdinand. "That's fair enough. Do the best you can for us, Freddy. We'll push off now."

"Hey, wait a minute," said one of the other crows. "How about these mice? How do we know they won't talk?"

"Say, listen," squeaked Eeny shrilly. "Just because we're small, you think we haven't got any sense, you big black useless noisy feather-headed bug-eaters, you!" His anger at the insult was so hot that he fairly danced about the porch on his hind legs. "Another one like that and I'll climb that tree and gnaw your tail-feathers off!"

"Oh, he didn't mean anything, Eeny," said Ferdinand, edging a little away from the enraged mouse. "Sure, we know you won't say anything."

"Well, let him keep a civil tongue in his head, then," grumbled Eeny. "Come on, Quik." And he started off home without waiting for Freddy.

The pig overtook them, however, a minute later, and they climbed up on his back, for it was slow going for such small animals across the fields. "I must say, Freddy," remarked Quik, "that I think you're letting the crows off pretty easy."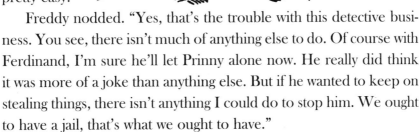

Freddy nodded. "Yes, that's the trouble with this detective business. You see, there isn't much of anything else to do. Of course with Ferdinand, I'm sure he'll let Prinny alone now. He really did think it was more of a joke than anything else. But if he wanted to keep on stealing things, there isn't anything I could do to stop him. We ought to have a jail, that's what we ought to have."

"You mean like the one in Centerboro?" asked Eeny.

"Yes. Then when we find any animal doing anything he shouldn't, we could lock him up for a while."

"You mean if a cat chased us, he could be locked up in the jail?" asked the mice. And when Freddy said yes, that was exactly what he did mean, they both agreed that a jail was certainly needed.

So that evening Freddy called a meeting of all the animals in the cow barn, where the three cows, Mrs. Wiggins and Mrs. Wurzburger and Mrs. Wogus, lived. It was one of the finest cow barns in the county, for when the animals had come back from Florida with a buggyful of money that they had found, Mr. Bean had been so grateful that he had fixed up all the stables and houses they lived in in the most modern style, with electric lights and hot and cold water and curtains at the windows, and steam heat in the wintertime. Even the henhouse had all these conveniences and such little extra comforts as electric nest-warmers, and little teeters and swings and slides for the younger chickens.

All the animals on the neighboring farms as well as at Mr. Bean's had by this time heard about Freddy's success as a detective, so the meeting was a large one. A lot of the woods animals, including Peter, the bear, came. There were even a few sheep, and if you know anything about sheep, you will realize how much interest the proposal for a jail had created, for there is nothing harder than to interest sheep in matters of public policy. Freddy found it unnecessary to make much of a speech, for nearly all of his audience agreed at once that the jail would fill, as Charles, the rooster, aptly expressed it, a long-felt want. Practically the only dissenting voice was that of Jinx. When Freddy threw the meeting open to discussion, Jinx jumped to his feet.

"I don't see what we want a jail for," he said. "We've always got along well enough without one before."

"We got along without nice places to live in, too," replied Freddy. "But it's nice to have them."

"Yes, but we aren't going to live in the jail."

"Some of us are," said Freddy significantly.

"You mean animals like the rats, I suppose," returned the cat. "Well, if you're such a swell detective, why don't you catch them and get Everett's train back? If you aren't any smarter at catching other animals that steal things than you have been about them, you won't have anybody in your old jail. And anyway I don't see any need for it. Let me get hold of those rats and you won't need any jail to put 'em in."

"I'll catch 'em all right," said Freddy. "Even Sherlock Holmes couldn't do everything in a minute. These things take time. I guess I've settled quite a number of cases since I started being a detective, haven't I?"

"Sure he has! Shut up, Jinx!" shouted the other animals, and Jinx had to sit down.

So the matter was voted upon, and it was decided by a vote of seventy-four to one that there should be a jail. But where? After a long discussion the meeting agreed that the two big box stalls in the barn would be a good place. Mr. Bean's three horses lived in the barn, but they had stalls near the door, and the box stalls were never used.

"How do you feel about it, Hank?" asked Freddy.

Hank was the oldest of the horses, and he was never very sure of anything except that he liked oats better than anything in the world. "I don't know," he said slowly. "I guess it would be all right. Some animals would be all right, and then again, some wouldn't. I wouldn't want elephants or tigers. Or polar bears. Or giraffes. Or—"

"Or kangaroos or leopards or zebras," said Freddy impatiently. "We know that. But there won't be any animals of that kind."

"Oh, then I guess it'll be all right," said Hank. "These prisoners, they'd be company for me, too. I'd like that."

"That's all settled, then," said Freddy. "Hank can be jailer and look after the prisoners and see that they don't escape. Then let's see; we'll need a judge, to say how long the prisoners shall stay in jail. Now, I suggest that a good animal for that position would be—"

"Excuse me!" crowed Charles, the rooster, excitedly. "I'd like to speak for a moment, Mr. Chairman."

"All right," said Freddy. "Mr. Charles has the floor. What is it, Charles?"

Charles flew up to the seat of the buggy, and all the animals crowded closer. The rooster was a fine speaker and he used words so beautifully that they all liked to hear him, although they didn't

always know what he was talking about. Neither did he, sometimes, but nobody cared, for, as with all good speakers, what he said wasn't half so important as the noble way he said it.

"Ladies and gentlemen," said Charles, "it is with a great sense of my own inadequacy that I venture to address this distinguished meeting. We have gathered here this evening to pay tribute to the genius— and I use the word 'genius'—without fear of denial—of one of our number, a simple farm animal, who yet, by virtue of his great talents, his dogged determination, and his pleasing personality, has risen to a position of trust and responsibility never before occupied by any animal. I refer, ladies and gentlemen, to Freddy, the detective." He paused for the cheers, then continued. "It has been said of Freddy that 'he always gets his animal.' But his career is too well known to all of you for me to dwell upon its successive stages.—"

"Yeah, I guess it is!" remarked Jinx sarcastically. "Why don't he get those rats then?"

"And," Charles continued without heeding the interruption, "who am I to come before you with suggestions concerning a subject about which he to whom I refer knows more than any living animal—?"

"I'll tell you who you are!" shouted the cat, who was always thoroughly exasperated by Charles's longwindedness. "You're a silly rooster, and if Henrietta catches you up there making a speech again, *she'll* make some suggestions you won't like!"

"Shut up! Put him out!" shouted the animals, and Jinx subsided. But Charles was seen to shiver slightly. For Henrietta, his wife, didn't approve of his public speaking, and she had been heard to threaten to pull out the handsome tail feathers he was so proud of if she caught him at it again.

Presently, however, he recovered himself and went on, though somewhat hurriedly. "I do not wish to detain you unduly, so I will proceed to the matter of which I wish to speak: the matter of selecting a judge. Now, it is not easy to be a judge. When the prisoner is brought before the judge, he must hear all the facts in the case, and must first decide whether the prisoner is innocent or guilty. If guilty, he must then decide how long the prisoner ought to spend in jail. Now, this is not an easy task. Whoever becomes judge will have a great responsibility. He will, moreover, have very little time to himself. I feel sure that none of you animals will really want the position. But I have thought the matter over carefully, and I am willing to sacrifice myself for the public good. I wish to propose myself as judge."

He paused, while some of the animals applauded and some grumbled.

"As to my qualifications for the position," he went on, trying to look as modest as he could, which wasn't very much, "it is hardly seemly for me to speak. You know me, my friends; whether or not I possess the wisdom, experience, and honesty necessary for this great task I leave it to you to judge. I have lived among you for many years; my record may perhaps speak for itself. I can only say that if you express your confidence in me by electing me to office, I shall do my utmost, I shall spare no labor, to be worthy of the confidence you thus express in me." And he flew down from the buggy.

The meeting at once divided into two parties, one for Charles and one for Peter, the bear, who was Freddy's candidate. Most of the animals who knew Charles well were for Peter, for though they were fond of Charles, they didn't think much of his brains. "He talks too much, and he thinks too much about himself to make a good judge," they said. But those who didn't know him so well made the common mistake of thinking that because he spoke well, he knew a lot. They thought that Peter had brains too, but there was a serious drawback to Peter. From December to March he was always sound asleep in his cave in the woods, so that any cases that came up in the winter would have to wait over until spring. Some of the anti-Charles party said that didn't matter; a good judge asleep was better than a bad judge awake. But the general feeling was that it wouldn't be a good idea to elect a judge that slept nearly half the time.

A number of speeches were made, and the argument grew so bitter that most of the sheep went home, and two squirrels got to fighting in a corner and had to be separated before the voting could start. When the vote was counted, it was found that Charles had won.

The rooster wanted to make a speech of acceptance, and he flew back up on the buggy seat, but he had got no further than "My friends, I extend to one and all my heartiest thanks—" when Jinx, who had disappeared during the voting, stuck his head in the door.

"Hey, Charlie," he called; "Henrietta wants you."

Charles's sentence ended in a strangled squawk, and he jumped down and hurried outside. But Henrietta was not there. Charles looked around for a moment; then, deciding that Jinx had played a trick on him, he turned to go in, when a voice above him called: "Hi, judge! Here's a present for you!" And plop! plop! plop!—soft and squashy things hit the ground all around him. He dashed for the door, but he was a quarter of a second too late. An overripe tomato struck him fair on the back and flattened him to the ground, while peals of coarse laughter came from the roof.

He got up and shook himself. But it was no use. The handsome feathers he had cleaned and burnished so carefully for the meeting were damp and bedraggled. He could make no speech now; he couldn't even go back into the cow barn. A fine plight for a newly elected judge! But he knew whom he had to thank for it. Jinx had got those mischievous coons from the woods to play this childish trick on him. And he'd get even with them, see if he didn't! They'd forgotten that he was a judge now. He'd put 'em in jail and keep 'em there, that's what he'd do. And half-tearfully muttering threats, the new judge, after a mournful glance back at the barn, where honor and applause awaited him in vain, stumbled off across the barnyard toward the hen coop.

VI
The Defeat of
Simon's Gang

ON one Side of the rail fence was

a ditch, on the other was a cornfield. Between

the corn and the fence was a lane, and down

this lane Freddy was sauntering. Although it was a windless day, there

were odd little rustlings and swishings all about him, and now and

and now and then a corn-stalk or a tuft of grass or a bush beside the fence would be shaken for a moment as if a breeze had passed over it. Freddy, however, did not seem to notice any of these things, but strolled along, stopping now and then, as a detective will, to examine a footprint or a stone or a mark on a fence rail.

Presently fence and lane and ditch turned sharply to the left. Freddy turned with them, but as soon as he was round the corner, he darted quickly aside into a tangle of bushes and vines in an angle of the fence. Here, completely hidden, he lay motionless for perhaps a minute. And then a rabbit hopped into sight. It hopped along quietly, peering about sharply; but it did not see the pig and went cautiously on. Following the rabbit came Clarence, the porcupine who lived up in the woods, creeping along and trying hard to keep his quills from rattling. A squirrel ran stealthily along the fence above Freddy's head, but so intent was he on keeping the porcupine in sight that he did not see the pig crouching below him. There was a rustling in the tall corn, and a goat stuck his head out, looked up and down the lane, then retreated as Robert, Mr. Bean's dog, came slinking along on the porcupine's trail.

"Very good," said Freddy to himself as he watched the animals go by. "Very good indeed. They're learning. But good gracious!" he exclaimed as a sound of trampling and crashing came from the corn-field. "That can't be Mrs. Wiggins again. My, my! Mr. Bean *will* be mad!" He got up, just as the cow appeared in the lane, leaving behind her a broad path of trampled corn.

"Where are they, Freddy?" she panted. "I've been shadowing that Robert, but I guess I lost him again." She sat down heavily. "Whew! This is certainly trying work, being a detective! And hot! I'm going to pick a cool day next time I try it." She looked back at the trail she had beaten down. "I'm afraid I've spoiled one or two stalks of Mr. Bean's corn."

"One or two!" Freddy exclaimed. "My goodness, you've wrecked the whole field! Mr. Bean will be good and sore, and I don't blame him."

"Oh pshaw, Freddy," said the cow, "you know perfectly well that you can't shadow anybody unless you hide from them, and an animal as big as I am can't hide behind one or two little spears of grass the way a cat or a dog can. And besides, you said yourself that an animal couldn't be a good detective without a lot of practice. What else could I do?"

"Why, you'll just have to give up being a detective, that's all," replied the pig. "At least that kind of detective. Because there's lots to detective work besides shadowing. You have to hunt for clues, too, and then think about them until you can figure out what they mean."

Mrs. Wiggins sighed heavily. "Oh dear!" she said. "You know thinking isn't my strong point, Freddy. I mean, I've got good brains, but they aren't the kind that think easily. They're the kind of brains that if you let 'em go their own way, they are as good as anybody's, but if you try to *make* them do anything, like a puzzle, they just won't work at all."

"Well," said Freddy, "detective work is a good deal like a puzzle. But I *do* think you ought not to try to do this shadowing. Mr. Bean certainly won't like having the corn spoiled this way, and he's been pretty touchy lately anyway. Not that I blame him, now that all the animals have started to play detective all over the farm. I heard him tell Mrs. Bean that he was getting sick and tired of having about fifteen animals sneaking along behind him every time he leaves the house. And whenever he looks up from his work, he says, no matter where he is, there are eyes peering at him—dozens and dozens of eyes watching him from hiding-places."

"Ugh!" exclaimed the cow with a little shiver. "I know how that is! Nothing makes me more nervous than to have something watch-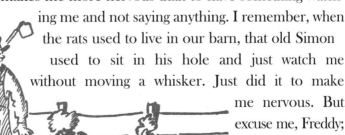ing me and not saying anything. I remember, when the rats used to live in our barn, that old Simon used to sit in his hole and just watch me without moving a whisker. Just did it to make me nervous. But excuse me, Freddy; I didn't mean to mention the rats."

"Oh, that's all right," said the pig. "I don't mind. Though I must confess I don't know just what to do about them. It's the only case so far that has given me much trouble."

"Nasty creatures!" exclaimed the cow. "If I could just get up in that loft, I'd show 'em!"

"I wish you could," said Freddy. "You could just pick the train up on one horn and walk off with it. But the stairs are too narrow. No, I've got to think out something else. Oh, I'll get an idea sooner or later."

"That's it," said Mrs. Wiggins. "Ideas! You've got to have 'em to be a detective. And I can't remember when I had my last one. But land sakes, there must be some way of getting the train. Couldn't you tie a rope on it and pull it out?"

"H'm," said Freddy thoughtfully, "that's an idea."

"An idea!" exclaimed the cow. "Gracious, Freddy, that isn't an idea; it's just something I thought of."

"It's an idea all the same," said the pig, "and a good one. But we'd have to do it quick, or they'd gnaw the rope in two. Come on, walk back to the barn with me and talk it over. I'd like to get at it tonight if I can."

So they strolled back, talking so earnestly that they never noticed that they were being rather clumsily shadowed by half a dozen animals of assorted sizes who dodged behind trees and darted across open places like Indians on the warpath. Mrs. Wiggins was so excited to find that she had really had an idea after all, and so flattered that Freddy was actually asking for her advice, that she hardly looked where she was going, and Alice remarked to Emma as they passed:

"I've rarely seen Mrs. Wiggins so animated. She looks quite flushed." "Humph!" replied Emma, who was a little upset that day because her Uncle Wesley had scolded her for eating minnows—"Humph! It always goes to her head when she gets a little attention!"

Jinx was up in the loft where he spent much of his time now, though there was very little he could do there but watch the train make its periodic trips to the grain-box and back and listen to the insults and ribald songs that the rats shouted at him. He came down at once when Freddy called him, and went into conference with the pig and the cow. And when they finally separated to go to supper, they had decided on a plan.

There was a door in the loft through which Mr. Bean took in the hay every summer. Over the door was a beam with a pulley at the end, and through the pulley ran a stout rope that ended in an iron hook. The other end of the rope came down into the loft, where it was coiled upon the floor. Late that evening, when Mr. Bean had finished the chores and had gone round to the barns and the henhouse and the pigpen and turned out the lights and said good night to the animals in his gruff, kindly way and had then gone into the kitchen to eat a couple of apple dumplings and a piece of pie and a few doughnuts before going to bed, Freddy and Jinx went up into the loft. The train was still going back and forth, for although the rats felt that they had completely outwitted the cat, they were wise enough to realize that the luck might turn any day, and they intended to lay away as big a supply of grain as they could. So they worked in shifts, night and day.

When they heard Freddy, who hadn't visited the loft since the night when he had broken his tooth, they set up a derisive shout. "Yea! Here's old Freddy, old curly-tail! How's tricks, pig? Who you going to arrest tonight?" And then they began to sing:

"Oh, we are the gay young rats
Who laugh at the barnyard prigs;
We can lick our weight in cats,
And double our weight in pigs.

"We live wherever we like,
We do whatever we please;
An enemy's threat can strike
No fear to such hearts as these.

"When the pig detective squeals,
When cats lash furious tails,
Our laughter comes in peals,
And our laughter comes in gales.

"We've done as we always did,
  We do as we've always done,
Though cats and pigs forbid,
  For we take orders from none.

"So, cats and pigs and men,
  If you want to avoid a fuss,
Stay safely in house and pen
  And don't interfere with us."

"Kind of like themselves, don't they?" remarked Jinx. Freddy said nothing, but went quickly to work. The loose end of the rope he threw out of the door to Mrs. Wiggins, who was waiting below, and then, after several trials, during which he nearly fell out himself, he got hold of the hook and drew it down into the loft.

The rats, meanwhile, in order to show their contempt for him, were marching all round the floor inside the train, shouting out their song at the top of their lungs. They felt pretty sure that neither of their enemies would make another direct attack, and they were so taken up with the effort to outdo one another in thinking up insulting new verses for the song that they didn't realize just what was going on. Suddenly Freddy said: "Let's go!" The two animals made a pounce for the train, and before the rats knew what had happened, the big hook was firmly fastened in the engine window, and Freddy had shouted to Mrs. Wiggins, who, with the other end of the rope looped about one horn, simply walked away from the barn.

There was a rattle and a great squeaking as the train was dragged across the floor. It reached the door, swung out, and was pulled up toward the pulley, the rats dropping from it like peas from a pod Jinx had

run downstairs, and as the rats picked themselves up and ran for shelter, he was among them, cuffing and slapping. Simon, unfortunately, had not been in the train, but his son Ezra was there, and Jinx grabbed him by the back of the neck and held on while the others made their escape. Then Mrs. Wiggins walked back toward the barn and the train came down to the ground at the end of the rope.

The rats who had not been in the train, desperate at the loss of their means of livelihood, swarmed angrily out of their holes as their comrades were dragged squealing and struggling across the floor, and Freddy, feeling that his work there was completed, saw no reason for staying longer. In fact he fell down the last eight steps of the stairs, so eager was he to get away. But outside, by the captured train, he recovered himself and thanked Mrs. Wiggins generously for her part in the victory.

"Everett owes his train to you and no one else," he said. "You don't have to bother with learning to shadow people if you want to be a detective. Goodness, you've got *ideas*. That's the important thing."

"Ideas!" exclaimed the cow in bewilderment. "Why, land of love, that wasn't an idea! I never have ideas. I told you that."

"It certainly was an idea," protested the pig.

"Well, if that's what you want to call it . . . it just looked like common sense to me."

Freddy didn't say anything for a minute; then he turned his attention to the prisoner, who had given up struggling and was lying quiet under Jinx's paw. "Good work, Jinx," he said. "We got one of 'em, anyway. Better take him down and have the judge sentence him right away. Then we can lock him up in the jail."

"Aw, what do we want of a judge?" demanded the cat. "You leave him to me. I'll see he don't cause any more trouble." And he glared ferociously at Ezra.

But Freddy and Mrs. Wiggins insisted, and Jinx finally gave in. "Come on, then," he said. "I shouldn't have caught him if it hadn't been for you, so I guess you ought to have the say-so."

The henhouse was dark when they reached it, but at the first tap on the door a head popped out of a window and a cross voice wanted to know what they meant by waking up honest chickens in the middle of the night. "Go along about your business," scolded the voice, "or I'll call my husband, and *he'll* soon settle you."

Jinx grinned at the picture of Charles trying to drive away a cat and a pig and a cow, but he only said politely: "Excuse us, Henrietta, but this is a very important case that won't wait. We've got a prisoner here, and we must see the judge."

But Henrietta was not appeased. "I'm not going to have my sleep disturbed by a lot of roistering cats and pigs, and you needn't try any of your soft soap on me either, Jinx. I know you! And who's that out there with you—Mrs. Wiggins? Take shame to yourself, Mrs. Wiggins, to be gallivanting about the country at all hours, like this, with a pack of disreputable scalawags and good-for-nothing disturbers of the peace—"

"Oh, come, Henrietta," boomed Mrs. Wiggins good-naturedly, "I guess you know me well enough so you don't think I'm up to any mischief."

"Birds of a feather flock together," interrupted the hen. "I can only judge you by the company you keep, ma'am. But of course nothing *I* can say would do you any good—"

"Oh, call Charles, will you?" demanded Freddy impatiently. "We've captured a prisoner and we want to have the judge sentence him."

"Give him six months," came the sleepy voice of the rooster from within the coop.

"Why, you don't even know who it is or what he's done!" exclaimed Mrs. Wiggins. "Come out, now, Charles, and do your duty as you said you would when you were elected."

"Give him a year, then," came the sleepy voice again. "And take him away. I want to go to sleep."

"There, you've got your answer," said Henrietta. "Now go along and stop your racket. What'll people think?"

"I know what they'll think," said Freddy angrily. "They'll think we've got to get another judge. You wouldn't elect Peter because you said he slept half the year. How about a judge that won't stay awake long enough after his election to hear the first case that comes up? Come on, animals; we'll go get Peter."

But this didn't suit the hen at all. She was very proud of having her husband a judge, though she wouldn't have let him know it for anything, and with a hurried "Wait a minute," she disappeared inside.

There was a rustling and flapping, a squawk or two, and then the door opened and a very sleepy Charles stood before them. "Wha's all this?" he demanded. "Very incos—inconsiderate, I call it." His tongue was thick with sleep, and he leaned against the door-post and closed his eyes.

But a sharp peck from his wife roused him, and he frowned at the prisoner. "What's he done?" he demanded.

They told their story, and when it was finished, Charles, finally awake, turned to Ezra. "Is there any reason why you shouldn't go to jail, prisoner?" he asked.

The rat started to say something, looked up craftily at Jinx, who held a

heavy paw in readiness, and, lowering his eyes, said meekly: "No, sir.

"Nothing to say for yourself, eh?" said the judge. "Well, it's your first offense—or, rather, it's the first time you've been caught, so I'm going to give you a light sentence. Three months in jail. And now I want to say to you, prisoner, that I hope you'll do some serious thinking during those three months. I hope you'll see the wisdom of living at peace with your fellow animals and of letting other people's property alone. I want to say to you—"

But, whatever else it was that he wanted to say, it was lost to the world, for at that moment Henrietta, who had little patience for speeches at any time, and none at all for them in the middle of the night, seized him by the tail feathers, yanked him inside, and slammed the door.

VII
A Crime Wave in the Barnyard

FREDDY
was
NOW a made pig.

His victory over Simon's gang and the return of the stolen train to Everett brought him a great many cases. He took Mrs. Wiggins into partnership, and it was an excellent combination, he supplying the ideas and she the common sense, neither of which is of much use without the other. They themselves handled only the more difficult cases, turning over the simpler ones to their staff, which consisted of several smaller animals who were good at shadowing and gathering information. Freddy printed a large sign and hung it on the shed which had once been the offices of Barnyard Tours, Inc. It read:

FREDERICK & WIGGINS
DETECTIVES

Plain and fancy shadowing. Stolen articles restored. Criminals captured. Missing animals found and returned to bosoms of families. Our unexcelled record makes it worth your while to investigate. Not a loss to a client in more than a century.

Mrs. Wiggins objected at first to the last sentence. "We haven't been in business but a week," she said.

"What difference does that make?" asked Freddy. "It's true, isn't it?"

She had to admit that it was. "But, don't you see, it sounds as if we'd been detectives for a long time."

"That's just the way I want it to sound," replied the pig.

So Mrs. Wiggins didn't say any more.

Pretty soon there were eight animals in the jail. There was Ezra, and there were two rabbits who had stolen some parsnips, and there was a goat named Eric, who had come to the farm to visit his friend Bill and had eaten Mrs. Bean's filet lace tablecloth and Mr. Bean's best nightshirt right off the clothesline. Then there were two snails who had come up on Mrs. Bean's freshly scrubbed front porch one night and left little shiny trails all over it. And there was a tramp cat who had chased Henrietta up into a tree one day when she was out calling. And finally there was a horsefly named Zero.

The capture of this fly had been a difficult matter. The two dogs, Jock and Robert, who had been appointed policemen, could of course do nothing about it. Zero was not an ordinary fly who bit and flew away. He had attached himself to Mrs. Wogus. He lived in the cow-barn, and as soon as it was light in the morning, he started biting her. When she went down to the pasture, he followed along and bit her some more. He was very agile, and when she swished her tail at him, he only laughed. Even when she climbed down into the duck-pond and lay in the water with only the tip of her nose showing, he would fly down and bite her nose. It got so bad that she appealed to Freddy.

Now, every night Zero slept on the ceiling of the cow barn. He was right over Mrs. Wogus, so that as soon as it was light enough for him to see, he could drop down without wasting a second and begin biting. "Perfectly simple matter, Mrs. W.," said Freddy in his business-like way. "Just you leave it to me." And he went into the house and borrowed a piece of flypaper from Mrs. Bean and put it in the cow-barn. "That'll do the business," he said.

Early the next morning he was awakened by a great commotion, and he ran out and saw a crowd of animals gathered about the cow barn. He hurried up to them importantly. "Where's the prisoner?" he demanded.

They made way for him and he saw, struggling feebly in the sticky paper, not Zero, but Eeny, who had gone into the barn to see Mrs.

Wiggins and, knowing nothing about the trap, had walked straight into it.

With some difficulty, and after getting a good deal of stickiness on his own snout, Freddy rescued the unfortunate mouse, while Zero buzzed round impudently overhead. After listening to all the unpleasant things that Eeny's family had to say to him, the pig went outside to think. Undoubtedly he'd have to try something different now. And he was wondering what it would be when he gave a sharp squeal and jumped into the air. Something had stung him on the ear.

He looked around angrily, and there was Zero circling above his head, and a thin, whining laughter came down to him. "That's something for *you,* pig, in exchange for the flypaper," buzzed Zero. "It'll be worse next time, so better leave me alone." And he flew off in search of Mrs. Wogus.

But Freddy had no intention of being intimidated by a fly. He got some jam and put it on Mrs. Wogus's nose. "Now," he said, "get into the pond with just your nose showing. Then when Zero lights, duck under the water for a minute. His feet will be stuck so he can't get away and he'll be drowned and that'll be the end of *him.*"

So Mrs. Wogus went into the water, and Freddy sat down on the bank to watch. Zero was not in sight for the moment, and Freddy started thinking how clever he was, and then he got to thinking how comfortable he was, and his head nodded and nodded—and he woke up suddenly with a squeal of pain, for Zero had quietly alighted on his snout and bitten him ferociously.

"There's another for you, pig," droned the fly as he swooped over the enraged Freddy's head. "Maybe now you'll let me alone. I don't eat jam. It makes me fat, and a fly can't afford to be fat and slow on his wings these days. Too many birds and wasps around. But pigs! Why, Freddy, you couldn't catch a blind fly with one wing. No, sir, you—"

But Freddy, although he was hopping mad, was too good a detective to pay much attention to empty insults. Zero's words had given him an idea. Off he went at a fast trot, stopping only now and then to rub his smarting nose in the cool grass, and presently he was talking to a family of wasps who were building a new house under the eaves of the barn.

"It's a bad time to ask our help now," said the father wasp when he had heard what Freddy wanted. "We've got this house on our hands, and the days are getting shorter all the time. Still—I might let you have George. Hey, George!"

George was a husky young wasp who was only too glad of any excuse to get away from house-building. Wasps build their houses of chewed-up leaves and things, and George had chewed until his jaws were lame. He listened to Freddy's instructions and then flew off toward the pasture. The pig trotted along after him.

When they reached the pasture, Mrs. Wogus was not in sight, and Freddy remembered uneasily that he had forgotten to tell her to come out of the pond. Good gracious, she had been sitting there for over an hour now! Sure enough, there was her black nose, smeared with jam, making a queer little island in the water. He threw pebbles at her until she came up; then he explained.

Mrs. Wogus was rather vexed. "You ought to have told me," she said. "It's no fun sitting there in the mud and the cold, with nothing to do but shiver. And the way the minnows tickle you, you wouldn't believe! I do hope I haven't caught a cold."

But she soon got warm in the hot sun, and Freddy went over with her into the pasture to watch proceedings. Pretty soon Zero came buzzing along. But this time as he dropped down to settle on Mrs. Wogus's nose, he heard the deep drone of George's wings and hastily went into a nose dive, flew right under the cow, then dashed off with the wasp in hot pursuit. It was like an airplane battle, with Zero dodging and twisting and George trying to get above him and drop on him, but it didn't last long, and presently Zero was driven down to the ground, where he took refuge in a small hole under a stone. George tried to go in after him, but the hole was too small.

"I'll dig him out," said Freddy. "You stand by to chase him again."

So Freddy turned the stone over, and up buzzed Zero into the air, and the chase was on again. But this time when the fly was driven down, he went into a crevice in the stone foundation of the barn.

"You can't turn that over," said George.

"Guess you'd better give up for today. Some time when I haven't got so much to do, I'd like nothing better than to catch that insect for you, but I ought to get back now. Father won't like it."

"Wait," said Freddy; "I've got an idea. You watch till I come back."

He went into the barn, and in a few minutes came out with the two spiders, Mr. and Mrs. Webb, who were great friends of his. In no time at all they had woven a web over the entrance of the crevice, and then they had Zero safe and fast. After that there was nothing for the fly to do but surrender, so he came out and the Webbs tied his feet and wings together, and Freddy carried him off to jail.

Freddy was very much pleased when they had eight prisoners in the jail. He wasn't so much pleased when, a week after the capture of Zero, they had thirty-four. "I don't understand it," he said to Mrs. Wiggins. "I suppose it must be one of these crime waves we read about."

"We'll have to enlarge the jail, at this rate," said Mrs. Wiggins.

"There'll be more animals inside than out," said Freddy.

They were strolling down through the pasture, and a number of strange animals passed them, going toward the barnyard. At last one, a motherly-looking Jersey cow, stopped and asked the way to the jail.

Freddy pointed it out to her. "Nothing wrong, I hope?" he said. "I mean, none of your family or friends *are—*er—*in,* are they?"

"Oh no," said the cow. "But I've heard of those poor animals locked up in jail, and I *do* feel so sorry for them, poor things! It's just *dreadful* not to be able to get out in the fresh air among their friends."

"If they'd behaved themselves, they wouldn't be there," said Freddy.

"Oh yes, I know," said the cow, "but it's so horrible to be locked up, isn't it? It makes me quite sad to think of them." And a tear rolled down her broad cheek.

"As a matter of fact, they have a pretty easy time," put in Mrs. Wiggins. "Play games and lie round and get lots to eat. I don't think you need be so sorry for them."

"I suppose it *is* silly of me," replied the other, "but I've always been that way. Anyone in trouble just wrings my heart strings. And it's better to be too tenderhearted, I always say, than to run the risk of getting too hard. Don't you think so?"

"Oh, undoubtedly," said Freddy. "But I wouldn't get very tender-hearted about that bunch of prisoners. They're a tough lot."

"Well," said the cow, "perhaps you're right. But I thought I'd just go down and see if there wasn't anything I could do to make things easier for them. I can't bear to think of them being unhappy. It hurts me here." And she tapped her left side with her right front hoof.

When the cow had gone on, Freddy said: "That's one reason—all these sentimental animals that come to visit the jail and feel sorry for the prisoners and want to do things for them. After all, they're there to be punished, not to have a good time. And we treat 'em well. There's no reason to cry over them and bring them better food than they ever get at home—why, what are you getting so red for?" he demanded suddenly. For a blush had overspread Mrs. Wiggins's large face.

You have probably never seen a cow blush. And indeed the sight is unusual. There are two reasons for this. One is that cows are a very simple people, who do whatever they feel like doing and never realize that sometimes they ought to be embarrassed. You might think that they lack finer feelings. And in a way they do. They are not sensitive. But they are kind and good-natured, and if sometimes they seem rude, it is only due to their rather clumsy thoughtlessness.

The other reason is that cows' faces are not built for blushing. But as Mrs. Wiggins was so talented above her sisters in other directions, it is not to be marveled at that she could blush very handsomely.

Her flush deepened as Freddy spoke. "Why, I—now that you speak of it," she stammered, "I see that you're right, but—well, Freddy—land's sakes, I might as well confess it to you—I got to feeling sorry for those prisoners myself yesterday, especially those two goats. It seemed such a pity they couldn't be jumping round on the hills instead of sweltering in that hot barn. And I went out and got them a nice bunch of thistles for their supper."

Freddy frowned. "That's it!" he exclaimed. "That's just it! Sentimentality, that's what's going to ruin our jail. I *did* think, Mrs. W., that you had more sense!"

The cow looked a little angry. "If I knew what you were talking about," she said stiffly, "perhaps I might agree with you."

"Being sentimental?" said Freddy. "I'll tell you what it is. It's going round looking for someone or something to cry over, just for the fun of crying. You knew you weren't doing those goats any good. You just wanted to have a good time feeling sorry."

The nice thing about Mrs. Wiggins was that she always admitted it when she was wrong. She did so now after she had thought about it for a few minutes. "I guess you're right, Freddy," she said. "I won't do it again—but, good grief, what's that rabbit up to?"

Freddy had noticed the rabbit too. It had hopped out of the long grass, turned and looked straight at them, then deliberately went into the garden where Mr. Bean grew lettuce and radishes and other vegetables and began nibbling at a head of lettuce. Now, no animals were allowed in this garden except the head squirrel and his gang, who did the weeding and could be trusted not to eat the vegetables. So Freddy was greatly shocked by such bold behavior.

"Come, come!" he shouted, hurrying up to the rabbit. "You're a bold one, I *must* say! You just come along with me. You're under arrest."

"Yes, sir," said the rabbit meekly. "Do we go to jail right away?"

"Jail?" said Freddy. "I guess we do go to jail, just as soon as the judge can sentence you."

The rabbit looked quite pleased at this and started hopping off, his mouth still full of lettuce leaves.

"Stop!" called Freddy, hurrying after him. "No use your trying to escape. Better come along quietly. You'll just make matters worse for yourself if you don't."

"I wasn't trying to escape," said the rabbit. "I was just starting for the henhouse so I could be sentenced—I really was, sir," he added, as Freddy stared at him in amazement.

The pig was rather puzzled. The rabbit was evidently telling the truth, and yet such eagerness to be punished didn't seem reasonable. "You're a queer one," said Freddy. "I don't believe you understand. You've been stealing lettuce, and it's against the rules, and you're going to be punished by being sent to jail."

"But I *do* understand, sir," replied the prisoner. "I know I've done wrong, and—well, sir, I think I *ought* to be punished. As a lesson to me, sir. I ought to know better than to do such things."

"H'm," said Freddy, "you're saying all the things *I* ought to say. Still, they're true, and I'm glad you see it. Only if you feel that way, I can't see why you stole the lettuce in the first place."

"I can tell you that," said the rabbit. "But—well, I'd rather wait until after I'm sentenced."

"All right," said the pig. "And I'll do my best with the judge to see that your sentence isn't a long one. I'm sure you won't do it again."

"Oh, yes I shall!" exclaimed the rabbit anxiously. "Yes, sir, I'm apt to do things like that any time. I'm quite a desperate character, sir, really I am. You'd better get me a good long sentence."

"Say, look here!" said Freddy sharply. "Are you trying to make fun of me, or what? If you're a good law-abiding rabbit, as you seem to be, I can understand your being sorry that you'd done wrong and thinking that you ought to be punished. But I don't believe that anybody, animal or human, ever thought that he ought to be punished a *lot*. Come on, now, tell me the truth!"

At this the rabbit broke down and began to cry. "Oh dear!" he sobbed. "I thought it would be so easy to get into jail! I thought all you had to do was steal something. And I wanted to go to jail—the animals there all have such a good time, and don't have to work, and they play games and sing songs all day long, and other animals are sorry for them and bring them lots of good things to eat! Oh, please, Mr. Freddy, take me to the judge and get me a good long sentence."

"I'll do nothing of the kind," said Freddy crossly. "And, what's more, I'm not going to arrest you at all. I'm going to give your ears a good boxing"—which he did while the rabbit submitted meekly— "and then you can go. Only let me tell you something. Don't go stealing any more lettuce in the hope that you'll be sent to jail. Because you won't. You'll get something you won't like at all."

"Wh—what's that?" sniveled the rabbit.

"I don't know," said Freddy. "I'll have to think up something. But you can bet it'll be something good."

Then he went back to where Mrs. Wiggins was waiting for him. "Can you beat it?" he exclaimed. "Did you hear that?"

"I certainly did," said the cow. "I tell you, Freddy, something's got to be done, and done quick. Let's go have a talk with Charles. Maybe he can suggest something."

VIII
The Judge Disappears

THEY found The henhouse in a great state of excitement. A flock of young chickens—Henrietta's gawky, long-legged daughters—were crowding about their mother or dashing in and out on errands, and the older hens were running round

distractedly, squawking and clucking, some of them bringing water in their beaks to sprinkle over one of their sisters, who had fainted, others merely hurrying aimlessly out of the door to stop and give several loud squawks and then hurry as aimlessly inside again.

At first the two detectives could get no answers to their questions in the general hubbub, but at last Freddy, losing patience, squeezed his way inside, seized Henrietta by a wing and pulled her over into a corner. "Come, now; what's the trouble here?" he demanded. "Pull yourself together, hen, and tell me what's wrong."

Henrietta glared at him for a moment without seeming to see him. Then suddenly she seemed to recognize him, and burst out wildly: "You!" she cried. "You *dare* come here, you wretched pig, with your fine airs and your lordly ways—you that's to blame for all this, you and all your smart friends that told him how fine it would be to be a judge! *You* are the one that got him into this, you imitation detective, you; you big chunk of fat pork!"

Freddy backed away a little. "Come, come, Henrietta," he said soothingly. "Let's not talk about me. I may be everything you say, but that doesn't get us anywhere, does it? I don't even know what's the matter yet."

But Henrietta's rage was quickly spent. She broke down and began to cry. "He's gone!" she sobbed. "My Charles, the finest husband a hen ever had! They've got him, my good, kind, noble Charles!"

Serious as the situation seemed, Freddy had to repress a grin. When Charles was around, Henrietta did nothing but scold him and tell him what a silly rooster he was. Outside the henhouse there was a strange whining, grumbling sound, and Freddy recognized it as Mrs. Wiggins's giggle. But fortunately the hen did not hear it and went on with her story.

There wasn't very much of it. Charles had been missing since late the previous afternoon. None of the animals on the farm had seen him.

Freddy suggested the only thing he could think of. "He may have gone visiting," he said, "and been invited to stay all night."

"He wouldn't *dare* stay out all night!" flashed the hen. "Just let him try it once!" Then she began to cry again. "No, he's gone. It's one of those animals he sentenced to jail. There were a couple of them that said they'd get even with him when they got out. And now they've gone and done it. And I shall never see him again! Oh, my poor Charles! My noble husband!" And she flopped round in a violent fit of hysterics.

Freddy shook his head dolefully and went outside. "Come on," he said to the cow. "Nothing more to be got out of her. We'd better get busy right away. Now, where in the world do you suppose he can be?"

"Off somewhere having a good time probably," replied Mrs. Wiggins. "Though it *is* funny. Henrietta would peck his eyes out if he stayed out a minute after ten o'clock."

"Yes," said Freddy, "and none of the animals he has sentenced to jail have got out yet, so it can t be that. Of course, he might have been carried off by a hawk, or had a fight with a stray cat. But, for all his bluster and boasting, Charles is too clever to be caught like that. I expect we'd better put the whole force on it to go round and find out all they can."

So they got all their helpers together and sent them out in different directions to ask questions and look for signs of the missing rooster. Both Freddy and Mrs. Wiggins went out too. But when they met again late that evening, nothing had been found. Charles had vanished without leaving so much as a feather behind.

The next morning Freddy was up and out before the dew was off the grass, for this, he felt, was a case on which his reputation as a detective rested. It wasn't just an ordinary disappearance. Charles was the judge, an important personage, and if he wasn't found, and quickly, nobody would bring any more cases to the detectives.

He was on his way down to the cow-barn to get Mrs. Wiggins when he heard a loud moo behind him and, turning, saw that animal galloping toward him as fast as she could come.

"Come with me over to the jail," she panted. "I've got something to show you. I went over there when I got up, to check over the prisoners and see that they were all there, because I thought some of them might have escaped and perhaps murdered Charles—though, goodness knows, none of 'em are mad at him for sentencing them. Quite the contrary. Just listen to them."

The sounds of shouts and laughter and songs greeted them as they approached. Hank, from his stall, turned a weary eye on them as they entered. "I do wish you would do something about this," he said. "I thought it was going to be company for me, having the jail here, but, my land! nobody wants company twenty-four hours a day! They just keep it up all night. I haven't had a wink of sleep for ten days."

Freddy nodded. "Yes, we'll have to make some other arrangements. This jail isn't a punishment any more at all. But we'll talk about that later. What was it you wanted to show me?" he asked the cow.

Without speaking she led him to the door of one of the stalls, hooked the wooden pin out of the staple, and opened the door. Inside, some twenty animals and birds were crowded together. One group was in a circle, watching two rabbits doing gymnastic stunts. Another group, with their heads together, were singing "Sweet Adeline" with a great deal of expression. Mrs. Wiggins raised one hoof and pointed dramatically at a third group. In the center of it was the missing judge, declaiming at the top of his lungs.

"On with the dance!" declaimed Charles.

"Stop! Silence!" shouted Freddy, and Mrs. Wiggins stamped on the floor to get attention.

"Let joy be unconfined!" went on Charles dramatically. Then he saw the visitors, and his voice flattened out into a whisper.

Heads turned; the song died down; the groups broke up and surrounded the detectives.

Freddy pushed his way through them and confronted Charles. "What on earth does this mean?" he demanded. "What are you doing here? Don't you know that Henrietta is half crazy with worry?"

"Why I—I'm in jail," explained Charles a little hesitantly; then, gaining courage at the immediate applause which this remark drew from his fellow prisoners: "Tell Henrietta I'm very sorry," he went on, "but I'm serving a six weeks' sentence, and I can't come home until my time's up."

"A sentence!" exclaimed Mrs. Wiggins. "But how can you be serving a sentence? You're the judge. Who can sentence you?"

"The judge!" said Charles triumphantly. "I'm the judge, and I sentenced myself!"

"What for?"

"Well, I'll tell you," said Charles, now thoroughly at ease. "You see, two or three years ago I stole something. It doesn't matter what it was. Well, then, when I was elected judge, that old crime worried me. Here I am, I thought, sentencing other animals to jail for crimes no worse than the one I committed, and yet *I* never served any sentence for it. It got on my nerves after a while. It didn't seem right, somehow. What right had I to set myself up as better than these other animals and punish them for things when I was no better myself? The only fair thing, it seemed to me, the only just thing, the only honest thing, the only noble thing, was to punish myself. And so I did. I'm serving my sentence now."

The other prisoners set up a cheer, but Freddy scowled. "Nonsense!" he exclaimed. "I'll tell you why you're here. You're sick of being nagged at by Henrietta. I don't blame you there—I shouldn't like it either. And so you thought this would give you an excuse to stay away from home and have a good time. But you can't get away with it, Charles. This jail isn't a club. It—"

"But I stole something, I tell you," insisted the rooster. "I'm only getting the punishment I deserve. I can't get out."

"You can and you're going to," said Freddy. "You never stole anything in your life. And how are you going to be of any use as a judge when you're in jail yourself?"

"I don't see why I won't," protested Charles. "Bring the prisoners down here and I can sentence 'em just the same, can't I?"

"No, you can't," put in Mrs. Wiggins. "Come along, now. Henrietta's waiting for you."

"I'm not going," said Charles.

Freddy turned and winked secretly at the cow. "Oh, all right, then," he said. "Let him stay here. We'll just have to elect another judge, that's all. We'll get Peter. There s a lot of the animals thought he would be a better judge anyway, and there'll be plenty more now, when this gets out."

But this didn't suit the rooster either. "You can't do that!" he shouted, hopping up and down in his excitement. "You can't do that! I was elected, and you can't put me out that way."

"Oh, can't we?" said Freddy. "Don't you know that a judge loses his job when he goes to jail? We don't have to put you out. You're just *out,* anyway. Unless, of course, you decide that there was some mistake about it and take back your sentence."

For a few minutes the crestfallen rooster thought this over in silence. He was having a very good time in the jail. On the other hand, in jail he was really just one of the prisoners. And outside he was a judge, looked up to and respected by the entire community. Still—

there was Henrietta. He knew that no story he could fix up would go down with Henrietta. And what she'd say—he shivered to think of it.

"Come on," said Freddy. "Henrietta is taking on terribly. You don't want her to feel badly, do you? She misses you, Charles." And he repeated some of the things Henrietta had said, about how good and noble he was.

Charles looked up quickly. "She said *that*!" he exclaimed.

"She certainly did," said Mrs. Wiggins.

"Well, then, I guess—I guess I'd better go back," said 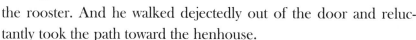 the rooster. And he walked dejectedly out of the door and reluctantly took the path toward the henhouse.

That evening Freddy and Mrs. Wiggins were strolling down through the pasture, talking over the new problems that confronted them in their detective work. From the hen-house came the angry clucking and gabbling of Henrietta's voice, going on and on and punctuated occasionally with Charles's shrill squawks. They listened for a few minutes, then grinned at each other and walked on.

"It's really a swell joke on us," said Freddy. "We were looking for a missing rooster, and there he was in jail all the time—the one place nobody'd ever look for him."

"We find 'em," said Mrs. Wiggins complacently. "Wherever they are, we find 'em."

Freddy grinned more broadly as a particularly agonized shriek came from the henhouse. "We'd have no trouble finding the judge tonight," he said. "I bet that's the last time he stays out all night."

"He won't have a tail feather left by morning," said the cow.

IX
Jinx Is Indicted

ALTHOUGH Freddy Had been successful with nearly all his detective cases, there were two things that bothered him a good deal. The rats were still in the barn, for one thing, and though they couldn't get to the grain-box any more without running the risk of being caught by Jinx, who was always on guard, they had stolen enough grain while they had the train of cars to keep them all the next winter. And, for another thing, the two robbers were still living in the hermit s house, and Freddy hadn't yet thought up a way of bringing them to justice. One of the mice, Cousin Augustus, had volunteered to go live in the house with them, and the reports he brought back were disturbing. They spent the day sleeping, or shooting at the chimney, or mending their clothes. But every night they went out and got in an automobile and drove off, coming back in the early morning with big packages of dollar bills, which they kept in an old trunk in the attic. They did all their own work—even made their own clothes—but the house, said Cousin Augustus, who was used to Mrs. Bean's neat housekeeping, was a disgrace. "Dirty," he said, "isn't the word for it! Crumbs all over the floor, and the stuffing coming out of the sofa, and the kitchen sink full of dirty dishes. And the window-curtains simply black! You'd think they'd have some pride!"

Cousin Augustus had succeeded in gnawing a hole through the back of the trunk and in pulling out a package of the dollar bills, which he had brought to Freddy. Nothing would be easier, he said, than to take a gang of mice up there some night and get all the bills; but Freddy decided that there wasn't much point in this, as they didn't know whom the money had been stolen from, and so couldn't give it back to its owners. And certainly a pigpen was no place for it. But he kept the package Cousin Augustus had brought, hoping that some day he might get a clue which would lead to the arrest of the robbers and the return of the money.

And then one morning, when Freddy was in his office, he heard a buggy draw up in the road opposite it, and, looking through the window, he saw two men lean out and read the sign he had printed. The man who was driving was the sheriff, who lived up near Centerboro. He was in his shirtsleeves and had a tuft of thin gray whiskers on his chin and a silver star on his vest, and Freddy knew him well because he owned some pigs who were distant relatives of Freddy's. The other was a rather cross-looking man with a hard face, who had the stump of a cigar so firmly clamped between his teeth that it looked as if it was a part of his face.

"It may seem funny to *you,*" the sheriff was saying, "you being from the city an' all, but I tell you these animals are *different.* They take trips to Florida in the winter, and they do all the work round the place without anybody tellin' 'em what to do, and there am 't one of 'em, so Mr. Bean tells me, that can't read."

"Bah!" exclaimed the hard-faced man so disgustedly that he almost lost his cigar stump. "I never heard such nonsense! You country hicks will believe anything. You can't tell me any animal can learn to read, to say nothing of setting up in the detective business and hanging out a sign. Who printed that sign for 'em? I suppose you'll tell me the animals did it!"

"Sure, they did it!" replied the sheriff. "I tell you, these animals are a lot smarter than some folks I know."

"Meanin' me?" said the other threateningly.

"I name no names," said the sheriff. "But I ain't goin' to quarrel about it. All I'm tellin' you is, if I had the say-so, I'd get these animals to help me catch those robbers. Of course, you're the boss, since you've been put in charge of the case. But you're a city detective. I don't mean nothin' against city detectives, nor against you, personal. I don't know nothin' about you, but you must be a good man or they wouldn't 'a' sent you. But detectin' in the city and detectin' in the country is two different things. I'm a pretty good sheriff in the country, I guess, but in the city I wouldn't be worth much, because I don't know city ways. And you don't know country ways, and that's why I'm tellin' you—"

"Oh, you talk too much," interrupted the detective rudely. "Why don't *you* catch these robbers if you're so smart?"

"Same reason you don't," replied the sheriff calmly. "I ain't smart enough. Only I'm willin' to say so, and you *ain't*. And I'm willin' to take help where I can get it. If a pig can help me, I call on a pig."

"A pig!" exclaimed the detective. He was so disgusted that he chewed a big piece off the end of his cigar. But he did not say anything more, for at that moment Freddy, who had been listening all the time, decided that he would show himself. He came slowly out of his office, walked over to the fence, and, getting up on his hind legs, leaned his forelegs on the upper rail as a man would have done, and looked inquiringly at the two in the buggy.

The detective gave a gasp of surprise and swallowed his cigar, and although he had chewed up so much of it that it wasn't very big, it hurt quite a lot going down and it was several minutes before he could speak. Then he pointed at Freddy and said hoarsely: "What's that?"

"That's one of 'em," said the sheriff, "the pig I was tellin' you about." He leaned out of the buggy. "Eh, Freddy? You're a detective, aren't you?" he said.

Freddy nodded solemnly, and the detective gasped again.

"I got a case I'd like your help on," continued the sheriff. "Come on over and sit under this tree while I tell you about it," and he climbed out of the buggy. When Freddy had got over the fence, they sat down in the grass, while the amazed detective goggled at them for a few moments before himself getting out and joining them.

"You see, it's this way," said the sheriff. "There's been a lot of robberies lately in this neighborhood. Robbers have been breaking in the back windows of banks and stores in nearly all the towns around here and taking all the money. We don't know who they are. So far we haven't got a clue, except that they nearly always wear rubbers, and that they travel in a car with one wobbly rear wheel. It's got so that the people are afraid to leave their places of business now at night, for fear they'll be robbed, and the bankers and business men are most of them sitting up all night with shotguns and pistols to protect their money. Yes, sir, Freddy, it's getting pretty bad. Because now, you see, the business men are so sleepy in the daytime that when you go in to do business with them, you find them sound asleep behind their counters. There's hardly any business bein' done in Centerboro, on account of the business men being so sleepy.

"That's only one bad thing about it. There's been a lot of accidents through fallin' asleep at the wrong time. Just yesterday my brother fell asleep when he was looking for something to eat in the icebox, and he lay there with his head on the ice for an hour till we found him, and froze both his ears. Right in the middle of summer—yes, sir! Froze 'em both solid. If you'd 'a' tapped 'em, they'd 'a' broke off like crackers. Course we was careful. We thawed 'em out slow, and they're all right again.

"Then there was old Mr. Winch. He fell asleep driving up Main Street, and his car ran right up on the porch of the Holcomb House and knocked four rocking chairs to splinters. That wouldn't 'a' been so bad, but Mis' Holcomb was settin' in one of 'em at the time. She was quite upset.

"But that ain't neither here nor there. What I wanted to tell you was that we're at our wits' ends to know what to do. We can't find hide nor hair of these robbers, even though we've got this special detective up from New York. Oh, I forgot to introduce you to him. Mr. Boner, this is Freddy."

Freddy bowed politely, but the detective frowned. "I ain't going to shake hands with no pig," he growled.

"Suit yourself," said the sheriff, winking at Freddy. "Pig or not, he's shook hands with the President in his time, and that's more than you've done, I bet."

"Oh, come on! Let's get going!" exclaimed Mr. Boner.

"Time enough," replied the sheriff. "Specially as we ain't goin' anywhere in particular." He turned to Freddy. "I just thought," he said, "that maybe, now you've started in as a detective, you'd be willing to give us a hand. I don't know just how you'll go at it, but we're stumped. What do you say?"

"Can he *talk*?" demanded the astonished Mr. Boner.

"Course he can't!" snapped the sheriff. "Who ever heard of a pig that could talk!"

"Well, according to you he can understand everything you're saying," said the detective, not unreasonably.

"That's different," said the sheriff.

While they were wrangling about this, Freddy got up, climbed the fence, and came back presently with the package of one-dollar bills that

Cousin Augustus had brought from the trunk in the hermit's house. As soon as they saw it, the two men became very much excited. They examined it carefully, and then the sheriff said to Freddy: "This is from Herbie's Hardware Emporium, that was robbed last month. Gosh, I wish you could talk! Do you know where there's any more of this money?"

Freddy nodded.

"Will you lead us to it?"

But this time Freddy shook his head. Lead them to it indeed, and let them get all the glory of the capture! No, he intended to capture the robbers himself. While they had been talking, he had thought of a plan. It was a good one, too, and he intended to try it out. If he failed, he could call in the sheriff later.

The sheriff was much put out at his refusal. "Oh come, Freddy," he coaxed, "you want to help us, don't you?"

Freddy nodded.

"But you won't show us where the rest of the money is?"

Freddy shook his head again.

"You mean you've got some scheme of your own for getting it back?"

Freddy nodded his head emphatically.

"You see," said the sheriff to Mr. Boner, "he'll help us; but he's going to do it in his own way. And I don't know that I blame him."

"Nonsense!" exclaimed the detective angrily. "Let *me* talk to him." He moved toward the pig, but Freddy was too quick for him and scrambled over the fence. Mr. Boner would have climbed over after him, but the sheriff caught his arm.

"You won't get anywhere that way," he said. "Let him alone. He said he'd help us, and he will. I know these animals."

"You know 'em all right," growled Mr. Boner. "You ought to be livin' in the pen along with 'em. I wash my hands of you. When you're ready to go along, let me know." And he climbed into the buggy and lit a cigar.

"Well, Freddy," said the sheriff, "I guess you'll have to do it your own way. I'll be back along this way day after tomorrow about this time, and if you've got anything for me, you be here. If you want me before that, you know where to find me. And do the best you can. If you can help me catch these rascals, I'll be grateful, you bet; and you know there's five thousand dollars reward offered for their capture. You'll get that, and I'll see that your name is played up big in the newspapers. So long. I'm countin' on you."

As soon as the men had gone, Freddy made his preparations. He got a pencil and paper and drew a plan which you will hear more about later. But to visit the hermit's house he needed a disguise, for he remembered how anxious they had been to catch him when he had been there before. Detectives did much of their work in disguise—workmen's clothes and false whiskers and so on—and Freddy had got together quite a large wardrobe for use in disguising himself, though he had never yet used any of it. Today he picked out a false mustache, a pipe, a cap like Sherlock Holmes's, with a viser in front and behind and ear-flaps that tied at the top with a tape, and an old suit of Mr. Bean's which was a trifle long in the leg, but otherwise fitted very well.

Walking on his hind legs, with the pipe in his mouth and the cap pulled well down over his eyes, Freddy might have passed for a very small tramp with a very long nose. As there was no looking glass in his office, he decided to go first up to the house and see what he looked like in Mrs. Bean's mirror. At the same time he would try the effect of his disguise on some of his friends.

To his surprise, he found no animals in the usually busy barnyard. He walked across to the house and rapped on the back door. Mrs. Bean answered. "Good morning," she said politely. "What can I do for you?"

Freddy touched his cap awkwardly and then brushed past her, walked across the kitchen, and started up the back stairs, while Mrs. Bean watched him with amazement and alarm. "See here, young man!" she began—but at that moment Freddy came to grief. By long practice he had learned how to walk on his hind legs, but going upstairs was a different matter. At the fourth step he lost his balance and came tumbling down.

Mrs. Bean stared for a moment, then burst out laughing. "My goodness, Freddy, it's you! For a minute I thought you were a tramp. I suppose you're up to some of your detective tricks again. What won't you animals be doing next!" She picked up his pipe and handed it to him.

"Land alive! In that suit you look enough like Mr. Bean to be his brother, except that your legs aren't long enough, and you haven't any beard."

She patted him on the back and went back to her knitting, and Freddy went upstairs on all four legs this time and was soon admiring his get-up in the big mirror in the front bedroom. As he turned and twisted before the glass, trying the hat and the pipe at different angles, and nodding and bowing to himself with little grunts of satisfaction, he heard a curious sound. He turned quickly. Someone, he thought, had chuckled. But there was no one there, so he went back to the always pleasant task of admiring himself.

And again came the noise—an unmistakable giggle this time.

He stooped and looked under the bed, and there, not an inch from his nose, was the grinning face of Jinx, who had been watching him all the time.

It is always embarrassing to find that someone has been watching you when you think you are alone, even if you haven't been doing anything silly; and Freddy knew that he must have looked very silly in front of the glass. So he said angrily: "What are you doing here? Why aren't you watching for the rats instead of sneaking around and spying on sensible folks?"

To his surprise Jinx, instead of bursting into his usual loud teasing laugh, came out from under the bed and said meekly: "Excuse me, Freddy; you did look funny, you know. But I wasn't spying on you. I was hiding. They're after me."

"Who are after you?" demanded the pig.

"Haven't you heard?" asked Jinx. "The policemen are after me—Robert and Jock. I tell you, Freddy, I don't know what to do. I wouldn't mind going to jail at any other time. From all I hear, they have a better time inside than we do out. But I *can't* go now—"

"What on earth are you talking about?" interrupted the pig.

"You haven't heard, then," said Jinx. "Well, let me tell you about it—or at least what little I know—for I need your help. You know that for the past few weeks, ever since we got Everett's train back from the rats, I have been spending nearly all my time up in the barn loft, guarding the grain-box. The rats have been trying every way they can to get into it, because, although they say they have got enough grain hidden in their holes under the barn to last all winter, I don't believe they've got very much, and when their supply gives out, they'll have to leave the barn and go back to the woods."

"That'll make old Simon pretty sick," said Freddy.

"Yes, and that's just what I'm working for. He's got to be shown who's boss around here. But if I go to jail, he and his family can just help themselves to all the grain they want. I can't go to jail, Freddy!"

"Well, why should you?" asked the puzzled pig. "You haven't done anything, have you—?"

"Of course I haven't. But just listen to this. This noon I left the barn and went to the house to get my lunch. When I got back, over in the corner of the loft where I usually sit, I saw something that hadn't been there when I left. I went over to look at it, and what do you think was there? Somebody had eaten a crow there and left nothing but his claws and feathers."

"My goodness!" said Freddy.

"Just what I said," went on the cat. "And I was standing there looking at them and trying to figure out how they could have got there, when in stalks Charles, very haughty—you know he's never forgiven me for throwing those tomatoes at him the night he was elected—and he clears his throat a few times and then says: "Ha, it was true, then, was it?' he says. 'This is a serious matter, Jinx,' he says. 'This will take some explaining.'

"'Well,' I said, 'if you can explain it, Charles, I wish you would. It's beyond me.'

"'Oh, is it, indeed?' says Charles, very sarcastic. 'Well, it looks plain enough, Jinx. Yes, it certainly looks plain enough.'

"'Oh, cut out the big talk, Charles,' I said; 'I come back here and find that someone has eaten this crow—'

"'Someone!' he interrupted. Then he laughed kind of nastily. 'Someone! Ha ha, that's good.'

"He made me so mad that I pretty near slapped him one. But I kept my temper. 'Look here, Charles,' I said, 'you don't think *I* had anything to do with this, do you? Gosh, you ought to know that even an alley cat won't eat a crow.'

"'They've been known to eat chickens,' he said meaningly. 'But I'm not afraid of you, Jinx. I warn you, it won't be wise for you to try any violence. Jock and Robert are within call. If you dare to so much as lift a paw against me, I have only to call, and they'll be here in a few seconds.'

"Well, Freddy, that kind of pompous talk from Charles, who has always been a good friend of mine, made me pretty wild. If I hadn't seen that there was something serious behind it all, I'd have given him the scare of his life. But I tried to be reasonable. 'Look here, Charles,' I said, 'that kind of talk is just silly. I never even chased a bird of any kind, to say nothing of eating one, and you know it. I found this crow here when I came back from lunch. Now be sensible and tell me what it is all about.'

"Well, then I got it out of him, though he wasn't very friendly about it. It seems that about the time I was having lunch, one of the young rats slipped out of the barn, ran down to the henhouse, and told Charles to come right away and bring the policemen. He said I had caught this crow in the barn and was eating it. Of course Charles came, and there I was with the crow. Charles must know perfectly well that I wouldn't do such a thing, but he's made up his mind to get even with me about the tomatoes, and so he wants to send me to jail. So I didn't wait for Jock and Robert to get there. They were waiting by the door. I ran down the stairs and got through the window in Hank's stall, and I've been hiding here ever since until I could get a word with you. You've got to get to the bottom of this for me, Freddy."

"Oh, we can get to the bottom of it all right," said Freddy. "But it may take some time. It looks to me as if it was a plot the rats cooked up to get you sent to jail so they could have all the grain they wanted."

"Exactly," said the cat. "But what can I do? I ought to be in the barn, not hiding here under the bed."

"You stay here a little longer," said the pig, "and I'll go down and see if I can pick up any clues."

"But you *do* believe I didn't do it, don't you?" asked Jinx.

"Sure I believe you," said Freddy. "But believing isn't enough to keep you out of jail. We've got to prove it. But you wait; I'll be right back." And struggling out of his disguise, he hurried down the stairs.

In the loft he found a crowd of excited animals, in the middle of which was Charles, who hurried up to the pig as he came in. "Aha, here's the detective!" he cried. "Now we'll get something done. The criminal has escaped, Freddy. You'll have to track him down for us. Spare no pains, in the interests of justice and the safety of this law-abiding barnyard—"

"Oh, shut up, Charles," said the pig good-naturedly. "I know all about it. I don't think for a minute Jinx killed this crow. Clear out, now, all of you. I want to take a look at things."

The animals went reluctantly downstairs, and Freddy looked carefully around. The crow's two claws were laid neatly side by side, and the feathers were in a tidy heap beside them. "Please note," he said to Charles, who, since he was the judge, had been allowed to stay, "that there are no signs of a struggle. If Jinx caught this crow here, the crow would have struggled, and feathers would be strewn all over the place."

"He may have caught it outside," said Charles. "What difference does that make? All this detective work of yours can't change the fact that he's guilty."

"Maybe they can. Maybe they can," said Freddy musingly. He walked around the pile of feathers, stopping to examine them closely every few steps, then sniffed at them. "Ha!" he said. "Hum! Very curious! Very curious indeed!"

"Very silly, if you ask me," said a harsh voice, as Simon stuck his nose out of a hole in the floor. "You'd be better occupied catching that cat and getting him locked up in jail, than poking around up here, Freddy. He's a friend of yours and all that, but we've got him this time!"

"What do you mean, *you've* got him?" demanded Freddy sharply.

"Oh, nothing," grinned the rat, "except that we all saw him catch the crow and eat him, right in front of our eyes. You can't get round that, I guess."

"No, it doesn't look that way, does it?" said Freddy. He picked up a claw and a few feathers and carried them over to the light, where he studied them for a long time. Then he said: "Charles, we'll just keep these things for a while. I'm not at all satisfied that this business is as plain as it looks—not at all satisfied. You can't sentence Jinx to jail until he has had a regular trial. We'll have to get a regular jury together, and all that. I'll leave that to you. But I want to have a few days first to make some inquiries. Let's say we'll have the trial a week from today."

Charles agreed, and the two friends left the loft, followed by Simon's malevolent glare. They took the claws and the feathers along and left them with Robert, who promised to keep them in a safe place. Before he left Charles, Freddy got the rooster to promise that Jinx should be allowed to go free until the day of the trial. "If he's found guilty," the pig said, "you can give him a good long sentence. But until then let's let him go on with his job. He won't run away."

"You talk as if you thought he wasn't guilty," said Charles; "yet the proof's as plain as the nose on your face."

"The nose on my face may be plain or it may not be plain," replied Freddy. "Some think one way and some think different. It's a matter of opinion, Charlie, old boy. And so is this matter of Jinx's guilt. My opinion is, he isn't guilty. But I'm not going to tell you why. You saw as much up there in the barn as I did. If you didn't see what I saw, you'll have to wait until the trial to find out what it was. Good-bye."

Then Freddy went back in the house and upstairs to where Jinx was waiting and told him what had happened. "You just go back to the barn and keep an eye on the rats," he said, "and leave the rest of it to me. I've got another job on my hands right now that will keep me busy for a day or two, but there's plenty of time before your trial to get the evidence I need to prove you didn't eat that crow. Don't you worry."

So Jinx went back to the barn, and Freddy put on his disguise again and set out on his adventure.

X
Freddy Becomes
a Burglar

FREDDY had Got such a late start that it was nearly dark in the woods, though above him the treetops were bright green and gold in the light of the setting sun. Since he could not swim the creek in his men's clothes, to get to the hermit's house

he had to cut through the woods to the bridge and then walk back on the other side. He walked on his hind legs, because after his mishap on the stairs he felt that he needed all the practice he could get if he was to make anybody think he was a man. But the trousers bothered his legs, and he stumbled over roots and tripped over vines and fell into holes until, long before he reached the creek, he was so bruised and hot and out of breath that he sat down on a log to rest. "My goodness," he said to himself, "I'm glad I'm not a man! How they ever manage to do anything or get anywhere in all these clumsy hot clothes I can't imagine! Lords of creation, they call themselves! Humph, I'd rather be a pig any time."

Pretty soon he got up and went on again, and at last he reached the bridge. On the farther side of the bridge a narrow grassy road ran off to the left toward the hermit's house. Freddy followed it. He began to feel rather nervous, but he was a brave pig and he had no thought of turning back.

By this time it was dark. The windows in the hermit's house were lighted up, but they were so dirty that Freddy couldn't see what was going on inside. He could hear music, however—someone was playing the harmonium and a man's voice was singing. The song was "Sweet and Low," but both singer and accompanist were going as fast as they could, and they were never together for more than one note. The singer would be ahead for a time, then the player would put on a burst of speed and pass him, only to get behind again when he stopped to take breath.

Freddy thought this was the funniest singing he had ever heard, and he went up to the front door and peeked through the keyhole, just as the song came to an end. The big man, who was sitting at the harmonium, was wiping sweat from his forehead. "You won that time, Looey," he was saying, "but it's the chords in that second part that slow me up."

"I'll race you on 'Boola Boola,'" said Looey.

"No you won't either," said Red. "You always win on that because you leave Out about six 'Boolas,' and I can't keep track when I'm playing. Let's take something where all the words aren't alike. Let's do 'Annie Laurie.' One, two, three—go!"

The noise was terrible. If you don't believe it, try singing "Annie Laurie" as fast as you can. Freddy couldn't stand it any longer, and he rapped on the door.

The musicians were going so fast that they couldn't stop for about four bars. Then there was a moment's silence, followed by the clump of heavy shoes, and the door was flung open. Freddy touched his cap and bowed politely.

"My gosh, what's this?" said Red. "Come in, young feller. What can I do for you?"

Freddy stepped inside. The room was lit by three kerosene lamps, but the lamp chimneys were so dirty that they gave very little light, and he felt reasonably sure that if he kept his cap on, they wouldn't know he was a pig. Nevertheless he was scared when they both came close to him and squatted down with their hands on their knees and stared at him.

At first they didn't say anything. They stared at him for a minute, then stood up and stared at each other, then squatted down and stared at him again.

"Well, I'll be jiggered!" said Red.

"So'll I!" said Looey. "He's a—what do you call those little men— a wharf, isn't it?"

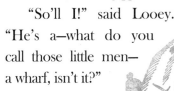

"A dwarf," said Red. "You ought to know that, Looey."

"Well, wharf or dwarf, what does it matter what we call him? The point is, what does he call himself? What's your name, guy?"

Freddy pointed to his mouth and shook his head.

"He's dumb," said Looey. "What good's a dumb dwarf? Let's throw him out and go on with the music."

Freddy had in his pocket the chart that he had prepared, but although from long practice in handling books and papers he had got so that he could use his forefeet almost as if they were hands, he was afraid that if he took it out and gave it to them they would see that he had hoofs instead of hands, and would realize that he was a pig.

Fortunately at this moment Red said: "Wait! I've got an idea!"

"I hope it's better than the one you had last Thursday," said Looey.

"This is a good one," said Red. "Listen, this dwarf is little, and he's dumb. That means he can get in places where we can't get in, and that he can't tell anybody about it afterwards. How about that back window in the Centerboro National Bank?"

"Gosh!" exclaimed Looey. "That *is* an idea!" He turned to Freddy. "Say, dwarf, would you like to make a lot of money?"

Freddy nodded enthusiastically.

"Fine! You come with us and do just what we tell you to, and we'll give you fifty cents. Come on, Red, get your things on." And almost before he knew what had happened, Freddy was walking back up the dark road with one of the robbers on each side of him.

He hadn't had a chance to show them his chart, and he hadn't the least idea what sort of adventure he was in for now. "Something pretty shady, I bet," he said to himself. "But no use worrying. I'm in with them now, and if I can't catch them after this, I'm a pretty poor detective."

At the bridge they stopped, Red dove into the bushes, and pretty soon there was the sputter of an engine and he drove out into the road in a badly battered open car. Red hoisted Freddy in, and they started off in the direction of Centerboro. Nothing was said on the way. Both the robbers had on raincoats, black masks, and rubbers and carried pistols in their hands. Looey had hard work driving with the pistol in his hand, and once when he had to shift gears, it went off. It was pointed at the windshield when it went off, and Freddy was surprised not to see the glass fly to pieces, but Looey only laughed.

"We don't carry loaded pistols when we're at work," he explained; "it's too easy to have an accident."

As they drove down Main Street, Freddy saw that there were lights in all the stores, just as the sheriff had told him there would be. They slowed up when they came to the bank, and he saw a watchman sitting on the front steps with a gun across his knees. But he paid no attention to them as they turned into the alley next to the bank.

Looey stopped the car in the alley, and they all got out. Red took a stepladder out of the back seat and put it against the bank wall under a small window. "There you are," he said. "They don't bother to lock this window because it's too small for anybody to get through. But you can get through, and when you're inside, we'll throw this sack in after you, and all you have to do is stuff all the money into the sack, throw it out, and then come out yourself. See?"

Freddy saw all right. He saw that he was going to be a robber in spite of himself, and there was nothing else to do. But he had reckoned without the stepladder. Climbing the back stairs at the farm with Mr. Bean's trousers on had been bad enough, but this was hopeless. He scrambled up three steps, then caught his left foot in his right trouser leg, stumbled, squealed, and Freddy and the ladder and Looey came down with a crash on the cobblestones of the alley.

At once the night was full of noise. Windows went up, police whistles blew, men ran out into the streets and began shouting and firing off their guns. Looey scrambled to his feet, tossed Freddy into the car, and climbed in beside him as Red started up the engine. With a roar they dashed out of the alley and up Main Street at full speed. Half a dozen cars swung out into the street behind them as they dodged and twisted to avoid the men who tried to stop them. Red drove magnificently; he almost seemed to dodge the bullets that were fired at them, for none of them hit the car. In less than a minute they were thundering back up the road on which they had come into town, with the pursuit streaming out behind them. In a few minutes more they came to the bridge and crossed it; then Red put on the brakes so quickly that they were all nearly flung through the windshield, swung the car around, snapped off the lights, and drove into the bushes where the car had been hidden before.

One by one the pursuing cars flashed past their hiding-place. When the last one had gone by, the two robbers climbed slowly out of the car.

"You can go on back where you came from, dwarf," said Looey in a disgusted voice.

"You ought to be ashamed of yourself," said Red. "Now we haven't got any stepladder, all on account of you. I was going to put up fresh curtains in the living-room tomorrow, but how I'm to do it without a stepladder I don't know."

"Go on," said Looey. "Beat it. We don't want anything more to do with you. You haven't got any more sense than a pig."

Freddy grinned to himself in the dark; then he took the paper out of his pocket and handed it to Red.

"What's this?" said the robber. He lit a match to look, then called in an excited voice to his companion: "Look, Looey, he's got a map of that farmer's place—the one that lives across the creek—and it shows where his money is hidden."

They bent over the paper, lighting match after match to examine it. "Map of Mr. Bean's barn, showing location of hidden treasure," it said at the top, and under this Freddy had drawn a chart of the barn, but from one of the box stalls he had drawn a long arrow, at the end of which was written: "Under the floor of this stall is hidden a box containing ten thousand dollars in gold."

The robbers were greatly excited. "This is what he came to give us," said Looey. "Maybe he ain't such a bad dwarf after all." He turned to Freddy. "I'm sorry I said that about your being a pig. Are you sure the money is there?"

Freddy nodded emphatically.

"It's worth trying," said Red. "But, just the same, I ain't taking any chances. We'll take this fellow to the house and tie him up while we go over and see if the money's there. If it is, all right; we'll give him his share. But if it ain't—" He glared at the detective. "Well, he'll regret it, that's all."

This didn't suit Freddy at all, but there was nothing else to be done. They took him back to the hermit's house and tied him in a chair and then set out—on foot, this time, as there would be too many people looking for their automobile on the road.

Freddy was almost in despair. He had made no arrangements for the capture of the robbers. If they went to the barn, they would find nothing in the box stall but a dozen or more animal prisoners. If they came back empty-handed a second time this evening, what would happen to him? To think about it made his clothes feel even more tight and uncomfortable than they already were.

But he didn't think about it long, for the robbers had not been gone more than a minute when there was a movement in a dark corner of the room, and a tiny voice said:

"That you, Freddy?"

"Cousin Augustus!" exclaimed Freddy. "Gosh, I'm glad to hear your voice! Gnaw these ropes through, will you, like a good fellow? I've got to get to the farm before those fellows get there or I'll miss an important capture."

Cousin Augustus's teeth were sharp; in a very few minutes Freddy was free and had thrown off his disguise. "Ha," he exclaimed, "this feels like something! Now I'm equal to anything! But I wonder if I can get there before they do. Tell me, Gus, is there any bird round here that you could wake up and get to take a message to Jock?"

"Sure," said the mouse, "there's a wren lives under the eaves of the porch. I'll just slip up and take a peek in his nest and see if he'll go."

Cousin Augustus wasted no time. In two minutes he was back, accompanied by a very sleepy and rather cross wren, who, however, when he realized that it was Freddy, the renowned detective, who wanted his help, was only too anxious to oblige.

"Fly over and wake up Jock or Robed," said Freddy, "and tell them to clear all the prisoners out of the second box stall right away. Tell 'em they mustn't waste a second. There are two robbers coming over there, and I want them to get into that stall without any difficulty. Tell Jock to get all the other animals up and have them hide in the barn and keep quiet until the men get in the stall. I'll be there before there's anything else to be done."

The wren repeated the message to be sure he had it straight, and flew off, and then Freddy dashed down to the creek, dove in and swam across, and galloped off through the woods toward the farm. It was much easier going on four feet than it had been on two, and it wasn't long before he reached the pasture. From there on he went more carefully, and by the time he reached the barn he was creeping along like a shadow.

Faint sounds came from the barn, and now and then a light flickered and was gone again. The robbers were there, then! Freddy slipped inside and into Hank's stall. "Hello, Hank," he whispered. "Everything going all right?"

"Far as I know," said Hank. "Though what it all means is beyond me. Just a few minutes ago Jock and Robert and Mrs. Wiggins came in here and made all the prisoners go into one stall, and then they hid— they're over there in the corner—and then two men sneaked in, and it sounds as if they were tearing up the floor. What's it all about anyway?"

But there was no time to explain. Freddy tiptoed across the floor to the door of the stall. Sure enough, there were Red and Looey, working by the light of a flashlight, heaving at a plank in the floor. With great caution Freddy pushed the heavy door slowly shut and dropped the peg into the hasp.

The robbers heard nothing, and Freddy made no noise, for he had a reason for letting them go on with their work. He went over to the corner where his friends were hiding.

"I guess you can come out now," he said. "We've got 'em safe and fast. This is a great night's work! But what I've been through since I left here you wouldn't believe!"

He started to tell them the tale of his adventures, but suddenly there was a great rattling at the door of the stall. The robbers had found out that they were locked in.

Jock laughed. "Let 'em just try to get out!" he said. "That door will hold an elephant. Anyway I sent down for Peter, in case anything should go wrong. He can handle 'em all right."

Freddy started to go on with his story, when they heard a car drive into the yard, and a loud voice shouted: "Hey, farmer! Wake up!"

"I know that voice," said Freddy. "It's the city detective. Well, let's see how many robbers he's caught tonight!"

The animals went to the barn door. A light had sprung up in an upper window, and pretty soon Mr. Bean's head, in its red nightcap with a white tassel, was poked out into the night.

"Stop raisin' all that rumpus, or I'll come down and take my horsewhip to ye!"

"I want to know if you've seen an open car go by here in the past hour," shouted the detective.

"I got something better to do at night than to sit up and watch for open cars," said Mr. Bean. "Now go "long about your business. I won't have my animals woke up an' disturbed this way."

"I'm huntin' for two robbers in an open car!" shouted Mr. Boner.

"Well, I ain't two robbers in an open car," replied the farmer. "I'm a self-respectin' citizen in a nightshirt, an' what's more, I got a shotgun in my hand, and if you ain't gone in two minutes—"

Just then another car drove into the yard, and the sheriff got out. Mr. Bean's manner changed as soon as he recognized the newcomer. "Oh, how d'e do, sheriff?" he said. "Who is this feller? Friend of yours?"

The sheriff explained. They were combing the countryside for the two robbers who had been frightened away while trying to rob the Centerboro bank, and they wondered if Mr. Bean had seen or heard anything of them.

"I been in bed for three hours," said the farmer. "But there's Freddy comm' across from the barn. Looks like he might have somethin' to show you. Now I'm goin' back to bed. Look around all you like, but for goodness' sake be quiet about it. I want them animals to get their sleep." And he shut down the window.

Meantime Freddy had come up to the sheriff. He raised a foreleg and waved it toward the barn.

"What is it, Freddy?" asked the sheriff. "You know somethin', I bet."

"Oh, that pig again!" exclaimed the disgusted detective. "Come along, sheriff, there ain't anything here."

"Not so fast," replied the sheriff. "I'm goin' to see." And he followed Freddy to the barn and up to the door of the stall, which was still being shaken by the imprisoned robbers.

"H'm," said the sheriff, lugging out his big pistol. "Looks like you'd caught something this time. Stand aside, animals." And he pulled out the peg.

The door gave way suddenly, and out tumbled Looey and Red.

"Stick up your hands!" said Mr. Boner, stepping forward. And as the discomfited robbers backed up against the wall with their hands in the air, he turned to the sheriff. "There's your prisoners, sheriff," he said dramatically. "I knew they were here all the time. That's why I stopped in here in the first place."

"Yeah?" said Looey. "Is that so! Well, let me tell you something. It wasn't you that caught us, city detective. You couldn't catch a lame snail."

"No back talk from you!" exclaimed Mr. Boner angrily. "If it wasn't me that caught you, who was it?"

"It was a little feller in a checked cap, if you want to know," said Looey. "And if all you detectives was as smart as him, you'd have caught us long ago."

"Here's your 'little feller,'" said the sheriff, pushing Freddy forward.

"There you go with your pig again," snorted the disgusted Boner.

"I drove into this barnyard to look for 'em, didn't I? And they're here, ain't they? Well, then, who caught 'em? And who's going to believe that a pig could have done it?"

"The pig done it," said the sheriff doggedly, "and the pig ought to get the credit, *and* the reward!"

Looey and Red were staring at Freddy in amazement. "A pig!" exclaimed Red. "My gosh, Looey, a pig!"

"Pig, all right," replied Looey wearily. "Gee, we're a hot pair of robbers. Caught by a pig!" And then as Mr. Boner started in again to argue that it was he that should get the reward, Looey added: "Well, take us away and lock us up. Anywhere where we won't have to listen to this guy talk any more."

Mr. Bean, in his long white nightshirt and carrying a lantern, had appeared a few moments earlier in the barn door. "Trying to take the credit from my animals, is he?" he muttered. "We'll soon fix that." And he put his head outside and called softly:

"Peter! Get rid of this fellow for us, will you?"

"And I want to tell *you* something too, Mr. Sheriff," Mr. Boner was saying. "You ain't done anything on this case, any more than your friend the pig has, and I'm going to give my own story of the capture to the newspapers, and don't you try to stop me. They're going to say that Mr. Montague Boner, the famous detective, was successful in putting an end to the depredations in upstate banking circles last night. With his brilliant capture of the two—"

Here he stopped, and abruptly, for something rough and furry had rubbed up against him. He turned to look. Peter, the bear, was standing on his hind legs beside him, his mouth wide open, his arms spread out, looking twice his size in the flickering lantern-light.

Mr. Boner opened his mouth almost as wide as Peter's, and out of it came a long yell. Then he dashed for the door. He yelled as he reached the yard, and he continued to yell as he turned out of the gate and dashed off up the road, with Peter loping along easily a few feet behind him. The animals crowded to the door; they could see nothing, but they could hear those diminishing yells dying away in the direction of Centerboro, until at last through the calm night they came back as a thin thread of sound, like the whine of a mosquito. And presently that was gone too, and there was silence.

"Thank you, Mr. Bean, and animals all," said the sheriff. "I'll be getting along now. I'll be up in the morning, Freddy, to have you show me where all that stolen money is. I'll bring the reward with me. Come along, you two. Couple o' nice cells all made up for you, with clean towels and flowers in the vases and everything. Night, all."

Mr. Bean said good night; then he turned to the animals. "Now don't sit up talking half the night," he said gruffly. "Lots of time to go over it all tomorrow. I'm proud of you, Freddy." He patted the pig clumsily on the shoulder. "Good night." And he stumped off toward the house.

"Well," said Mrs. Wiggins with a deep sigh, "*this* has been a night, I *must* say. But Mr. Bean is right; we must get off to bed. Only I want to hear all about it first thing in the morning."

The animals dispersed slowly. But Freddy drew Jinx aside, and as soon as the others were gone, "Look here, Jinx," he said, "the boards those robbers pulled up in that stall are just about over where the rats store their grain. Better have a look at that before you turn in, eh?"

Jinx twitched his whiskers twice, clapped Freddy on the back with a paw, then winked broadly, and as the pig left the barn, he glanced back and saw Jinx creep like a shadow through the open door of the box stall.

XI
The Trial

AT last

Came the day of the trial. From early morning the roads and field paths were full of animals, streaming toward the cow-barn, where Jinx was to be tried for the murder and subsequent eating of the crow. Many of them had brought their lunch with them, for there was no question that the trial would be a long and hard-fought legal battle. The general opinion through the countryside was that the cat was guilty, but Jinx's friends had stuck by him loyally, even in face of what seemed almost certain guilt. "For," said they, "we stand on Jinx's past record, as well as on the general nature of cats. Jinx has never been known to chase, much less to eat, even a sparrow. And it is a well-known fact that no cat will eat a crow. We don't care what the rats say. We believe him innocent."

The trial was set for two o'clock. From the door of his office Freddy, in the intervals of his work, could see the animals streaming by. But he was very busy that morning. The capture of the robbers had made a great impression, and accounts of it had been published in every paper in the country. The day before, a deputation of Centerboro citizens, headed by the mayor in a silk hat, had come to tender him their official thanks and to pay him the reward of five thousand dollars. After the ceremony, which included speeches by several prominent bankers and business men, a number of the deputation had stayed behind to engage his services in various matters which they wanted cleared up. Many animals, too, from distant villages, who had now heard for the first time of his remarkable ability as a detective, had brought him their troubles, so that he had work enough to keep him busy for a year or more. He listened to them all with courteous attention, giving as much of his time and interest to the cousin of Henrietta's from whom a china egg had been stolen as to the wealthy banker from Green's Corners who wanted assistance in finding his long-lost daughter.

He sat inside the shed, listening gravely to his clients, exchanging now and then a word with his partner, Mrs. Wiggins—who had to sit

outside the door because there was not room for her inside—giving orders to his subordinates, the mice and squirrels and other small animals to whom were given the less important tasks of detecting, and receiving the reports of other birds and animals who hurried in and out on his errands. Beside him the money he had received as a reward was piled up in plain sight—"for no one," said Freddy, "would dare to steal it now. They know that if they tried it, we'd catch 'em and have 'em clapped in jail within twenty-four hours."

Pretty soon Jinx himself came along. He sat down and waited until Freddy had finished with another client, then went in and said good morning.

"Good morning, Jinx," said Freddy. "How's everything up at the house?"

"Oh, all right, I guess," replied the cat. "But I tell you, Freddy, I'm a little nervous, and that's a fact. Are you *sure* you can get me off? As I told you, I wouldn't mind so much going to jail at any other time, but right now it's as much as my job's worth not to be where I can keep those rats in their place."

"I thought you'd got the upper hand of them since the other night," said Freddy.

"So I have. I captured Ezra and two of Simon's nephews and locked them up; and where those boards were ripped up, I found nearly a bushel of grain, which the mice carried back to the grain-box while I stood guard, but Simon is still there, and this morning, while Mr. Bean was getting the boards ready to be put back in place and nailed down, Simon stuck his head out of his hole and gave me the laugh. 'You'll never drive us out of the barn, Jinx,' he said. 'I admit you got most of our supplies, but by this time tomorrow night,' he said, 'you'll be locked up safe and tight, and then, boy! Won't we have a feast! And by the time you get out,' he said, 'we'll have enough more stored away so you'll never get us out.'"

"Well, as I've told you before," said Freddy, "you aren't going to be locked up. I've got this case just where I want it, and the trial will prove some things about those rats that will surprise you. It isn't just what I believe—it's what I can *prove*. And I can prove you didn't kill any crow."

"Well," said the cat, "I wish you'd tell me—"

"No," interrupted the pig, "I'm not going to tell you anything. It's a long story and you'll hear it all in court. There isn't time for it now. Just be patient, and don't worry, and everything'll come out all right, I promise you."

"I hope you're right," said Jinx with a sigh. "Oh, gosh!" he exclaimed suddenly, glancing out of the door, "here's Charles. I'm off, Freddy. I'll lose my temper if I talk to that big stuffed shirt, and goodness only knows what might happen then."

"Yes, you'd better go along," said Freddy. "See you in court.— Morning, Charles, how's everything in the henhouse this morning?" he said as the rooster, with an indignant glance at the departing cat, entered the office.

"Everything is all right, thank you," said Charles stiffly. "I must say, Freddy, I can't approve of your hobnobbing with criminals this way."

"Oh, hobnobbing with your grandmother's tail-feathers!" exclaimed the pig good-naturedly. "Don't try that high and mighty stuff with me, that's known you since you were a little woolly chicken that couldn't say anything but 'Peep, peep,' like a tree-toad!"

"That's all very well, Freddy," said the rooster, "but, fond as I have been of Jinx in the past, it is my belief that by committing this crime he has forfeited the friendship and esteem of all decent animals, and I cannot—"

"Oh, save the speech till later in the day," interrupted Freddy. "But just let me tell you this: Jinx is innocent, and I can prove it, and I'm going to prove it this afternoon, and you're going to feel very silly when you know the truth and remember all the things you've said about him. And now let's talk of something else. I've been wanting to see you to ask you what you thought about conditions in the jail. It isn't as overcrowded as it was before we threw out all the animals who hadn't been sentenced at all, but it seems to me that we could make it a little less like a club if you pardoned any animals who seemed to be having too good a time there, and put them out. I think that if the animals knew that they weren't going to be allowed just to stay there and enjoy themselves, they wouldn't

be so anxious to get in, and there wouldn't be so many of them stealing things just so they'd be put there."

"An excellent idea, Freddy," said the judge. "And I'd like to start with that Eric. You know what he's done? He's been making speeches to the other prisoners, telling them how silly they are to want to stay out of jail when they can have so much better fun inside, and he's organized a lot of them into a club called the Hoho Club. To join it you have to give your word that as soon as your sentence is up and you're free again, you will commit some crime so you'll be put right back in."

"What does "Hoho' mean?" asked Mrs. Wiggins.

"Hilarious Order of Habitual Offenders," said Charles.

"Which leaves me right where I was before," said Mrs. Wiggins. "What does *that* mean?"

"An habitual offender," explained Freddy, "is an animal who makes a habit of committing offenses, so he'll go to jail."

"Oh!" said Mrs. Wiggins.

"They've even got a song they sing," said Charles angrily. "It goes something like this:

"Habitually we offend
Against our country's laws.
It works out better in the end
Than being good, because—

No home has a superior
Or cheerier interior
Than this old jail,
The which we hail
With constant loud applause,

For—

Be it ever so crowded
     There's no—o place like jail!"

"It's not a very good song," said Freddy. "Or perhaps it's the way you sing it."

"Not enough expression," put in Mrs. Wiggins.

"Oh, who asked you to criticize my singing?" asked Charles crossly. "I was just telling you—"

"Sure, sure," said Freddy soothingly, "we agree with you. Something's got to be done. But wait till after the trial this afternoon. I've got an idea how we can fix this Hoho Club so they won't be so anxious to come up before the judge. I'll see you then, Charles."

"Everything is in now except Eeny's report, isn't it?" asked Mrs. Wiggins, as soon as Charles had gone.

"Yes," said Freddy, "and he'll meet me at the courtroom. I suppose we'd better be getting on over and see that all our witnesses are there. Here's the evidence." He dragged out a market basket in which were the claws and feathers that had been found in the loft, along with several other small objects, and Mrs. Wiggins hooked it up with her horn and they started off.

The cowbarn was full, and a big mob of animals who could not find room inside were crowded about the door. Mrs. Wiggins pushed her way good-naturedly through the crowd, and Freddy followed. "What you got in the basket?" called a horse. "You going to use it to carry out what's left of Jinx after the trial?"

The crowd laughed, and Freddy turned around. "Listen, horse," he said, "we've got the proofs of Jinx's innocence in this basket, and what do you say to that?"

"Why, I say I hope it's true," replied the horse, and the other animals raised a cheer.

At the far end of the barn was an old phaeton, which the animals had brought back from Florida two years before, and on the front seat stood Charles, very dignified and grand, only occasionally exchanging a few words in an undertone with Peter, the bear, who was foreman of the jury.

Charles had selected the twelve members of the jury, and they sat in a double row to the left of the phaeton: Peter and Mrs. Wogus and Hank and Bill, the goat, and two sheep in the back row, and in the front row, because they were smaller, Cecil, the porcupine, and Emma's Uncle Wesley, and two mice, Quik and Eek, and Freddy's sister's husband, Archie, who was so fat that he snored, even when he was wide awake. The twelfth juror, Mr. Webb, the spider, had spun a thread down from the roof and hung there, just above the rest of the jury, where he could see and hear everything, but wouldn't be in danger of being stepped on. In the back seat of the phaeton was the prisoner, Jinx, looking much worried.

Every available inch of space in the barn was occupied. Windowsills, beams, and rafters were lined with field mice, chipmunks, squirrels, and birds, and the pressure of the crowd on the floor was so great that even before the trial began, several smaller animals fainted and had to be carried out. Just in front of the judge a space had been kept clear, and as Freddy moved up to one side of this, Eeny darted out from under the phaeton.

"I found it at last, Freddy," he said. "They didn't get it from Mr. Bean's house at all. It was Miss McMinnickle's. Something Prinny said put me on to it, and I went down there and got in the house, and, sure enough, they'd tipped it over on her writing desk and spilled a lot, and you could see their footprints on the blotter."

"Fine!" said Freddy. "That's great work, Eeny!"

"I brought a piece of the blotting paper along," said the mouse. "Jock has it for safe keeping.

"Good. Now stick round. I'll need your testimony before very long. Believe me, we're going to give those rats a surprise!"

"Order in the court!" called Charles in his most important voice. "Silence, please. Now, gentlemen of the jury—"

"Ladies, too," whispered Jock, pointing toward Mrs. Wogus.

"You can't say 'ladies' when there's only one," snapped Charles.

"Well, you've got to say *something,* you can't just leave her out entirely."

"Lady and gentlemen of the jury," said Charles, "you are here to decide from the evidence presented to you at this time upon the guilt or innocence of one, Jinx, a cat in the employ of Mr. Bean, who is charged with the murder, and subsequent eating, of an unknown crow, in the barn on August seventh last. Ferdinand, as a member of the great crow family, will conduct the prosecution. Frederick, the well-known detective, will conduct the defense, with the assistance of his colleague, Mrs. Wiggins. Mr. Ferdinand, will you call your witnesses?"

Ferdinand hopped up to the dashboard of the buggy, cleared his throat with a harsh caw, fixed the foreman of the jury with his sardonic eye, and said:

"As you doubtless know, ladies and gentlemen, the chief witnesses for the prosecution are Simon and his family, a band of rats who are living illegally, and without permission from Mr. Bean, in the barn. This in itself constitutes a misdemeanor which may well in time bring them as prisoners into this court. Nevertheless, their crimes and offenses have nothing to do with the case which we are now considering, and I wish you, in listening to their evidence, to make up your opinion without reference to any prejudice you may have against them on that score. It is Jinx who is being tried now, not the rats. Do I make myself clear?"

Mrs. Wogus spoke up. "No," she said bluntly, "you don't."

"I will try to make myself more clear," said the crow. "You believe these rats are thieves, don't you?"

"Yes," said the cow, "I certainly do."

"Probably a good many of us here agree with you," said Ferdinand. "Still, they have a story to tell of what they saw, and in judging of the truth of that story you must not be influenced by that belief. In other words, just because you think they are thieves, you mustn't also think they are liars."

"But I do," said Mrs. Wogus. "How can I help it?"

"Because it hasn't anything to do with *this* case," said Charles.

"Certainly it has," said the cow.

"You'd better get on with your case," said Charles to Ferdinand, and the crow, seeing that he was only throwing doubts on the truthfulness of his witnesses by continuing his efforts to explain, nodded his head.

"Well," he said, "I can only ask you to judge by the evidence that will be presented to you. I may say that the rats were reluctant to come here and testify, since it meant leaving their homes under the barn, where they feel themselves safe. In order to get them here at all I have had to get a promise from the judge that they shall not be molested until the trial is over. I will now call my first witness, Simon."

The old gray rat crept out from under the buggy, where he and his family had been waiting, and took his place in the open space reserved for witnesses.

"Tell the jury in your own words what you saw," said Ferdinand.

Simon's whiskers twitched and his eyes slid round toward Jinx, who was crouched in the backseat of the buggy, his tail moving gently from side to side. "I'd like to have your word, your honor," he said to Charles, "that my children and I will be allowed to give our evidence and go back home without being assaulted. I'm a poor rat, and I am 't done harm to anybody. We rats have to live.

That's something that you animals don't ever seem to think of—"

"Silence!" said Charles sternly. "We're not trying *your* case now."

"No, sir," said Simon humbly. "But if you'd just give your word—"

"The judge and the jury and all the animals, including myself and the prisoner," put in Freddy, "have agreed that until the trial is over, no harm shall come to you. Am I right, Your Honor?"

"That was the agreement," said Charles.

"Yes," said Simon, "but will you give me safe conduct back to the barn after the trial?"

Charles was about to speak, but Freddy interrupted him. "Unless you commit some crime between now and the time the trial is over," he said, "you'll be allowed to go back with your family."

This seemed to satisfy Simon, who, with an uneasy eye on Jinx, began to tell his story.

"At noon on August seventh, I and my family were peacefully eating our dinner when we heard a great commotion in the loft. We rushed up through our secret passageways in the walls and, looking out from our holes, saw one of the most terrible sights we have ever witnessed. This cat, who now stands before the bar of justice—this wicked felon, whose vile sins have at last found him out—this evil—"

"Come, come, Simon," interrupted Freddy, "get on with your story, and don't call names."

"Ah, forgive me, Your Honor," said Simon, with a hypocritical leer at Charles, "for letting my feelings get the best of me. It is my hatred and loathing for such detestable crimes that has led me into saying more than I intended—"

"And if you say much more like that," put in Jinx with an angry swish of his tail, "there'll be a *real* murder to investigate in about two seconds. One good overhand swipe at you, you oily old rodent, and there'll be one less at breakfast tomorrow morning under the barn!"

"Order!" shouted Charles. "Continue with your story, rat, and keep your opinions to yourself."

"Yes, Your Honor," said Simon with mock humility. "As I was saying, this—this cat had pounced upon a poor, inoffensive little crow and, when we had reached a point from which we could see what was going on, was tearing him limb from limb with unparalleled ferocity. We shouted, Your Honor; we called upon him to stop; but he merely grinned wildly and went on with his butchery. I sent one of my grandchildren to notify the police at once, but then there was nothing for us to do but watch until the horrid deed was done. We wept, Your Honor—I will not conceal it from you that in our horror and indignation, in our helplessness and in our sorrow for the fate of this wretched bird, we wept bitter tears. But they were as unavailing as our threats and warnings. The cruel and relentless animal was—" Simon stopped suddenly as Jinx leaped to his feet. "That, Your Honor," he said hastily, "is my story."

Following Simon came eight other rats who testified to having seen the same thing; then Charles took the stand and told of having been summoned to the barn, where he found Jinx, evidently terrified at having been discovered in his crime. Then, Freddy having said that he would like to cross-examine Simon, the rat again came forward.

"How large are the rat-holes that lead into the loft?" asked the pig.

"You've seen 'em; you ought to know," replied the rat with a grin.

"That's not what I asked you," snapped Freddy. "Are they big enough for a cat to get through?"

"No cat ever got through 'em."

"Just about big enough for one rat, then?"

"Just about."

"And how many are there?"

"Three," said Simon. "There ain't any harm in my telling you that."

"Oh, isn't there?" said Freddy. "Well, will you tell me how nine rats, with only three holes big enough for one rat each, managed to see everything that went on?"

Simon snarled and twitched his whiskers. "Trying to make me out a liar, are you?" he demanded. "Well, let me tell you, smarty, that three rats can see out of one rat-hole all right."

"How do they stand when they're looking out?" asked Freddy. "They can't stand beside each other, and if they stand one behind the other, how can they see?"

"How do I know how they do it!" snarled Simon. "They did it all right, didn't they? You heard 'em say they saw it, didn't you?"

"Sure, I heard 'em," said Freddy pleasantly, and, turning to Charles: "That's all, Your Honor," he said.

Simon retreated under the buggy, where a chatter and squeaking of excited rat voices could be heard, while the jury examined the claws and feathers of the crow. Evidently Freddy's questions had disturbed the witnesses somewhat, but they quieted down when Freddy announced that if the prosecution had no other evidence to present, he would like to call a few witnesses in the defense.

The first was Ferdinand himself, who testified that he did not know who the dead crow could be. So far as he knew, no crows had been reported missing within a day's flight in any direction from the farm.

"At this time of year crows are not likely to fly more than a day's flight in any direction, are they?" asked Freddy.

"No," said Ferdinand. "But this crow might have been going on a visit to relatives in another district. It is probable that this was the case."

"Crows don't usually make such visits, do they?"

"No."

"Have you ever known of a crow doing it?"

"No," said Ferdinand, "but that's no reason why one might not do it."

"True," said Freddy, "but I would say that it is *possible,* rather than probable, wouldn't you?"

"Why, yes, perhaps," said Ferdinand unwillingly.

"Thank you, that's all," said Freddy. "I will now call Eeny."

The mouse took the stand and told how he had been sent by Freddy to inspect the writing desks of all the neighbors within half a mile of the farm. At none of them had he found anything unusual or out of the way until he had visited Miss McMinnickle's house. Here he had found signs that the ink bottle had recently been overturned, and although Miss McMinnickle had evidently sopped up the ink and washed and cleaned the desk, the blotter on which the bottle had been standing showed several large blots, and the inky prints of many small feet. He had brought away with him a piece of this blotter, which Freddy presented to the jury for their inspection.

Freddy then called Prinny, Miss McMinnickle's dog, who testified that on August 5 Miss McMinnickle had had chicken for supper. Charles shuddered at this, and his daughter Leah, who was perched on a beam over the jury-box, fainted dead away and fell with

a thump to the floor. When she had been carried outside and order had been restored, Freddy said:

"When did you last see the claws of this chicken?"

"I object!" exclaimed Ferdinand, before Prinny could answer. "Your Honor, the question of what this Miss McMinnickle had for supper on the day before this brutal murder has nothing to do—"

"And *I* object, Your Honor," shouted Freddy suddenly. "It is not yet proved that any murder has been committed, and I submit that Ferdinand is endeavoring to prejudice the jury."

"Order in the court!" crowed Charles, as the animals surged closer so as not to miss a word of this clash between the opposing counsel. "You *can't* both object at the same time! What did you object to, Ferdinand?"

The crow repeated his remark.

"I intend to show, Your Honor," said Freddy, "that the question of what this lady had for supper has a very close bearing on the case. May I proceed?"

"Proceed," said the judge, who was somewhat flustered and couldn't think of anything else to say.

Freddy repeated his question, and Prinny said: "I last saw them on the rubbish heap on the morning of August sixth."

"And did you visit the rubbish pile later on the same day?"

"I did."

"And they were there?"

"No," said Prinny, "they had disappeared."

Ferdinand did not cross-examine this witness, and Freddy then called Simon's son Zeke. There was a flutter of interest as Zeke took the stand,

and the animals pushed forward until Charles threatened to have the court-room cleared unless they were quiet. Even Archie opened his little eyes, which had been tight shut for some time, and stopped snoring.

"Now, Zeke," said Freddy, "I suppose you are anxious to answer all the questions I ask you fully and truthfully?"

"Oh yes, sir," said Zeke, opening his eyes wide and trying to look truthful, but only succeeding in looking as if he had a stomachache.

"Very well," said Freddy. He paused a moment, then suddenly he glared at the rat. "Where were you on the morning of August sixth?" he shouted.

Zeke looked startled. "Why, sir, I—I was at—home all day. Yes, sir, at home."

"You were, eh?" roared Freddy. "And what if I tell you that I have witnesses to prove that you were *not* home?"

"Why, I might have been out for a little while, sir. I can't exactly remember. I do go out once in a while."

"You *were* out, then?"

"Yes, sir. I—I may have been."

"Good," said Freddy. "Now cast your mind back to the morning of August sixth. You were out taking a walk, let us say. You went up along the side of the road to Miss McMinnickle's house. Am I right so far?"

"Why, honestly, sir, I can't remember. I was just out getting a little air. I might have gone up that way. I—"

"You *might* have gone that way?" said Freddy. "I suggest that you went directly to Miss McMinnickle's house, to which you gained entrance through a cellar window. You then went upstairs and got up on the kitchen table and ate part of a ham—"

"Oh no, sir!" exclaimed the rat. "I wasn't in the kitchen at all. I—"

"Shut up, you fool!" came Simon's snarling voice from under the buggy, and immediately Ferdinand began fluttering his wings and shouting: "Stop! Stop! I object! Your Honor, I object on two counts. First, Zeke's whereabouts on the day before the mur—I should say, the alleged crime—have nothing to do with this case. Second, Freddy is trying to intimidate this witness."

"Objections not sustained," snapped Charles. "Even if this rat's whereabouts have nothing to do with the case, I guess everybody here wants to know what he was doing at Miss McMinnickle's. And, second, if anything can be done by Freddy or any other animal to intimidate him, I want to see it done. Proceed, Freddy."

"Oh, shucks!" exclaimed Ferdinand disgustedly. "That isn't any way to try a case, Charles. Use a little sense, will you?"

"If you don't like the way this case is being tried, crow," said Charles with dignity, "you are at liberty to leave. This court will not be dictated to. I'm here to sentence Jinx, and sentence him I will, but I shall do it in my own way."

"Perfectly satisfactory to me, Your Honor," said Ferdinand.

"But it's not to me," said Freddy. "You are *not* here to sentence Jinx, Charles; you're here to see that justice is done."

"Well, justice is done if I sentence him, isn't it?" demanded the rooster.

"Not if he's innocent."

"But he isn't innocent," exclaimed Charles. "Everybody knows that."

"No free-born American animal," said Freddy, "can be convicted of a crime until he is proved guilty. I appeal to the audience in this courtroom. What should we do with a judge who condemns a prisoner before he has stood trial?"

"Depose him! Throw him out! Elect another judge!" shouted the animals.

"Order in the court!" screamed Charles. "My duty here is to give judgment—"

"You can't give what you haven't got!" called a voice. "You never had any judgment, Charles, and you know it!"

There was a shout of laughter, but Freddy stood up on his hind legs and motioned for silence, and the noise quieted down.

"I'm sure," he said, "that our worthy judge spoke without thinking. He knows as well as you do that a prisoner is considered innocent until he is proved guilty. I merely wished to call attention to the fact that he is letting his dislike of Jinx interfere with his sense of justice. You see that, don't you, Charles?"

"Oh, I suppose so," replied the harassed rooster. "Get on with your trial, will you, and quit picking on *me.*"

"Very well," said Freddy. "Now, Zeke, by your own admission, you were in Miss McMinnickle's house on the morning of the 6th. Will you tell us what you did there?"

"You don't have to answer that," called Simon from under the buggy. "You don't have to answer any question if you feel that the answer would tend to incriminate or degrade you."

"All right, I won't answer that," said Zeke.

"You feel that the answer would incriminate or degrade you?" asked Freddy.

"Yes. A lot."

"Good," said Freddy. "Consider yourself incriminated and degraded, then. Ferdinand, do you wish to cross-examine this degraded witness?"

"No," said Ferdinand crossly. "He hasn't anything to do with this case. I've said that all along."

So Freddy called two more witnesses. The first, a squirrel, testified to having seen a rat carrying a bird's claw of some' kind going toward the barn on the morning of the 6th. The second, a blue jay, testified that on the same day he had come home to his nest unexpectedly and had found two rats looking into it. He had flown at them and driven them away and had then looked about carefully, but could find nothing missing except a number of long feathers which had formed part of the lining of the nest. Later in the day he had seen two rats, who might or might not have been the same two, running through the woods carrying in their mouths a number of feathers of different kinds. They had evidently been gathering them for some purpose of their own.

The crowd, which could not see what all this had to do with the case and had been getting restless, became quiet again when Freddy announced that he would call no more witnesses, but would sum up his case for the jury.

XII
Freddy Sums Up

"I will Show you, gentlemen of the jury," said Freddy, "not only that Jinx is innocent of this crime, but that no crime has been committed. I will show you further that certain animals have been guilty of a conspiracy to deprive Jinx of his liberty and to cause him to be sentenced for this nonexistent crime.

"Now may I ask you to examine carefully the claws and feathers which are alleged to be those of a crow, killed and eaten by Jinx. You will remember that two chicken claws disappeared from Miss McMinnickle's rubbish heap on the 6th, and that, by his own admission, Zeke was near that house at the same time. I suggest to you that those claws you have there are not crow's claws at all, but the chicken's claws, which were taken by Zeke or one of his relatives and placed in the barn."

"But these claws are black," said Peter.

"True," said Freddy. "They have been colored black with ink. They were taken into the house by the rats who tipped over the inkbottle on Miss McMinnickle's desk while they were dyeing the claws. Here is a portion of the blotter taken from that desk. You will see on it the plain prints of rats' feet.

"Furthermore, you have heard evidence to the effect that several rats were gathering feathers of various kinds in the woods on the sixth. Now please examine carefully the alleged crow's feathers. I think you will find that they are of very different kinds. They are all black, true; but if you will smell of them and then smell of the ink-soaked blotter, you will find the two smells exactly the same. The smell, in fact, of ink. They have been dyed, just as the claws were dyed."

Some confusion was caused by the efforts of the jury to smell of the feathers, which are very difficult things to smell of without getting your nose tickled. There was a tremendous outburst of sneezing in the jury-box, in the course of which the feathers were scattered all about the courtroom, but when it was over and the feathers had been gathered together again, it was plain that the jury had accepted Freddy's theory.

"I will ask you now," went on the pig, "to remember several facts. There was no sign of a struggle in the barn, as there would have been if Jinx had actually caught a crow and eaten him there. The claws and feathers were laid out in a neat pile. Again, although there was only room in the three rat-holes for three rats to see what was going on in the loft, nine rats testified to having seen Jinx catch and eat the crow. Lastly, no crow is known to be missing, although, as all of you know, if one crow so much as loses a tail-feather, you will hear the crows cawing and shouting and complaining about it for weeks afterwards.

"Now, what happened was this, as you probably all see by this time. The rats wanted to get Jinx out of the way, so they could get a fresh supply of grain from the grain-box in the loft. They got the feathers and claws as I have shown you, dyed them black with ink, put them out on the floor, and then when Jinx came in, accused him of the crime. There is not a word of truth in their evidence. It is one of the most dastardly attempts to defeat the ends of justice which have ever come under my notice. I leave the case with you, confident that your verdict will free the prisoner."

There was much shouting and cheering as Freddy concluded, and then Ferdinand rose to make his speech to the jury. He knew that he had a weak case, so he said very little about the facts. His attack was rather upon Freddy than upon the evidence that had been collected.

"A very clever theory our distinguished colleague and eminent detective has presented to us," he said. "A little too clever, it seems to me. After all, it is the business of a detective to construct theories. But what we are concerned with here is the truth. We are plain animals; we like things plain and simple. Here is a dead bird, and beside it a cat. What is plainer than that? Do we need all this talk of ink and blue jays and chicken suppers to convince us of something that gives the lie to what is in front of our very noses? I think not. I think we all agree that two and two make four. I think we prefer such a statement as that to a long explanation why two and two should make six. With all due respect and admiration for the brilliance of the theory which Freddy has presented to us, I do not see how your verdict can be other than 'Guilty.'"

There was some cheering at the end of Ferdinand's speech, but it was more for the cleverness with which he had avoided the facts than because the audience agreed with him. And then Charles got up to speak. His speech was perhaps the best of the three. He referred to the grave responsibility which rested on the members of the jury, to the great care which they must exercise in deciding on the guilt or innocence of the prisoner. They must not be swayed by prejudice, he said, but must look at the facts as facts, must remember that—But it was a very long speech and, though beautifully worded, meant very little, so I will not give it in full. If you are interested in reading it, it will be possible to get a copy, for Freddy later wrote out an account of the trial on his typewriter, with all the speeches in full, which is kept with other documents in the Bean Archives, neatly labeled "The State vs. Jinx," where I have seen it myself.

The jury whispered together for a few minutes while the audience waited breathlessly for the verdict, and Jinx sat quite still, looking rather worried, but with one eye on the dark space under the buggy where the rats were chattering together. Then Peter got up.

"Your Honor, our verdict is ready," he said.

"What is it?" asked Charles.

"Not guilty!" said Peter.

At the words there was a burst of cheering that shook the barn and knocked two chipmunks off the beam where they had been sitting. Mr. Webb ran hastily up his thread and watched the rest of the proceedings from the roof. Jinx had jumped down from the buggy to receive the congratulations of his friends, who were crowding round him. But Freddy spoke to Charles, who crowed at the top of his lungs for order, and presently there was quiet.

"Ladies and gentlemen," said the detective, "there is another matter before this court before it adjourns. I call for the arrest of Simon and his family on the charge of conspiracy, perjury, and just plain lying."

The squeaking and chattering under the buggy became louder, and Ferdinand said:

"You can't do that, Freddy. We promised 'em they could go back to the barn in safety."

"If you remember what I said," replied the pig, "it was that unless they had committed some fresh crime before the trial was over, they might go back in safety. But they *have* committed a fresh crime. They didn't tell the truth about Jinx, and that's a crime, isn't it?"

"H'm," said Ferdinand, "I guess it is. Simon, come out here."

Simon was no coward; he could fight when he had to. He came out now, grinning wickedly. He knew better than to argue, however.

"You're all against me," he said. "Fat pig and stupid cow and silly sheep and stuffed-shirt rooster and all of you. Well, go ahead; sentence us to jail and see if we care. That's all you can do. Come on out, Zeke, and the rest of you."

The other rats were not so anxious to come out, but they were more afraid of Simon than of any of the other animals except the cat, so presently they crept out into the open space beside their leader.

"We'll have this trial in order," said Charles. "We've got a jury here, and you can pick somebody to defend you."

"I'll take care of my own case," snarled Simon.

"All right. Jinx, you see that none of them try to get away."

"Yeah!" said Jinx. "Watch me!" And he walked up and sat down beside Simon, who bared his teeth. But Jinx, who was a goodnatured cat and couldn't bear a grudge for very long, even when he had such good reason for it as he now had, merely winked at the rat. "Be yourself, Simon," he said.

One by one the rats were questioned, their names and ages taken, and the question put to them whether they had any reason to give why they shouldn't be sentenced. Acting under Simon's instructions, they all said no. The smallest of the rats caused some amusement when he gave his name as Olfred.

"There isn't any such name!" said Charles.

"There is too!" exclaimed the rat. "I've got it, haven't I?"

"How do you spell it?" asked the rooster.

"O-l-f-r-e-d," said the rat.

"It ought to be spelled with an A," said Charles. "Alfred—that's what it is.

"It isn't either. It's Olfred," insisted the rat.

"Nonsense!" exclaimed the judge sharply. "Don't you suppose I know?"

"No, you don't. Just because you never heard of it don't mean anything. There's lots of names you never heard of."

"Is that so!" exclaimed Charles angrily. "I bet you can't tell me one that I don't know."

"Yes I can," said Olfred. "There's Egwin and Ogbert and Wogmuth and Wigmund and Wagbert and—"

"You're just making them up!" said Charles.

"Of course I am. But they're names just the same."

Charles gave up. "All right, all right, get on with the case." And the questioning went on.

Simon was the last. Asked if there was any reason why he should not be sentenced, he said yes, there was, but that he had no objection to going to jail, so he would say nothing about it. "We've been living under the jail for some time," he said. "We have no objection to moving up one story into the jail itself. It's a pretty good place, from all I've heard, and you'll have to feed us. I don't see what you gain by sending us there, but that's your affair."

"There's one thing we gain," said Charles. "We have had a good deal of trouble with the jail, I'll admit. Many animals have so good a time that they commit crimes just to be sent there. Some animals have even got in who haven't committed crimes or been sentenced at all. But Freddy has suggested a remedy. All sentences, from now on, will be *at hard labor*. There'll be no more playing games and carousing; the prisoners will work all day. The jail won't be so popular from now on."

The rats looked rather crestfallen at this. They whispered together for a minute; then suddenly, at a signal from Simon, they made a dash for the door.

They had been so reasonable during the questioning that even Jinx had been thrown off his guard. He made a pounce, missed Simon by the width of a whisker, then dove in among the legs of the audience after the fugitives.

"Let 'em go, Jinx," Freddy shouted after him. "Keep 'em away from the barn, but let 'em go!"

Jinx gave a screech to show that he had heard, and scrabbled on among the legs of horses and sheep and goats and all the other animals who had jammed into the cowbarn to hear the trial. Even outside, the crowd was thick, but he made his way as quickly as he could to the edge of it nearest the barn. Not a rat was in sight. "Lost 'em, by gum!" muttered the cat, but he went on cautiously toward the barn, from which came the sound of hammering. Evidently Mr. Bean was repairing the floor that the robbers had torn up.

"They won't dare go in that way," he said to himself. "This hole under the door is the most likely one. I'll watch that."

He crept up toward it and then, to his surprise, saw that a piece of tin had been nailed across it. "Golly!" he thought. "If Mr. Bean has found out about the rats, I'll be out of luck. He must have, too, if he's found this hole and nailed it up."

But there was one other hole on the other side, so he went round to watch there. He was pretty sure that the rats hadn't reached it ahead of him. "If I can keep 'em out—" he thought, and then he saw that the second hole was nailed up too.

Inside the barn the prisoners, unaware of the hard work in store for them, were singing and laughing and carrying on.

"We raise our voices and shout," they sang,
"And call the judge a good scout,
For he puts us in
And he keeps us in
And we'd rather be in than out."

Jinx grinned; then, as the song finished, he heard someone talking. He stopped to listen. ". . . didn't realize there were all them rat-holes in the old place," Mr. Bean was saying. When I saw 'em, I was kind of mad. "Jinx ain't doin' his duty,' I says to myself, "to let them rats get a holt in here again.' But there ain't a rat in the place. I stomped all over the floor and took up a couple more boards and there wan't a sign of 'em. So I nailed up the holes, case any should come wandering along looking for a home."

"Oh, Jinx is a good cat," said Mrs. Bean. "He wouldn't let any rats get into the barn. Best mouser we ever had, Mr. B."

"You always *was* fond of that cat, Mrs. B.," replied her husband,

"and I guess you been right. Takes a good cat to keep rats out of a barn with two big holes into it like I nailed up. Guess we might set him out an extra saucer of cream once in a while."

"I'll set out one for him this very night, Mr. B.," said Mrs. Bean. "What do you suppose all that rumpus is down at the cow-barn this afternoon?"

"Oh, another of their meetin's. I like to hear 'em shoutin' and bellerin' an' havin' a good time. I do hope they ain't goin' to take any more trips, though."

"You must 'a' read my mind, Mr. B.," said his wife. "But they're all taken up with this detective business now. That Freddy, he's a caution. Brighter'n a new penny! But then, so's Jinx."

"So's all of 'em, for that matter," said Mr. Bean. "There ain't a finer lot of animals in New York State, if I do say it myself."

Jinx crept away. He was a very happy cat. All his difficulties had been solved at once. The jury had declared him innocent, and the rats had been shut out of the barn. Lucky the trial had been going on while Mr. Bean nailed up the holes, or he'd have nailed 'em inside, and then there *would* have been trouble. But everything was all right now.

That evening he and Freddy and Mrs. Wiggins sat down by the duck-pond, watching the moon come up. The water rippled white in the moonlight—just the color, Jinx thought, of fresh cream.

"I've been working pretty hard the last few weeks," said Freddy after they had discussed the day's happenings. "I think I'm going to take a little vacation. Like to get off somewhere where it's quiet and there's nothing to do but loll on the grass and make up poetry."

"I'm tired, too," said Jinx. "All this rat business has got on my nerves. What do you say we take a little trip?"

"I think that's a good idea," said Mrs. Wiggins. "I can look after the detective business while you're gone, Freddy."

Freddy yawned. "Sure you can," he said. "Gosh, I hate to think of going back to that office tomorrow morning and interviewing clients and figuring out cases. Funny how tired you get of even the things you like to do."

"Like watching for rats," said Jinx. "I know."

"The open road," said Freddy dreamily. "Remember that song I made up about it when we were going to Florida?"

"You bet I do!" said Jinx. "Let's sing it, out here in the moonlight."

"It's a travelers' song," said the pig. "Ought to be sung when you're *on* the open road; it's sort of silly to be singing it when we're sitting here at home."

Jinx jumped to his feet. "Well, *there's* your open road." He pointed dramatically toward the gate, whose white posts glimmered in the moonlight.

Freddy stared at him for a moment; then he too jumped up. "You're right," he said. "What are we waiting for? Let's go!" He turned to the cow. "Good luck, Mrs. W. Expect me back when you see me, and not before."

Mrs. Wiggins watched them go through the gate and off down the road together. Long after they had disappeared, the sound of their singing floated back to her through the clear night air.

Freddy sings:

O, I am the King of Detectives,
 And when I am out on the trail
All the animal criminals tremble,
 And the criminal animals quail,
For they know that I'll trace 'em and chase 'em and place 'em
 Behind the strong bars of the jail.

Jinx sings:

O, I am the terror of rodents.
 I can lick a whole army of rats
Like that thieving, deceiving old Simon
 And his sly sneaking, high squeaking brats.
For I, when I meet 'em, defeat 'em and eat 'em—
 I'm the boldest and bravest of cats.

Both sing:

In our chosen careers we'll admit that
　　　We haven't much farther to climb,
But we're weary of trailing and jailing,
　　　Of juries, disguises and crime.
We want a vacation from sin and sensation—
　　　We don't want to work all the time.

And then they broke into a verse of the marching song that they had so often sung on the road to Florida.

Then it's out of the gate and down the road
　　　Without stopping to say good-bye,
For adventure waits over every hill,
　　　Where the road runs up to the sky.
We're off to play with the wind and the stars,
　　　And we sing as we march away:
O, it's all very well to love your work,
　　　But you've got to have some play.

Mrs. Wiggins hummed the tune to herself for a while in a deep rumble that sounded like hundreds of bullfrogs tuning up. Then with a long sigh she got up and walked slowly back to her comfortable bed in the cow barn.